ACCLAIM FOR WHEN GOOD MEN FALL

"...a gripping read with many unexpected turns in the plot, and the suspense kept me on the edge of my seat. The tension builds up to an exciting end that exceeded my expectations by far."

~Alma Boucher, Readers' Favorite

"Readers will be kept off-balance as Bergman and his team sort through a chaos of clues. Ms. King has created another winning character."

~Capn. Lee Sneath, the Rough Writers Academy

"King's readers have come to expect the twists and turns in her novels, and this one does not disappoint!"

~Lisa Petrocelli, Author of *When the Gloves Come Off*

"*When Good Men Fall* is filled with gritty page turning twists and turns..."

~Tank Gunner, Historical Fiction Author

"Deanna King has expertly woven a thought-provoking plot line that kept me on the edge of my seat... I look forward to reading more by Deanna King."

~Frank Mutuma, Readers' Favorite

"...a truly immersive experience into the world of FBI investigations. *When Good Men Fall* is a gripping crime thriller. I'd highly recommend it to readers everywhere seeking clever, exciting crime fiction."

~K.C. Finn, Readers' Favorite

"*When Good Men Fall*, the brand new thriller from Deanna King, is a rip-roaring read you won't want to put down. Fast-paced, and with terrific character development, the author weaves an intricate web that with each fresh page, you'll relish untangling."

~Robert E. Kearns, author of *A Donnybrook Affair*

"A standout addition to the FBI procedural genre, a team of diverse Quantico classmates join forces to track down a surprising serial killer."

~Genevieve West, owner of A Wicked Read, Canton, Texas

ACCOLADES FOR DEANNA KING

Twist of Fate – A Jack West Novel

"Ms. King's novel reads like a good Netflix crime series – an engaging story with compelling characters making the reader want to binge from chapter to chapter. Best part of it all: It all takes place in Texas and really captures the diverse, yet unique character of the state."

~Samantha Calimbahin, Fort Worth Magazine

Lethal Liaisons – A Jack West Novel

"Smartly written and hauntingly entertaining."

~Fort Worth Magazine

"...another tumultuous Texas thriller."

~Lisa Petrocelli, author of *The Heart of Rome*

Vicious Vendetta – A Jack West Novel

"Deanna King's cinematic writing style will keep you intrigued from start to finish!"

~Samantha Calimbahin, Managing Editor, Fort Worth Magazine

"Jack West tackles his most brutal case in Vicious Vendetta; a case where he ultimately will be forced to push through fear and pain that will alter the detective's personal life forever."

~Lisa Petrocelli, author of *The Gloves Come Off* and *The Heart of Rome*

"The narrative grabbed my attention from the beginning and kept me captivated until the end. This series is something to look forward to!"

~Genevieve West, owner of A Wicked Read Bookstore

Trust No One – A Jack West Novel

"Trust No One – A Jack West Novel is a fast-paced thriller that flows effortlessly. It is impossible to put this book down once started. This thriller just works so fantastically well. There is no indication of deceleration to King's limitless supply of ideas or more extraordinarily, her striking characters. She truly is a runaway train on a course to strike the mainstream literary world."

~R. Hill, Manager of Half Price Books, Waco, Texas

"Detective Jack West's reputation for solving crimes has him stepping outside of the Houston P.D. and into an inside D.E.A. criminal operation. Will this bring him closer to finding the person responsible for his unsolved triple homicide? Ever resourceful and tenacious, he will use his skills, partnering with brilliant and competent women in his professional and personal life. Join this bulldog of a detective as he solves the crime and drags men into the world of gender equality and mutual respect."

~Genevieve West, Owner of A Wicked Read Book Store, Canton, Texas

"*Trust No One* by Deanna King is the fourth installment in her Jack West series, and it does not disappoint. This is a high-octane thriller that will have the readers up until well after bedtime. Strong characterization, a cracking plot, and a fast-paced easy-to-read style, that will more than satisfy existing fans and win over some new ones. I recommend Trust No One to all lovers of the detective genre."

~Robert E. Kearns, Award-winning author of *Ossuary*

"Deanna King once again brings the reader into the world of Detective Jack West, this time with a host of new characters to shake up the Houston Police Department and the D.E.A. Fans will recognize the older characters from previous novels, as all have a role in helping to solve the latest round of homicide cases, involving drugs, human trafficking, deep deceit, and betrayal. Trust No One will keep you guessing till the end!"

~Lisa Petrocelli, Author of *The Gloves Come Off*

Saving A Sioux Legacy – The Story of Blaze

"Blaze is wonderfully spunky, quirky and brave – a character you root for in a unique and original journey that marries fantasy and history."

~Samantha Calimbahin, Fort Worth Magazine

"Fantasy, romance, and action...this book's got it all!"

~Leslie Farin, 50Plus-Today Online Senior Lifestyle Magazine

ALSO BY DEANNA KING

JACK WEST NOVELS

Twist of Fate

Lethal Liaisons

Vicious Vendetta

Trust No One

Saving a Sioux Legacy

Gracie's Stories

WHEN GOOD MEN FALL

DEANNA KING

ISBN: 979-8-9856982-5-1

Edited by Lisa Petrocelli

Cover by Chandra Fry

https://stainedglasspublis.wixsite.com/bookpublisher/ppromoting

Formatted by Staci Olsen

staciolsen.com

Published by Deanna King

deannakingwriting.com

For my readers who have believed in me.
Thank you for your support and the confidence you've given me.

CHAPTER ONE

Quantico, Virginia - July 2013

Intense competition ensued with the FBI New Agent Trainees (NATs). Students, both male and female, were competing in hand-to-hand-combat training. Trainees trying to best each other physically and in the classroom, proving they were the smartest.

Eighteen men ready to battle it out on the wrestling mats. There were plenty of females, but Kasper landed in a class full of testosterone-laden men with attitudes. Mick Townsend, a real *gnat,* the kind who buzzed you and aggravated the piss out of you; spelled G-N-A-T, an acronym for Gorilla New Agent Trainee. Ninety percent of the time he mimicked an ape, throwing his muscles around, and while apes were more intelligent, Townsend performed as if he had no discernible brains.

Mick, always posturing, Bergman guessed the idiot was attempting to be labeled a badass. Maybe his plan was creating a badass rep. What a moron. All he got was a terrible start with the other NATs.

Most perceived Kasper as a nerdy tech guy, somebody they could whip up on, and it pissed him off. His plan was to prove he wasn't a weakling. He might not emerge victorious in every challenge, but he didn't intend to lose each match either. In recent weeks, he'd done well. Today was his unlucky, yet lucky day, facing Townsend as a sparring partner. They had never faced each other before.

"Bergman, Townsend," Robbs bellowed.

Mick stepped into the center with the facial expression of a tough guy. "Lookie here, fellas, I get to mop the mats with Bergman's face. This'll take me two whole minutes. I won't even have time to break a sweat." His lips curled in a menacing sneer.

"Stow it, Townsend," the teacher barked as he tossed a prop knife to Mick. Then, "Bergman, today Townsend's the bad guy and he's gunning for you. Take him down."

Bergman squared his shoulders, muttering, "Gonna do my best to take down this baboon."

After backing away, Robbs blasted his whistle.

They danced around, Mick snarling like an idiot. Kasper locked onto his opponent's face, anticipating his moves. An expression in Mick's eyes conveyed to him, *you're mine,* and he moved forward, but Bergman was faster than the cheeky baboon. Chalk knife in hand, Mick advanced, lunging, giving Kasper just the right angle to get his attacker in an armlock. Bergman brought his knee up, catching Mick in the gut, causing him to double over and knocking the wind out of him. He grabbed Mick's hand, bending his thumb back, and inflicting immediate pain. Kasper used the front end of his tennis shoe to kick the knife out of reach, sweeping Townsend's legs up from under him, knocking him flat. Without missing a beat, Kasper was on his haunches yanking Mick by the arm, rolling him, and cuffing him like a calf-roping contestant at a rodeo. None of the students expected it to end this way—most of all, Mick Townsend.

Dazed, the bigger man couldn't believe what just happened. Infuriated, he bucked and screamed. "Somebody take these motherfucking cuffs off me right now!"

"Townsend, watch your mouth. You know I don't tolerate bad

language." Fishing keys from his pocket, Robbs tossed them to Kasper. "Uncuff the lout, then move back; he's probably gonna take a swing at ya." Their instructor grinned.

Townsend rocketed up, rubbing his wrists, scowling at Kasper. He didn't swing, he didn't speak. Mick stepped back into his spot and waited while Robbs gave Bergman his props. The instructor dismissed them after a brief discussion.

In the gym's doorway, Townsend shot his arm out, blocking the exit.

"You caught me off guard this time, *Boogerman*. Next time, I'll own your ass. Robbs will hafta carry you to the infirmary afterward. Got it?"

"Step aside, Mick. Whatever you've got against me, get over it. It ain't worth it." Bergman's face was stony, his tone matched.

Mick let Bergman pass, but he made sure he bumped his shoulder into Kasper's, in an act of aggression.

"He's an ass, Bergman, ignore him." Lefty walked next to him as they left the Quantico Training Facility heading to the dorms to hit the showers.

"Yeah, Townsend's got a shriveled-up penis between his tiny balls. It's why he acts like a big dick; only way he'd have a big dick is to be one. Men like him, with muscles, are compensating for lack of other tools." Pete Casbury walked on Kasper's left.

"I just can't figure out why he has it out for me."

"Better work on those figuring out skills. Dude, you know you're in training here to become an FBI agent, right?"

Corneal snickered, and Kasper's eyes rolled.

Corneal Sebastian, known as Lefty, was an odd one. He wasn't left-handed. Everyone called him Lefty because of the constant razzing saying most of his ideas were out of left field.

"Yep, you shit, I know. Hey, got an idea. We should head to the range; I'm in the mood to put holes into faceless silhouettes."

"Sure, Bergman, and if we could visualize what you did when you pulled the trigger, we'd catch sight of Mick Townsend's rotten mug." Pete Casbury jogged toward the dormitories. Kasper and Lefty followed in strong pursuit, turning it into an out-and-out race between three good up-and-coming FBI Agent buddies.

Posted on the bulletin board outside the classroom were NAT's scores. Students swarmed in front searching for their names, but not Kasper. He stayed at the back, waiting. No reason to shove; besides, he wasn't as antsy as most of these yahoos. He stood against the wall, observing the others, with Pete and Lefty also patiently waiting off to the side.

After seeing the board, each NAT stepped aside. Justin Plumes, Bobby Tibet, Missy Short, and Earl Karson's sad faces said they needed to step it up a notch on the bookwork or fail. Townsend wasn't too smart, and this had Kasper wondering how the dude got the scores he'd made. It seemed suspicious. Hell, this was the FBI. If they didn't catch him cheating, Townsend might deserve to be here, or possibly he should join the CIA.

A select few stood in the hallway after the crowd dispersed. Mick Townsend, Pete Casbury, Lefty Sebastian, Jay Greenburg, Chad North, and Greg Spokane, with three female NATs, Francine Ryder, Karney Logan, and Harlowe Bishop.

Kasper relaxed against the rear wall watching and listening as they interacted.

Chad North elbowed Mick. "Amazing, man, you're still here. Wow, who'd have figured you had any smarts in your fat head?"

"Fuck off, North, I understand you passed by the skin of your teeth, same teeth you got wrapped around instructor Robbs' dick."

"Hey! Some of us don't like that kinda talk, Townsend. Cut it out." Karney Logan turned, hands on her hips, frowning.

"Jealous your lips aren't on Robbs' skin flute, Corny?" Jay sneered, his only facial expression since a smile never reached his lips.

"It's *Karney*, and I'm betting someone tells Robbs about the stuff you guys say. Personally, I can't wait for that day to happen. He'll rip you guys up for being so disrespectful."

"Gonna be a little tattletale are you? Besides, how will you prove I said anything? You think these guys give a shit what I say?"

"It's called a wiretap, you fuck-shtick, or aren't you paying attention in class?" Harlowe drew herself up to her full height of five-foot-four and challenged him. Kasper kept his laughter in check. Unlike Karney, Bishop had a mouth on her rivaling most men, and she was gutsy.

"Any of us finds out you're wearing a wire, little Miss Harlot, and I'll make sure you get the boot, or worse. I promise you—" It was Mick talking this time, his body language hostile, but he stopped when he realized eight pairs of eyes stared directly at him, listening to his threat to Harlowe. In his line of sight, he spotted Bergman, who'd hung back. Great, it was nine sets of eyeballs and the same number of ears.

Kasper straightened not advancing his position, nor did he speak. Harlowe looked from Townsend to Bergman, then the others.

"Sure, Townsend," she began. "No one wants to be your enemy. And look here, you might outweigh me by over ninety pounds and be a half-foot taller, but don't think I can't hold my own where you're concerned. I've dated fellows bigger, and meaner, and handled them all when they got out of hand, *capiche*?"

"Fine, prove it on the mats if the instructor ever lets you girls in. And well, if not, then keep filing papers, and your fingernails, and let the real agents handle this stuff. And by real agents, I mean us men."

Time to step up and show Karney, Harlowe, and Francine he was neither apathetic nor a misogynistic creep. After working with DEA Agent Sophia Medina and Agent Janet Spears, from the OAG, Kasper knew women made excellent agents. Spears and Medina were two of the finest he'd worked with.

He cleared his throat taking the few steps to be in line with the group at the bulletin board.

Mick's brows crinkled in aggravated annoyance. Bergman rubbed him the wrong way. Spokane and Greenberg didn't like the guy either. None of them had a valid reason, they just didn't like the guy. Greg Spokane and Jay Greenberg were men's men—tough—and Mick Townsend semi-bonded with them, but he didn't really like them. Funny, as a kid he'd watched the *Harry Potter* movies and somehow got typecast in his young life as belonging to the house of Slytherin. Just great, here he was an adult male typecast with Greenberg and Spokane as the dumb trio, Malfoy, Crabbe, and Goyle.

"Here to see if you passed, Bergman?"

"Yeah, Mick, I passed. I suspect my name's within the top, perhaps six or less." Kasper wasn't being narcissistic or a braggart, he had no doubt he had made the grade. "Be nice if you'd apologize to the ladies. Females make excellent agents. It's time to pull your head out of your 1940s ass and into this age. Or don't you believe in equality?"

Their eyes locked—whatever war was raging inside Townsend's head baffled Kasper. Perhaps this was a test for him. He *was* in training at Quantico, wasn't he? He hadn't been interested in the Behavioral Analyst Unit (BAU), but sizing Mick up, profiling him would be great practice to decide if it suited him or not.

"Oh yeah, equal rights, of course, women's lib, lest I forget." Mick eyeballed his watch.

"Gotta leave, running late. See you freaks later. You coming, Greenberg?"

"Yep, right behind you." As he passed Karney Logan, Jay leered. She flinched. He chuckled.

Mick was an enigma. They watched the duo disappear through the corridor, leaving out the door. No one spoke for a minute.

"Where're they rushing off to?" Pete leaned against the wall.

Greg Spokane moved from the bulletin board and walked past the girls. Positioned in the center of the hallway, he faced Kasper with a stare of hostility, answering Casbury's question.

"Is it anybody's business where they're off to?"

"You can't say where your so-called buddies are going? Guess they never invited you, huh?"

"No, and I ain't a busybody like you are, Pete, and shit, I ain't their mother," Greg clipped. He squinted, watching the hallway. "Those two go somewhere every other day. Sometimes they're gone for an hour and a half. I've asked what's going on, both of 'em tells me, it's none ya, and well, it isn't, so I back off."

Corneal Sebastian smirked. "Maybe Mick's getting tutored since we know the guy's a bag of brainless muscles. Greenberg, though, who knows, the guy's a freak by himself."

Francine Ryder, the shy young woman with frizzy hair, who stood at the back watching quietly, spoke. It shocked everyone, because she only spoke in class when called upon.

"My roommate Missy Short heard Mick has been leaving campus every weekend for the past nine weeks, and gets back sometimes just before curfew on Sunday night."

"Well, Frizz Head, you and soon-to-be dropout Missy Short need to mind your business," Greg spoke out in their defense.

Francine locked eyes with him raising her shoulders slightly, not wanting to let the man intimidate her. Heck, she was in training to be FBI; she couldn't be a coward.

"Look, Greg, it's called sharing information, not gossip, because it's the truth. Everyone has to sign in and out. Besides, the log's not top secret. I've seen your name on there, and a few of your other pals, even Greenberg's several times, well, more than several times, but who cares? Students go places on the weekends, ain't no biggie."

"Why are you looking at it if you're not signing out? Why do you give a damn?" Greg stepped toward her, but Francine didn't flinch, at least outwardly.

"Missy will kill me for this. She had a crush on Townsend. Let me repeat, *had*, as in past tense. She couldn't find him one weekend, so she checked the logs to see if he'd left the campus."

This information surprised them. Not because Missy had a crush

—this happened with students—but her attraction to the asshole Mick Townsend shocked them.

"Checking to see where the guy was, holy hell. When we sign out, it never says where we are. Missy's just a stupid broad who's stalking him like a lovesick woman. Mick's right. You ladies ought to be at home cooking dinner and having babies. Not here having crushes like wimpy girls. You females are so predictable."

"Stow your attitude, Spokane, and your outdated views on women in the workplace garbage," Kasper said with authority. "You, Mick, and Jay are all ignorant."

"I gotta agree with Mick. Bergman, you're just a brownnosing jackass, and do-gooder. Whatever makes you feel as if you're better than any of us is a mystery. You think you're a big shot for bringing down DEA agents a few years back? Hell, Kasper, the unfriendly ghost. You were a tech nerd, not a cop. I hear tell some guys say you're here because there's an ex-DEA agent who is now on the FBI's Ten Most Wanted who's gunning for you. Is this true? You're a chickenshit who needs FBI protection?"

Kasper's head dipped slowly, closing his eyes. He counted to ten. Greg Spokane was a moron, same as Townsend and Greenberg.

"Since y'all obviously hate my guts for no apparent reason, any of you three protecting me or having my six is a damn out-and-out, far-fetched idea. "

"I'd say it sounds like jealousy, doesn't it girls?" Kasper took up for them. Bishop wanted to return the favor.

"Butt out, Bishop. Just leave this to the men. No one cares about you or your two girlfriends, except for what you've got between your knees; it's all women are good for. And you, Bergman, stop acting high and mighty. You no longer have the Houston Police Department in your back pocket." Greg paused for a beat, snickering. "All you've got is a pocketful of pussies. Counting the men you hang out with."

"Yep, a lot more than what you've got. You've got Mick. We don't like the guy, so who else ya got? Jay Greenberg, Ned Stovall, and possibly Bobby Tibbets? Crud, Bobby might not make the grade. Hell, even our resident loner, Leo Sutton, steers clear of you boys."

Kasper, done bantering with this moron, sidestepped him, moving alongside the bulletin board. Spokane walked past Kasper with a nasty smirk and a one-fingered salute, and the others watched him trudge through the hallway, leaving out the same door Mick Townsend had. No one uttered a word.

Harlowe Bishop broke the silence. "Umm, uh, Kasper, uh, thanks for taking up for Karney, Frankie, and me. We appreciate it, but it's unnecessary. "

"Oh, I don't know. Kinda sweet to have a guy say nice things about us lowly women." Karney grinned.

"I'm, uh, hey, girls, I know y'all can fend for yourselves, but my mentor wasn't a narrow-minded type of guy. He was fair and knew women made great cops and agents."

"Yeah, Bergman's right. The grades on the board prove it. You gals outranked all but two of us. Kasper sits at the top. And by damn, I can't believe Lefty's right under him. Fuck, Lefty, oh, sorry, ladies, my mouth. But Corneal, I had no idea you were actually smart." This amazed Pete Casbury.

"I presume this is a flattering comment from you, correct, Pete? You can be a real shit, you jackass. And no, I won't apologize for my mouth. Like good ole Mick stated, equal rights. I have no intention of verbally beating you down, but I ain't gonna treat you gals with kid gloves just cuz y'all are girls either."

Harlowe frowned. "First, stop this shit about girls, females, and this gal crap. Me and Frankie are NATs just like you boneheads, and we aren't constantly talking about your gender since we don't fucking care about your body parts. And yeah, I have a potty mouth too." She elbowed Karney. "Miss Goody Two Shoes here, she's the prude. Sorry, bestie, but I still think you're a tough broad."

"Whatever. I cuss, just not every second word. Besides, I really gotta be flaming mad," Karney Logan huffed.

Harlowe let out a spurt of laughter. "Flaming, y'all know this is code for Karney—it means fucking."

"So, fellow NATs, how about we grab grub and sodas? Afterward, let's head over to the main dormitory. We can veg out watching the tube till lights out." Lefty was ready to relax.

"Yep," "yeah, uh-huh," "I'm in, sure thing," and "let's go," phrases were called out.

"What do we wanna watch tonight? Chad called over his shoulder as they filed out of the main classroom hallway.

"How about we watch *J. Edgar* or *Silence of the Lambs*? Maybe we can learn something new." These were Pete's choices.

"I vote for *Criminal Minds*." Frankie liked the darker series.

"What about *X- Files*?" Lefty liked the- it-ain't-ever-gonna-happen-with-FBI along with ghost series.

"How about none of those and we watch a *Rocky* movie instead? Get away from FBI and law enforcement?" Karney threw out as an alternative.

Kasper couldn't help it. "Okay, sure, but is his manager dead or alive?"

The seven of them broke up with laughter.

CHAPTER TWO

January 2014

Quantico graduation was less than a week away; spirits were high. Eager to get their badges to become official FBI Agents, yet sadly, not everyone made the cut. One surprise was Mick Townsend.

Kasper did some digging on Townsend and Greenberg—unofficially, not inclined to become an adversary to anyone. This was their choice, but he felt it wise getting to know his chief nemesis, Mick Townsend, and his henchman, Greenberg.

He found little on Jay Greenberg, who was older. This was strange enough since Quantico's cutoff age was 37 and Greenberg was almost 36. For a few years, Greenberg worked as a Deputy Sheriff in Bastrop County. Not much else in his work files, blank spots with little other work history. Prying a little deeper, he looked into the SSA files, careful to obliterate his footprint, but it did him no damn good. It was as if Greenberg didn't exist until he began working at the Bastrop County Sheriff's Department. Was Greenberg part of an undercover program to protect him from unresolved enemies?

Mick Townsend's story: ex-vice from Chicago. The FBI was his one way to progress since his advancement at the Chicago PD wasn't working out like he'd figured. Townsend was a pure misogynistic pig, not for any reason except he grew up in that atmosphere. Mick's father, hardcore military, where and men were men and women were at home waiting. However, recently, Mick had lessened his macho misogynistic outlook all because of one NAT. During the sparring, a trainee of the opposite sex showed zero fear when she'd faced him. Harlowe Bishop was going to make a remarkable FBI agent, male or female it didn't matter; she was a cut above the rest.

Six Weeks Before Graduation

Harlowe Bishop, part of another group of mostly women, joined the all-male close combat training class Bergman and Townsend were part of. Mick, what an idiot he'd been uttering snide remarks under his breath showing off for what few buddies he had. Instructor Robbs, with his ears like a dog, didn't miss a beat.

"Townsend. Front and center," Robbs' voice boomed.

Brawny and cocky, Townsend sauntered to the mats.

Robbs turned. "Bishop, join Townsend on the mats."

She stepped up facing Townsend, who outweighed her by almost one hundred pounds and was a half-foot taller, with a confident look in her eyes.

Robbs tossed them each a chalk knife. "Bishop, put your knife in your waistband and turn your back."

"Townsend, on my mark, come at her, disarm her, and then abduct her." Robbs used his whistle, and they began.

He advanced, confident this was gonna be a breeze. In a sudden move, snaking out his right arm, he grabbed her around the neck. When she felt his arm on her neck, she turned her body toward him, twisted, and ducking her head she pulled out of his hold. This move threw him off balance for a second before he advanced. Thrusting his knife hand forward, he stepped in for the attack. Harlowe ducked under his outstretched arm, reaching behind her she yanked out her chalk knife and in a quick unexpected movement, she head-butted Mick in his solar plexus. He doubled over as her right foot swept his left foot, sending him to the ground. In a brief two seconds, she'd put an X on his torso and backed away.

It was an action-packed few minutes. A thunderous applause erupted, breaking the silence in the training room as the class celebrated Harlowe's victory. She'd outmaneuvered a man six-foot one, 225 pounds, and her five-foot-five, 123 pounds, soaking wet.

Robbs blew his whistle to end the exercise. "Agent Trainee Bishop, good job; those quick reactions will save your life." He shifted his gaze toward Mick who had stood and was gingerly trying to wipe off the chalk X from his gray sweatshirt.

"Townsend, remember, just because you're the size you are, doesn't mean you have the advantage. Bishop is a black belt in Judo and has attained high-level mixed martial arts training."

Harlowe noticed several jaws drop. This wasn't information she'd even shared with her new best bud Karney and now their instructor was telling everybody in the class.

"That was a Judo move she made?" Mick regarded her intently.

The instructor waggled his head. "No, but it was a smart move. I asked her not to use any Judo in this class. She's in a special tactical class with other female NATs. These women are proficient in self-defense: Judo, Muy Thai, Karate, and Jujitsu. Everyone needs to remember this; there are no genders at this academy. We aren't genders here at the FBI. We're Special Agents who work together to keep our country safe. Got it?"

Enthusiastic hands applauded his comment—everyone but the one NAT, or better-known GNAT, Mick Townsend—who clapped reminiscent of a feeble old lady giving Harlowe Bishop the worst stink-eye stare in history.

Twenty weeks later, 239 of 251 students crossed the stage to receive their diplomas. The last NAT walked across the stage, credentials and badges in hand; the FBI Director took to the podium.

"Please stand and raise your right hands," the Director instructed.

Lifting their right hands, in unison they repeated word-for-word the FBI Oath, making it official.

"Students, you're duly sworn in to keep your pledge to defend the Constitution of the United States. However, tonight I want you to relax. Have a few drinks, but drink responsibly. Have a few laughs because you've all earned it. After tonight, your new job is to keep the world safe. Congratulations, Agents!"

Whoops were yelled and applause rang out. Merriment and enthusiasm drifted in the air as graduates along with their families and close friends enjoyed the festivities.

Kasper, Lefty, and Harlowe were seated across from Karney, Francine, and Chad, listening to Harlowe's father tell stories about his days as a Navy SEAL, before and during the Persian Gulf War. He had funny and deeply interesting stories. The most interesting tales ended with, "I can't tell you any more, it's classified." They let out groans in sync, and Mr. Bishop snickered. "Use your imaginations, kids. It's what I had to do when my grandfather told me stories."

Harlowe's great-grandfather had been a WWII veteran, stationed at Pearl Harbor. Later, it came out that Benjamin Oscar Bishop, whom everyone called Bob because of his initials, was a WWII flyboy who took part in the fire bombs over Tokyo after Doolittle's Raid. They were awestruck.

Kasper watched them at the after-graduation party—Mick Townsend, Greg Spokane, Jay Greenberg, and Ned Stovall—off to themselves, heads together, almost as if they were plotting. Here he was, twenty-minutes after reciting the oath, thinking like an agent.

Although he would miss Houston, he wasn't too far away. Dallas, Texas, was where he'd call home. In his peripheral vision, he noticed Mick staring. Kasper wanted to know what his problem was, but left it alone. Nobody knew what was up his rump.

Dan Robbs was on his way to the refreshment table when Kasper caught up with him.

"Bergman, are you enjoying the festivities?"

"Yes, sir, I am. Actually, I wanted to thank you for your mentoring and for, well, everything."

"You're welcome, Bergman." Robbs took a mouthful of his hors d'oeuvre, chewing in thought, and Kasper waited, noting a display of concentration on the instructor's face. Once he swallowed, Robbs said, "The Bureau's got good people, although not everyone follows the correct path. You're a top-notch guy, Bergman, with strong convictions. I never said this, but keep your guard up around certain classmates. Be wary of who you put your trust in, but always trust your gut, kid. Not gonna say any more."

Kid. Instructor Robbs called him *kid.* This took him back to his initial encounters with Detective Jack West of Houston, who also called him kid. He smiled.

"Thank you, sir. It means a lot, coming from you."

"About this *sir* business, call me Dan. You've earned it, Special Agent Bergman."

"Yes si—uh, of course, Dan. It was my honor to be in your class. And I learned from the best back in Houston to watch my six, with everyone and everything."

Robbs' eyebrows arched, and he motioned to the empty chairs next to a far wall. "Seems you have a story, Bergman. Care to share?"

Kasper grinned. "How about I grab us a couple of brewskies first?"

Couple of beers later, munching on chips, cheese, and crackers,

Kasper told him about working undercover with Jack West. Under the table at first. Then OAG and DEA, approved. Robbs listened intently, interested and amazed, knowing Bergman was gonna make one helluva FBI Special Agent.

CHAPTER THREE

Two nights before departing to head their separate ways, most of the students congregated at a local microbrewery off campus called Flavor Brewing, Inc.. Oddly, FBI for short.

Kasper positioned himself against the wall in the back near a corner table, sipping his third flavor of micro-beer, which he didn't care for, but drank anyway. He listened to the conversation between a few guys he didn't consider friends and stayed in the shadows.

"Yeah, right, like you'd have a chance at hitting that. She's all work and no play. I can attest to that," Greg Spokane enlightened Jay Greenburg.

"Yeah, same thing Earl Kason told me. He asked her to dinner, and she was flat-out rude to him. Hell, it was only dinner, not a marriage proposal," Greenberg scowled.

Townsend finished his beer wiping his mouth. "Females should be home, waiting to fuck their men, not out catching bad guys. By the way, where's Ned? Didn't he take her out for drinks once?"

"Stovall had to hit the head. Yeah, he had a date with her, said she was a cold fish. He told me, and I quote, 'No one will get his hands on her beaver, not without getting his fingers bit off.' "

Kasper watched Greg's eyes cut over to where four of the girls stood. Spokane focused on Harlowe. She was the prettiest. Karney and Missy were both cute and Francine, poor girl, everyone called her Freaky Franky. She wasn't pretty, but she was one helluva smart girl and this intimidated even the nerdy guys, who were all over the cyber-shit, as they called it. Kasper felt in the years to follow, Francine could be running a terrorist cyber unit blindfolded, kicking butt. He'd talked to her when others didn't give her the time of day, and he knew her dream was an overseas gig. Bergman wondered if the others knew she spoke four languages other than just her computer language skills—probably not, no need for her to show off.

The men salivated over Harlowe who was attractive, smart, built, and tough. Because she didn't react to any of their advances, they all talked about her unfavorably.

He continued to listen.

"So, Stovall mentioned she'd gone out with him for drinks, but when he got friendly, she damn near broke his hand."

Greg snorted his nasty laugh. "Yeah, she crossed her legs and nearly broke his fingers."

"Spokane, you're a pervert. He didn't say that."

"More colorful said like that."

"What sounds more colorful?" Back from the men's room, Ned Stovall carried a fresh beer.

Mick explained, and Greg continued his yammering. "Yeah, since Stovall said she didn't put out I didn't ask her for drinks. Hell, I wanted a gal who'd give me some action in the sack. I've had to be celibate since I got here and was getting blue balls."

"You should've gone for the obvious if you were so hard up."

"What are you blathering about, Greenberg?" Mick followed Jay's gaze as he took a quick look at Francine, winking. She blushed and broke the eye lock quickly.

"Francine Ryder, freak-geek, and you?" In his mind's eye, he envisioned it, and Ned Stovall laughed at the image it made.

Greenburg finished his orange-spice beer, plopped his glass down heavily, wiping his mouth. "Me and freakozoid Frankie. Shit, no way. Now, Bishop, yeah I'd tap her or Goody Two Shoes Karney, who I'm betting would be a she-devil in the sack, cuz her prudish little piece of ass ain't fooling anyone."

"Shoot, I like my women with more meat on 'em, staying home with no panties on, spread-eagle waiting for me to just slide the rails."

Jay's lip curled in a half snarl. "You like fat chicks, Spokane?"

Greg frowned. "I said more meat, not a fucking tub of lard, Jay. Did you hear me say fat?"

"No, Greg, you said more meat, same as fat to me."

Mick jumped in. "Nah, what Greg meant is have sumtin to hold onto, that's all."

Stovall kept a straight face. "So, Mick, you like 'em big too, ain't that right?"

"You're a bastard, Ned."

Jay Greenberg spurted a laugh.

Greg and Mick frowned and Greg asked, "You find this funny, Jay?"

"Nah, but you two shitheads carrying on about overweight chicks when we all know you both fucked Laurie Bassett, the big gal who left the program six weeks in."

"Nah, she wasn't huge. She was healthy," Greg argued.

"She had extra weight, Greg. I saw her without all her clothes, too." Mick snickered. So did the others. An awkward silence followed.

Kasper made no noise, sitting in the shadowed area, sipping a nasty warm micro-beer, apple-butter flavor, which tasted neither like apples nor butter or a mixture; all it did was leave an unpleasant aftertaste. He silently set his mug on the table and leaned back further into the darkness to listen to these four boneheaded agents making fun of Francine. They called her the biggest geek at Quantico and not a "real" girl. They yakked about how Missy Short and Evie Jordan were there to find men.

Several fellas agreed having women in the Bureau was a step up out of the Middle Ages. Most guys thought women had a great deal of value to offer the agency. He'd even learned Lefty and Francine had bonded over their keen interest in crimes associated with banking institutions, money-laundering, and the ever-growing Bitcoin cryptocurrency dollar. Kasper predicted Sebastian and Ryder would make an excellent team one day.

Kasper had only scratched the surface of what he knew about his classmates. There was no one he was ready to forge a meaningful relationship with yet. They weren't there to make lifelong friends, their purpose was becoming FBI Agents. He wasn't blabbing it all over Quantico, but thanks to Mick Townsend, everyone learned about his stint with the Houston Police Department and him working with the DEA, plus the crap about Theo Sykes. Townsend spread the rumor he was in hiding and using the FBI as cover to save his ass. The guy was a nimrod.

"Where've you been hiding?" Harlowe pulled out the seat next to his.

"Not hiding, listening to chatter."

She glanced over his shoulder where the four creeps sat. "Hope you don't believe everything you overhear."

"No, never have, never will."

"I know what they're saying, all us girls do."

Kasper gathered their belittling misogynistic attitudes and beliefs genuinely hurt her.

"Bishop, not all men think that way. Just guys who're afraid you ladies are gonna take over the world." His lips arched into a slight smile.

"And here I'd thought all men had risen above those 1940 attitudes and learned to accept women as equals."

Kasper gave her a toothy grin. "Smart men, yeah. Men with zero smarts are gonna take time."

"Come on, I know a place. They sell real beer and stronger shit. We can sit and talk. You game?"

"Uh, sure, Bishop, I guess."

"Oh, cripes, Bergman, I'm not coming on to you. I just need a friend." The frown she gave him was real enough.

"What about Karney, she's—"

"Totally into Neal and has been since they met on the mats. You're oblivious, aren't you?"

Kasper gazed over to witness Neal and Karney with their heads together, doing who knew what.

"Yeah, I guess I am. Okay, Bishop, let's go talk shop and shit, like two good old buddies over a coupla brewskis and I mean real beer, not this micro crap—which I hate—I'm talking about Miller, or Budweiser, and possibly a few shots of Jose if you think you can hold your alcohol."

That night, Kasper, and Harlowe became Bergman and Bishop, trusted comrades and lifelong friends. No romance, just an honest relationship between two coworkers. Everyone thought they were "doing it." Not a fact, but absolute fiction. Even though, as a red-blooded male, he found her attractive, he didn't consider her a romantic interest. Bishop made it plain in the beginning that romantic relationships weren't on her to-do list.

CHAPTER FOUR

He sat staring at his hands. A solitary image appeared in his head. In the last moments all he focused on was the eyes, watching them roll back into their heads with their final breath. Eyes unable to see. He didn't exist, neither did they any longer. Their panic and fear ceased with their final breath. No longer struggling to breathe, they were now at peace and so was he.

He lifted his head looking out his windshield into the starry night, thoughts careening him backward to the days of his youth.

1981

What had his father seen in her? She was a vampire, sucking the life out of them.

They were fine after Mom died of breast cancer. His preparedness to be a single dad with a three-year-old was a culture shock. It'd become his pop's mission to create a family life, find a new wife and a new mom for his baby son. Stan Wallen did it one year after his wife had passed.

Even when Jason was a preschooler, Lydia wasn't Mom material. He hated his stepmother. When his dad was watching, she pretended to act like a loving mother, but as soon as he left, she turned nasty. She made him stay in his room all day, ignoring his most primary needs.

After a spanking, Pop would say, "Son, mind your mother, she's doing what's best for you."

The spankings were frequent, each time hurting worse than the last, but he refused to cry making her even madder. His evil stepmother never left a scratch; she was careful. Jason never told anyone—not his dad, not a teacher, not even a friend at school.

Soon, Lydia was weepy every day and sick, with zero energy to beat him. She was getting fatter, but he never said it aloud for fear of getting clocked in the mouth. A few months shy of a year into this farce of a marriage, along came brother number one, and then less than ten months later, brother number two came along.

In between caring for a baby and being pregnant the second time, she continued to hurt him, physically and emotionally. "You aren't mine. Stay out of the way, and don't cause me any trouble, brat."

Five-year-old Jason didn't say a word, but when she turned away, he put his finger up like a gun, wanting to kill her, wishing her dead. The seed was planted.

1986

After Pop lost his job, unemployment rolled in, but it wasn't enough, and they resorted to food stamps, church charities, and handouts. They ate cheap-ass food and did what needed to be done to survive. Of course, Lydia was no help at all, always complaining and making Pop feel worse. Life was a struggle for two years. Then one day Stan

Wallen came home with a spring in his step and the worry lines gone from his face.

"Hey, Liddy, got good news."

Yuck, Liddy, his pet name for her. Jason wanted to throw up and always wanted to call her Liddy Piggy, but decided a beating wasn't worth it. He followed his dad into the tiny apartment kitchen. "Hey, Papa, what's the good news?"

Stan stared at his wife anxiously. "Got a job, ain't that great?"

Lydia lit a cheap generic cigarette, huffed, blowing out smoke. "Where and what's it pay?"

"It pays more than unemployment which is running out. Job's in Oklahoma."

"Oklahoma City. Huh, it's a decent town, be nice to—"

"No, the job's on the outskirts of Marietta."

"A fucking farm, you're no farmer, Stan." Lydia's double chin wobbled with her hateful scowl.

Jason glanced at her, then him, waiting for Dad to tell her to kiss his ass, a job was a job.

"Not on a farm," he said, clearing his throat. "Landed a job as a groundskeeper and backhoe digger at a cemetery. Money's decent and there's room for advancement."

Lydia's coarse, bitter, smoker's laugh rang out. "Right, advancement, sure! Guess the perks are a free grave plot." With extra force Lydia crushed her cigarette butt out. "Sounds fan-fucking-tastic. So, when we gotta move?"

1988

Jason found the letters written by his ugly stepmother, letters to other men. Slinking around he nosed into her things, finding the letters they wrote back. He read every letter, before stashing them away and hiding them from the lard-ass whore.

The lovie-dovie words paired with nasty things they'd like to do made him want to hurl. She told them how bad her life was with her stupid husband and his brat kid. She wanted a real man to satisfy her, not a lame dick like Stan. Next, she asked them what their plans were after their release. His disgusting stepmother also wanted to hear about their crimes; she wanted more excitement, she wanted more money, she wanted a different life. All Lydia ever did was "want."

His hate grew twofold. His pop was an honest, hardworking man who'd ended up with a cheap hussy of a wife. A hussy corresponding with men who didn't deserve to live, who had gotten themselves arrested, and were rotting behind prison bars. He shut his eyes—he'd just turned eleven when he faced her.

"I'm just a friend to men, men who need a friend, and it ain't bad and it's not illegal either."

What bullshit!

"Did you tell my father you're writing love letters to these scum buckets?" Jason stood, resolute, crossing his arms glaring at the obese bitch.

Her jowls wiggled with the shake of her head. "I ain't cheating, just giving those poor guys some happiness, that's all."

"Uh-huh, it is too cheating. I read some of those letters. It's nasty. If you're just being friends, why talk about sex? And you talk bad about Pop. It's like, it's, well, you're cheating on him in your heart. You ain't nuttin' but a greasy whore and I hate you."

Before he could stop her, she smacked the holy hell out of him, sending him backward, his head banging to the ground. Lydia smiled an evil smile, leering at him. "You ain't gonna tell him squat, you got me, cuz somebody will pay for it if you do, someone like poor Matty, you want that on your head?" She swayed her head and an insignificant evil smile sprung up on her wrinkly smoker's lips. Lydia's double chin shook when she spoke again. "Besides, kid, I give your dad anything he wants, you hear me, *anything*." The word "anything" was highly emphasized with her snort of laughter. If Dad wanted a blowjob or anal sex, he'd get it from this tubby broad and by damn, she'd offer it up to keep him on her side too, or she'd deny him any sexual favors. Either way, he was beat.

Jason's voice, a low growl, "Fine, but you'd better keep your word, you don't touch Matt or Den, cuz if you do, I swear I'll kill your flabby ass."

The idle threat of an angry young preteen boy—little did he know the fruitless prophecy would one day bear fruit. With a heated glare at one another, they turned and left the room, each detesting the other fiercely.

1992

The case made national news.

Red-Light District Killer Caught in Texas

Preston Munn was apprehended last night in Frost, Texas, a small town just outside of Dallas. Police were alerted to his whereabouts after finding a second prostitute dead a week prior. Munn is allegedly responsible for the killings of several call girls in the States of Arizona, Nevada, New Mexico, Utah, and Colorado, before ending up in Texas. The detectives for all States are pulling their resources...

At fifteen years old, this mesmerized Jason. The story drew him in, consumed him, and he followed it for almost two years. Next came the sentencing. Munn ended up sentenced to life without parole in the maxim security penitentiary in ADX, Florence, Colorado.

Dennis and Matt hated their mother too. Lydia treated her biological sons like second-class citizens, suffocating them with her neediness; they had no way of breaking free. The obese tramp had no other family. They'd all moved off and were several states away. Years before, she'd alienated her family.

Their father barely acknowledged his wife, repulsed by what she'd become. Lydia, now weighing over 300 pounds, wasn't just slothful, she was revolting. The woman hardly ever bathed; all she did was cry and bellyache.

"No one cares about me and how I feel," she whined.

"Lydia, care about yourself, then others might care about you. I'm going out. Clean yourself up and for God's sake, take a damn bath, you smell." Stan Wallen slammed the door, headed to the bars and another night of drinking himself into oblivion, as he'd been doing for three solid years.

Pop didn't believe in divorce and just because his wife had become a chubby slob wasn't grounds for divorce. His pop also didn't believe in irreconcilable differences. What a shmuck. The boys watched their father die more every day because of her. At a young age, Jason had already lost his mother, and he'd be damned if he was gonna lose his dad too.

Late Fall 1994

At seventeen, Jason was old enough to leave home, but if he left, he'd have to leave them alone with her. Dennis thirteen, Matt almost twelve, neither would survive if he wasn't there; they were too weak. Lydia Wallen used intimidation and extortion to leave them completely drained.

"Shut the hell up, both of you boys, cuz if ya don't get me some money, I'm gonna beat the hell outta Matty, and you know he ain't gonna say I did it. He'll blame the school bullies like he always does."

Matt had endured her wrath on more occasions than the others had. She hated him with a passion no one understood.

"Come on, Jason, get her some cash. Levi's mom had some money in her purse. Please?" Matt was in tears.

"I'm tired of stealing cash for your fat ass." His hatred was palpable and his eyes shot daggers at her.

"Find something to sell, then, and stealing for me, shit, you're already a thief, you stupid punk. I know what you're doing at the cemetery." Her fat face jiggled, and a sneer curled her nasty lips. "Get me more money this time, cuz, ten fucking dollars ain't gonna cut it. I'm not kidding, Jason, or your dad's gonna get wind of your pint-sized enterprise."

"Shit, Mom, he'll never fucking believe it, and you ain't gonna ruin Dad's job," Dennis burst out.

"Watch your mouth, Dennis, or I'm gonna tell him you were involved too, then Matt's gonna suffer because of you two dildos." She turned her 315-pound ass around leaving the three boys in the kitchen alone.

"Jason, we can't let Dad find out. He'll lose his job and we can't sell the stuff, not yet."

A simpering Matt crumpled to the floor. "I can't again. She doesn't just beat me anymore, you guys just don't know, you don't!" His wailing muffled as he covered his face.

Jason placed his arm on the shoulder of his youngest half-brother, hugging him. "Yeah, we do know what she does, and I swear, Matty, I ain't gonna let her touch you, never again. I swear, Den and me, we'll make sure she don't hurt you anymore. Just let me think, I promise to fix this."

How the fuck did Lydia find out what they'd been doing? The others would never tell. They were all in too deep and he'd beat the hell outta RJ to prove to them what would happen if they blabbed.

Lydia threatened to ruin everything, and this was no minor thing, pissing him off. Today was the breaking point. He finally saw red, opening a door to a demon he never knew existed. Lydia's threats to expose them were bad. Her threats to beat Matty were the last straw. He had to do something, and it had to be drastic.

Spring 1995

Lydia Wallen was gone. Stan assumed she'd had enough and ran away, so no one reported her missing. She was a grown-ass woman, perhaps she'd hightailed it with another man. He sorta hoped she had, he actually didn't care. When a full week passed without a word and no answer to any of his calls, Stan Wallen filed a police report. The boys knew it was to keep up appearances, because they knew their pop felt a sense of relief. She was gone. Everyone joined the hunt for Lydia Wallen, but there were no clues where she'd run off to, and no signs of foul play.

"How you gonna work this, Jason...uh...about her just disappearing? Won't it be weird if she just ups and leaves?"

"Don't worry, RJ, gotta plan. The fat bitch was writing letters to prisoners so I'm gonna make it look like the whore ran off with one. They're crooks, let them talk their way out of it, or prove it wasn't them. You two can't tell anyone, ever, especially Matt, he'd cave. Got me?"

RJ and Annie couldn't ever utter a word to anybody about what he'd done, hell, they'd helped, so they were just as guilty when they'd watched him drain the life outta his fat stepmother.

He placed a handful of her more lurid pen pal letters strategically where his dad would find them. Once found, it hurt Stan, but it was fleeting. He turned the two letters over to the local police, which led the community to believe she'd run off and was in hiding with her ex-convict lover; what a joke. It worked like a charm.

Time passed. No one searched for Lydia Wallen any longer—she was off living with an ex-con—and nobody cared. Until Mera came into Jason's life in 2010, eleven years later, and his world began a slow spiral downward.

CHAPTER FIVE

Austin, Texas 2008

Vice Detective Jason Wallen made a few critical mistakes in judgment early in his career. His first infraction was having sex with one of his snitches, and the second was beating the hell out of a suspect. The first incident, eh, men were men. It got him a slap on the wrist and a warning to keep it in his pants. The second transgression got him sent to anger management classes. Therapy was a good thing; perhaps it would help him drive out the past and his old sins, which still haunted yet thrilled him.

He didn't worry about Lydia Wallen, his fat stepmother. He'd made sure no one found a physical body—no corpse, then no murder. Not a soul could connect him to her disappearance. Fact was, nobody bothered to look into his stepmother's disappearance, until Mera prodded and poked into his life.

Spring 2011

Thirty-four-year-old Jason Wallen stood six-foot-two, 215 pounds of muscle, very athletic. Mera Soon-Lee, his polar opposite, was six years his junior. He was brawn, she was brains. She'd been a columnist on *The Daily Texan*, the UT Austin student newspaper, and a journalist major with dreams of investigative reporting.

Half-Black, half-Asian, Mera Soon-Lee was a tiny thing and a sex kitten behind closed doors. They'd never stated their relationship was exclusive; it was just implied. Four months into the relationship he was smitten but not in love. He wasn't sure love existed for him. By damn, she was sexy with a fantastic body. But love? No, his heart wasn't involved. He'd miss her if she were to break if off, but mostly he'd miss fucking her and her fucking him back with just as much enthusiasm.

Saturday afternoon, they were at Mera's apartment. She was immersed in her research notes, and Jason bored while waiting began pestering her.

"Jason, stop. I have a work assignment due and don't have time to play your stupid games."

"Mera, you're a tease. You sit there in those fucking short shorts, and a top your luscious hooters are spilling outta and you expect me not to get worked up?"

She rolled her eyes, her pen tapping the notebook she was writing in. "Stop acting like I'm a sex toy for you, cuz if you don't, I'm gonna, uh..." She was trying to think of something gross to dampen his arousal. "Eat like a pig, get fat and nasty, and stop shaving my pits!" She turned back to writing, ignoring him, not expecting him to react.

This was a trigger, one he hadn't known he had. "You bitch!" Raising his hand he smacked the living shit out of her with his open palm.

Mera spiraled backward, her pen and notebook went flying, her eyes wide in disbelief.

"What the motherfucking fuck, Jason?" With her open palm she rubbed the side of her face as tiny tears formed at the corners of her eyes. Her face stung. "What was that for?"

He sat dumbfounded. He'd never hit a woman before, not even Lydia, his cunt stepmother. No, he hadn't hurt her, hell, he'd killed her, but it wasn't the same. He hated his stepmother, he didn't hate Mera.

Her voice tight, "You gonna answer me, you bastard? Why'd ya hit me?"

"Uh, I, well, I'm sorry, Mera. I didn't mean to."

"You didn't mean to? What the fuck? Didn't mean to but did! Why?"

His larger shoulders jerked upward. "Dunno. Sorry."

Her hand rubbed her offended cheek, still sensing the sting. A tear, only one, eked out the corner of one of her hazel almond-shaped eyes. "You're a shit, Jason Wallen!"

His thoughts turned to Lydia, his missing stepmother. He'd never told Mera the story because he never talked about the obese whore, or his childhood. But, oh, he remembered vividly what happened, reliving it, and each time he experienced profound sexual gratification. Only he knew—this was his dark secret.

He offered his hand, but she refused it. The diminutive woman stayed seated, legs crossed, distancing herself.

An inconsequential frown creased his brow, and Mera regarded him in a new light. It scared and intrigued her and her inner reporter was determined to find out what Jason Wallen's real story was.

"J," she crooned. "Go to the gym. Work off your frustrations. When you get back, we'll go for a nice dinner. Whatdaya say?"

Unbeknownst to him, this would begin of his spiral downward. It would rip the scars of his past open releasing the ugliness of who he was. For Mera, though, her time was up.

CHAPTER SIX

As she helped Cal Thompson, an investigative reporter, with research and police reports involving a serial rapist preying on the University's young coeds, Mera was also on a private mission investigating her current boyfriend of nine months.

He'd never introduced her to his family; all he'd said was his real mom passed away when he was three and his stepmother was mean. When he was seventeen, Lydia ran off, leaving his father wifeless and the boys motherless. It was a hard life, and he didn't care to talk about it. She'd let it go because she realized it bothered him immensely. Seven months into their relationship, they'd been a semi-family with her parents, but his family was still nonexistent.

As a good girlfriend, Mera never pried—until now.

"You've gotten to know my mom and dad, they're fond of you, and well, I believe it's time I get to know *your* family and have our families meet."

"Now's not good, cuz I gotta undercover thing I'm working, and I'm on call, so—" He gave her his usual *I'm sorry* facial shrug with a slight head tilt.

"Jason Wallen, this is the same tired old excuse you give me every damn time. Why not plan a four-day weekend, drive up to Oklahoma, it'll be fun?"

"No, I can't right now. When I get time off, we will." He couldn't keep putting her off, but damn it, he didn't want her meeting his dad or Dennis and Matt, not yet, possibly never. Shit.

A month later, his undercover sting ended. The case was ready to go to court, his part done, yet still he had more excuses, pissing Mera off. Her anger, though, was short-lived when he told her his COD chose him for a workshop in the prison system and he'd be in and out of town for the next month.

"Sorry, babe, but they want me to go with a group to Huntsville."

"Just vice going, or what?"

"Vice, homicide, sheriff's department, CSU techs, a few spooks, that's what I heard."

"To do what, preach law to convicts?" A laugh escaped her as her insides quivered. He'd be gone—road trip to Oklahoma!

"Nah, we're supposed to learn something from those bastards."

"Back in the day the FBI learned a lot from prisoners, didn't they?"

"Yeah, they got books on it—profiling killers and crap." This was so much more him. Preston Munn was at Huntsville. In 1994, as an impressionable already angry teenager, this case kept him glued to the television. Munn had no connections to his stepmother, but the idea of doing to her what Munn had done to the whores appealed to him at fourteen. Once he had the proper clearance as a police officer, he'd studied Preston's files. Reading the case files now, he hadn't realized how insightful he'd been as a mere teen by using the prison letters to leave a broken and useless trail to his long-gone stepmother. This was his chance to talk to Munn, find out what made him tick. Jason was giddy about this opportunity.

"You gonna miss me, or you gonna be too busy being Cal Thompson's bloodhound, doing his work making him look good for the newspaper?" He grabbed her pulling her close to hug her.

"Hey, sure, I'll miss ya," she lied, but this time away from him gave her a chance to dig into his life—perfect. "And, for your information, it's my job to be his so-called bloodhound. I find the facts, do interviews, and it's gonna help to further my career. I get credit for some of his story, might not be a byline, but credit is credit, you toad."

"Mera, you're hunting a rapist, be careful, would ya?"

"I'm not hunting him, per se, just facts about the case. The cops are hunting him, hell, Jason, you should be hunting him, right?"

She had a point, but he wasn't in the mood to argue. "Wanna go get some pizza?"

He never wanted to discuss cases, as well as never talk about his family, and it drove her nutty.

"Sure. Pizza and beer, I could use a few."

"I need a week off, Cal."

"No problem, Mera, you've been working your tiny tail off. Is everything okay?" He'd noticed a subtle change in her.

"Oh, sure, I, uh, just want to visit relatives." She didn't want him to know what she was doing. Cal could be intrusive and she didn't care to discuss this with him, plus he didn't like Jason. Cal never said why; Mera figured it was a male jealousy thing.

She snuck Dennis and Stan Wallen's numbers off of Jason's cell, and the next morning after a quick goodbye, he was off to Huntsville. Mera waited all of fifteen minutes before dialing the first number.

"Dennis, this is Mera Soon-Lee, Jason's girlfriend. I'm planning a trip to Oklahoma, and was wondering if I could come by to meet you, Matt, and your dad. I'm putting together a scrapbook for Jason and I wanted to see if y'all could help me."

"Uh, yeah, I suppose, but, ain't J coming with ya?"

"No, no, this is a surprise. Please don't tell him, okay?"

"Sure, I can keep a secret." A hint of a smile played on his lips.

Mera prearranged her flight to Lawton, Oklahoma Regional Airport the week before. She arranged a rental car to drive to Ardmore, where Dennis, Matt, and Stan Wallen lived. Stan moved to Ardmore after being diagnosed with liver disease. His years of drinking finally took a toll on him. Old man Wallen retired early taking disability. Neither Dennis nor Matt ever left their father's side, supporting him and caring for him. Sadly, she'd learned all of this from Dennis since Jason never spoke of his father or brothers. Odd and unnerving, bothering her for many reasons and making her wonder if it wasn't about her and who she was. Was he ashamed of her? She was a mix of Black and Asian. He was from a lily-white family; was he embarrassed by her? She'd let it go for now.

It was nine-thirty when she arrived at the Lawton Airport. In no time she'd gotten her rental and was driving to Ardmore to meet the Wallen boys at a Starbucks on Holiday Drive.

"You must be Mera." Dennis extended his hand, and she took it; his grip was firm.

"I am, and since there's a Whataburger next door, I'm famished. You wanna a get a burger?"

"Yeah, sure, I'll text Matt, let him know where we are."

"Great!"

Over flame-broiled burgers, fries, and colas, the three of them got acquainted. Small talk ensued—where they were born, what they did for a living, and then Mera said, "I'll bet you two have some good and bad stories about my Jason, dontcha?"

Sniggers between the brothers sounded as old stories, school, and at-home anecdotes were told. It was funny learning about the man she was living with, his childhood and unruly teenage years, stuff he never talked about.

Dennis was aware, as he watched him talking to her, that Matthew was smitten with Jason's girl.

"Tell me more about Jason growing up. You know, he's so closemouthed about his childhood. I mean, he knows about every scraped knee I've had." Sipping her cola she looked at them, waiting.

"Our dad can tell you about when Jason was a little boy. Not much I remember, he was almost six when I came along," Matt said.

"Yeah, we were too young to remember much," Dennis concurred.

She didn't miss the odd exchange between them and her instincts kicked in. Whatever they were hiding wasn't good. Mera didn't want to know, but she *wanted* to know.

"You're going to visit with our dad?" Matt changed the subject.

"Yes, tomorrow morning, he has doctor appointments today."

Dennis squashed up his empty burger wrapper and fry container, his forehead puckered. "My big brother's a shit for not bringing you around sooner to meet all of us. I mean, we're the only family he has.

"If you were my gal, I'd have told the world," Matt confessed to her shyly.

Dennis's frown became more pronounced. "Matty, he ever heard you say that, you'd get a walloping."

This comment had Mera wondering if Jason had anger issues all his life. He'd already smacked her once, would it happen again?

"Mera, I've got old photos and stuff I can share. How about I meet you after work? I get off at five." Matt eyed his brother with his *don't fuck with me* look.

"Sounds like a plan. How about I meet you guys, at my hotel tonight, say, oh, around six, it'll give us more time to chat?"

CHAPTER SEVEN

Dennis declined meeting later, saying he had other plans, but Mera didn't believe him. Hell, they'd just met so she couldn't outright call him a liar.

"How about I take you to dinner tomorrow?" Dennis picked up the remaining empty burger wrappers.

"Sure." Her smile didn't reach her eyes and her stomach tightened with her gut instinctively warning her to get back to Texas.

Dennis said, "Marvelous. I've got a meeting and can't be late."

They watched him pull out of the parking lot and something sent a shiver up Mera's spine. Matt noticed her reaction, and he patted her arm.

"Don't worry about Den, he's protective of Jason. Of me too, but Jason's different."

"Oh?" Mera slurped the dregs of her cola.

Matt sighed, watching his brother's taillights disappear. "He saved us. Our mom used to beat us, especially me." He shook his head. "Don't wanna go into details, but she ran off and we were glad, even Dad was happy. Please don't ask about her or that time in our life. Jason didn't tell ya, did he?"

Mera tilted her head a smidge puckering her brows. "No, Matt, and I suppose it's his place to tell me." She paused. "Hey, you got time for ice cream before you head off to work? I saw a Braum's, how does a sundae or a banana split sound? I'm buying." End their meeting on a pleasant note, she thought.

Matt hadn't disappointed. He had a box full of old photos, mementoes from Jason's school days, including old love letters from his high school sweetheart.

"He was smitten, wanted to marry her." Matt's voice faded. He just sat staring at the photograph of him, Jason, Gloria, Dennis, and a few other kids in the front yard of a friend's old house. One kid perched on the tailgate of an old blue Ford Truck.

"Where was this taken?" Mera eyed him wondering what terrible memory he was harboring.

"Here, in Oklahoma. Tiny town our dad was working in. He was a groundskeeper for a park." He couldn't bring himself to say *cemetery*. "Back then our pop thought we'd like living out in the country. Small-town values, free space to roam. Mom hated the place, and she hated Dad for moving us out to the middle of shitsville." He eyed her, wondering if she'd perceive them differently—*him* differently—regarding them as a poor country family.

"Well, seems like a fun group, the four of y'all."

He exhaled. "Yeah, guess so."

"Uh, what happened with the girl?"

"Her family shipped her off to relatives up North, I think." Matt wasn't about to spill the beans. Big brother Jason got the girl pregnant and right after, Gloria up and disappeared.

"Guess Jason was sad, huh? What was Gloria's last name?"

"Yeah, he was sad, and her last name, gosh, lemme think, uh, hmmm, ain't that funny, I don't remember. It's been forever, and she wasn't *my* girlfriend."

As they talked, Mera could tell there were holes in his stories and Matt kept hem-hawing at certain questions, like innocent inquiries about Gloria, Jason's ex-girl, and their mother. What was this family hiding?

Stan Wallen was a nice old man. Mera instantly liked him and enjoyed their light conversation and his witty humor.

"You know," he said," I gotta box full of Jason's old stuff. If you want, I'll get it for you. Let you dig through it, long as you bring it back."

"Uh, that'd be fantastic, Mr. Wallen." Her heart thudded. What secrets would she find?

The old man chuckled. "Call me Stan, or Dad. Hell, Mera, we're family now."

"Yes, of course. Stan."

Family, my ass, she thought. Jason never brought her around, not once, and it pissed her off.

He helped her load a banker's box full of stuff that belonged to Jason from birth through his college years, into the trunk of the rental car.

"So, you're okay with me taking this stuff tonight to go through? I mean, I promise to get it back to you before I head back to Texas."

"Yeah, yeah, sure, ain't like I need the stuff to live; it's just memories I wanna keep, that's all. Ya know, haven't seen my boy in a while. He sends me money when I need it, and he might call me once in a blue moon. Seems he wrote his brothers and me off after Lydia left. Jason went to college, never looked back. Our family unit fell apart back then, was never the same."

Stan opened a door for her, or a Pandora's Box, but she asked, "Would it hurt too much to talk about it, Stan? What happened, exactly?"

The old guy scratched at his ashen stubble, and his shaggy eyebrows dipped together. He hadn't talked about Lydia's disappearance to anyone since 1999, back when it happened. Stan coughed dryly and motioned to his kitchen table. Mera knew Stan suffered from cirrhosis of the liver but what stage, she wasn't sure. He was gaunt with tummy bloat and some spider vein blood vessels. Otherwise, he didn't seem frail. She also wasn't gonna blurt out, "Hey, what stage is your cirrhosis," either. She'd not seen any booze in his kitchen, and hoped he'd stopped drinking, for the sake of his sons.

He pointed to the ancient 1960's kitchen table and chairs. "Why don't we set a spell? You got time?"

"Yes, I do. Not leaving for a day or so. Even then, for you, Stan, I'd make time." Mera pulled out an ancient chair. The vinyl had ripped, and he'd patched it with duct tape. She liked him, even though it was a sad situation. Stan, with his dying liver and empty life, *his golden years, my butt*, she thought. Nothing about his last years were golden. Soon she'd learn that nothing about his younger years had been anything to write home about either.

Stan began, "Jason was three when his mom died. A year later, I met Lydia. It was all okay, I guess. But then it wasn't—"

In the hotel room, alone, she lifted the lid off the box—papers, pictures, cards, letters, even old bills scattered throughout the mess of papers haphazardly piled inside. Letters he'd written to his dead mother; she figured some kid's therapist had him write them. Newspaper articles regarding sporting events from high school as a star football player and some about his accolades, both in high school and college. The oddest newspaper clippings concerned the trial of a man named Preston Munn, rapist-killer. Wow, this happened when he was fourteen. Had this gotten him interested in police work?

Mr. Wallen had a few pictures of him in his toddler years and some older photos of him with his real mother before she got sick, then sadly some of them together once she was sick, withering away. Mera found school photos and a few of him with Dennis and Matt.

There were pictures with friends, and several with Gloria. She came across other photos of different girls, but Matt said Gloria had been the one. The box was a treasure trove of real life. Until she found the notebooks. Jason's diaries were deeply personal, and she felt like a voyeur, but as she read a few pages her heart raced.

The date on the front in black Sharpie was 1989, he would've been about twelve, and as she read, it drew her in, like reading a horror novel in the making. Stories from the mind of a twelve-year-old boy, and they scared her. Were they just stories? As she thumbed through them, her insides cringed. After putting them in chronological order, several years were missing, and the books had pages torn out—that too was a mystery. Why had he kept them, and did he know his father had them? She set the composition notebooks aside and dug into the box finding letters written to inmates. He hadn't written them, but why did he have them? Stamped with *Return to Sender*, these were letters written by his stepmother, Lydia, along with the replies from some of the convicts addressed to her, with things written that unnerved her. Surely, Stan hadn't known about this or he would have burned the entire box to ash. Or would he have turned them over to authorities, along with his son's diaries?

She couldn't confront Jason. That would be a huge mistake and possibly dangerous.

Think, think, who can I talk to? Who would I—then it hit her. Dennis. She had to talk to him, get him to tell her the truth, and then she'd promise to help them. If he wouldn't listen, then she'd speak with Matt, get the brothers together. She needed to keep a few things for proof. She'd mail them to herself. No, she'd mail them to who...ah, her dad; he wasn't a nosy busybody like her mom was, and he'd keep them for her, no questions asked.

Dennis would be here soon, so Mera got busy sorting mail, keeping a few of the original unopened *Return to Sender* letters. Of the replies his stepmom had gotten back, four were disturbing. She set them aside, planning to make a trip to Office Depot to get them laminated. Afterward, Mera's plan was to hide them underneath her purse lining, sewing it up so no one would find them. She set aside the journals from 1988, 1994, and 1996. If he'd kept one for every year, several were missing. Since she had to give a box of something back to Stan, she'd only kept these three. They weren't just worrisome, they horrified her. Were they ramblings of an adolescent boy? Made-up stores of his deepest desires? Surely, Jason couldn't have been writing about his real life; it had to be fiction. She'd read horror, true crime, even ghost stories and zombie apocalypses. But these chilled her to the bone.

After purchasing a flat mailing box, she addressed it to herself, using her parents' mailing address. In a separate envelope she wrote a brief note to her father, asking him to keep it hidden and safe for her to retrieve at a later date.

Dear Dad, Please do not open this box, but keep it hidden and safe until I retrieve it. Don't let Mom nose around or open the box. You know Mom! Toss this letter into the shredder and give Mom the second letter. Hugs!

Letter number two for her dad to let her mom read:

Hey guys, just a note to tell you I love you. I've been really busy on this case with Cal. I really hope we catch this rapist. What a nightmare for my Alma Mater, right?

She lifted the pen. Should she tell them she was in Oklahoma? No, no need for them to worry, and her dad would ask why she mailed them from Oklahoma when he saw her next. Pen to paper, she wrote:

I'll call y'all to set up WOK night. How about some Kimchi, Japchae, and Kimbap? Sounds good, doesn't it?

Your favorite daughter, Mera

She hurried to the nearest post office then headed back to her room to wait for Dennis.

One leg crossed over the other, pumping her foot, Mera sat on the edge of the bed nervously while Dennis occupied the guest chair in the corner. His eyes were taking in all the papers, letters, and journals she had spread out over the queen-sized bed.

"I understand why you'd be concerned, but this was years ago, just the mere ramblings of a kid. And Mom was a piece of crap. She was never a mother to us. We were in her way. Her running off and my brother's journals are a bunch of nonsense, Mera. Think about it. His real mom died when he was barely three, and Dad told us Jason was in the room when she passed. Poor kid watched the life drain out of her, and Dad took him to her funeral. It traumatized him."

Her eyebrows V'd at the center of her forehead as she gnawed her lower lip. "Despite all this, I suppose Jason seems pretty normal."

"He *is* normal, Mera, for Christ's sake, our brother is a cop."

She released a shaky chuckle. Dennis relaxed some. She was digging where she ought not to be digging. He wanted to smack his father on his balding bony head. Didn't his dad know what was in the fucking box? He guessed dear old Dad never dug inside the box.

"Yeah, well, we all know cops are human too, but this stuff..." Her hand waved over the journals, photos, and letters scattered over her hotel bed. "So much of this is far from normal, though, Dennis, and it scares me, and well..." Her gaze moved to the mess on the bed, and she shuddered.

"Are you in love with him?"

Her head shot up.

"What?"

"I asked you if you're in love with my big brother."

"Uh, we've never said the words to each other, but yeah, I love him. Why?" she lied.

"Then believe in him, and don't tell him you ever saw this stuff. All you'll do is revive his past and upset him. Let it go, Mera."

"Dennis, he slapped the shit outta me the other day for something I said, and we weren't even fighting. His expression afterward scared the fuck outta me."

"Shit, he used to beat the crap of Matt and me, laughing the whole time, and he still loves us." His hand moved to halt her from speaking. "Before you say it, yeah, we hardly see each other; it doesn't mean he doesn't love us. We've got hectic lives, plus, his work keeps him on the go. You should know how it is with his job."

Her face expressionless, she studied her hands. This wasn't like the chicken pox where once you had them they went away. No, this was a disturbing part of Jason's personality living profoundly within him, so why was Dennis shoving it under the rug? He just said he'd beat the crap outta him and Matt and laughed about it.

Mera stopped pressing the issue because he wasn't willing to face the facts. Maybe Matt would listen to reason. Jason needed help; it could be he needed to be locked up. Either way, they were over.

He knew she wouldn't back off, and now, damn it, he had no choice but to act.

"Mera, I've got an early morning and need to run a few errands, so let me box this stuff up, I'll take it to Dad." He would burn this box of nonsense to a crisp, but had no idea she'd already confiscated certain items. Dennis watched her face as he placed the last scrap of paper in the box, plunking the lid on. He asked, "Staying in Ardmore long?"

"I'm gonna head back in the morning. I came to meet you guys to get stuff for a scrapbook, it's a moot point now," she lied.

"Yeah, best not to dredge up his boyhood traumas. But I got an idea if you're game?"

"Sure, I suppose. What do you have in mind?"

"How about we surprise Jason with a visit? Matt and I was gonna take Dad fishing weekend after next, how about we come visit y'all instead?"

Well, it wasn't the worst idea. She had to tell Jason she was breaking it off. Hell, what was one more weekend? Besides, Jason would be in Huntsville for the next full week.

"Okay, Jason will be gone during the week, I'll let you know if he's gonna be home for the weekend." Something inside her stomach churned.

"Great, give me your address and Dad, Matt, and I will come down on a Friday night. I'll call ya, and we can surprise our big brother. Sound good?"

Her head bobbed. "Alright we'll set up a dinner, surprise him. I don't know Jason's schedule, but we can work around it."

They had a plan, but the truth was, Dennis had his own plan.

CHAPTER EIGHT

Vanished—Mera Soon-Lee was missing. It had been almost four months. No clues, no leads, nothing. She had been on an investigative fact-finding mission regarding a so-called serial rapist in the UT Austin area for her boss, reporter Cal Thompson. She'd interviewed a few of the victims, those who'd talk to her. The suspect was raping, not murdering. Who knew if he'd finally snapped? Was she the serial rapist's first murder victim? Although the so-called University serial rapist went dormant, law enforcement frantically searched for him, suspecting he was the reason Mera Soon-Lee was missing. It was the story she'd been working on and somehow she'd gotten too close.

Lead reporter Cal Thompson blamed himself, losing his mind with the responsibility of her abduction. The cops' leads dried up, and they were nowhere near finding her or a body. Another issue Mera never foresaw was her dad taking this proof with him when he traveled back to Korea, unopened and forgotten, after they buried their daughter.

Late Fall 2011

"Listen, I'm going nuts, J. Can we go somewhere else, please?" Dennis whined.

"Stop, Den, no one suspects. Even though I wanna thrash you till you're almost dead, I understand why. I mean, we both gotta lot to lose."

"They think it's the rapist, ya know."

"I know, Den."

"My boss has a cabin on the lake. Why don't we go down there? Get the hell outta Austin for a couple of days. Whatdaya say?"

"I can't just leave work whenever I feel like it, Dennis."

"J, I gotta go or, well, you know, I just can't. I gotta get outta town."

His eyes slanted, Jason Wallen looked at his little brother. What was he supposed to do, hang him out to dry? If he did, then his own personal dark secrets would come out. Shit. Shit. Shit.

"We can get Matt and..."

"*No!*" Jason grabbed Dennis by the shirt, shaking him. "Leave Matt out of this, got it?" His eyes bore into Dennis's light-gray, weak-minded eyes.

"Sure, J, sure, sorry, I just get, well, you know."

"Where's this cabin?"

Dennis inhaled. "Oklahoma, Leeper Lake. I'm thinking we can do some fishing—relax, drink beer, cook on the BBQ—might be fun, ya know?"

Oklahoma. Why not? Jason was considering a career move. Maybe a mini vacation, yeah. Give him time to think. Plus, he needed to contemplate what to do with Dennis. Dennis, his flesh, and blood by design of the heavens, but also bonded by the flesh and blood of others—a fact which would never change.

He was bored. The cabin was too quiet, the fish were nil, but Dennis enjoyed the peace, for it gave him space to let the darkness ebb slowly from his being.

"Too quiet. Think I'll drive over to Thackerville, drop a few hundred in the slots. Wanna come with?" Jason dangled his keys.

Dennis's eyes opened into slits. "Nah, I'm enjoying the silence. Don't want the sound of coins dropping and bells ringing in my ears. You should stay here, J, you need to relax, know what I mean?"

"During the week, the casinos are quieter. Wednesdays, there's just a bunch of old ladies tossing away their Social Security checks filling the nickel and penny slots. I'm gonna go nuts, just need civilization for a few hours."

Dennis squeezed his eyes shut, waving his hand in the air. "Be back to eat dinner with me, okay, bubba?"

"Yep."

"Jason?"

"Yeah?"

"Uh, I never told you how sorry I was about what happened, just trying to protect you, you know, right?"

Jason's insides cringed. He knew. He hated it, but he knew. Man, he was gonna miss her—not her, but Lord, her body, Gawd Almighty —and the sex.

"It'll be okay, Den."

Dennis swallowed hard. He knew she'd been special to his big brother. But she knew. She'd found the letters and the photos, and if she read the journals, she could put two and two together. Why the hell had his brother kept them? Well, shit, he had his own mementoes, so he understood.

"Jason?"

"Now what?"

"Nothing, just want you to know I love you, big brother."

At the bar, he nursed a scotch, watching people. They made him want to retch. He saw Lydia in all these women—poor, fat, and nasty. His focus was on the far side of the bar, watching the bulky Indian woman chatting up the man next to her. She touched his arm, her fingers running the length, then she fixed her hand upon his. Jason wanted to puke.

Swallowing hard, he couldn't. Not again. Lydia. Gloria. Something inside him stirred. Mera. Dennis. Damn him to hell. He knew their secrets had to stay hidden. This Indian woman. There was no need, but desire pulled him. A desire so deep-seated, one he couldn't control. Lydia's death thrilled him, gratified him. Her eyes losing their life turned him on. Jacking-off in her face had been the cherry on top, and this had unchained a demon.

The other man walked away; he sidled up striking a conversation. Something about her seemed familiar and in a short time he learned her life sucked. She was a high school dropout. That's when it clicked. He knew her from high school in Marietta, Oklahoma. She'd known Gloria but hadn't recognized him. Funny thing about her spilling her life story—he already knew it. What a whore, just like Lydia. Overweight, broke, no education, and jobless. Desperate women hunting for a man—begging or whoring was the same to him.

He thought about Mera. The first girl since Gloria he'd enjoyed fucking, all the others a disappointment in the sack. Mera had a job, an education, and Lord Almighty, she was sexy. It had all been so friggin' fantastic until she got nosy and started asking questions. Damn her. Damn Dennis too.

It was easy. A few bucks and Sylvia slithered on her back, lying on the bed in her bra and panties, her fat rolls spilling out. She hadn't been a bad-looking girl in her high school youth and even then she'd been willing to slip off her panties anytime, for free. He remembered that nearly every boy in high school had fucked her, but he wasn't gonna ask if she remembered him. He'd never fucked her, he had Gloria. Fifteen years gone, he'd changed and so had she. His insides seethed. It was her fault things with Gloria had messed up. Shit, he owed her.

"You don't have a friend to help you?" He unbuckled his belt then unsnapped his jeans, pulling the zipper open, all the while thinking how he wanted to hurt this woman, make her pay for Gloria.

"Had a BFF in high school—Gloria—but she vanished. They never found her. It mentally messed me up."

It was her who got Gloria all revved up about not getting an abortion, trying to ruin his life. He thought about the day at the cemetery. The young girl watched them from behind a gigantic oak tree. He'd fucked Gloria, then made it a point to find out who the young girl was who'd watched.

How in the bloody hell had his life become so complicated with all this death and destruction? There was a part of him that enjoyed watching his victims' lives ebbing away, and the peace set in.

"You gonna stare into space or what?" Her stringy dark hair was tied back in a ponytail; her voice brought him out of his thoughts as he regarded her chubby brown face. Fucking her was a revenge fuck, only she'd never know it.

While helping her slip off her panties, he pretended and laughed, despite feeling nauseous at the sight of her naked body, and she responded with a seductive glance. At thirty-three she looked sixty, and again, the bile rose in his throat, but his man parts rose too, despite his absolute repulsion. However the biology of the man's sexual arousal, with a naked female underneath you, your Johnson will react. He rolled on the condom and then plunged in; as he did, he lay against her, slipping the panties under her neck. His thumbs hooked into the elastic on both sides and he rose slightly. With a grip on one end then the other, he brought the sides together, pulling tight as he thrust as hard as he could, not in pleasure but in pure anger. Her hands pinned behind her back, his weight crushing as he choked her, watching her eyes roll back in her head. Right before she went limp and lifeless he released himself with one final hard plunge.

Ditching the body was a breeze. Familiar with the area, he drove all the back roads and with only his parking lights on, he drove through the familiar gates knowing there were no cameras monitoring the vicinity.

In a short time, he was back in his car, headed to her house. Hell, he knew where she'd lived—same place—only now her parents were dead. He snapped on a pair of thin work gloves and gently pried the bedroom window open. In the partial moonlight, he saw the bed, same bed he'd laid in taking Gloria's virginity while her best friend Sylvia stood watch in the front room. These memories pained him; he thought he might've loved Gloria. He walked toward the sliding doors on the back wall. Sliding the door open to the small cube-shaped closet, he found a box stuffed on the top shelf, lifted the lid, and shoved in two crumpled envelopes underneath papers and old photos. After replacing the lid he stood in the semi-dark smiling. Sex he could get, sex he could take. God, the sexual gratification he got watching their life ebb away as their eyes rolled up until all you saw was white. Taking a last breath, they never saw again making this almost as satisfying as fucking them.

News Headlines

33-YEAR–OLD CHOCTAW WOMAN GOES MISSING—POLICE FEAR FOUL PLAY

WINONA AMOS-GARZA, OF DURANT OKLAHOMA, REPORTED SYLVIA AMOS, A LOCAL WOMAN FROM THACKERVILLE, OKLAHOMA, MISSING…

They relaxed in the cabin's main room after dinner. Dennis on the couch, feet propped up, a beer in his hand, Jason in the old beat-up recliner, footrest propped up and his long legs stretched out. He'd just finished his third beer. He shut his eyes, worried about Dennis after he'd read the news of the Choctaw woman from Thackerville. His little brother had become sullen and quiet.

Dennis sat straighter and discarded his empty beer bottle. He pulled a pillow over his lap, covering his hands.

"Jason."

"Dennis." Jason's eyes were still closed.

"You know we knew her."

"Yep."

"Gloria's best friend, remember?"

"Yep, Den, I remember, yes, sir, I do."

"It won't change anything, not with Gloria or Mera."

"I know."

"Jason, you know, I, well..." He was choking up.

"What's done is done, Dennis. Let's try to forget it, okay?"

"I'll try. Jason, do you need help? Do you have to go back?"

"Nah, I'm good, got it covered, little brother."

"Jason?"

He opened his eyes into tiny slits glancing over. "What?"

"I can't do this anymore. It's making me sicker."

"Okay, let's get you some therapy." He re-closed his eyes.

"It won't help. I want to end it."

Another night like this. Jason sighed, keeping his eyes closed.

"Okay, then end it."

To Jason's horror, his baby brother did just that.

CHAPTER NINE

FBI Office, Dallas, Texas, Early Fall 2016

Chatter, twenty-four hours a day. Agents listening to chatter around the world from nooks and crannies (and no one had a clue there were nooks and crannies), locations people thought didn't exist, or no living person or animal inhabited. Voices over voices, words over words, and ears trained to hear specific keywords, utterances, or watchwords. Marking dates particular things were uttered, noting where these phrases came from. Logging dates and times the communication traveled. Agents listened for repeating loops and watchwords tagging continuation of conversations over the airwaves for conspiracies, planned or thoughts of plots against the United States, or any other nation.

It was tedious work, since most conversations weren't a threat to our nation or any other fraction of the world. Most chatter was laughable. You might hear an embarrassing conversation, however, most were entertaining. Other times certain types of dialogue put agents on high alert, as it could be a channel of communication disguising the real message being sent.

Eyes closed, Kasper listened as part of a training exercise, picking out keywords, phrases, and various tones of voice. His ears deciphered stress points or aggravated tones; sometimes voices with even tones suggested a leader was speaking.

He was learning to recognize definite tones of voices—sweet, rough, demanding, edgy, or angry. With an upward glance, he noted the exact times. World clocks lined the far wall. Dallas time was 12:55 pm. He was ready for a break. He'd been listening since early that morning, wanting to catch the chatter in several places with over six to eight hours in time difference. It was funny, not "ha-ha" funny, but weird funny. These days there was no rhyme or reason for phone chatter. Internet VoIPs were always heavier than normal; people talked to each other 24/7—friends, family, business, telemarketers—scam callers were nonstop.

This entire clamor with 800, 888, 877, and 900 calls was bad enough, flooding the wires with what they considered mostly harmless dribble, unless you were the butt end of a scam. Add in email scamming and computer glitches, which weren't real glitches but a way to hack into your computer to get vital information, sometimes costing you your life savings, or just your week-to-week paycheck.

Greedy people with nothing better to do than cheat or steal from you. Oh, they could get honest work, but crime was easier. Alongside his colleagues, he'd learned certain personalities were easy to sway to the dark side. People lured with promises of false security. So many liars and gullible personalities walked amongst us. There were many talented criminals—dangerous people, the type no one saw coming until it was too late—able to reel in unsuspecting victims.

Kasper pulled his headset off and leaned back to stretch when his phone rang. He snatched it up with his eyes shut. "Bergman. TCA Task Force."

"Victimless crimes, I call bullshit," Harlowe Bishop popped off.

"Well, howdy to you too, Bishop. How are you? I'm fine, by the way."

"Oh, sorry, Kasp, but I'm a little pissed off. Need to vent a minute. Uh, you got a minute? And what the hell's a TCA Task Force?"

"Technical Chatter Awareness. Yeah, sure, I've got about sixty to spare. I need a lunch break. So what's this nonsense about victimless crimes bullshit?"

"Get your lunch. Can't have you starving now, can I?"

"Let me warm up my leftover pizza. Give me five and I'll call you back."

"You've got five. Give me time to get another cup of this shit they call coffee."

"Five," he repeated then hung up.

No sooner had he reached his desk than his phone started ringing, and she was calling him.

"Bergman."

"How long does it take to heat a couple pieces of hamburger pizza? Gee whiz, slowpoke!"

"I was about to call you, damn it."

Kasper saw the time. He'd been gone six whole minutes. What was her deal? "Look, Bishop, I promised I'd give you sixty. We're at fifty-two. My advice is don't waste anymore of *your* time." He chomped into his leftover pizza and chewed. He waited and heard her snicker.

"Yeah, yeah, you're right. I called you and you're giving me your lunch hour, or what's left of the hour. Okay, straight to it then. I'm coming to Dallas, can you put me up?"

He took another bite and chewed. Huh, this was a first. He heard her expel a hefty breath into the phone.

"No, I don't want you or your body, you're safe, Bergman."

"Gee, thanks, you know how to bolster a guy's ego. And what if I have a girl?"

"You don't or I'd know. Good Lord, Kasper. If you had a girl, you'd have told me."

"You're right, I don't have a girl, and although it's none of your business, I haven't dated in a while." Kasper had zero desire to discuss his last relationship with her or anyone else. "What's bringing you to Dallas? And don't give me the regular smart-ass answer and tell me a plane is. Also, what did you mean when you first called? What's this about victimless crimes and bullshit?"

"My boss wants me in Dallas. I'll fill you in when I get there, you know, Big Brother's listening. Oh yeah, you're Big Brother, right? Oh M gee, I crack myself up."

"Shut up, Bishop. Tell me when, where, flight number, cuz I'm on the last nine minutes of my lunch. Besides, I gotta hit the head first and grab a fresh cup of Joe and get back to work on time."

"Okay, okay, I'll text you my itinerary and you'd better pick a decent place to eat, because I'm sick of Las Vegas buffets." Laughing, she hung up leaving Kasper shaking his head, a small grin pulled at his lips. His phone buzzed. A text from Bishop popped up:

Flight AA218, Terminal C, Gate 26 @ 4:10 pm tomorrow afternoon.

Find me at the baggage carrousel; don't be late; I hate waiting in airports.

We can talk victimless shit on the drive to a nice steak dinner, you're buying.

After another quick text of: *Okay, see ya tomorrow night,* he pocketed his phone.

She hadn't expounded on her trip, possibly for safety or security. Her showing up in Dallas didn't mean they'd work together, but it'd be gratifying to visit with a trusted classmate. In this "women's libber age," as he still called it, Bishop didn't need to prove herself. Her focus was on the job and reminded him a little of DEA Agent Sophia Medina. He'd loved working with Medina when he'd worked with the Houston Homicide Department, first off the books with Detective Jack West, then as a deputized agent for the DEA. It'd be interesting to see Bishop and Medina work a case together.

“Okay,“ he muttered, ”back to work.” Headset on, leaning back he turned up the volume listening to the world, chuckling. He was an only child, but right now you *could* call him Big Brother.

CHAPTER TEN

The airport was busy as usual. Kasper got there early, parked, and proceeded to the terminal to hang around. Dressed in nice slacks, he'd removed his suit coat and rolled up his shirtsleeves, unbuttoning the top button of his shirt. He walked casually through checkpoints with everyone else, as a regular civilian. The line was long. Several flights had arrived back-to-back, and he decided for once he'd use his credentials to move up faster. Why the hell not? At Security, he discreetly flashed his FBI badge and told them he was picking up another agent who was flying in from Nevada.

"Of course, Special Agent Bergman, I'd be glad to let you pass ahead,"—the officer smiles—"and your sidearm?"

"No need for me to carry. You guys got it covered, right?"

"Yes, sir, we got your six. You can go around. I'm sure you know your way around our fair city's airport." He motioned with his arm, allowing Kasper to pass.

"Much obliged, Officer Davis. Thank you for your service." Kasper did a tiny hand salute and headed to the baggage pickup for gate number twenty-six.

Harlowe was a little disheveled and frowning when Kasper saw her walking to the baggage claim. She had a carry-on slung over her left shoulder and a large purse/computer carry case over the other. He watched her eyes searching for him and raised his hand to wave. She waved back not smiling. Her eyes darted to the carousel, watching for her luggage as she beckoned him over.

"Hunt for two black hard-shelled cases with red, white, and blue ribbons on the handles." Her voice sounded strained. Was she pissed off or was it flight stress? He'd ask later, concentrating on looking for her luggage.

"There, here comes one with your patriotic ribbon configuration." Kasper stepped to her right, headed for the suitcase and she followed, passing him. "There's the other one. Let's get out of this airport." She took her suitcase handle, popped it up, and stepped beside Kasper. "Where did you park? What direction are we headed?"

"Hi, great to see you too. I parked in lot E in the garage." He pointed.

A chuckle slipped out as she set her luggage down to hug him.

"Sorry, dude. I had the joy of flying with two crying brats. Not to mention I've got other crap on my mind. Fantastic to see you, now let's leave this fucking airport, okay?"

"Yeah, sure. Oh, and you look good too, Harry. A stressed-out Harried Harlowe equals Harry."

"Okay, but you'd better be spelling it H-a-r-r-i and not H-a-r-r-y, you jackass."

"Yeah, okay, Harri without a *y*, let's scoot. Get you hot food and a few adult beverages so you can unwind."

Suitcases were stored in the Yukon, his official FBI vehicle. Harlowe buckled in, leaning against the seat, closing her eyes. "Can we not talk for a minute? Once we leave the airport, then you may riddle me with questions. Deal?"

"Yeah, sure, I'll even turn off the radio." Kasper started the Yukon and switched off the radio backing out of his space. He headed for the north exit of the airport to connect to 635. First, get her food. Second, order her a stiff drink so she can relax. Then they'd head to his apartment in Coppell. Bishop was lucky he had two bedrooms. Otherwise, he'd have said no to her staying at his place.

He exited the parking terminal and made his way toward the airport's main entrance and ticket booths. Fees paid, Kasper was northbound on Interstate 121, thankful for once traffic wasn't a nightmare.

"Steak, sushi, Mexican, burgers, none of which are Vegas buffets...what's your mouth set for?"

She exhaled, opening her eyes, cutting them toward the driver. "Any bar serving beer on tap and respectable whiskey. And positively no to sushi, hate the stuff. How about burgers and fries, or Reubens?"

"Yep, know a place, kinda reminds me of home. Good food with darts and beer. Sequestered in a commercial area, it's a great place to unwind. And, if you wanna just chill, no questions till after we get a drink in ya, deal?"

She let out a deep breath and relaxed into the passenger seat, trusting her driver and saying, "Deal."

At first look, you wouldn't suspect it to be a pub. The small building was partially hidden from view by the fenced-in dumpsters of the McDonald's on one side, which butted up to the other gated area of dumpsters owned by the twenty-four-hour gas station/convenience store aptly named, Al's All-Nighter.

The small rectangular sign above the double doors advertised the name, *A Bit O' Dublin*. A non-imposing storefront, the blacked-out windows painted white simply read, *Play Darts - Eat Good Food-Drink Cold Beer - The Fun Starts Here.* There was parking on both sides. A public self-storage company was on the opposite end and a metal fencing company ran alongside Al's All-Nighter.

Sequestered near the warehouse district of Coppell, Texas, a few blocks away, were several stores touting wares such as tiles, flooring, and rugs. There was a tool company, an appliance warehouse, several one-off shops for commercial painters, an exterminator's supply store, and off to the end, a huge restaurant supply warehouse. Across the way sat undeveloped land, next to an empty lot with construction vehicles, trucks, excavators, backhoes, and lifts.

"Wow, Bergman, this is definitely off the beaten path. How'd you find it?"

"A guy who lives in my complex works for the heavy equipment company over there." He pointed. "He told me about it. I came here one night to explore. Remember the pub I told you about in Houston called Quinn's?"

"Yeah, you mentioned it repeatedly." She gave him a sarcastic look.

"Okay, Harri, don't get snarky with me. I loved Quinn's Pub, it was where I finally learned how to drink. Anyway..." He released a sigh. "This place makes me think of Quinn's. The barkeep's an older fella, but he's not from Texas. Luke's a good old boy from Georgia, believe it or not, and he moved here after his wife passed to be nearer to his son- and daughter-in-law and their three kids. He's told me some funny stories."

"Sorry. Look." She twisted her head around. "Let's get food and drinks. Afterward I should be good."

He turned his head toward her after turning off the engine and unbuckling his seat belt. "You okay?"

"Yeah, but look, there are things. Hey, let's eat then talk, okay?"

"Perfect! Food, beer. Then we chat, gotcha."

The pub had a darker atmosphere with low lighting giving it an old-time atmosphere. Kasper directed her to a tall pub table near the backside of the bar. He dragged out the tall chair for her. "Place meet your approval?"

Her eyes wandered over the area. Small, quaint, and she felt relaxed. It was nice.

"Wow, yeah, great place. Better than the ones crammed to the hilt with drinkers, so noisy you can't hear yourself think."

Four older guys lounged at the front drinking, three younger dudes playing a friendly game of darts, and a handful of construction workers sat enjoying hot food, cold cerveza. None were overly boisterous. Two guys in pants and dress shirts, ties undone, sleeves rolled up, and no blazers, three women at a back table chatting. Lots more people walked into the pub—men and women in pairs or groups. Friday, six p.m. happy hour was the onset of a weekend.

"Howdy." A woman wearing a t-shirt touting an outline of Texas with a shamrock where Dallas was located and *A Bit O' Dublin* written underneath, walked up, handed them menus and silverware. "What can I get y'all to drink today?"

"What's your poison?" Kasper asked her.

"Pint of Guinness and a shot of your best whiskey."

"Great choice, and you, sir, what'll you have?"

"I'll have the same."

"Be right up." The hostess left for their drinks while they looked over the menus.

"How are the corned beef and sauerkraut sandwiches?"

"Good. Add in the owner's special horseradish sauce. It's got a bite, but not too spicy. Order sweet tater fries. I'm getting the same and I'll order a side of his potato salad. He makes it with small cubes of potatoes and his own special secret recipe. It's delicious. We can split a bowl if you like so you can try it."

"Sounds yummy." Harlowe closed her eyes, exhaled, and Kasper watched the stress melt from her face, but not all of it.

The hostess placed their drinks on the tabletop. "We're a little shorthanded tonight, so I'll take your orders." As they read off the menu, her head bobbed. "Good choices. Becky will bring your food in a jiff."

Harlowe took her shot, waiting for Kasper to do the same. A half-smile curved her lips when she said, "Boilermaker time, Bergman, so here's to dropping a shot o' whiskey into my pint of beer and not my panties on the floor."

"Good grief, woman! What kinda of toast is that?"

"Drop your shot, swig, after we drink, we'll talk."

They released their shot glasses going bottoms-up with their pints. Harlowe was already wiping her mouth when he plunked down his empty.

With his hand aloft, he called out to the bartender, "Two more pints."

Kasper waited as the waitress placed refilled mugs down, taking the empties.

"Okay. What's up your craw or has pissed you off? Start talking. And why not start about this victimless crime comment you made? Wait. First. What in the devil kinda drinking toast was that? Spill it, Bishop."

Her expression became contemplative as she took another healthy gulp, wiped her mouth with a napkin, pushed her glass back, and leaned onto the table. As she balanced her forearms on the edge, she relaxed her body between her bent elbows.

"The toast was just to shock you. It meant nothing. Honest. I haven't dated for months. Dropping my panties is a very moot point. And so's ya know. I don't drop them just anytime because that's not the person I am. Besides, I've been so busy at work. No time to meet anyone." She compressed her lips dropping her gaze to the table.

Kasper is quiet, sipping his beer letting her think. He had no reason to hurry anyone unless it was a suspect. And then you did so to keep them off guard hoping they'd slip up because they were in a hurry to lie, trying to think fast on their feet.

She released a deep sigh and looked up. "Victimless crimes don't exist. Like prostitution. People call this a victimless crime. Oh, I'm not talking about sex slaves or human trafficking. I'm talking full-on streetwalker, man, or woman who's selling you a piece of ass. A customer shells out cash because they're desperate for it and have to buy it, damn the cost. It's a mutual arrangement. It doesn't matter why a person, regardless of gender, sells their body. For drugs, rent money, gambling debts, or whatever."

"Coming from Nevada, there are several counties where prostitution's legal with active brothels, right? "

"I'm aware, but even if it's mutual, it isn't victimless."

Kasper hushed her. "Our food's coming. Let's continue this conversation after our server is out of earshot, okay?"

Harlowe's lips turned downward, and she nodded in agreement. Becky placed baskets with food smelling like heaven on the tabletop, and her semi-frown changed into a full-blown grin.

"Y'all gonna split this yummy potato salad?"

"You know if she doesn't like it, I'll eat it."

Becky's face lit up. "I know. You never *not* order it. Afterward, your bowl's as clean as a whistle, like a dog licked it."

Kasper rolled his eyes at her. "Becky, this is my coworker from Nevada. Harlowe, meet Becky, the best waitress in town, well, at this pub anyway."

"Hi, Harlowe, good to meet'cha and as you might guess, Kasper comes in here a lot. Anyway, this is my uncle's place. I work here part-time. Y'all enjoy your supper, holler if ya need anything else."

Becky took the empty tray, heading back to tend to other customers.

"Bergman, you sly rascal, Becky, huh? She's cute."

"Uh-uh, it's not like that. First, she's a college student at the University of Texas, Dallas, getting her bachelor's degree in nursing to become a pediatric surgical nurse; second, she's way too young for me. Also, she doesn't have time for dating."

"Ah-ha, does this mean you've asked her out?" Harlowe picked up her Reuben, took a bite, closing her eyes, savoring this wonderful heaven on earth. "Oh, yum, you were right, a slice of heaven."

He let her chew, savoring her Reuben, and he did the same; he was famished. Harlowe gave him the third-degree in-between bites. "Alright now, about Becky. What's the story between you two?"

"Try my potato salad first. Then I'll explain crap even though it's none of your business." He pushed the bowl over to her.

One bite and she pulled the bowl over confiscating it.

"Hey, Becky, bring an extra dish of potato salad, will ya?"

"Sure thing, Kasper, coming right up." He heard Becky's laugh as she proceeded to the kitchen.

After popping another forkful of spud heaven into her mouth, she looked at him. "Stop sidestepping, fill me in about Becky. What's the story?"

"No, I didn't ask her out, and we're not dating, if that's what you thought. She was working the bar one night, the place was dead. I drank a couple of beers, and we chatted. My last romantic relationship didn't end well, but I don't want to discuss it further. It's over, I've moved on. Becky's a nice kid who doesn't need an FBI agent boyfriend. Besides, she's twenty-two years old, and me, I'm, well, enough about this crap. What's this stuff you're griping about? Tell me about this prostitution and victimless crime shit. Wassup?"

Kasper took a bite of his sandwich and waited for her to finish chewing.

"Fine, don't tell me about your love life. Let's eat, and then we can talk about gross shit afterward, okay?"

"You'll get no argument from me." Kasper dug into the extra bowl of potato salad.

As they ate, the only thing they discussed between mouthfuls of wonderful food was what secret ingredient might be in this little container of cubed spud nirvana.

CHAPTER ELEVEN

"So, what happened was, we were working a sting on human trafficking outside a small place in Nye County, where prostitution's still legal, with certain restrictions, of course. Anyway, the place was a disaster. There were sick girls of all ages—a spattering of them barely in their teens, and a few were pregnant. I wanted to throw up. Some girls wanted to be there. This utterly astounded me. They were of age. So, all legalities went out the window."

"I take it you broke up the ring? Made arrests? What?"

"We apprehended a few handlers. Not the big boss. You know how it goes. This isn't the end of their business, though. It's a shame because now they're on the lookout for new girls. We just can't protect them all."

"So, Bishop, these girls kidnapped and forced into sex slavery are not victimless. Just what are you referring to?"

"Legal or not, consensual prostitution's what I'm talking about. This leads to venereal diseases, HIV, and unwanted pregnancies. Then a crackhead sells her body for dope and has a crack baby and the legal system takes it, or this person passes on a disease to another and it becomes a domino effect. While our tax dollars take care of this crap. Please don't get me started on the married man who steps out on his wife. The shitty hubby gets a deadly disease and afterward passes it on to his unsuspecting wife who gets sick and dies. Thus leaving this scumbag with three small children he ignores, and they get sent to foster care and..." The words were coming hard and fast and he wondered if she was breathing.

"Whoa, whoa, Harlowe, slow down, breathe—" He brought up a hand then noticed the tears rolling off her cheek.

She sniffed then wiped her eyes and drained the last of her warm beer. "I gotta go to the ladies' room. Order me another Guinness and a shot of Jameson, please?"

His brows dipped and his eyes never left her face. "Uh-huh. Sure, of course. Another for both of us and I'm gonna make it a double shot for you. When you're back, you can have your boilermaker. Then damn it, you're gonna tell me what happened. *Comprendo*?"

She gave him one of those sad, *I'm sorry* sorta frowns with a head tilt. "Yes, I will, and thanks, Kasper. Be back in a few."

She grabbed her bag, and he pointed her to the women's restroom. Harlowe walked, her head bowed, disappearing behind the door with the word *Lassies* stenciled in white paint.

Kasper had never seen his friend this way. Emotional, shaken to the core, pissed off and sad, rolled into one enormous ball of a raging storm. He knew she was on the verge of eruption. The Harlowe Bishop he knew was tough-as-nails no nonsense. Business to a T. They'd formed a bond at Quantico and he considered her family. He was worried about her.

Face splashed with cool water, she ran a brush through her hair pulling it into a ponytail. Both hands on the sink, she stared at her reflection. Lines of anger played on her forehead. A morose, dead feeling swam behind her brown eyes. She felt rage, sadness, hatred, and bitterness—not an nth of happiness. She knew in time her spark would return, however, for now she needed to put her emotions into her work. There was nothing more she could do. It was imperative for her to set her personal drama aside and do her job. With a deep breath, she squared her shoulders, hiked her purse strap up over her arm, and walked to the table to drink with her friend and unload but not explode.

Two pints of Guinness and three shots of Jameson whiskey awaited them. Kasper stood when she arrived at the table.

"Bergman, such a gentleman, but you don't have to, you know."

"My Army dad raised me to be respectful of the opposite sex. Note I didn't refer to you as the weaker sex either. Besides, it's just good manners."

"Well, you could give some bums a lesson or two, or ten. You run circles around most men. I'm glad we're friends." She grabbed her first shot gesturing to his, and they kerplunk'd the shot glasses into the pints and upturned them drinking until they were empty. Harlowe toyed with her other shot glass, taking a small sip, then shot the rest and drank half of her second Guinness.

He wiped his mouth with his knuckles and leaned back. "I'm not gonna pry. Seems whatever it is, is personal and none of my business."

"It's okay. You're not just a friend, you're my family, like a brother, you know?"

"Yeah, I feel the same, Bishop."

"Like I'm your brother?" A grin tugged at the edge of her mouth.

He couldn't help it; he chuckled. "Yeah, cuz you're one tough-ass female."

Her face grew pensive, and she shot her last whiskey, then drained her mug of the remaining Guinness. "No more alcohol for me." Harlowe pulled her water glass closer and asked him, "Have I ever mentioned my cousin Monica to you?"

Without speaking, he shook his head sipping his stout.

"She was married to Kevin Eastman. He was from Kansas. They met at Iowa State his senior year. Monica fell hard for him. They married, stayed in Iowa, had three children, who are now ages four, seven, and nine. Two girls; the oldest is a boy. "

"Was? Are they—?"

She lifted a hand. "I'm getting there. I guess I should preface this by telling you Monica and I were like Siamese twins growing up. Our mothers are sisters, and her mom died about nine years ago of heart failure. We grew up living less than ten blocks from each other in Iowa. From first grade to our senior year in high school, we were inseparable. Monica was a year older than me but her birthday was in late fall, so it put us in the same grade. We were both only children, and I felt I had a sister in her. It was great to have a sister. You know?"

"Yeah, I'm an only child. I'd always wanted a brother or sister"—he waved his hand at her"—and I finally got a brother."

She spurted a laugh.

He laughed too. "I'm happy to have a sister like you, Bishop. Now, back to your story."

"Yep, let me jump ahead several years. Monica and I stayed in touch even though she studied at Iowa State and I received a scholarship to the University of Western Illinois. I made the Dean's list and got three separate smaller scholarships. One in debate, one in martial arts, and don't laugh, theater arts. I also worked through my first and second years. I received three different financial scholarships during my third and fourth years and had to take out a student loan for the remaining amount. Afterward my parents got a windfall from my dad's dad when he passed, so they paid off my student loans."

"Terrific, Harri, good to know you have no student loan debts from the government."

"Sorry, TMI, I get carried away. Okay, back to my cousin Monica. I was her maid of honor and after her kids were born she was a full-time mom while Kevin worked teaching and coaching at the high school we both graduated from. Again..." She stopped, taking a drink of her room-temperature water. "More than you needed to know. I'm just giving you backstory. After the last baby, Monica got her tubes tied. With three young children, her life was full and busy.

She was supportive of Kevin, going to all the football games. She was a hostess for the team and their parents. My cousin earned a degree in English and was super smart in math, so she tutored any player who wasn't making the grade. Her fees were minimal, but it took up her time. Lots of stupid football players." Harlowe shrugged her semi-apology to Kasper, him being a male.

"Okay, I gotta ask, why does all this make you mad and cry?"

"Because Kevin couldn't keep his pants zipped, and got caught screwing another teacher. The other teacher got fired cuz God forbid they lose the coach who took them to the State championship two years in a row. To keep his job safe, he started paying for sex from hookers, escorts, pure street filth, and ended up with gonorrhea which he gave to Monica, who got really sick before he finally confessed."

His brows dipped. "She stayed with him?"

"They separated, but Monica took the bastard back because she loved him. A year later, Kevin began waggling his penis all over the place again. Allegedly, he was playing both sides of the fence; then add in he started gambling. Not only did he lose three quarters of his 401K, he contracted HIV, passing it on to Monica. Kasper, she was too frail to handle the illness." Tears flooded her eyes. "We buried her two weeks ago. I've been numb. I was until I saw all those young girls. It was awful. The sex slave trade's killing girls. Then it hit me, Kevin was this type of guy—a brutal asswipe, not caring about anything except whichever direction his little head led him. Because of him Monica is dead. He killed her just as if he'd put a gun to her head."

"And his HIV...is he dying?"

"Hell no, lucky bastard's in remission. And the bastard pawned his kids off. Told the family, his and ours, he couldn't take care of them, it was too much, so the kids got fostered out, thank God to immediate family. I wish I could help. I...I'm...I, clearly I..." She covered her face with her hands and wept openly not caring who saw her falling apart.

It'd anger her if he coddled her, he knew her that well, but was unsure of what to do. Should he hug her? Pat her arm? Harlowe was like a sister to him, so he scooted his chair over, putting his arm around her, pulling her into him. She laid her head on his shoulder and cried, letting it all out; she hadn't even cried this hard at Monica's funeral.

Several minutes passed. She snuffed up her tears, wiped her splotchy face with a napkin, letting a sad crooked grin play on her mouth.

Kasper repositioned his chair to get a better look at her. "It'll be okay, I'm sorry men are—"

"No, don't apologize for the male race, Kasper. Kevin's a weasel, a piece of shit, not a man. I've been so damn mad and not able to let it all out. In my opinion, Monica was a casualty—a sad casualty of prostitution. She didn't consent to get HIV or gonorrhea, none of it. Yet, prostitution took her life, and to me that's not victimless. Does that sound logical to you?"

"Yeah, when you put it that way, makes sense."

"Our recent case is over for now. I had a long talk with the SAC about Monica's death. I turned in my reports, told him I needed time, and luckily, he understood."

Kasper bowed his head then looked up. "Bishop, I can't imagine how you feel, never having lost anyone close to me. So I can't lie telling you I understand."

"Here, with you listening, this is what I needed."

"Time heals everything, so they say. You never said why you're in Dallas...you on vacation, work, what?"

"Let's drop my personal drama and get ice cream on the way to your place. I'm emotionally bushed and need shut-eye. I'll explain my trip to Dallas tomorrow. Ice cream awaits, I'm buying."

Kasper never refused free ice cream. Lucky for her he wasn't impatient, or he'd badger her until she spilled.

CHAPTER TWELVE

FBI Headquarters Dallas, Texas

"Wow, nice digs, Bergman."

"It's an office. You know Dallasites got to be upscale. No expenses spared on décor."

Harlowe wrinkled her nose. "Well, of course, dah'ling."

"Come on, I'll show you the most important room in the house."

"The ladies' room?"

"Nope, our luxurious breakroom. Come on, I'll buy you a cup of Dallas FBI coffee. Then..." He turned, giving her the eye. "You *will* enlighten me on why you're in Dallas."

She gave him the old eyeball roll and sighed. "Good grief, you're a bulldog with a bone."

"No, I'm not. What I am is a very curious FBI agent. Let's get coffee and I'll show you to my cubicle."

"If it's all the same, you got an office we can snag?"

"Uh-huh. Sure. Coffee, then follow me."

Grabbing her briefcase she followed.

"Good old law enforcement Joe—has a bitter bite, even with sweetener."

"Yep, love me some ground-up sludge, pops my eyes wide open." He put his cup on the edge of the desk, leaned back and crossed his right ankle over his left knee. "Well?"

Clearing her throat, she began, "In the spring of 2011, a Black/Asian woman named Mera Soon-Lee disappeared in Austin, Texas. Her body was found in 2014. In 2013, a Caucasian transgender woman, Rayna Anderson, formerly Raymond Anderson, from Marietta, Oklahoma, was reported missing; they found his bones last year. June 2014, two years ago, Trina Robinson, a Black woman from Mansfield, Texas, was also reported missing, her remains discovered outside of Dallas ten months ago. Another Caucasian woman named Annelle Mackey vanished ten months ago from a little town called Itasca. Her body was discovered three months ago. "

"So, you have four homicides, and this means what to the FBI? Aren't homicide detectives working these cases?"

"Let me finish."

Uncrossing his leg, he crossed his ankles, slouching, waving his hand for her to carry on.

"Sylvia Amos, a full-blooded Chickasaw Indian from Thackerville, Oklahoma, missing the fall of 2011, and her body hasn't been located. Three months later, Nora Mendez-Finch, Hispanic woman from Azle, Texas, vanishes. Both presumed dead."

She stopped to take a gulp of her lukewarm java. Kasper gazed at her, brows lifted. "And you are telling me about these cases why?"

"Because we're the FBI."

"Yeah, and homicide detectives are homicide detectives. Humor me. Elaborate."

"Fine. We have four murders. Killings that cross the Texas and Oklahoma State line which might be linked to the two missing persons. And we believe there could be more. This attracted the attention of the Bureau."

"Why haven't I heard about it since I'm in Texas?" His frown deepened as he crossed his arms mulishly.

"Stop it. We don't need to be kept up-to-date on every single case; besides, my boss gets scores of information before the news comes out and to be clear, this case hasn't hit the wire yet. Now, get a freaking grip."

He stared looking deep into her brown eyes, watching her face. She was hard to read, a worthy talent for an agent.

"And you're here because why? Did this case somehow cross over to Vegas then back to Texas?"

A long sigh slipped between partially closed lips. "No, I requested to be transferred temporarily because of Monica's death, and me wanting off the sex trafficking squad for a while. The SAC told me there wasn't another team he could transfer me to in Vegas."

Kasper didn't buy it. Wordlessly he watched her, his arms still crossed, eyes boring into hers.

Closing her eyes, she cleared her throat. "Ya got me, okay? There were some other cases I could've worked, but I told my SAC I needed a temporary change, away from Vegas. I requested a new assignment here in Dallas to work with you."

Kasper eyed the ceiling tiles, the square grids, and the one water leak stain in view. Assigned to a special task force, even though monotonous, was an important job to track potential terrorists. Bishop was his peer, and here she was prancing to Dallas to run an operation, and he was—shit, in his mind he was playing the role of a misogynistic creep. Stupid. He needed to get over himself.

"Fine, I get it. You needed a change, now to stop this hem-hawing around and spit it out."

"The Bureau's been compiling data on each case, and we have some obvious connections. If it's okay with you, I'd like to give you the details of one case first. "

"So, tell me."

"Three years ago a Black woman named Trina Robinson vanished from Mansfield, Texas."

"Yeah, it's a small town outside of Fort Worth. Go on."

"Robinson was last seen near a trashy motel outside of Dallas. Nobody understood why she drove to Dallas. She was unemployed. Didn't have many friends, her family is all in Mississippi, what family she had left."

"Who filed a missing person's report for her?"

"Her next-door neighbor did. Ms. Robinson's cat yowled for days, so she went to see what the deal was. Her cat got locked in the laundry room for six days. Poor thing ran out of food and water. Mansfield police put out a missing person's flyer with Robinson's photo. One person who'd been at the motel recalled seeing the victim close to the time she disappeared."

"Did she rent a room? They have cameras?" He uncrossed his arms leaning one elbow on the armrest.

"No, she didn't, and no cameras. Someone saw her near the backside, so they swept rooms. Can you believe they recovered her DNA?"

"You're kidding? How could they have found her DNA?"

Her thin eyebrows knitted together. "They got lucky, I'll admit. After searching half a dozen rooms, Dallas CSU found a locket wedged behind the dresser, between the wall and the nasty carpet. It was Trina's, had her name engraved on the backside with her date of birth. There were strands of her hair caught in the catch; fortunately, the roots were intact."

"Yeah, DNA, what else?"

"After a more thorough search, CSU found blood."

"Hers?"

"Some of it was. The other, well, it'll be hard to match any DNA to it unless the perp's listed in NDIS or CODIS. Besides, who knows how often they clean these shithole rooms?"

Kasper found it sick, yet understandable. "Prints?"

"Any usable prints weren't in AFIS. Again, could be anyone's prints, even from months ago."

"And they found her body. Where, exactly?"

"Six miles from the motel buried on an empty acre of land, nothing but brush and weeds. Couple of boys were out dirt biking. Wild dogs or coyotes dug up part of her corpse. Anyway, DNA testing proved her to be Trina Robinson."

"Signs of sexual assault?"

"Likely, but we can't prove it; perp wore a condom, *if* he raped her. There was no sign of a scuffle. He might've drugged her."

"Cause of death?"

"Strangulation."

"So, she was at the motel, probably killed there, then dumped six miles away. What about the desk clerk? Had he seen her?" Kasper felt he was following the lead of his expert tutor, Homicide Detective Jack West, as he uttered each statement or question.

"We questioned him, and the DPD checked out the few names on his register. Three were aliases; the other names checked out, so did their stories. The detectives said the desk clerk rented a room around eleven-ish to a big guy wearing wrinkled jeans, a ratty t-shirt, a dark jacket, and a ball cap. He had thick-framed glasses and the ball cap was pulled down, covering his face so the clerk couldn't give a good facial description. All he told them was the guy was clean-shaven. The fella registered with a name, but it wasn't his real name."

"How does this involve the Bureau?"

"Murder victims crossing State lines."

"The agency thinks these killings connect to each other? They think we have a serial?"

Again, she heaved a sigh. "Yes, but not your normal serial."

"Shit, Harri, no serial's normal. What the fuck does that even mean?" Kasper's attitude took a dive. Her story was dragging on.

"Keep your jockey shorts on. First, these women all had diverse looks, hair color, races. One of our victims wasn't a woman by birth. Her legal gender was female when she vanished. It seems our perp likes big girls mostly, but his crossover into various races is out of the norm."

"Okay, I grant you everything about this is odd. Serials rarely veer, they stick to a certain type. Are there any commonalities between the victims we can pinpoint?" Uncrossing his legs, he straightened and leaned in, a furrow between his brows. "Were they all raped? Could they tell?"

Her shoulders jerked up then down, her head tilted slightly.

"No proof of rape for Soon-Lee or Anderson because their clothing degraded, and there were only bones. I mean, we can't rule out rape, nor can we prove it. The woman from Itasca, we only suspect rape, no semen—again, the perp likely used a condom."

"Strangled?"

"Yes, they all were. Each had something twisted around their necks, underwear, or bra."

"What else?"

"Most of the victims share social and physical commonalities—poor, unattractive, and in each case the woman was overweight. None of 'em had close family or friends, not any real friends, I mean. Mackey and Robinson, single mothers, neither got child support. The missing Azle woman, Mendez-Finch, was in divorce proceedings with two kiddos at home. Sylvia Amos, the woman from Thackerville, never married, no known kids. The one victim with any kind of real money was Anderson. She got a payout from a hefty lawsuit. Seems she was involved in a big truck accident. All the other women came from poor working class."

"You left out the woman from Austin. What's her name?"

"Mera Soon-Lee. She was the first. At least we think so."

"Was she another heavyset single mom, without friends, family, or money?"

"No, oddly enough, she was a young, pretty, college graduate from an upper middle-class family."

"So, she differs from the others. The question would be, why? And why target these women? Four murders committed across two State lines and two missing women. These missing females, do we believe they're part of this equation? What'da we got going on here? The Bureau thinking it's another Ted Bundy? Honestly, we'll never know all the facts, but he was a monster among the many monsters we've seen fry."

"Yep, they think the missing women are part of our guy's trail. And yeah, Bundy had a certain type. But then he veered from his type, killing a very young girl." Her frown deepened.

"Yeah, the bastard had a type—young girls he sucked into his spiderweb of death. Innocent girls with budding lives ahead of them, and he snuffed them out. What he did to them, oh my God, makes me want to fry the bastard all over again!" His body stiffened as his fist pounded the arm of the chair. "I hope he's burning in hell, and he..." Bergman looked up to see a wide-eyed Harlowe staring at him. She felt the same way he did. But for Kasper it was like it happened yesterday, not thirty years ago.

"Kasp, hey...uh...you okay?"

His stiff posture relaxed. "Sorry. It's just—I'm fine, no worries. Sometimes, you know, it makes you crazy. Christ, Bundy kept victims' heads in his home. Dahmer piled bodies in a spare room, and John Wayne Gacy buried young boys in a crawl space, and no one knows about it. How does this happen? Plus, Bundy escaped, twice! It just beats fuck all. Jumping out a second-story window, wish he'd broken his neck. It would've ended sooner. But the second time from his cell fitting his body into a one-foot-square light fixture hole, I mean, how the hell? The guy's not Houdini. Worse of all, we couldn't catch the sons of bitches—Gacy, Bundy, or Dahmer—to keep 'em from killing. Shit, murder just hits an overly sensitive nerve with me, the waste of life. Know what I mean?"

Special Agent Harlowe Bishop smiled. Kasper had a deep commitment to keeping the public safe. It wasn't only his duty to catch the bad guy, it was his promise to his badge—his oath.

"Bergman, I think you have what it takes to be a terrific profiler."

"Profiling interests me, but it doesn't mean I'd be exceptional at it. I'm more of a techy type of guy, you know?"

"Nope, don't want to hear excuses. You were in the top five of two-hundred-fifty students at Quantico. Remember what the Behavioral Science instructor said about your keen ability?"

Kasper huffed. His brain worked like a machine, understood the machine, but he wasn't sure he could read another man's psyche to figure out how his brain ticked. Could he see beyond the man? Could he dive into the mind of a criminal, a morbid killer?

"Remember what the instructor said?" she repeated herself.

"He said heaps of stuff and not just about me either; he was kinda ruthless in the beginning." An itty-bitty smile flitted on his face, then he frowned. "Yeah, I remember. Instructor Laramie said I knew stuff I didn't even know I knew."

"He's right, I think you do too. Here's the deal, Bergman. My boss wants me to assemble a task force to work these cases, so you in or what?"

His tone was playful, joshing as his arms swept the open area. "Oh, Harri, I don't know. I mean, I sit here all day listening to the chatter in the world. How could I possibly leave this?"

Her eyes narrowed, so he got serious. "Alright, I'm in. Other than what you noted was obvious, what else connects these murders? What one special telltale thing makes up this killer's signature?"

"Letters."

"As in ABCD, like the alphabet?"

"No. Prison pen pal letters."

She had his full attention.

CHAPTER THIRTEEN

"I'm all ears, Bishop."

"When they found Trina Robinson's remains, they unearthed her purse and a letter."

"From who?"

"An inmate at Huntsville, who was writing to a lady in Mississippi."

"The letter had a Mississippi address? But she got it in Mansfield? Post office overshot a bit, didn't they?"

"Somebody crammed it into another envelope then sent it to her."

"Is someone tampering with the mail? That's a federal offense; did we open a case?" He attempted to keep the amusement out of his tone, but didn't quite manage it.

"You know, Bergman, you are just a barrel of laughs, aren't you?" Her heavy exhale summed it up. She wasn't in the least amused with his unspoken humor.

"It's a real thing, you know, messing with the mail, but alright, I'll let that go. Okay, who was the letter intended for?"

"A gal named Maggie Stone, from Yazoo City, Mississippi."

"Did she know our victim?"

"The Dallas County Sheriff's office contacted the woman in Mississippi and she'd never met our dead girl."

"And this letter supposedly to this Maggie Stone...was it correspondence from a family member, or was it a prison love hookup?"

"Maggie wasn't writing to prisoners even though she was part of a church outreach group. These ladies only correspond with minimum and low-security prisoners. Stone wrote one letter, that was it, said she wasn't comfortable writing to those men."

"Did they question the inmate?"

A wry smile turned her lips up. "The inmate who allegedly wrote the letter died. Get this. This con's letter got mailed a few days after getting shanked over a cigarette dispute. Come to find out, he didn't write it."

"How could anyone possibly know this?" Kasper shifted in his chair, reaching for his lukewarm coffee draining the cup.

"According to his prison files the man was illiterate, couldn't read or write."

"This letter he couldn't write had his name on it, so who wrote it and mailed it if he was dead? It seems like a good 'who done it' for TV."

"It sure has us stumped. Add in who redirected this mail to our victim? They had to have had her name and address, and why change addressees? "

"And the dead con not being able to read or write doesn't have anyone stumped?"

"He could've had another inmate do it for him. It's the only plausible answer." Her brows knitted in thought.

"The letter, what'd it say?"

"It was a poor me, I'm so lonely message, how he needed a friend and he'd found Jesus. You know all the crap inmates spout. He didn't do it, he was in the wrong place at the wrong time, yadda-yadda."

"The guy gets shanked, bad luck for him, especially if he really didn't do it. Are they investigating his murder?"

Harlowe is quiet; her facial shrug says it all.

"Fine, I'll leave it alone, let the homicide detectives in Huntsville handle it. One letter has the Bureau thinking these letters are the key to these victims? Really?"

Kasper relaxed, extending his legs, crossing his ankles, and folding his arms over his chest, staring at her.

"No, not just one flipping letter, you dork. They found two others in the missing Chickasaw woman's belongings."

"No dead body and no other items found either, I'm assuming. So are they currently still working her case?"

"Her sister, Winona Amos-Garza, is still working her sister's missing person's case, without police help. They gave up since there were no fresh leads until now."

"This Sylvia Amos, the missing woman, had prison mail. How do you know this?"

"Her sister rifled through her stuff after she vanished, found two letters from a Huntsville inmate, and turned them over to the Thackerville police."

"And who was this inmate?"

"Another dead end. The guy died in a car accident four months after his release, which was less than a year ago. He was still in lockup when Sylvia Amos went missing, so he's not connected to her missing person's case."

Kasper's brows lift. "Well, well, well. How convenient for the dead convict. Were the letters really from him?"

"The detectives in Tulsa located a family member, a cousin in Nashville, the only immediate family who hadn't disowned him, asked if he knew about any letters. Seems his cousins had a girl he was writing to in Rockwall, Texas. After his release, they were getting married, but a drunk driver ended his plans."

"The letters for a chick in Rockwall, rerouted to a lady in Thackerville, Oklahoma? We don't think the post office is screwing up?"

"Nope."

"Why not?"

"Neither had beginning salutations. So, no proof either letter was for either woman."

Kasper blew out a breath of irritation. This was all sorta stupid, passing notes kinda crap in junior high.

"So, three letters in total: one to Robinson, two to this missing Oklahoma woman. So, did they match up the handwriting? Is it from the same inmate?"

"No match, and neither dead guy wrote them, so the big question's this: how did their inmate numbers get on them? Before you ask, we did DNA testing on the flaps and the stamps, and got nothing. Not an ounce of DNA. The paper and envelopes were handled repeatedly, so fingerprinting got us nil."

"Two letters to this Amos woman, one to the Robinson woman, that's it? This is what we're making a case on?" Kasper was attempting to grasp how this all fit together.

"No, damn it, that's not all. Cheese and rice, Kasper. Keep your shorts from knotting up inside your butt crack, would you?"

A laugh spewed from him. "Really, you just said cheese and rice? Wouldn't this be a Karney Logan curse?"

"Yeah, okay, I'm trying to work on my potty mouth, you motherfucker."

Silence ensconced the room for a millisecond before they laughed.

"Alright, what else you got?"

"We called the sheriff's office in Okmulgee County, Oklahoma, where they discovered the remains of Rayna Anderson." Harlowe saw his posture change; she held up a hand. "Wait. Yes, we believe she's part of this same victimology. Her bones turned up outside of Okmulgee County, Oklahoma, twenty-five miles from Tulsa. A man was bulldozing a building he owned getting the land ready to sell. The killer buried the victim under a dumpster, but they didn't get an ID until a week later, when the demolition crew dug up a suitcase buried six hundred yards away. Her passport, among other types of documentation, ID'd her. Dental records confirmed. Oh, and just a side note, the sheriff's office in Okmulgee passed the case on to Tulsa Homicide."

"They've got a bang-up homicide team. So, tell me about this Anderson person."

"Rayna Anderson got a huge settlement after winning a case with a large trucking outfit and this helped pay for his gender reassignment surgery. So, our victim was clinically and psychologically considered a woman. She was a nurse, a home health care provider. Anyway, Anderson was reported missing by three elderly clients. Three different male clients called to complain because Rayna never showed up at their homes. Several days later, the agency reported her missing. Afterward, no one cared, and her missing person's case just sat."

"Her clients knew he was a man? I mean, before his surgery?"

"Yeah, so did the agency. That's how we located her medical records. The autopsy told a tragic story. She was big-boned, a tad short of being six feet tall and weighed in right at about 225. The man, er, uh, lady, didn't get sexually assaulted, at least the forensic guys don't think so. With the surgeries he'd endured to become a she, it was hard to say, and bones don't always scream sexual assault, but someone beat her badly. Bones don't lie. Andersons's rent was paid ahead a month, but since she never came back to her duplex, the landlord never reported her missing."

"And just why not?" His forehead crinkled. "Don't people give a damn about another person anymore? Anderson hadn't given the guy a notice to vacate. What about the furniture? Personal stuff? Wasn't it all still there?" Scum-bucket landlords. Kasper dealt with these types in Houston.

"It was a furnished duplex. The owner re-rented it and kept the security deposit, told the cops he thought Anderson just jumped ship."

Kasper nodded. "What about her belongings? Did the landlord keep it all? "

"Men's clothing and shoes, but she was no longer a man. There were no other items, because she was renting a furnished duplex. Her emergency contact was a cousin from Georgia. The landlord called Anderson's cousin, and he came and got the items. He didn't seem concerned about Rayna and told the landlord, Ray, as he still called her, met someone and he figured they'd run off together. The family was dysfunctional to the max. Seems they did not approve of Ray's lifestyle choice. Anyway, even before then, theirs was a family filled with issues. The cousin Danny said they would've excommunicated her after the sex change anyhow."

"Why's this case considered part of this?" Kasper uncrossed his ankles to sit up straighter and he propped his elbows on the armrests.

"They found letters, yes, from an inmate's love letters, in Rayna Anderson's suitcase, no name, just signed, 'from your lover.'"

"The suitcase was all she had, like she was planning to leave town?"

"Uh-huh. From what the cousin said, Rayna downsized, sold everything worth selling. She was moving in with a new man she'd met, they were planning on getting married."

"They interview this new man, his fiancé?"

"No. No one knows, not even the cousin. Seems it was an enormous secret."

"Well, that's not the least bit suspicious, is it? We think she told this unknown man, probably an ex-con, about her sizeable chunk of money. What about the money?" *Money*, Kasper thought, *great motive for murder*.

"Currently it's the property of the State of Oklahoma until they figure out who the rightful heirs are. So far, a will hasn't materialized."

Kasper's next question, "How about the victim in Austin? What makes her a victim?"

"Mera Soon-Lee was a diminutive woman, of dual heritage, Korean, and African American, and according to what they've concluded, she could've been the first victim. She might still be missing if it weren't for some kids. Anyhow, after they found her skeleton, they panned out and did a wide search of the area. In a ravine less than four hundred yards from where they discovered her bones, they found a medium-sized plastic purse, and honestly, how the contents survived the elements amazes me."

"You're not telling me they found letters, are you?"

"Yeah, I am. Four letters stitched into the lining of her purse."

"She was corresponding with inmates, really? This many years later, you could read the letters found in her purse...you're joking, right?"

Harlowe had to be messing with him because letters written on paper buried at least four years would be unusable, it was impossible.

"They found letters rolled and rubber-banded and stuffed at the bottom of her purse, under the lining. Someone cut them, sewed the lining up by hand, and you'd think paper would've deteriorated over time, and it should have, but weirdly enough, someone laminated them. Forensics used light filters to read them clearly. Two letters came from the State pen in Florence, Colorado, two from Huntsville, Texas."

"Odd, so my next question is, why?"

She shrugged. "That, too, is a mystery."

"Back to these letters. Did the inmates or alleged inmates who wrote these letters check out?"

She stood to stretch out her back. "Yep, nobody popped. Two guys in lockup wrote letters, but only to family. The other two were paroled with ironclad alibis. Forensics did a handwriting comparison. Neither one's handwriting matched. They checked this against correspondence the other victims received. No match."

Kasper's head bobbed absently. "This accounts for all the victims except Annelle Mackey from Itasca and the missing woman from Azle, Nora Mendez-Finch. What do you have to link them to the others?"

"When they found Mendez-Finch's car, her purse was in the floorboard and they found letters inside, but in the other cases the killer buried the victims' personal items, so why was her purse still there?"

"You're saying, then, until now he's been in character, same MO. He's changed it up so something's off."

"Spoken like a true profiler, Kasper."

"Whatever. You said letters in the Azle woman's car, there was more than one? Tell me about them."

"Two found under the driver's seat—one from Huntsville, the other from the State prison in Hutchins."

"Hutchins? Same place they found the body of Trina Robinson?"

"Yeah, odd, ain't it? Oh, and they found Ms. Robinson's car parked in a wooded area outside the city limits a few months later. After another thorough search of her trailer, they found another letter in a purse stored in a shed in her backyard. Letter written by an inmate locked up in Louisiana, who's dead."

Kasper's eyes popped with a discernible headshake. "Jesus H. Christ, sounds like a horrible movie plot."

She handed him a list. "Here's the list of current victims. I've included the one missing woman who fit our victimology."

1. *Mera Soon-Lee*, 28, Austin, Texas: Travis County, missing in 2011, remains found 2014 near Marietta, Oklahoma, Love County—active homicide.
2. *Trina Robinson*, 35, Mansfield, Texas: Tarrant County, missing in 2014, remains found 2015 in Hutchins, Texas, Dallas County—active homicide.
3. *Rayna Anderson*, 35, Marietta, Oklahoma, missing in 2013, remains found 2015 in Okmulgee/Tulsa County—active homicide.
4. *Sylvia Amos*, 33, Thackerville, Oklahoma, Love County: missing 2011, believed to be an active homicide.
5. *Nora Mendez-Finch*, 35, Azle, Texas, Tarrant County: missing in 2016, believed to be an active homicide.

6. *Annelle Mackey*, 36, Itasca, Texas, Hill County: missing in 2016, remains found 2016 in Itasca/ Hill County—active homicide.

"From what I understand, Annelle Mackey, the newest victim, was not writing to a prisoner. You mentioned nothing about any inmate correspondence."

"Don't know. Her case is fresh, the Hill County sheriff's office has been investigating."

"If they didn't find prison mail, why's she lumped into this case?"

"The Bureau's keeping tabs on recent missing women who fit the victimology, and women strangled with an undergarment got flagged as the MO. Annelle Mackey came up. She fits the profile, and they found her strangled to death with her own underpants. "

"Makes sense, I suppose. So, let's talk timeline. He starts in 2001, with Soon-Lee. At the end of 2011, they report Sylvia Amos missing. They report Rayna Anderson missing 2013. In 2015, they discovered her remains. March 2014, they find Soon-Lee's remains. Then seven months later, still in 2014, Trina Robinson vanishes. Her remains are discovered in the fall of 2015. Eight months ago this year, early March, Annelle Mackey goes missing. Her body is discovered end of June. Nora Mendez-Finch went missing in late July and it's now early October. She's still missing. We're considering her a victim."

"Yep." Harlowe's short fingernail tapped against her empty ceramic coffee cup watching him working something out.

"So, there's a three-year break from his first supposed killing to his next. This doesn't count the Thackerville woman. And Mera Soon-Lee doesn't fit our killer's current victimology. Makes me wonder why her? What triggered his initial rage?"

"Well, he has a solid profile of his victims and she doesn't fit, so perhaps she was his first opportunity and she was accessible."

Kasper focused his stare on a scratch on the front panel of the desk across from where he sat. "This person travels between Texas and Oklahoma...any chance these two cases don't connect?"

She pushed the porcelain mug to the center of the desk. "Maybe, but I doubt it. The letters are a keynote. Add in the other factor, the victims have similar life circumstances. So, it seems they're targeted by the same person. Rayna Anderson, though, is unusual. I'm not sure how she fits in."

Another dead body found and two women still missing; this was more than worrisome. More bodies were likely to show up. Killers like this didn't just stop, they usually increased the frequency of killing. The clock was ticking.

"Alright, my next question," he began, and she finished for him, "Who else do I want on our team?"

CHAPTER FOURTEEN

Two days later, using a conference room at the Dallas FBI headquarters, they'd established a task force office. Four desks arranged in the center with two eight-foot tables on either side. Last, a smaller table with a Mr. Coffee, Styrofoam cups, creamer, and sweeteners. A water cooler in the back corner, a large, detailed US map on the rear wall, and instead of a whiteboard on wheels, they had two rolls of 6x4-foot peel-and-stick magnetic whiteboard paper on either side of the conference room. Along with a passel of dry-erase markers in a large plastic container and rolls of scotch tape.

Pens, pencils, notebooks, message logbooks, and landlines were on each desk. There were four computer monitors with docking stations for each agent to use their own FBI-issued laptop.

Kasper looked around their new HQ. *Great workspace*, he thought and grinned, and it would be fantastic to see Corneal Sebastian AKA Lefty and Francine Ryder again. Bergman hadn't seen her since graduation. He wondered if she was still called Freaky Frankie behind her back. Kasper hadn't kept up with any of his classmates; he knew people changed.

He'd Skyped with Lefty a few times so he was aware of how

much Corneal had changed, which wasn't much sans a few pounds and a new receding hairline. Lefty and Francine were both traveling from DC; Kasper wondered if they'd formed a bond like he had with Harlowe. Hell, the DC office alone had over 36,000 employees, so who knew if they'd seen each other?

"It's shaping up in here," Harlowe announced walking in and around him to the desk nearest the US wall map. Kasper walked up beside her as she stood back eyeballing the map. Harlowe grabbed a plastic box with colored pushpins, then placed a white pushpin in each town a victim lived and a yellow one for each missing woman's hometown. With red pushpins, she marked the place where each body was located.

"The white denotes the town our victim was from, yellow, the missing women. The red shows where each body was located. From what we can tell..." She paused as the door squeaked opened. In walked Corneal Sebastian.

Smiling, he extended his hand, clasping Bergman's, pumping it like an oil rig pump jack so hard oil was bound to shoot out his nose. "Good Lord, good to see you in person, feels like forever." Hauling him in with one quick jerk, Lefty hugged him as men hug, shoving him back just as fast. He turned to Harlowe. "And look at you, girl, you look fantastic." His long legs took a few strides, and he had Harlowe in a tight bear hug, then he stepped back beaming.

Harlowe laughed. "Nice to see you too, Sebastian. It's been what, three years?"

"Closer to four, but hey, who's counting?"

"Does everyone still call you Lefty these days?"

"Well, duh, of course they do, but now they call me Agent Lefty." He glanced over her shoulder. "I see four desks. Who else is joining us?"

"I figured you knew because she works in DC, too."

"Oh, for Heaven's sake, gimme a break, Lord, the DC office has over 36,000 employees, and even as good-looking as I am, I can't know every employee. Besides, don't have time to meet everyone. Who else is coming?"

Harlowe was ready to spurt out a name, and the door opened. Their fourth agent walked in, computer bag slung over her shoulder, a large purse dangling from her wrist and a hang-up clothes bag draped over the suitcase she was wheeling behind her.

"Godawful traffic at the airport and the cab driver was a nightmare! I can't believe there wasn't one blasted rental car for me." She stared up at Harlowe. "What's more, I can't believe nobody came to pick my ass up!"

"Frankie, uh, I mean, Francine?"

"Yeah, it's me, Kasper, the nasty girl they called Freaky Frankie. They all treated me like a ghoul, not a real girl."

"Well, shit, Agent Ryder, don't get your panties wadded up in your butt crack. Just for the record, I never called you any nickname; I thought you were a cool, very smart girl. I...well..." He stopped talking and rubbed his head in frustration.

"Bergman, sorry, didn't mean to bite your head off. I knew you were a good guy. Shit. Quantico was a lifetime ago; I need to let it go. Hey, though, you can still call me Frankie, but only if you leave off the *freaky*, we got a deal?"

"Umm, yeah, sure, Frankie it is, sans the freaky." Kasper grinned.

Francine Ryder winked at him as she hoisted her computer bag and purse up higher on her shoulder dropping the handle of her suitcase. Her hanging clothes bag slipped off crumpling to the floor.

"Here, let me help." Lefty bent to retrieve her bag, slyly glancing up. "Wow, it's been a while since I've seen you, Francine. I hear you're in DC too." Corneal laid the clothing bag across the back of a chair, and then he took the computer bag from her, setting it on top of the desk.

Kasper watched, and his gut instinct kicked in. This wasn't the only time they'd been in contact since Quantico. No siree, bob! He watched Francine's eyes light up, if only momentarily. He noted the smile reaching Lefty's eyes but not his lips. An expression telling him his good pal Corneal had seen this aggravated side of her plenty of times before. He stared at them.

Francine wheeled her suitcase up to the desk, plopped her purse on top, then sighed, looking at Lefty. "Thank you, Corneal. My-my-my, it's been a while, great to see you again." An insignificant blush rose, then faded quickly when she shook Lefty's outstretched hand.

"Oh, you two, cut out the malarkey." Harlowe said. Her back to them, she was staring at the map.

"What malarkey, Bishop?" Francine took a seat and leaned back. She shut her eyes, releasing the airport stress through an eight-minute yoga breathing technique—inhaling for eight, exhaling for eight.

Kasper laughed aloud. "You mean them, the two of them, really? Hell, Lefty never said a word, you dumb shit, and Bishop, how did you know?"

"Gossip runs rampant in the circle I work with and the people I know love office gossip. Besides, girls talk and tattle. Oh, never about agency things, just about personal crap." She glanced at Francine. "Karney was in DC two years ago. She told me she saw you together in a stairwell. Y'all were—"

Francine stood quickly. "Never mind what we were doing." Her face blushed beet red.

"I was just fixing to say it. You guys were pretending about how long it's been. It shows all over your damn faces. Why are you trying to hide it?" Kasper's forehead wrinkled.

"We aren't in the same department, wanted to keep our seeing each other low-key. It's not in the regs saying we can't date, we just keep this to ourselves. Only a few friends we work with and our SACs know. Who else needs to know?"

"I'm not your friend?" Kasper sounded a little offended.

Frankie pushed the chair out of her way and walked up to Harlowe. "It's wonderful to see you, Bishop." She hugged her and then walked to Kasper. "You too, Bergman, and hey, you can blame me. I told Left not to tell you, and no, I didn't tell Harlowe. I didn't even know Karney was in DC until you just told me. She didn't look me up." Frankie scowled. "We were being pretty closemouthed about our dating, we didn't want it to cause any issues if we worked together, you know, like now. Man, if Karney told y'all, who the heck else knows? Crap." Francine was distressed their secret was out.

"Awe, Frankie, who even cares?" Lefty placed his arm around her shoulder

She shrugged it off, looking up at him. "I care. What if we end up working together 24/7 and we have a terrible breakup? Then what happens?"

Lefty took her hand in his and kissed the back of it. "You ain't ever getting rid of me," he said in his best Sylvester Stallone voice, just like Rocky said to Adrian in *Rocky II*.

She giggled. Corneal Sebastian the romantic.

Harlowe rolled her eyes while Bergman was trying to take it in. Francine and Corneal, Frankie and Lefty—wow! Francine had been a mess at Quantico. She wore no makeup, was not your average girly girl. Not overly athletic either, even though she'd passed physical strength training, surprising the hell outta everyone. Francine was the stereotypical frizzy-haired extremely smart geek. Who was this woman with her medium-brown hair cut in a long bob wearing makeup? The used-to-be-shy girl who never spoke her mind, the Francine Ryder he knew was an introverted nerd.

"If you try to break up with me I have a gun and cuffs." She blew him a kiss then blushed.

Lefty waggled his brows lecherously. "We did that already."

"Keep it business, you two. Behind closed doors, who cares if handcuffs play into your fantasies?" Harlowe pretended to scowl.

Frankie gave an eye roll. "Leave our fantasies outta the mix, Lefty. Bishop, you want to explain why we're in Dallas?"

"Yeah, I'm clueless about this, so I second her motion." Lefty stood, arms crossed, looking from Bergman to Bishop. Harlowe took the lead.

"Frankie, with your experience in the technical aspect, and knowing how to obliterate your footprints—"Bishop began.

Kasper's mind wandered back to a case he'd worked with Detective West and the DEA. He'd worked alongside a DEA agent who ended up being a hitman for the Mexican Cartel, making a vicious enemy. Sykes was currently still on the lam, and likely gunning for him. He brushed it off. Today wasn't the day to think about ex-DEA Agent turned Cartel Hitman Theo Sykes. He opened his ears back up to hear Bishop talking.

"Frankie, you'll help backtrack all the paperwork, all the files, do some confirming, fact-finding, and gathering. You understand how this works."

Francine Ryder nodded, jotting notes.

Bishop looked at Lefty. "Corneal, you're our out-of-left field kinda agent. A dude who sees things everyone else might overlook. You think out of left field, coming up with the darnedest ideas. We expect you to connect dots no one else would ever connect. Plus, you get to work with Frankie. Don't make me sorry I put y'all on the same team. Got me?"

"Look, Harri, for your information, we've worked a few cases together and—"

"Forget it, Lefty, she's just messing with you." Frankie smirked. "You are, aren't you, Harlowe?"

"Yeah, I'm messing with y'all. I know y'all are professionals. Besides, you wouldn't be on this team if I thought you weren't, so I'll stop kidding you guys."

In between questions Frankie and Lefty had, and a pot of coffee Kasper brewed, Harlowe brought them up to speed. "You two getting any type of picture in your heads?"

Frankie got up to stretch and inspect the map, followed by Lefty, whose eyes crinkled in concentration.

Her finger tapped on a particular rural area letting her fingernail slide to the next small town. "Small towns are havens for men preying on women and children. Residents in Itasca, Azle, and Thackerville, places where no one locks their doors and everyone-knows-everyone sort of mentality, but not in bigger towns like Tulsa or Austin. Even Mansfield ain't a Mayberry-type town anymore."

Lefty stood back, getting the complete picture. "Did they live there all their lives?"

"No. Most of them moved to these areas later in life. From their histories, we know they grew up poor with minimal education. Four of them—Robinson, Mackey, Amos, and Mendez-Finch—are high school dropouts. Mackey and Robinson were single moms, never married. Mendez-Finch got pregnant her junior year of high school and married Stanley Finch. She'd just filed for divorce. And before you ask me, yes, the husband is on our radar. Nothing's come of it, not yet anyway. Our victims, Anderson and Soon-Lee, are the only two with college educations. They don't match the other profiles, but they didn't want to be dead either. Listen, before we get into this any deeper,"—Bishop cleared her throat—"I'm handing the reins to Kasper."

Bergman's head snapped up, and he pointed to himself. "Me? Hey, this is your show, Bishop. Why are you pawning it off on me?"

"Not pawning, you jackass, following order." She heaved a deep sigh. "Here's the deal. They wanted the case worked by the Dallas office. The reason is three murders happened in Texas and there's one missing woman from Texas."

They glanced back. There were three red pushpins planted in Texas: Austin, Hutchins, Itasca, and one yellow for the missing woman in Azle. A pushpin in the above State of Oklahoma marked one dead from Tulsa, and another missing from Thackerville.

Lefty slapped him on the shoulder. "So, our killer prefers Texans. Congrats, Bergman, your state wins the prize."

CHAPTER FIFTEEN

Murder books and the files from the missing person's cases lined the back table, with information gleaned by the homicide teams who'd worked each case initially. Correlated by dates and bound in three-ring binders.

Kasper took charge knowing Bishop could've easily run this unit with her eyes closed, so why was she really backing away? He intended to ask her.

Kasper addressed his team. "Frankie, dig into each victim. See if they had anything in common. Had they ever met, ever gone to the same stores, churches, banks, you know the drill. Work up a profile on them. If you need help, there's a secretarial assistant. Call downstairs." He looked at Lefty. "Left, dig into their financials, get background checks. See if you can establish a financial pattern which might have connected them. We've got a guy in the building who can help you if needed. Travis is a financial forensic wiz."

Two heads nodded. They went to work. Then there was Harlowe.

"What about my assignment?"

"Pull all the initial reports for each homicide and the missing person's reports. Get copies for all of us. But first, I need a private word."

Frankie and Lefty minded their own business. Theirs was not to question why, they were there to follow the leader.

At the end of the hall, in a corner office, Harlowe stepped in first. Kasper pushed the door closed.

Pointing to a chair he said, "Sit."

Her hands neatly folded in her lap, quietly she waited for him to speak.

Kasper watched her from the opposite chair where he could see her entire face. She was calm, docile, reserved, not the Harlowe he knows. It was high time she explained what the heck was going on. A worried look etched his face. "Talk to me."

Closing her eyes, she shook her head only slightly. "When my SAC approached me about heading up this task force in Texas, I was like hell yeah, and see my buddy Kasper. But I told him I had to decline being the lead, and look, it won't be the last time they offer me this type of position. Truthfully, I'm emotionally not up to it. Ever since Monica's death, I haven't been myself. I wanted to work on this task force, but not run it. Like I said before, I trust you. I know you. You're not like the flipping agents I worked with in Vegas. Those assholes figured I should just get over her death, move on like a fucking machine. I'm experiencing a bit of burnout but ain't gonna admit it, only to you, and I'll call you a liar if you repeat me. Listen, take it as a compliment that I requested you to lead the team, will ya?"

He stared at her before saying, "Harlowe...Harri, come on. It'll help get your mind off Monica."

Her brows dipped in sadness, and in her eyes there was a haunted look. "No, not yet, I can't. And Lord knows Monica's upstairs with the Big Guy shaking her finger at me telling me to get on with my life. I know she is."

"Then do it, Harri. I'll step aside and let you lead. I don't mind." He leaned in touching her arm.

Eyeing his hand, a wistful smile formed on her lips. Kasper Bergman was a real gentleman, and she was fortunate to have him as her friend.

"I wanna be on the team, not in charge. Besides, my SAC and the Washington office were right in sending the case here to Texas-land. With the bulk of our victims being Texas residents, your state earns the right to get the justice they deserve."

"Alright, I'll head this operation. Only because you asked me to, but you stay on the team."

"Done, and I hope we bring whoever this murdering bastard is to his knees!"

"Agreed. Now let's get to work."

Bergman felt there might be more than Monica's death keeping her from taking the lead, but he'd forgo giving her the fifth degree; it was time to catch a man who was killing women across state lines. His fervent hope was there weren't more women to add to the tally. Afterward, he trusted a jury would vote in favor of giving the bastard the needle.

CHAPTER SIXTEEN

When they returned, Frankie was gone and Lefty was up to his armpits in financials.

"Where's Frankie?" Harlowe looked toward the back.

"Upstairs. There are two computers, plus a copier. Said she'd be back by lunch."

"Good," said Kasper. Then, "Harlowe, start with Trina Robinson's case. Dig into it, see what you can find that everyone else might be missing. I'm gonna go over all the initial reports and interviews."

Everyone went to work.

Papers strewn, files up on files, and heads bent reading when the door opened and Frankie walked in, followed by the smell of burgers and fries.

"Are y'all hungry?"

Lefty looked up. It was two. "I can't believe I missed lunch."

"You didn't miss eating, Lefty. Look in your trash. There's a Cheetos bag, two candy bar wrappers, and a small empty bag of cookies."

"Fine, Harri, I had a few snacks. You gals never eat." Frankie's eyes widened at his statement. "Okay, okay, I know you eat, Frankie, but not as much as I do, alright?"

"How about we eat the burgers and keep working?" Kasper stood helping her sort out the burgers and fries, and they went back to work as they filled their stomachs.

Kasper dug into the files and reports and his food, and as he read, something about the letters jumped out.

He scooted his chair back. "We've got two letters mailed in a new envelope, and original addressee was not the recipient."

Harlowe looked up. "Are you talking about the letter supposedly written to a woman in Mississippi but stuffed into a different envelope and sent to Trina Robinson in Mansfield, and the letter intended for some chick in Rockwall, which ended up in Sylvia Amos's belongings?"

"Yep," Kasper said, "both letters addressed and stamped but no postmark on the second envelope, at least not an authentic one. It's a manufactured postmark and looks damn near real. How did the post office allow this?"

"If it went out of the prison, no one looks at the outgoing mail. They only check incoming," Harlowe voiced.

Lefty's head bobbed. "It's an issue, alright, but it's an issue for the Post Master General to figure out, right?"

"Dunno, Lefty, seems like we should figure it out. I mean, we're working the case, aren't we?"

Frankie stopped what she was doing to join the conversation. "Kasper's right, you guys, we should look into this. Were any of them sent to the intended recipient and received by said recipient?"

Harlowe opened the file with the copies of the letters, thumbing through them. "They never began with a person's name, just Dear

Baby, Honey, or Sweet girl, never an actual name, so who knows who they're intended for?"

Pushing her seat back, Frankie looked over her reading glasses at Harlowe. "And all the letters had the same vibe?"

Harlowe replied, "Yeah. How they've found God and how they can't wait to meet. Just how much it meant to them to have met someone who might give them a second chance. How hard prison life has been, all the sad sack, sad shit a convicted criminal deals with. "

"Addressed to one person, mailed to another, why? And another question: how does that happen?" This left Agent Sebastian doing a head scratch.

"Someone starts the letter off with Dear Baby or Honey, and these women believe the letter is to them and I mean, why not? It got mailed to them. Dontcha think Robinson and Amos wondered why they got mail addressed to another woman. I mean, who stuffs someone else's mail into another envelope and mails it to a different person?" Kasper had a valid point. No one had an answer, and he resumed, "And why go through these channels? If you had her address, why not send it directly to her? This makes me wonder if we're missing a message from the killer."

Harlowe's lips pulled as she asked, "From the killer, really, Kasper?"

"Yeah, I got a theory, well, sort of anyway."

Frankie's eyes widened. "Do tell. We'd all love to hear what you've come up with and so quickly, I must say." So, explain, would'ja."

"Count me in. I want to hear this too." Lefty leaned back, folding his arms staring at Bergman.

"Shit, okay. Look. The inmates who purportedly wrote the letters are either dead, illiterate, or out on parole and have concrete alibis. Harlowe said the tone of each letter sounded familiar. I'm wondering if the same guy is writing all the letters."

Frankie's brows dipped in question. "One man?"

"Yeah, one," Kasper told them.

Frankie blew out a huge exhale of disbelief. "You wanna tell us how one convict could write these letters if they originate from—" She stopped to count inside her head. "Three different prisons?"

"Haven't figured it out yet, but it's possible if you have the right contacts."

"Kasper's right. Prisoners have outside contacts and do things we'd never think of, shoot, some of 'em work scams while they're incarcerated." Harlowe had a valid point.

"So, we've got one dirtbag writing letters but not using his name. Why?" Kasper's head was hurting.

Harlowe watched his face. He was putting something together, or hoping he was. Bergman shifted his chair back from his desk, crossing one leg over the other before he spoke again.

"Unquestionably, we've got someone writing letters—call them love letters—to these women. This con, whoever it is, has them snowed into believing they've got a connection. You think these women, all of them, were honest about their weight problems, or social and financial status in life?"

Harlowe bobbed her head. "Yeah, why lie, what do they have to lose, they're not in jail? So, whatcha thinking?"

Kasper went on with his theory. "If they sent him a photo he'd recognize them, and if they'd corresponded for a while, and she felt she'd met her soulmate, she'd tell him stuff—personal stuff—and I'm betting the scumbag has a phone number too."

Lefty jumped into the mix. "So, Bergman, what you're saying is whoever got these letters got a photo and a phone number making it easy to find their victims. These ladies were sitting ducks."

"Yeah, so it seems. But it makes little sense, since the inmates connected to the letters are either still incarcerated, deceased, or have alibis. None were in for rape or murder, they're in for burglary and assault. Did they step up their game? It's not likely, realistically, I mean."

Harlowe made her way to the coffeepot. "What if there's somebody else, you know, on the inside?"

"Inside, as in not a criminal, you mean?" Lefty turned to stare at her.

"Yes, and no."

Lefty frowned at her. "What the hell does that mean, Bishop?"

"Whoever's involved might not have a police record. It opens the door to tons of suspects."

Frankie sipped her drink, gazing over the rim of her cup. "What makes you think someone on the outside is involved?"

"Because whoever it is has access to prison records."

"Why would they need this access?" Frankie asked.

Kasper replied, "To get information about inmates would be my guess. Cons who are illiterate or ready for parole, or they already wrote to a pen pal...or anything they could use as bait to reel the victim in."

"So, they reel in a fish. Then what? I guess I'm not getting it?" Frankie commented.

Lefty chimed in, "They're using an inmate's BOP number and prison address. Then someone intercepts the mail in the mailroom. Whoever is really writing the letters continues corresponding with the victim, but not as themselves."

Kasper's right elbow rested on the arm of his chair. His hand came up, and he stroked his chin, feeling stubble. "This creates a large pool of people being this involves three prisons. What's our guy doing moving from prison to prison?"

Harlowe's face scrunches up. "Nah, it has to be someone on the outside because cons don't travel from prison to prison."

"Lord, this could involve the post office." Lefty couldn't believe how deep this might go.

"I doubt the postal service is involved, not directly, could be an employee, but not the entire institution." Kasper believed investigating the entire postal system was unnecessary, but he couldn't discount the possibility of involvement from a postal employee.

Were the letters really a key, or were they a useless lead pointing them to nowhere? Were they a deliberate misdirection? Was whomever they were looking for aiming to confuse them, having them focused on something as trivial as letters, with the simple salutations of Dear Honey, Sweetheart, or Baby, and not one person's name?

CHAPTER SEVENTEEN

"This jailhouse mail motivates him to kill?" Frankie's nicely coiffed eyebrows puckered.

"Not his motivation, no. Why he's motivated to kill is unclear; it's how he's finding his victims, or it's what I'm leaning toward," Kasper responded, then, "Let's drop the issue about letters and see what else we've got. Lefty, how about the financials, any luck?"

"Travis and I found out they were all living paycheck to paycheck. Trina Robinson was on welfare and food stamps; actually, they were all on food stamps except Mendez-Finch. And Sylvia Amos, although we can't add her to the actual victim list, was on unemployment when she disappeared. Annelle Mackey had two jobs, and Nora had a new job at Walmart, but hadn't gotten her first paycheck. She'd only been working for three days prior to her vanishing. Plus, she was still living with her husband. He didn't want the divorce and hadn't moved out." Lefty flipped a page over. "Misses Robinson and Mackey's bank accounts were both tagged with overdraft fees. Other than Mrs. Mendez-Finch, they all had maxed-out credit cards, with credit scores dipping below five hundred, or barely in the four-hundred ranges. Travis just started looking into the, uh, into Rayna Anderson's financials. We know she had a job, wasn't on welfare or food stamps and his, um, I mean, her credit scores were decent. We're also looking into the lawsuit with the trucking company, her medical records, and bills, just in case."

"So, Soon-Lee, what about her? How does she fit in?"

"We haven't started digging into her yet." Lefty picked up a file.

Peering up from her notes, Frankie frowned. "So, are we thinking Mera was his first?"

"Maybe, probably. She vanished seven years ago, and after a year, her case went cold—until four years ago when they came across her remains. It's an active homicide and the letters are her only link to the others. But it's just odd as hell, because the letters hidden in her handbag were laminated. And get this." Skimming through his notes Lefty continued, "For four years at UT Austin, she got her degree in journalism. Her dream was to be an investigative reporter. Checking, we found her first job outta college was as a flunky for a publication in Austin called *American Statesman*. She worked there for a year as a copy flunky. After getting promoted to researcher she worked with an investigative reporter, Cal Thompson, who worked the police beat back then. I reached out to the newspaper, asked them what she might've been working before she disappeared."

Harlowe asked, "What'd they say?"

"Thompson was doing a story on a serial rapist terrorizing the UT Austin campus; she was his assistant. Not too long after she vanished, the rapes stopped, which is odd. Thought maybe she'd been researching a story on prison letters but no one knew about any story."

"Cal Thompson, you question him?" Kasper glanced at Lefty.

"Yeah, I tried. The guy lives in Vermont now. I have his number. Called and got his voicemail, left a message."

"You mentioned she got this job right outta college. What about finding a classmate, someone who knew her—a best friend, boyfriend, or a college professor? I know everyone's moved on. It's been seven years, actually, nearly eight if you wanna split hairs, but it's worth a shot."

"I'll look into it." Lefty scribbled his notes.

Then Kasper asked, "You checked with her parents—did she have siblings she might have confided in?"

"No siblings, parents divorced. Her dad returned to Korea a year after her disappearance. The mother stayed in Austin. I'm gonna set up an interview with her. I'll do what I can to find Mr. Soon-Lee too."

Frankie stood and walked over to the map. "Mera Soon-Lee is an anomaly, she and our trans woman. She wasn't a heavy woman, or poor. Although she might've been a poor college graduate with student loans out the wazoo, but not poor like our other female victims. I'm thinking if she was his first victim, then it wasn't random. It could have been personal, ya think?"

I'll delve as deep as I can into her life since she's an odd one out of this equation," Lefty assured him.

"Yeah, Mera, and the man are the peculiar ones. Could be they hold answers to questions we haven't thought about asking." Francine returned to her desk, letting her hand skim the sleeve of Lefty's arm in an affectionate manner as she passed. Lefty grinned while giving her a side glance, thinking how much he loved her and how happy he was to be working alongside her.

"What information did you and Travis discover about Anderson's finances, if anything?" Bergman's lips formed a straight line.

"Seems she got into financial trouble with school loans, was pinching pennies pretty hard until the hefty settlement came in. The surgery took a big hunk of the money, but he, um, oops, she got her student loans paid off and was finally seeing daylight. Her sexual reassignment surgery paid for per *her* banking records. Finally, I got the pronoun right. Good grief. Anyway, the rest of the settlement money is sitting in her bank account."

"What about the victims, Lefty?" Harlowe scribbled a few notes not looking up.

"Pizza delivery, convenience store counter help, nursing home laundry room and the kitchen, motel maid, part-time at a daycare, counter clerk at a hardware store, unskilled jobs mostly. Minimum hourly wages, menial jobs close to home. So, y'all are getting the commonality here, I'm sure."

"Yeah, most of them not educated, and poor." Kasper looked back to Frankie. "Were you and, uh, what's her name, the assistant, able to find anything we can use? Did any of them have any connections?"

"Her name's Russell."

"My bad, didn't know it was a man."

"Did I say *she* was a man?" Frankie winked. "I'm just kidding, Kasp, sorry."

Kasper rolled his eyes up with a snort. "Okay, smart-ass. What did you and *Russell* find out?"

"Amos, born in Durant, Oklahoma, lived in Thackerville, Oklahoma, in the house her parents owned, not too far from the casinos. Never married and no children. Mackey, born in Ardmore, Oklahoma, moved after her parents died to live with family in Itasca, Texas, on the Mill Block, never married, one son, Henry Garcia, eighteen. Rayna Anderson, grew up in Marietta, Oklahoma, lived in a duplex near town, had a decent job, never married, also no children. Nora Mendez-Finch, our missing woman, born and raised in Azle, in the throes of a divorce, two young kids. Then there's Trina Robinson from Buras Triumph, Louisiana, and like the many displaced after Katrina hit, she ended up in Texas. She's divorced and her ex-husband passed away from pulmonary embolism ten years ago. She had one son, who's twenty-four, was in East Texas, but seems per the DMV he went back to Louisiana." Frankie stood and stretched file in hand. "Russell couldn't find a book club, prayer group, or Facebook, Myspace, LinkedIn, Twitter—not any on social media linking them."

Kasper asked, "Anything else?"

"Um, they were all big women, apart from Soon-Lee, who was

also unmarried and no children, and her job with the newspaper was a good gig. The others, if they worked, had unskilled jobs except for our trans woman, Rayna, the former Raymond Anderson, who was also a sizable person, not obese but burly. He, uh, *she* stood just a tad under six-foot tall and was in decent shape, or so her personnel records stated. If I'm not mistaken, she was around 225 pounds and worked in a job usually done by women as a home healthcare nurse."

"Were any of them attractive women?"

Frankie eyeballed Lefty with a wrinkled forehead, not believing what she'd just heard.

"Hold on, will ya? Don't get all fired up. I asked because if they were overweight and didn't care about themselves they might've not had high self-esteem or confidence. Women like this are vulnerable."

"Frankie, he's right, low self-esteem because of being, well, let's call it what it is, guys, because you're *heavy*, gosh I'm trying not to say fat." Harlowe blew out a deep breath. "What's unfortunate is uneducated women who grow up poorer, or come from poor backgrounds, deal with this type of issue—personalities who can't escape this kind of life. As time passes, they let themselves go. Frequently, after a child's born, certain women can't lose the weight and end up not caring. Eating healthy isn't affordable since they have low-paying jobs and have to feed two or more mouths and clothe them as well. Sorry, Frankie, but this is a pretty accurate profile."

"Yes, it is, Harlowe. Although it never has to mean the woman or person's unattractive." Off her seat, Francine Ryder glanced over at her coworker/boyfriend.

"Lefty, in answer to your question, no, these women weren't raving beauties, but they had all the right woman parts for our rapist killer. When he was done, well, fuck, they were too!" She couldn't help it; she shoved her chair against the wall, it banged, bouncing back and with her foot, she stopped it from crashing back into the desk.

Three sets of eyes were on her. Two pairs belonging to Lefty and Kasper whose mouths were gaping. Harlowe's eyes narrowed as she bobbed her head, knowing exactly where Miss Francine Ryder was coming from, understanding her anger.

Smoothing her pant leg, Frankie brought her hand to her hair, tucking the longer sides in behind her ears, the sudden silence broken by her heavy sigh.

"Sorry, guys. You know, I get it, and understand these women, at least some of how they feel. Freaky Frankie, the other person I was back at Quantico." She exhaled, grabbing her chair, plopping down, setting her elbows on the desk, her face planted on top of her open palms. She stared at the wall. No one spoke. Two minutes went by. She lifted her head rolling her eyes up. "I hated being called Freaky Frankie, but truthfully, at least then I knew someone noticed me. I was the gross girl in high school everyone made fun of, or pulled pranks on."

Lefty rolled his chair over to hers and put his hand on her shoulder.

"Hey, come on, Fran, you're beautiful, and I'm not saying this because we're together. Back in Virginia I had a crush on your brain, and your beautiful eyes."

A giggle gurgled in her throat, and she bit the inside of her cheek to keep from out-and-out smiling. Corneal Sebastian, her superhero, always made her feel special.

"Apologies for my awkward outburst, however, as far as victimology goes, our victims had low self-esteem, no money, and felt unloved. These women were begging for companionship. They just wanted to be wanted. It didn't matter if it was a male or female. From what I could find, none of them had close family ties, even if they had family living nearby. It seems these women were castoffs, and all they had were the kids they supported. Even then, they had troubled children because of their lifestyle."

"Paints an insightful picture of each victim and how they were easy targets to reel in."

Three grim faces nodded in agreement to Kasper's statement.

Those females carried around an inner self-loathing. This killer was a narcissist, and he had physical power with a manipulative personality. He preyed on those who craved love and acceptance.

"Why don't we call it a day, go rest and recharge? We can meet back here seven sharp. All in favor?"

Three hands shot up. Kasper added his hand to the air, and it was unanimous.

CHAPTER EIGHTEEN

"G'morning. Who wants hot cinnamon rolls with their crappy Bureau coffee?"

Two hands went up as Lefty set a box beside the Mr. Coffee, poured himself a cup, sipped it, and scowled. "We need a Keurig. I hate this crappy generic coffee."

"Yeah, you spring for it, but they won't reimburse you for a Keurig." Harlowe scooped out a warm cinnamon roll, taking a bite. "Yummy. Where'd ya buy these?"

"Found the place by accident. Took a wrong turn when we stopped to get gas."

"Well, thanks, they're scrumptious. Oh, and Left, if you buy the Keurig, we'll spring for the pods, deal?" Harlowe looked around to get everyone's yea or nay.

"I'm in." Kasper snatched his wallet and extracted a twenty and a ten. "Get some strong Columbian coffee with the other girlie coffees." He handed the money to Harlowe. "This enough to get us started?"

"Lordy have mercy, Kasper, you still carry cash? And, sure, thirty is plenty."

"Yeah, nothing beats cash." He gave her the two bills. "Can we work now? Or we gonna jabber about cinnamon rolls and coffee all morning?"

Frankie dabbed the sugar from the cinnamon roll off her lips. "Okay, mighty leader, what's on the agenda today?"

"Couldn't sleep and had an idea."

"Why the hell didn't you wake me up, you dork? I'd have come up here too."

Frankie looked first at Harlowe, then Kasper. An incredulous look crossed her face. She pointed at him, and then at Harlowe. "You, him, y'all are, you're—"

Harlowe's eyes widened. She opened her mouth but couldn't form a complete sentence. "We, um, uh, didn't I, I guess I didn't—"

Lefty's deep laugh bubbled up. "No, you didn't tell us you two were shacking up." He shifted his gaze to Kasper, who'd turned pink in embarrassment.

"You guys stop it. We aren't shacking up. I mean, yes, Harlowe's staying at my apartment, but in the damn spare bedroom. For God's sake, we aren't sleeping together!"

She nibbled her lower lip; it wasn't the time to discuss Monica, so she coughed, getting their attention. "Hey, guys, listen up, will ya? I asked to crash at his place. I never made other arrangements. Frankie, how about I room with you until I get another place?"

"You can't."

"Why not?"

Francine Ryder's face flushed, her cheeks reddened. Kasper not able to contain his laughter, shot out, and loudly, "Are you and Lefty sharing a room?"

"Yeah, and y'all know we're dating, have been for two years." Lefty was slightly indignant.

Kasper raised his hands, palms forward. "Hey, makes no difference to me if you two are sleeping together. It's no skin off my nose. Harlowe, you can stay at my apartment as long as you want. We know we're only friends. Matter of fact, as long as Lefty and Francine's relationship doesn't interfere with Bureau business and you staying at my place don't either, then really, fellas, just who gives a flying fuck?" Kasper, the voice of reason, the damn voice of a task force leader bellowed.

Looks of surprise crossed the others' faces. Had he just hollered at them? His job was to keep his team on track, not give a damn about who was sleeping with whom or where. "Since we've got this settled, y'all gonna let me tell you what I did last night?"

Frankie and Lefty nodded, articulating a "sure" and a "yeah." Harlowe swallowing the last bite of her cinnamon roll said, "So, Bergman, tell us, what'd you do last night?"

"I mulled over the victims and the actions our perpetrator could have taken before or after their deaths, and I'm certain sexual assault was involved. Then I conducted a database search for offenders who are currently serving time in a high-security prison for aggravated sexual assault."

"Wait," Frankie stopped him. "These aren't just aggravated sexual assault. We're dealing with murder."

"Exactly, and not all killers start out as killers, either. Maybe he was only raping his victims in the early stages of his criminal career. We've read case files, had to at Quantico. Not every killer is the same. Some serials even start with acts of arson before murder."

Out-of-Left-Field Lefty chimed in, "Like he raped first, then something changed, and he killed because it was necessary, or he got angry during the rape. Is this where you're going, Bergman?"

"Uh-huh, so what if something made him lash out and the rape alone was no longer sexually gratifying, and he stepped it up to meet his sick needs? Then I searched for violent rapists." He heard a snorted "huh," come from one of the girls. Looking back, he noted Francine and Harlowe staring at him with a hand-on-your-hips stink-eye look.

"Hey, girls, look, I'm not saying rape isn't violent, but some offenders are crueler than others."

"Go on then," Harlowe said.

"Thanks for your permission," he mocked. "So, I entered

'murdering serial rapists' and narrowed down to 'men serving life without parole in Texas'—"

"Uh," Frankie interrupted him. "Sorry to cut you off, but how will this help? I mean, if they're locked up and not eligible for parole?"

An annoyed sigh blew from his partly compressed lips. "I'm trying to get there, Frankie."

She looked over at Corneal. "Left, you're right, you said I was and I am." Frankie closed her eyes, pinching her lips together, tucking her head to her chin. When she looked up, they were staring at her.

"You're what and I'm right, really?" Lefty's eyes widened.

"Yes, you dope, for once. I'm too impatient. Sorry, Kasper, please go on."

"Next, I entered this data into the National Crime Information Center (NCIC) and got a list of hits as long as the phone book, so I did some tweaking, adding in specific facts pertaining to our cases and victims' type, a backward profile if you will. This shortened the list by thousands."

"Humph," Harlowe sniffed. "Betcha it's still a long-ass list."

"Yeah, so I got busy fine-tuning it even more."

"We're all ears, Bergman." Lefty let out a weighty moan, wondering if his story ended somewhere.

"Yeah-yeah-yeah, keep your shorts on, would'ja? Our victims were a certain type, all but Soon-Lee and the dudette from Oklahoma."

"Hey, I like it—dudette—easier than my trying to keep the he's and she's straight." Harlowe did a golf clap aimed at Kasper, who did a mock bow and continued. "And the other thing I wanna mention is our guy has no issue with going from one race to another—Black, White, American Indian, Hispanic, Blasian, skinny, chunky, and transgender woman. It would seem our guy isn't real picky in some aspects."

"Blasian?" Lefty asked.

"Yeah, mixed Black, and Asian heritage," Kasper clarified.

"She's the exception, because she was petite," Frankie said. "Even the transgender woman had been large. So, the basic traits he's looking for are overweight, poor females. Oh, and you might add in lonely as hell. I'm curious, did you find anyone who fits this profile?"

"Not completely, but I wasn't expecting to find a perfect match. One con got my attention: guy's name is Preston Munn, was a lifer at ADX Florence."

"Ah, the Alcatraz of the Rookies, tough place I hear," Lefty commented, then, "But you said *was*."

"Yeah, he started his sentence in 1994 at ADX, and then transferred to Huntsville eight years ago in 2010."

"Alright, tell us about Preston Munn. Why does this dude interest you?" Harlowe leaned in and propped her elbow up on the desk. With her chin in her palm she watched Kasper distribute copies of printouts to each of them.

Frankie reached for hers. "Ooooh, I love handouts."

"Nerd, you would." Lefty stretched his hand for his copies.

"Preston Munn—serial killer, currently doing life without parole, convicted of killing prostitutes in motel rooms, said a monster made him do it. I'll give you a few minutes to read, then I'll tell you guys what I think."

They read an appalling story. The only sound besides them breathing was paper rustling as pages turned.

"Munn played a bargaining chip to take the death sentence off the table. He gave them one more case to close the hitchhiker. I want to interview this sick bastard."

Frankie shrugged. "And what about the gals he killed before her, the prostitutes? Do you think these victims factor in, because our victims aren't hookers?"

"The hitchhiker was heavyset. She was also a pen pal of a convict," Harlowe stated.

"You're basing your need to interview this guy on these letters, is that it?"

"No, Lefty, there's more." Kasper stood and walked to the table with the half- empty coffeepot still on the burner and started a fresh pot. "The court transcript where he talks about her is why I want to interview him. During cross-examination, you could tell the murder bothered him yet also thrilled him. He says how powerful he felt during the rape, almost bragging, then withdraws, saying it made him feel bad. A split personality, or so his legal team tried to run through, working on an insanity plea. Once he was out of gen pop, they interviewed his cellmates."

Harlowe frowned sifting through her pages. "Kasper, did I miss a page?"

"No, it's in another report I haven't copied yet. Sorry."

Lefty passed his empty cup to Harlowe. "Pour me a cup after the fresh pot's brewed, will ya, please? Okay, Kasper, give us the scoop on what his cellmates said."

"Several believed Munn had a dark monster inside of him. Munn told them how he treated the hookers. He paid top dollar, flashing big money around. The hookers did everything he wanted, even the abnormal requests, like saying he wanted to feel like he was raping them. Some girls they interviewed stated he got too rough and mean, and they didn't care how good the money was, cuz playing a rape victim wasn't worth the money he was flashing around."

"Still ain't gelling for me. This sort of sicko crap goes on in the normal non-hooking world; it's called S and M." Frankie pointed to her cup and Harlowe nodded, bringing a fresh pot of Joe over along with Lefty's fresh cup.

Frankie and Lefty uttered simultaneously, "Thanks."

"Reading and re-reading his court transcripts, I got to thinking about how the hitchhiker he killed bothered him. Munn stated the only whores he killed had snickered or made fun of him."

"So, the guy kills streetwalkers because they laughed at him, or..." Harlowe thumbed through the transcript reading, "or it was a facial expression he felt degraded him."

"Good grief, this gives another meaning to the phrase, 'if looks could kill', now doesn't it?" Lefty's brows dipped.

Frankie's head bobbed. "Preston was the guy who got pranked and teased his entire life, so one night he snaps and kills his first victim, a hooker named Wendi Hicks, because she laughed at him and belittled him. How does this fit in?"

Kasper leaned back eyeing them. "Let's keep the momentum going. Don't focus on how it relates to our case. Since we've been agents, none of us has worked a serial. Right now, let's just keep hypothesizing about Munn and his killings. Okay?"

Three heads nodded, so Kasper continued.

CHAPTER NINETEEN

"I know you just read this, but humor me while I talk it out," said Kasper.

"Hey, it's your dime," Lefty quipped.

"Talking it out is good. Go ahead." Frankie gave Lefty a light punch in the arm. "Shush, would'ja?"

Kasper resumed, "This guy's on the Ten Most Wanted, his picture's posted nationwide. He'd reportedly been responsible for the murders of a prostitute in Arizona, two in Nevada, one in New Mexico, and Utah, and then three in Colorado before he landed in Texas six months later. Once his face was out there, several working girls came forward claiming they'd had him as a john. It scared them to death, but they were happy to be alive. But the bastard kept killing. He hides in a small town called Frost on the outskirts of Dallas. Somebody reported seeing him in the red-light district in Dallas, not long after they found another prostitute dead."

Lefty glimpsed Francine's notes over her shoulder. "New Mexico and Colorado—neither had the death penalty like the other states. The guy's lucky to still be breathing."

Kasper's head bobbed. "Yup, and since they tried the shitbag in all five states and convicted him of first-degree murder, twelve counts, the prosecutor opted for the death penalty. But the sleazebucket struck a deal telling them he'd give them one last body if he got life without parole and got to pick which state to be incarcerated. Honest to God, why he picked ADX Florence is anyone's guess."

"Maybe the creep likes snow." Lefty hated murderers getting deals. "But how'd he get sent up to Huntsville?"

"Shit-bag's getting death threats. Got the living hell beat out of him several times, ended up in the infirmary half-dead, twice."

"Be better off if they'd shanked him, got it over with, better for him, anyway," Frankie stated matter-of-factly.

"Nope, it'd be his easy way out. This POS needs to stay locked up till he dies an old-old man," Kasper remarked coolly.

"How did he wind up in Texas?" Lefty yawned, trying to squelch it without success.

"His attorney jockeyed for him to be transferred. Munn picked Texas. Don't know why."

Lefty smirked wryly. "Maybe he enjoys riding sidesaddle for the cowboys. Get me?"

Frankie and Harlowe rolled their eyes, and Frankie said, "Yeah, we know whatcha mean, Left. Good grief!"

"So he gave up the hitchhiker's body." Harlowe redirected them to the case.

Kasper continued the story, "Nobody filed a missing person's report, so she wasn't on anyone's radar. The slimeball gave them the exact location of her body and her backpack. Here's what's odd, or is to me: the letters from the convict she was corresponding with. Munn still had them, which by this time were pretty worn because he'd read them and reread them. Short story is..."

"Short story, you gotta be kidding. If this is the short version, you suck at short stories, Bergman."

"Lefty, you're an ass."

"Uh-huh, I know."

Kasper exhaled. "What I'm getting at is this: raping hitchhiker and the prison letters is a big thing with this sick bastard. Munn's either sorely bothered by it, which I doubt because I've got the notion the bastard loves reliving it, or the rape made him feel powerful. He wasn't playacting with a hooker, this was an actual rape. The murder, though, this wasn't his control over sex, it was a superpower. To this creep it was the epitome of his sexual aphrodisiac, and—"

Lefty cut in, "Wait, he'd already killed hookers. He'd already had ultimate power of life over death, so what made this time different?"

Harlowe gazed over the rim of her cup. All this talk about sex and hookers was hitting a nerve, triggering thoughts of Monica, but she kept it in check and her voice steady. "How he tells it is, he finally got laid and afterward he dove into sex with the hookers, until one laughed at him, then he killed her for laughing. But he says he didn't kill them all, cuz not all of them disrespected him. Only this young hitchhiker ain't laughing at him. She's too damn scared, just wants to get away from him."

"Of course," Frankie said, "she wasn't like the hookers, she's not out strolling on the corner in the red-light district, so it's another power he has over her. Corrine's running away. Poor thing's in a situation she has zero control over. She's in his car. If she tried to run, what was she gonna do, jump from an automobile going sixty-five to seventy on the freeway? Munn craves control. He knew when he stopped he was gonna rape and kill her, there's not a doubt in my mind. But then he gets caught. This motherfucker offers one more body to get the death sentence commuted to life with no parole. So, he's still in control, the asshat. "

"It's more than killing and sex; it's all about control over another human being." Harlowe's caught up in this theory building.

"Serials have triggers and being in control of their situation is paramount. They'll also punish anyone who disrespects them, but Munn never said Corrine DeSoto laughed. She was the one person who never needed to be punished." Kasper was sad for the young girl, but pleased his team was functioning as a team, building a profile of their unknown subject. He got the impression whomever they were searching for was like Munn—a major control freak, amongst other personality traits serial killers possessed.

"Munn's MO isn't always the same, though. Some of his victims died of blunt force trauma, or suffocation, and some by strangulation," Harlowe pointed out.

"What caught my attention was how he killed the hitchhiker. Munn shoved her panties in her mouth to keep her from screaming during the rape, then strangled her with the same panties," Kasper detailed.

After upturning his coffee cup and draining it, Lefty asked, "Did Munn spill his story to another con? This other con hears the story about Corrine and the letters and just for fun he starts his own pen pal group? What's he thinking? He's gonna get these lonely women all worked up, think they're in love. Even poor women will help a man they're supposedly in love with. Women like this would be easy targets."

"So," Frankie said, "our killer takes this information and uses it to target women? The question I have is, if he's in jail still writing letters to these women, how the hell would he be able to commit rape and murder?"

"Good question. And these letters were, it appears, written by different convicts who are either dead or alibied out. Makes no sense."

"I agree with Harlowe, we can't convict a dead man or a man who's still in lockup, it's impossible," Lefty groused.

"Fine, let's get back to Munn's story, cuz something about it is pulling at my gut." Kasper got back on track. "I understand he's not our suspect here, but let's look at him a little deeper. He was an outcast growing up, ugly and sorta gross, stated he got teased a lot up through his teenage years."

"So what? Lots of kids are, don't mean they all turn out to be murderers."

"I agree, Lefty. Shit, I was Freaky Frankie, not just at Quantico either. I was a wallflower as a kid. But hey, look at me now."

"But you're not Munn, his head's messed up, has been a long time, and who knows, maybe his dad beat the hell outta him, or his mom was a drunk."

"Really, he felt unloved all his life so these hookers make him feel like he's loved, is that it?" Hookers and love—this was pissing Harlowe off—she was ready to burst in anger. "Well, color me shitfaced, cuz whores and love go together like peanut butter and dirt in a sandwich. Who would associate this shit with love? Oh, I know someone who did, that cheating, lying son of a bitch, I hope he burns in hell!" She banged her empty coffee cup against her desk with a resounding thud. Kasper understood, but wide-eyed Frankie and Lefty were clueless at her outburst.

Bergman saw a sad look in Harlowe's eyes.

"Uh, Kasper, can we get off track for a second?"

"Of course, Bishop. What's on your mind?" She had to be the one who brought it up, not him.

"Monica."

"You sure?"

"Yes."

He gave her the go-ahead look.

"Frankie, Lefty," she began, "I want to explain to you about my cousin Monica, and how I really ended up here in Dallas."

"We're so sorry for your loss, honey, and if we can help, please reach out anytime." Francine walked to Harlowe and hugged her.

"I appreciate it." Harlowe swiped the last tear from her cheek, sniffing. "I'm a blubbering mess. Sorry." She blew her nose.

"Not making light of this, Bishop, but I'm glad to see you're human. At Quantico, you were such a tough bitch...uh, I mean gal, my bad." Lefty's face pinked in embarrassment.

A shaky laugh escaped Harlowe's lips. "No worries, Left, it's a compliment coming from you, you oddball. And don't act hurt, my calling you an oddball, cuz we love you as our own personal oddball."

Over their desks, Harlowe, and Lefty clasped hands in a gesture of genuine friendship.

Kasper was relieved. Harlowe had gotten this off her chest, letting the others in; now she didn't have to carry this pain alone. They'd all be there for her emotionally and she'd have three shoulders to cry on.

"I'm grateful for all of you, but it's time I buck up. Let's continue with the case, okay?"

"Yep, that's why we're here. So, Red Leader to Blue Leader, what's next?"

"Lefty, you're goofy."

"Nah, Bergman, *Goofy* would be a Mickey Mouse thing. Red Leader to Blue Leader crap would be a *Star Wars* thing."

The other three rolled their eyes.

CHAPTER TWENTY

"When they found the letter with Trina Robinson's body, they kept the info under wraps. A letter written by a con was suspicious and their only clue. This meant the cops didn't want some news rag to publicize the information. They blew these stories out of proportion. When Sylvia Amos disappeared from Thackerville, it was highly coincidental when her sister brought in her prison pen pal letters." Kasper stood at the whiteboard, looking at the victims' photos. "Then Mera Soon-Lee's case comes up. Who the hell knows how, but she had four letters. Coincidence, nah, cuz we know no law enforcement agency believes in coincidences. If the letters were public knowledge, someone, even a con, would've known about it and used this tactic to hunt for their next victim."

"Also, after reading these letters," Harlowe observed, "they all bear the same tone as though a single person wrote them, but as per the reports, the attached inmate numbers belong to various men who were of no help. We checked. The inmate croaked, or is still in prison, and if paroled, has a solid alibi."

Frankie pushed her chair back with her feet, looking up at the ceiling. "Yeah, and all but one victim was overweight. Two of 'em weren't dirt poor. I also want to point out another obvious fact. We've got multiple races as victims. Black, Caucasian, Hispanic, American Indian, and Ms. Soon-Lee—half Korean, half Black. Adding a transgender woman throws a wrench into everything that makes any sense."

"Our guy's not killing his victims in their homes; he could've if he wanted. Since they've been writing back and forth, he has an address. Each of our victims used a physical street address for mail and no signs of a struggle at any of their homes. I think this person persuaded them to have their first meeting in a crowded location, making them believe they were safe. Then what happens?"

"Good theory building, Bishop, so let's run with this. So, after they meet up, he subdues her, taking her where?" Kasper asked.

Lefty spoke next, "Maybe a seedy motel, the kind you get by the hour, like Munn did. No one's the wiser cuz the employees who work at these places don't give a shit, money is money. He overpowers them, rapes then kills them, now he's got a body to dump."

"Wait, a minute here. What's he doing, talking the girl into sex? I mean, on the first date?" This appalled Harlowe, just how men could treat women and play on their sympathies.

"No, it's not a first date, "said Frankie. "Because they've been writing and think they've got a connection. To them they've been dating on paper. Maybe he tells her she's his soulmate. Men can be smooth talkers, we girls know this for fact. "

Harlowe commented next, "Oh yeah, we do. We also know he wants to get her alone. Problem is he can't if he's living in a halfway house. They can't have female visitors and unless he's allowed to live with family, and even then, not an ideal situation."

Frankie asked, "You think he's gonna take her to dinner? Play it out like it's a real date?"

Harlowe shook her head. "Nu-uh, cuz if she's a big gal, she'll feel self-conscious eating in front of him. Nope, I mean, she's already told him about her weight. This'll bother her."

Frankie came back with, "I'm gonna say he's a buff dude. I'm betting he's been working out, staying in shape. I mean, if he's gonna subdue a big gal, he'd have to be strong, not a skinny con."

The guys glanced at each other, listening to the girls theorizing between themselves, completely ignoring them. Lefty did a head/shoulder tilt at Kasper whose eyes had widened with a "let them give it a go" expression. So, the guys listened as the girls built a theory.

Frankie went on, "So, they meet up, he tells her he can't take her to his place and why. Next, what he suggests is they find a place to be alone. No crowds so they can talk."

"Except," Harlowe stated, "he isn't gonna take her to the freaking Hilton because this dude's an ex-con, so he takes her to a dump, someplace close by."

"Uh-huh, someplace in her neck of the woods, hoping to make her feel safe."

Harlowe nodded. "Yeah, yeah, and she gets nervous once they're alone in the motel room and then...*bam*! Now he has her where he wants her."

It got quiet, as they worked this scenario out in their heads separately.

Kasper spoke first, "Might be crazy, yet it sounds almost conceivable. What do you think, Left?"

Corneal Sebastian's eyes glued to his desk, his head just moving. "Could be, but then what? The guy carts the body off, and no one sees him do this? How's he get away with it?"

Frankie noted, "There aren't many women drifters our guy's gonna find walking around with prison pen pal letters readily on their person, and not all hitchhikers are big girls. Besides, girls aren't hitchhiking anymore because of men like Ted Bundy and Ed Kemper. However, men like them still prey on innocents, sick men with different names raping and killing women of all ages."

Thinking about these two monsters, Bundy, and Kemper, ignited urgency in this case since discovering the last victim three months prior. Add in the two missing women, and it felt like they were playing Beat the Clock. Timing was vital because nobody had any idea what might come next.

Kasper's fingers drummed his desktop as everyone looked to him for the next step. "Here's the plan. Frankie and me are going to Huntsville to interview Munn."

"Based on one murder?" Frankie asked.

"Yeah, the letters are a key here, and it's bugging me."

"Lefty and I, what'll we do?" Harlowe asked.

"You guys look into the victims. Start with the one from Itasca, Texas. I know they found no letter, but she fits our victimology. Afterward, do the same for Trina Robinson. There's a list of names, numbers in both murder books. Maybe someone will give us a new lead this second time around."

"Yep, we're on it. "

"Uh, Kasper," Harlowe interjected. "We need to discuss the man, well, uh, technically, he was a woman."

"This is an anomaly which has me stumped." Frankie's face puckered in thought.

"It's been niggling at me, too," said Kasper. "Why did this killer, who was picking mostly overweight single poor women, murder a transgender woman, and I got no answers either?"

Lefty leafed through Rayna Anderson's files looking for something to get his creative juices flowing and a few pages in he'd created a theory, completely out of left field, the very reason he'd earned the nickname Lefty.

"Alright, team, let's discuss our transgender woman, Rayna Anderson, who was initially a big man with feminine features, and had come out two years ago. She was a nurse's aide in a rest home in Marietta, Oklahoma. Working the night shift can mean a lonely daytime life, but at any rate before coming out physically, he might've been a man, but I'm betting emotionally he wasn't. The singular differences between Anderson and the others, besides the fact his, um, *her* life began as a man, were her education status and cash flow from a large truck accident, giving her enough money to pay for the sex change. From interviews, we've learned Anderson was supposedly busy with work and school, so she had few friends. His family wasn't very supportive of his, uh, sorry, *her*, choices." Lefty was trying to keep his pronouns straight.

A teeny facial movement lifted Harlowe's forehead, and she said, "It still gives us no connection to the killer, or why she was a victim. Rayna started life as a man, a tall, fit man, not living in squalor, educated, with a decent job."

"What about love? Rayna, the former Raymond Anderson, lived in Marietta, Oklahoma, all his life, a small town. A place where, you know the saying, everyone knows your name and your business. Anderson's officially a woman now. How would it work if he's trying to date men in the area? He'd been a man first, everyone knew that." Lefty thinking outside the box might be on target with this idea.

Kasper articulated, "Love, huh? I'd never connected this to this victim. I mean, the others, sure, but not Anderson."

Lefty's lips pinched in a smirk, and then he said, "Uh-huh, it might not even be the reason. It's only my hypothesis. Could be he met someone in prison, too."

Harlowe concurred, "Yeah, he could've kept certain facts about himself a secret until they met, hoping for the best."

"Anderson could've met someone other than an inmate. It's not like there aren't places to meet men interested in a transgender woman." Frankie looked at Corneal. "It's a decent theory, Lefty, and the love angle brings it into perspective; just don't see it as a jailhouse romance, do y'all?"

"Whatever it is, our victims all must have something in common and this includes Rayna Anderson, and for the life of me, I ain't seeing it yet," Kasper stated.

Lefty asked, "Okay, the plan is?"

"Frankie and I are gonna drive to Huntsville. The warden's expecting us tomorrow."

"Is there another SUV we can borrow, Kasper?" Harlowe asked.

"Bishop, you keep my Yukon. I'm gonna get a rental. Now, be nice to it and don't drive like a crazy person."

Her response was typical Harlowe, "Oh, so you want Lefty to drive it? I heard he doesn't drive crazy, I heard tell he drives like a grandma."

"Huh, I've got a tattletale, girlfriend." Corneal Sebastian gave Frankie the eye.

It was the best way to end their day—relaxed and laughing.

CHAPTER TWENTY-ONE

They stood outside the FBI building on the front steps. Lefty moved Frankie's suitcase and hanging bag into the rented grayish Nissan Rouge.

"Where are y'all staying, or did the warden have rooms at his special motel open for you guys?"

"Oh, ha-ha-ha. Hilarious, Bishop. Can you see me staying where seventeen-hundred men who haven't seen a female in multiple decades live?"

"You scared, Fran?" Lefty's concern was real.

"Corneal Sebastian, no, I'm not scared. Bishop's yanking my chain." Frankie winked at Harlowe, who winked back. Frankie looked at Kasper. "So, you get a king-sized bed or two twins?"

Lefty's facial expression was priceless, and the other three broke up in fits.

"You guys are assholes, you know that?"

Kasper joined the teasing, "Come on, Left, lighten up. I promise to lock the adjoining room."

"Y'all stop teasing Lefty. He'll have a complex." Harlowe smothered a giggle.

"First, to squash your fears, Special Agent Sebastian," Kasper used his official-sounding voice. "You needn't worry about your girl, I'll make sure she stays safe. As the task force leader, I've got zero intentions of putting my team into harm's way, or to have a sexual harassment suit to deal with—"

"Kasper, I'd never in a million..." Frankie sputtered. Kasper stopped her with a raised finger. "Yeah, I know I'm pulling your leg. Seriously, though, if I had any reservations about you being able to cope, you'd stay and I'd take Lefty."

"Francine will do great. She always does." Lefty gazed at her with pride.

"Here." Kasper handed Lefty and Harlowe a copy of their itinerary. "We're staying at the Fairfield Motel and Suites. It's around two miles from the penitentiary. We'll be back on Thursday, and hopefully Munn will be useful, but no guarantees. "

"You have copies of the files?"

"Of course I do. For Christ's sake, Bishop, you'd think I was a first-grader and needed my milk money pinned to my underwear or something."

"Hey-hey, Bergman, you'd better snap outta your foul mood. Got a long drive to Houston and I'm not putting up with crabby, got it?" Frankie spurted a semi-laugh.

Kasper's face fell. "Sorry, Bishop, didn't mean to snap, just keyed up. Never done this shit before. Look, you guys know I'm not a profiler. My worry is this damn killer will kill again before we catch him."

"Kasp, it'll be fine. You're better than you think. Have faith." Harlowe's face crinkled in sincerity.

"Bergman." Lefty stuck out his hand. "We do our jobs as best we can as a team. Let's nail the bastard. Drive safe, oh, and take care of my girl."

"Will do." He yawned, closing his eyes. His entire body shook, getting the blood pumping. "Also, check any crappy motel fitting our scenario within a twenty-five-mile radius. Anywhere he could've taken the Itasca woman. Don't think she'd go off with him any further, check on cameras, see how far back the recordings go. I doubt this will happen, but anything is possible. Question the staff. Oh, shit, you guys know the drill. I'm just blathering now, aren't I?"

"You were up all night long thinking? Is this why you got no sleep?" Harlowe muffled her laugh with a hand. Kasper, ever diligent even when he wasn't on the clock. Work ethics learned from his employment at the Houston Police Department, especially under the guidance of Detective Jack West. Bergman was a pit bull, his teeth embedded so firmly he might well splinter one.

Harlowe nudged him. "We're on it, Kasp, don't worry."

"Yep, and uh, Francine, we gotta go. Just because we're with the Bureau we get no special privileges. It ain't like the show, *Criminal Minds,* and we've got a private jet at our beck and call. Let's boogie." He jiggled the keys. "I'll drive, unless you wanna?"

"Nah, you can drive. I'm good."

Harlowe and Kasper did the short friendship hug, and she said, "Be safe."

"You, too."

Pulling away she saw Ryder and Sebastian in a lip-lock and a blush rose on her face. Feeling like a voyeur, ducking her head with a knowing grin, happy Francine and Corneal had each other.

"Awe, come on, guys. Is this how special agents act, all kissy-huggy?" Kasper joshed as Corneal deepened his kiss, dipping Frankie over like the iconic picture of the sailor and the nurse on V-J Day in 1945. Only Corneal added his own sauce to the moment. Had somebody been photographing the scene, they would've caught Special Agent Corneal Sebastian flipping Kasper off, and Bergman doubling over in laughter.

CHAPTER TWENTY-TWO

Hillsboro, Texas, Same Day, Late Morning

Lefty took the next exit, circling under the overpass to get to the northbound service road and their destination—the Royal Motel.

"This is the only motel close to Mackey's address. Not saying they went to a motel, but we can check it out and afterward cross it off our list. Sorta a dive, huh?" Harlowe's nose crinkled in disgust.

"Glad we're never gonna be customers." Lefty pulled into the parking lot which needed re-striping, potholes filled, and a trash detail. The building was old and falling apart; no one was putting money back into this establishment. "This place is minus two-star rating. Can you imagine the rooms being processed by a crime scene investigating unit and what all they'd find?"

"Not something I wanna even think about." She pulled a face.

Junkier cars dotted the old asphalt lot, and she shuddered, imagining the insides of the rooms. The sign offered rooms by the night, weekly and monthly rates. In all her life, she'd never envisioned calling a place like this home. Sad that poorer people had little options, options costing them more in the long run.

"Well, I'm not gonna organize it," she told him, her palm on the door handle. "You ready to see what we can shake out?"

"Uh-huh, and I've got some hand sanitizer in my jacket pocket, just so you know."

Rashid Bhalla, the front desk clerk, greeted them. "Good day. Can I help you?"

"I'm FBI Special Agent Bishop, this is Special Agent Sebastian, we're—"

"Oh my God, what, what, oh, dear, I'm just, oh my!" The man fell to pieces before they even flipped open their badges.

"Sir, take it easy, we need to ask you a few questions, nothing more." Harlowe kept her tone stern to keep the man from going off the deep end.

"Yes, yes, my apologies, I understand. Most of my guests aren't the most law-abiding, I know. But I never thought the FBI would show up on my doorstep."

"Your name is?" Lefty flipped open his notebook, pen in hand, looking at him.

"Rashid Bhalla." There was a tremor in his speech as he spelled out his last name. "B-h-a-l-l-a."

Sweat beaded on his upper lip as Harlowe laid an enlarged DMV photo of their victim on the counter. "Have you seen this woman, sir?"

Rashid looked at the photo. "Yes."

Harlowe glanced at Lefty, hopeful. "When did you last see her?"

"On the nightly news. She's missing, and this was the photo they used. Wasn't her body found three months ago?"

"Yes. Was she ever here?" Harlowe put the photo back into her pocket.

"No, ma'am, never. Why do you ask?" His voice shook.

"You have outside cameras?"

"Sorry, no."

Harlowe's eyes swept the room. No inside cameras, either.

"Mr. Bhalla, you work during the day, sir?"

"I work three to three."

"And, sir, who works the night desk?"

"My nephew, Bajit Bhalla."

Bishop wrote the nephew's name. "Sir, we'll need copies of your check-in registration for the last five months."

"Of course, yes, yes, we run a respectable business, and our records are in order." He wasn't gonna cause waves asking for a warrant; he wanted no trouble. Rashid Bhalla felt the sweat building up around his neck. This was crazy! How did his motel become involved?

Bishop handed him her card. "Sir, I'm sure there's nothing for you to worry about, but if any information comes your way, please call us."

"Oh, yes, of course, yes, absolutely I'll call," his words nervously rushed.

Both agents shook the nervous innkeeper's hand, and they set off for Itasca, relatively certain Royal Motel was a dead end.

Lefty had never worked with Bishop and he found her impressive —Joe Friday impressive.

"This guy's place isn't involved." She shrugged. "And places like this have more than their share of DNA, prints, and whatnot. Lord, how would a CSU team ever sort it out?" She thought about the seedy joints in Vegas, the call girl business, hourly rates, and no cleaning in-between customers. Yuck.

"Nah, the place is clean, rather in the clear, I suspect. Boy, the owner's a nervous Nellie, though."

"Nelson."

"What?"

"He's a guy, so not Nellie. He's a nervous Nelson."

"Oh, alright, Sergeant Friday, Nelson it is."

Harlowe's face puckered up. "Who's Sergeant Friday?"

Lefty shook his head and a tiny grin tugged at his mouth.

"Working for the FBI, and you've never watched *Dragnet,* the old black-and-white TV show?

"Good grief. I haven't thought about that show in ages. My mom used to watch the old reruns. Huh, so you think I'm like Friday?"

"Yeah, shooting question after question, straight-faced and so very formal saying, 'yes, sir' or 'Mr. Bhalla, sir'."

Harlowe rolled her eyes. "Well, my mom raised me right."

Seat belts buckled, sunglasses on, Harlowe pulled out her notebook, flipped over a few pages, and reeled off their destination. Lefty sped up when the light turned green. Putting on his left blinker he entered the on-ramp of the interstate, merging with crummy traffic. Constant roadwork kept drivers bunched up and stressed, a daily grind for Texans.

"You know, I've got another theory I've been working on—" She stopped mid-sentence to yawn.

"What's cooking in your noggin?" Lefty's foot tapped the brake in this stop-and-go traffic.

"Thinking our killer meets up with them in a populated place, like a well-lit gas station with a convenience store. The girl ain't gonna wanna meet at a motel for their first physical meeting. She might be anxious, but she doesn't want to appear desperate. She also wants to be cautious, especially in these times. At least you'd hope."

"I follow you. So, yeah, she wants to seem, what do y'all call it, aloof?"

"We call it not acting desperate, like I said." Harlowe huffed. "Anyway, she tells him she wants to meet him in a public area, but not anywhere like a decent restaurant, because she hasn't got a nice wardrobe. Second, she's self-conscious about her size. Having a meal with this man—nope, not the first time they meet, she won't do it. There's the other factor. This man's an ex-con. She's never laid eyes on him and if it were me, a bunch of what-ifs gotta be filling her head."

"Uh-huh, I see what you mean. Lots of lights, busy, people coming and going, so she'll feel safer, at least for the initial meeting.

Then what? They plan a date? Nah, I don't see it. Great storyline, but I also see something else."

"Alright, Corneal, let's hear what ya got." Harlowe Bishop loved building theory with a fellow agent and talking it out. It had been exciting with her team back in Vegas, before Monica's death, spitballing ideas, each trying to think like the offender, seeing what he might see.

"Let's presume they've talked on the phone first and set a date to meet. He tells her how excited he is and how he can't wait. At first, this POS suggests a public place to make her feel at ease. He tells her he doesn't want to make her uncomfortable. They meet and she doesn't get into his car. She has him get into hers and this makes her feel more in control."

"Yeah, sounds reasonable. Then what, they decide if there's a connection?"

Lefty's head bobbed. "Yep, and the guy's a scumbag. He tells the poor woman he feels a real connection and has since they began corresponding. Feels like he's met his soulmate, tells her she's a beautiful woman inside and out, and he's attracted to her, has been from the start, laying the BS on thick."

"Ah, I see, playing on her womanly heart to soften her up. Dude gives her the old 'it's been so long since I've had a woman in my arms' bullshit, then he suggest dinner and afterward a motel for privacy, get to know each other, something on that line?" Harlowe could see this happening.

"Exactly. This guy isn't interested in a relationship. He's looking for what turns him on—violent sex—and killing them becomes necessary because they've seen his face. Bishop, what are your thoughts? Possible?"

"Absolutely, anything's possible, and there've been weirder and less believable situations involving murder. Lord knows there are cases upon cases."

"Yeah, there's a statement truer than most," Lefty concurred with little thought.

"Since we're headed back to Itasca, take the exit to FM 934. There's an Exxon station. It's fairly lit up, see if they have cameras, and check it out. This woman lived near the Mill Block outside of Itasca. I'm betting she frequented that station and the convenience store."

"Looks like a good place to start. Who knows, we might get lucky." Lefty moved to the right. He proceeded to the exit for FM 934.

Her brows squished up in irritation. "Get lucky. It's a comment a man makes when he thinks he's gonna get laid. Maybe we need another phrase."

Lefty felt bad for forgetting about the story of her recently deceased cousin Monica, so he quickly interjected, "How about, hope we catch a break, then?"

"Much better choice of words, partner."

CHAPTER TWENTY-THREE

The Exxon station was a bust. They had cameras, but only backed them up for sixty days before recording over them. With recent turnover in staff, no one remembered her. Only what had been on the news.

Harlowe shut the Yukon door with force. "We're getting nowhere fast. I find it hard to believe no one knew this lady. Itasca isn't a hopping metropolitan city."

Lefty flipped open a file he picked up off the console. "You know, there's something I'm thinking."

"Lefty, talk, and drive, will ya? I have to get some food. Turn around, head to the chicken place we went past a few miles ago, I gotta eat."

She was right. Lefty's stomach suddenly prompted him it was well after the lunch hour. He silently cursed his stomach. This was his second instance of missing lunch. "Yeah, chicken, gravy, mash taters sound great, heading there now. In case you're wondering, I can talk, walk, and chew gum, so driving and talking is a cakewalk."

Turning the Yukon around, Lefty got back on FM 934 then headed toward I-35.

"They discovered her body behind the old cotton factory less than six blocks from the single-wide trailer she was renting."

"And this has you thinking what?"

"Why didn't he suggest they go to her place? He could have followed her in his car. This has me wondering about his vehicle. The report from the sheriff's department of Hill County says they found her car abandoned behind an old farmhouse off Highway 81."

Lefty turned left on the service road after passing under I-35. His foot pressed the gas picking up speed to move over to the on-ramp, getting back on the freeway and merging into traffic.

Harlowe pointed. "Take the third exit—food and a bathroom."

Lefty complained to her, "Anything you want, Boss."

"Zip it, goofball, and get back to your theory."

"If they were in her car, he must have returned to his car on foot. First he kills her, but where since there are no indications they returned to her trailer? We have jack for a crime scene. He places her body in the trunk, drives to the cotton factory, then buries her in a shallow grave, abandons her car several miles away." He spots the chicken place and turns in, still talking, "And his car is back where they connected, so how did he return?"

Harlowe was doing a Google Earth on the factory's location. "The old factory is on...oh, good, we're here. Let's go inside to eat, because I gotta go potty. Order me the three-piece original and coleslaw with fries, will ya? Oh, and a medium unsweetened tea." She jerked a twenty from her pocket, handed it to him, and said'll be back in a jiffy. Then she headed directly to the restroom, her eyeballs floating.

He set the tray with their meals on the far back table, grumbling. A pissy Corneal Sebastian muttered when she reappeared.

"What's up?" She saw his expression when she opened the box with chicken and fries and began eating.

"By damn, I guess nothing," he said with a pissed-off attitude. "Just you women, always ordering us fellas around when you hafta go pee. Makes me wonder if you females ever think us guys might have to pee?"

Boy-oh-boy, she was glad she hadn't taken a bite because a laugh spewed out spontaneously. "Christ, Corneal, get a damn grip! Next time, you go pee first and I'll order the food. Jesus."

Lefty went to the men's room.

Back at the table, after relieving himself, he opened the small container of coleslaw.

"Sorry I grumped at ya, Harri."

"No prob." She garbled her mouthful of fried chicken. "Don't mean to eat like a ravenous hog, but I'm starving." Taking a sip of tea, wiping her lips, she glanced around. No one was inside the fast-food joint. The lunch hour was over. "Alright, let's continue with the unsub and his car. He left it somewhere after they met up, and then he got her alone."

"How did he get in control? Did he sweet-talk her or did he hold a weapon on her after he got into her car?"

Harlowe dipped fries in ketchup and stuck them in her mouth, thinking while she chewed, swallowed, and wiped her mouth again. "Yeah, sounds more realistic, him holding her at knifepoint, threatening her. It could have been a gun, but Texas men all carry knives."

Lefty's eyebrows, shoulders, and mouth shrugged all at once. "Alright, so he gets her to an isolated place, alone. Could've been her trailer, but with no definitive proof they were there, we have no clue where her murder took place."

Stripping the last bit of chicken off the bone she chewed. "Yep, crime scene would be helpful. We'll just hafta work with what we got."

After sucking up a drink of Diet DP, Lefty continued, "So our guy ties her up, gags her in case anyone is nearby—he can't have her screaming while he rapes her—and then puts her in the trunk of her car to get rid of the body."

Harlowe verbalized an end synopsis: "They discover her body six blocks from her home, personal effects still in her car—purse, wallet, ID, and stuff. The guy ditches her car off Highway 81." She tapped her fingers, lost in thought.

Lefty tossed in, "Yep. Now he's on foot, because she met him at a public place, and they took her car, which is what we assume happened."

She nodded. "He needs his car, so how does he get there? On foot, call a cab? He's gonna wanna steer clear of being seen even though it's dark. Highway 81 isn't a main road, but I'm sure a few cars and trucks travel that stretch of road, and shit, other drivers would've seen a man walking alone at night."

Lefty crumpled up his napkin. "So, where'd our unsub leave his car? The guy wasn't flying around like Superman."

"What if he's already scoped it out? He's got her address from her letters. The guy knows where she lives. It's conceivable he's stashed a vehicle for his ride back. "

Lefty nodded negatively. "You think our creep has two cars? Where's the car he was in when he met up with her, Harri?"

"Look, Left, I don't know. All I know is the guy ain't walking five or ten miles or even twenty to return to where he met her. Hell, someone would have seen him for sure."

There was a momentary lull in their discussion. "Could be he has an accomplice, or..." She didn't finish her thought.

Lefty propped his elbow up on the edge of the small table. "Or? I like or, let's hear your or."

"Or, what if the perp's using cars he considers throwaways?"

"Throwaways, like a burner cell? Harri, how do you get a throwaway car?"

"Cars break down and then get stickered and after forty-eight hours they're towed. They search for rightful owners and if no one's found, the cars are either sold at auction, or if a certain age, junked or crushed."

"Those cars aren't running, so how would he use them? Shit, that's why the owner abandoned it."

"Nope, I'm saying he leaves a car there on purpose to use later. He knows when he's planning to rape and kill his victims, and he'd know how long the cars would sit there afterward."

"Jesus, Harri, how much money would this ex-con need? He'd have to purchase an extra car, he'd—oh crud, what the hell am I saying? This freak's a con, so he could be stealing older cars." Lefty raised his arm, rubbing the nape of his neck. Had Harlowe possibly hit on something?

"Okay, then," Harlowe tells him, "We'll call the DPS, have them print out a list of stickered cars off the nearest exits leading in both directions into Itasca and off Highway 81. All towed or unclaimed vehicles during the time the Mackey woman went missing."

"Good idea. Plus, we should get a CSU team to go over her car again. I'm sure the perp wiped it down, but again, like Kasper said, another look-see can't hurt." Lefty took his phone out, looked up the number for the Hill County Sheriff's office, jotting it in his notebook. "I'll call the sheriff's office, see where they impounded her car, and send a tech over ASAP."

Harlowe squished her wrappers. "That chicken hit the spot. I was ready to keel over from hunger."

"Yeah, it'll hold me until dinner back in Dallas, cuz I don't wanna get a room at the Royal, got it?"

Harlowe punched his arm playfully. "Not what I had in mind. Don't want Frankie mad at me either. You know how gossip goes?"

"Yeah, I do, I really do. Some of it started back at Quantico. I admit, I agree with you. Men can be shits."

"Ned Stovall. What a pig, him, Jay Greenberg, Greg Spokane, and the asshole Mick Townsend." Harlowe's nose crinkled in disgust at the thought of the men.

Lefty's brows shot up. "What kinda gossip did you hear about these dudes? Nah, calling them pigs sounds better. Well?"

She scowled when she thought about those days. She should've forced the sexual harassment issue, but decided not to. The idea was these boys, as she saw them, might one day mature, and make decent agents. Not having followed any of their careers, she only hoped they'd at least matured into honorable men.

"Those men, anti-feminist pigs, think female agents will never get promoted, or do well, unless we work on our backs. We'll never amount to anything but being glorified secretaries. Girls are good for baby making, cooking, and housework. God, such backward misogynistic thinking. Makes me wanna puke. We lowly females would never get ahead of them. I even heard Greenberg say he'd keep his foot on any female agent who stood in his way, unless she was to lay her skinny ass down for him with her feet in the air. What a creep!" The coldness in her words could freeze a warm summer rain.

Lefty looked at her, his brownish eyes softened. "We're not the smarter sex. Since I've been with Frankie, I've apologized for those creeps and a million like them in the world, so I get it. Have you seen any of them again? Stovall, Greenberg, Spokane, or Townsend, in the last four years?"

"Nope, not a one, and I'm fine with that. I haven't heard about any of them since we left Virginia, either. Good riddance to them."

"Me neither, nor heard where they even ended up, don't care."

"Honestly, I don't give a rat's ass. With over thirty-five-thousand employees in the Bureau, not much chance we're gonna just run into some of those dicks we trained with. Can we just drop this subject?"

Bishop was thrilled not to discuss Quantico. Some things needed to be left unsaid. Bagging up her empty food containers, she slurped the last of her watery iced tea, taking out her notebook. "Our victim has a cousin living in Itasca. Let's go talk to him."

"Then onward to Mansfield, shake the trees regarding Trina Robinson. Got a lot of ground to cover, so let's pick up the pace." Lefty felt her unease about these dickheads from their pastime at Quantico. He was certain Bishop had a story, but he wouldn't push. Harlowe had been through enough with her cousin's death.

CHAPTER TWENTY-FOUR

Itasca, Texas

Lefty backtracked on I-35 to get to old US Highway 81, a two-lane paved road, a lonely highway where a few beat-up pickup trucks and cars traveled. One time long ago, US State Highway 81 was a main road, so adding Interstate 35 in 1956 had expanded the roadway. Afterward, travel on US 81 was limited and used primarily in the Hill County area. The road was a means to get from Grandview, Texas, to Hillsboro, Texas, and in between, also smaller towns, such as Mayfield, Osceola, Woodbury, and Loveless. A little-known fact about Loveless was this small Texas town's name was misspelled and was now called Lovelace with a whopping population of twelve people in 2000.

GPS guided them on HCR 4281 for about seventeen miles, past the Itasca cemetery. Lefty took the turn onto FM 66, a two-lane asphalt road where undeveloped land loomed ahead. Developers hadn't snatched up the land, and it was nice to see countryside left. The decedent's cousin lived on an unpaved road off Highway 66. The house was in the sticks. There was absolutely nothing but empty land sans a few head of cattle and a few plowed acres where some farmer planted rye grass for winter.

Rains from last week caused the black dirt to ball up turning into clay with a pungent smell, getting stuck in the tread of the Yukon's tires. Good old black Texas soil clinging to your tires like cement.

"Damn, are any of the roads out here paved, like real roads? Or have they considered graveling them? Man, once Kasper sees his Yukon he's gonna think we went mudding." Lefty maneuvered around potholes the best he could.

"If we've got time, we can run it through a car wash." Harlowe thumbed to her right toward a driveway and a trailer setting back off the road. "Up there. Gotta be his place, ain't nothing else around."

Lefty slowed, turning onto an equally muddy driveway with its own set of potholes.

The single-wide trailer had long ago seen better days. A few hundred feet off the narrow one-car driveway sat a faded black prehistoric Ford truck parked under an old tin roof overhang. An old light-blue Chevy Saville, running or not, was the question, parked beside the pickup. There were three or four push lawn mowers. Three looked like junkyard fodder. One looked like it might run; who knew? Three large oak trees grew behind the old rusted archaic trailer. No nice green lawn, just weeds, and oak leaves which needed raking. The small yard, closed in by a chain-link fence encompassed a larger tree with a tire swing, held up with an old chain draped over the largest and most stable limb. Fire-burning barrels sat further away from the trailer, three in a clump, all corroded with rust.

Lefty parked the mud-splattered Yukon, cutting the engine.

"You think he's home and alone?" He scrutinized the surrounding area.

Harlowe checked her gun, chambered a round, and re-holstered, lifting the door handle of the Yukon to exit. "Have no idea, but I'm not taking a chance and neither should you. You got my six, Lefty?"

Copying her actions Lefty chambered a round, re-holstered, and gave her a nod.

"You bet, oh, and about him, or whomever is home, I saw the curtain move and someone just looked out."

Bishop lifted the handle swinging the gate open, and he shut it after walking through. With caution, they stepped around old broken toys and trash, avoided the muddier areas, and got to the front steps. Three steps up before Harlowe could knock, the old metal door opened. Ernie Gorman greeted them. "Howdy, folks, I'm guessing you two are with some law agency, FBI? You're here to ask me some questions about my cousin, Annelle Mackey, right?"

"Yes sir, I'm Special Agent Bishop. He's Special Agent Sebastian."

The inside smelled dank, moldy, and like a wet dog. If one hired a maid, it wouldn't have worked, a blowtorch, yes. His furniture was torn, stained, old, and covered in dog hair as the aforementioned pooch ran around wagging its tail, sniffing both agents' feet.

"Get back, Tiger," the old guy commanded but Tiger didn't comply. Thankful it wasn't a yappy licky dog, Harlowe bent and petted the mutt, then shooed it away, but the dog refused to leave, and Lefty, with no affinity to animals, ignored the poor pooch altogether.

"Let me lock Tiger up in the back, he won't stop iffin I don't." He carried the mutt to another room. The little fuzz ball barked twice. "Hush up, Tiger." The old fella eyeballed the closed door. His dog magically fell silent.

Harlowe took note of the array of trash, junk, old boxes, canned goods, and whatnot piled on the kitchen counter and on his small table. There were boxes lined against the wall, sitting opposite the old torn and threadbare sofa and the timeworn recliner. The containers looked to be filled with clothing, shoes, and housewares. But who knew for sure? Was this old gent a hoarder? It was quite possible by the amount of junk.

"Tiger's got his bed and a few old bones. He'll stay busy," the old guy supplied. He shuffled through the small kitchen and into the junked-up living area. "Uh, here, ma'am, move the basket of clothes off the sofa. You can sit there, and uh, sir, if you'll grab one of those folding chairs behind the door, I gotta sit and don't wanna be rude."

Lefty grabbed the folding chair, while Harlowe moved the basket and sat. The man looked up after getting settled.

"Mr. Gorman, I'm curious. Why did you immediately think we were FBI?" Harlowe pulled her notebook out of her inside jacket pocket.

Ernie Gorman inhaled, coughed like an old man for a second, and grunted. "By the way y'all dress and your ride. It ain't a police or sheriff's car, who have already been to see me weeks ago. No one else ever comes this way. Some of my kin come around, three, four times a year, making sure I'm still a kicking. Nell—uh, that's what I called Annelle—she, uh, lived the closest to me and we saw each other regularly as we could. Boy, I miss that gal."

"I take it you and Annelle were close?" Harlowe jotted the nickname Nell.

His head bobbed. "Yeah, we were, and call me Ernie. Mister sounds awfully official." He looked around his cramped, untidy place. "You know, my place was already a mess, I must admit, but once the courts finally freed up Nell's place, I had to go get all her stuff before her a-hole landlord tossed it all. All these boxes..." He gestured to the opposite wall. "They're filled with her stuff, and her furniture's stacked up in the shed out back. Hoping to get rid of this crap in here and move her stuff in. Her couch and chair are a little nicer than mine, not so torn up."

"Your cousin lived alone? I thought she had a son?" Lefty leafed through the notes he'd jotted back at the office from her personal information.

"Uh-huh, she did, and her boy just turned eighteen. They'd fostered him out for a few months, after her, uh, death. Since his last birthday, he took to living with his girlfriend and her dad. It was quite a mess cuzin he didn't want to leave the area or his girl."

"His name's Henry Garcia, correct?"

"Yes, ma'am. Nell never married his dad, but gave him the man's last name. Henry's biological father was an illegal who ran off to who knows where. Shmuck never met his son, so I was the closest father figure Henry had. Shit, pardon my language, but now he's too busy for me."

"You tried. That counts for something. I take it Henry was born and raised here in the Itasca area?"

"Yes, ma'am. Kid was born at Hughley Hospital. His birthday was last month, the fifth. You can figure the year out since I tole ya he's eighteen."

Lefty peered into a box. "Mr. Gorman, was your cousin involved with a man? Had she been dating anyone?"

A lengthy exhale sounded from the older gentleman before he answered.

"There were a few men. Not a heap of good men, though. See, Detective, um, I mean Agent, uh—"

"Sebastian," Lefty supplied.

"Yeah, right, Agent Sebastian, sorry. Annelle was a beautiful girl on the inside, but during her pregnancy she let herself go, gained a lot of weight. The girl was huge, and after Henry was born, she tried but couldn't lose the extra pounds she'd put on. Plus, coming from a low-income household, well, ya don't eat too healthy. Man, look at me... shoot fire, I need' a lose thirty pounds, be healthier if I did, but I live on a fixed income, too. It is what it is. The gal put every extra penny she earned into her son. School clothes, sports, whatever he wanted Henry got, and she did without. My Nell stopped caring about herself."

"That's understandable, sir, it is. Had she been dating recently?" Harlowe got back to Lefty's unanswered question.

His eyes seemed sad when he came back with, "Mainly men who used her and then they were done. Scum from this Podunk town, or what I call drifters. Nell was vulnerable. She'd buy into a person if they said they really cared for her until it happened one time too many. Then she got smart and stopped seeing the few dickheads who were using her for free sex."

"I'm sorry. Men can be pigs, present company excluded. I've dealt with this type of behavior before, too." Harlowe frowned.

"I imagine it happens to women of every walk of life." Ernie Gorman nodded in agreement. "Only just before she went missing, I've gotta tell ya, my Nell was happier, had a spring in her step. No one might've noticed but me, but she'd lost a few pounds too."

"What changed?" This tidbit of information for Harlowe was monumental. She knew the signs. A new man had entered her life.

"She never told me anything except she'd been writing to a friend. Heck, she was all secretive, and I couldn't get much outta her." He stopped and thought a minute. "You know, Nell didn't always live here in Itasca. Years ago she lived up Oklahoma ways. I got the feeling she hooked up with an old buddy. She was from a small town called Overbrook; her and her folks lived out in the sticks. Town ain't got a population of six-hundred, don't think. She went to school in Marietta...when she went. The girl cut class a lot."

"Her parents still in Overbrook?"

"Nah, died in a car crash right after Nell turned seventeen, and her older brother brought her here to live with our cousin Lannie. Then he joined the army and got killed in a military exercise a year later. Freak accident they said. Nell was twenty when Lannie passed. She had no place to go. I was here—her only family—so she stayed."

"Ernie, were there any letters in her belongings?"

"Miss Bishop, um, uh, sorry, I mean, Agent Bishop. I didn't go through her things, haven't had the heart to." He eyeballed the boxes, looking back at her. "Iffin' you got room in your nice SUV, why dontcha take these boxes so's you can dig through 'em, cuz iffin her son wanted anything, he would've got it already. Will that work for ya?"

"Of course, Ernie, we've got forms you'll need to sign giving us legal permission to take these items."

It gave them something to get better acquainted with their victim, and Bishop thought it was a chance worth taking.

Lefty's heart sank, not enthused about sifting through any of these cardboard cartons, or dealing with roaches or any bugs.

"Agent Sebastian, please get a release form while I sort through a few boxes."

Harlowe sifted through boxes. Boxes with clothes, shoes, trinkets, or housewares she left, only taking boxes with papers—mail, notebooks, loose photos, photo albums, and several three-ring binders —ending up with a total of five long banker boxes they loaded into the rear of the Yukon.

"We'll return this stuff once the FBI is done."

"I'll be here, Agent Bishop, and thank you."

"Please accept our sincerest condolences, Ernie, for your loss."

Harlowe got into the car, shut her door, and then turned to wave at Ernie Gorman. Ernie's old withered hand lifted, and he waved back, then slowly ambled up the three steps back into his cramped trailer, shutting the door.

Lefty cranked the engine to life. "Let's drive past Mackey's house since it's on the way, just wanna see where she lived, then head to Mansfield, see if we locate anyone who knew Trina Robinson, before heading to Dallas."

"Sounds like a good idea. Ernie's a sweet old guy, but I need a shower to scrub his place off me." Harlowe did the yucky shimmy.

"Uh-huh, he was a nice old dude, only I don't do grubby well either. Feels like bugs are crawling up my back right now." Lefty shuddered as he turned back onto the dirt road, heading toward US Highway 81, to the small town of Itasca, known as the Big Little Town.

CHAPTER TWENTY-FIVE

An accident on I-35 had two right lanes blocked causing all traffic to merge into one lane. It took creeping for two miles before cars could move to spread out over three lanes, making the drive to Mansfield slow. Damn drivers. No one was polite, and Lefty cussed a blue streak while Harlowe empathized, telling him she'd driven the Vegas strip during concert night when the Elvis impersonators flooded Las Vegas, so she understood congested streets.

Lefty took the loop off I-35 on to FM 1187. He headed east toward the mobile home park off the FM road where Trina Robinson once lived. The place was a cash cow. You might own the trailer one day but the land you perched it on would never be yours, and rent would be ongoing until you bought your own land, flushing good money down the toilet.

Trina Robinson had rented a single-wide trailer someone abandoned, confiscated by the park owner who'd made the bank holding the lien an offer. They didn't want it back, along with the cost of moving and reselling, so the park owner bought it for a song and a dance.

Harlowe pointed it out. "Not much nicer than Ernie Gorman's place, but at least she had a home, when she was alive, that is."

"There's a truck and an old car next door, hope her neighbor's home." Lefty looked around. "It looks like she only had this one neighbor since the other lots are empty."

His knuckles rapped on the frame of the door. The porch was small, so he stood on the top step with Harlowe positioned on the bottom step.

An elder woman peered out the small opening, the security chain still hooked.

"Yeah, whatcha want?" her voice cracked then she coughed.

Left held up his badge. "FBI, ma'am, we'd like to ask some questions about your neighbor, Trina Robinson."

The old woman, less fearful, closed her door, removed the chain, and reopened it.

"Not a lot I can tell ya that I didn't tell the sheriff's office but you're welcome to come and sit a spell."

"We promise not to stay long."

She pointed after letting them pass the threshold. "I enjoy sitting at the kitchen table, much nicer and cozier, and I got my smokes over there but won't smoke if it'll bother ya. I have a fresh pot of coffee made, iffin you want a cup."

A smile crossed Harlowe's face. She liked this old woman. Her home smelled like a smoker, but she wasn't a slob. Her house was tidy, thank goodness.

"Yes, please. A fresh cup of coffee would be nice, black." Harlowe took a chair, as did Lefty.

"How about you, young man, cup of coffee?"

"Yes, thank you, Mrs..."

"Nah, not Mrs. anymore. I haven't been Mrs. anyone in thirty years, widowed so long ago don't feel like I was ever married. Call me Rose—Rosemary—but always went by Rose."

"Alright, Rose, tell us about Trina Robinson." Lefty took the cup she handed him, waving off cream or sugar, having it black, just like his partner.

"Nice girl, kept to herself, was quiet. I mean, she didn't have any wild parties or lots of visitors. She was looking for a job. I knew she was having a hard time financially. So I'd cooked a pot of chili or stew, always took her over some with my homemade cornbread. Made her so happy, and she'd thank me and thank me. That's when I knew times were tough for the poor thing."

"Did she say anything about a fellow or a pen pal she was writing?" Harlowe sipped at her coffee.

"Nah, I...wait, yes, she did. Something about an old friend she was gonna meet up with. She never said who, just said she was getting reacquainted. I never asked questions, cuzin' it weren't none of my business, I don't pry." Rose's eyes saddened and her face fell. "Wish I'd been a busybody, asking her a bunch of questions, then she might still be alive."

Harlowe reached over patting the older woman's hand. "No way could you have known, Rose. It's not your fault. Just tell us what you know because it might help us catch her killer and bring him to justice."

Rose took a tissue out of her sweater pocket to dab her eyes, blew her nose, and then stuffed the tissue back into her pocket. "I'll try." She closed her eyes for a brief second, then reopened them. "Uh, right after she told me she'd reconnected with an old friend she mentioned she was going to a job interview. She was struggling to make ends meet on unemployment and food stamps, making monthly payments on a beat-up old car constantly needing to be repaired. Add in rent, utilities, insurance, who knows what else, before she even bought food. So you know money was short."

Lefty asked, "Did she work odd jobs? Get paid under the table or—"

Rose cut him off, her eyes snapped. "She wasn't into drugs or doing anything illegal. Trina was a respectable, sweet girl, and I find it insulting you'd think—"

Harlowe jumped in. "Rose, I am sure she was very nice. What my partner meant was did she have little part-time jobs, you know, clean houses, babysitting, anything like that?"

"Oh, sorry...I just...never mind, then. It's just..." The old woman frowned. "Trina was overweight. It was hard for her. Sweet child was trying to lose weight. But it's hard to do when you're poor. You don't get to eat the healthiest of foods. Her son would show up for a handout and she gave him what she could."

Harlowe jotted, looking back up. "Where'd her son live? Did he have a job?"

A snort shot out of Rose's nose. "A job, oh, hell, no. Uh, pardon my language. He was living with a girl on the other side of Mansfield, coming here every week to panhandle off his mom. Then the girl dumped him. Afterward he moved off. Someplace up in East Texas. Trina said he got a job on a road crew."

"Did Ms. Robinson...uh, Trina, have any family here, I mean, other than her son?"

"No, sir, no other family, at least none she talked about. Her and her boy moved here after Hurricane Katrina tore Louisiana apart. She told me her ex-husband passed away from a pulmonary embolism." The elderly woman prattled on. "Her parents were in a freak car accident when she was about twenty-five. Let's see...Katrina was in 2005, Tobias must've been around eleven. He's twenty-four now. Trina got pregnant a month before her sixteenth birthday, and right after her family moved them to Louisiana. I'm not sure from where, though; she never said, I never asked. It seemed to pain her to talk about when she got pregnant. I met her when she moved into the park in 2012, two years before they reported her missing."

"She ever talk about a boyfriend, best friend, anything?"

Rose looked at Lefty. "No, like I told ya, I wasn't a busybody. Never gave the woman the third degree. Something was bothering her a few days before she disappeared, though."

"Did she tell you what it was?" Harlowe asked.

"One day I found her crying out there on her steps. She'd gotten a letter and it upset her. Told me an old friend had written, and she was homesick, but like I told ya, I wasn't the prying type and if she needed to talk, I was here. Sorry I can't give you more."

Harlowe stood, Lefty followed. "We know a little more about our...er, uh, Ms. Robinson, after talking to you, Rose. It helps us to know her better." Harlowe didn't want to call Trina a victim, it was dehumanizing.

"You got a card? Just in case I hear something, or remember anything?" Rose stuck her hand out.

Harlowe handed her a card, in case the old gal might want to call a woman and not a man. They thanked her and left Breezy Creek Mobile Home Park.

Back on the interstate Lefty prayed for smooth traffic and a quick return to Dallas. They were quiet for a few miles, each thinking, Lefty concentrating on the cars ahead, anticipating the worst, gritting his teeth every time the driver ahead of him tapped his brakes.

"We got squat, not one solid lead. Shit." Lefty blinkered to move over with the faster-flowing traffic.

"Oh, I dunno, Left, we did some theory building and the car stuff is worth looking into. We've got boxes of junk belonging to Mackey. Who knows what we might find?"

"Sure, but I need a shower. Add in hot food. Then chill a bit after driving all day. Let's pick up again in the morning. Come by early, pick me up about seven, I'll spring for muffins and coffee."

Sounded like a splendid plan to her.

CHAPTER TWENTY-SIX

Same Day, Driving to Huntsville

Frankie buckled up, and they were quiet, Kasper maneuvering through Dallas traffic past the business district to get to the IH-45 exchange. Past the crunch of commuter traffic, the drive was smoother without brake lights flickering every three seconds like Christmas lights with a bad bulb.

Francine straightened in her seat and got comfortable. "You know, it'll be a first for me."

"What'll be a first for you?" Kasper looked right, moving from behind a cement truck.

"Interviewing a prisoner who's in lockup for life. Made me wonder why you didn't ask Lefty instead of me. I mean, a female in an all-male environment. Men locked up for decades who've not seen the light of freedom. And most never will again. You think I was the wisest choice?"

"You didn't say you didn't want to. What's up?" His eyes darted to see her profile, trying to read her. Francine Ryder, hands in her lap, leaned back, her eyes closed, didn't act worried or panicky. Kasper moved into the left lane into faster-moving traffic.

"Okay, ya got me, yeah, I wanted to come. That's not to say you made the wisest choice, picking me."

"Fine, I'll explain my reason for wanting you, but you gotta have an open mind and not take offense." He watched the road ahead.

"Nah, I'll tell *you* why you wanted me, then you can tell me if I'm right."

"Alright, Ryder, tell me why I selected you then."

Francine Ryder inhaled deeply, letting it out slowly. "At Quantico, I was the nerd outcast, on the outside looking in; it was the same for me growing up, but I'm sure you've read my personnel jacket. I can relate to Munn because he was an outcast, too. I understand how it was growing up. In the past few years, I've become...well, my real self. I've always known who I was. In the past, I was too introverted to show others who I really was. Quantico changed me." She lifted one eyelid to glance at him.

"So far, you're spot on. What else?"

"Working on this task force is a great opportunity for me. It'll give me an idea of this aspect of the Bureau. An opportunity to learn about profiling, and task force work of this nature. Oh, yeah, I still want an overseas gig working cyber. I love the technical aspect of FBI work, won't give that up. I get on well with women. The men, though, another issue because they treated me pretty shitty, teasing and making fun of me. Truthfully, though, my relationship with Corneal has helped me understand men. The good ones, I mean." Her head swiveled, and she opened her eyes to see his reaction, watching his lips tug upward into a grin.

"Yep, bout sums it up. You can use that kinship when talking to Munn, but you're as different as night and day. Frankie, you're a good, moral, decent human being. Munn's a depraved sick man with no viable conscience. I admire how much you've grown since Quantico. You're attractive, well groomed, and I think you're one sharp cookie with inner FBI capabilities you've yet to tap."

"My goodness, Kasper, you do carry on." She gave him the girly wave. "I appreciate being taken seriously. Thank you, it means a lot."

"With that being said, uh, you need to minimize your femininity, uh, I—"

Special Agent Francine Ryder's body shook with the laughter she held in, muffled noises coming from her closed lips. "No worries, Bergman. I've got a nondescript baggy pantsuit, I can slick my hair back, wear no makeup, have some ugly framed glasses, the entire enchilada. Shucks, I can change right back to Freaky Frankie for this special occasion!"

Kasper gestured with his head. "Our hotel is a few miles from the pen and although check-in isn't until three, we're FBI and I'm gonna use it to our advantage. We'll stop so you can transform, but, hey, uh, don't revert too far. I need you to communicate with this guy, not scare him."

Her fist shot out punching him in the arm.

"Ow!"

"You shit."

He laughed, then so did she.

Checked-in early, the front staff was ever so accommodating to a "big shot FBI agent," as they called him with a grin. Frankie went to her room and transformed, then met him in the lobby.

Kasper eyeballed her. Matronly, stern, and no-nonsense, the woman hadn't been joking at how she could transform her looks.

"Impressive. You look like you'd fit right in a women's prison."

"Uh, well, thanks, I think. Hey, while I was transforming I had an idea. We should keep it formal with Munn. You call me Ryder, I call you Bergman, taking the equation of my girl name out of play. Also, don't wanna be called Frankie either cuz I don't want Munn to see me as masculine or too feminine. Make sense?"

"Yeah, actually, it does. Good call, Ryder. You ready to roll?"

"Yup, as I'll ever be. Uh, a little scared, too. "

Huntsville Penitentiary, Huntsville, Texas

In the administration office, they sat, waiting for the deputy warden to fetch the warden.

The warden was a hulking man at six-foot-five, 252 pounds of muscle, not fat. Aaron Swisher just celebrated his fifty-second birthday and nobody'd dare call him an old man. He kept in tip-top shape, his job demanded it. His sheer size was intimidating; he could scare even the biggest con in the joint with one menacing look.

They stood as he walked over, his hand outstretched. "Special Agents Bergman, Ryder, pleasure to meet you." His eyes lingered on Francine, sizing her up. "Good choice of hairstyle and the loose-fitting pantsuit. Perfect." The warden looked at her feet. "Motorcycle boots?"

She lifted the hem of her pant leg to reveal the zip-up army-style boots. "I wear these more often than you'd think. They're comfortable. And me wearing strappy heels in your prison, no way."

"Yeah, only in TV shows do women run in six-inch heels, what a damn joke. Let's go to my office. A quick talk before we get you guys set up and we can go over protocol." He took his place at the desk, motioning for them to take a seat in the guest chairs.

"Warden Swisher, thank you for your hospitality," said Kasper.

"Sure, whatever I can do to assist the FBI." Then Swisher went over prison protocol. Standard stuff, they knew, but he was at liberty to explain.

"Now, how about we discuss why you're here to interview Munn? I'm in the dark and shit, it's my prison and no one's telling me anything."

"Warden Swish—"

"Aaron, call me Aaron."

Kasper took the lead. "Aaron, we're working a serial. I'd uploaded some facts of the cases into ViCAP and got a hit on Munn, his MO, and saw some things which interested me."

The warden bobbed his head, thinking he understood. "So, you have some dead streetwalkers? The shrinks never got him talking. I've got a dozen dead out-and-out killers who'd love to chat. Does it gotta be Munn?" His eyes went from one agent to the other.

Kasper pursed his lips, his eyes on the warden bobbing his head, subtly understanding the warden's desire to know why Munn. They knew the asswipe wasn't the brightest color of crayon in the box, more of an off-white with no personality by most standards. Munn was invisible, the type of person one looked at without seeing. Interviewing a crazy such as Ed Kemper made more sense. A seven-foot soft-spoken giant, scary figure, yet he was a genial man with an IQ of 145—a highly intelligent deranged, violent murderer. Scumbags like Munn with an IQ of a fourteen-year-old boy were a dime a dozen, like Charles Starkweather, with a below average IQ of 68, or Derrick Todd Lee, the Baton Rouge serial who had a purported IQ of 65.

"There's a specific reason we want Munn."

"And why, may I—"

Kasper didn't let him finish. "Aaron, this doesn't leave this room, understood?"

Swisher frowned, put off by Kasper's warning. Hell, he wasn't a gossip.

"Let's get this straight, I know how all this works. Munn could refuse to see you. That being said, discretion is part of my job and I take offense you'd think I'd go off and blab your secrets to any Peter, Dick, or crotch-puller in my prison."

"My apologies, Warden, didn't mean to offend you. This is my first time leading a task force and I want to make sure I do it right. Hope you understand I meant no disrespect."

Aaron Swisher's head bobbed as he extended his hand. "We're good. Sorry I barked, you have a tough job catching these creeps."

"Yeah, and you gotta deal with 'em and take care of their sorry asses, don't envy you. Let me fill you in on what we have."

"A letter from my prison brought you here? Why not talk to the prisoner who wrote it?"

"He's dead," Kasper explained. "Shanked in the yard over a cigarettes dispute of sorts. This letter got mailed days after they killed him, but even though his name was on the letter, he didn't write it."

"Quite a few inmates get shanked in this prison, even though we try to keep it from happening." The warden flustered a little. "I hope you don't think I'm running this penitentiary poorly, I mean, the guards do what they can, I assure you."

"Hey, it happens. Not much you can do to stop it if it's gonna happen, not an effing thing you can do," Frankie assured him. "It's one dirtbag down with thousands to go." She winked, and he gave her a knowing facial shrug with a nod.

"Can you tell me who the inmate is?"

Bergman pulled out his notes and gave the warden the inmate's ID number but divulged nothing about their current victims or the missing woman from Azle, or the letters found by the missing Thackerville, Oklahoma, woman's sister. With his thoughts about someone on the inside—Swisher was a good guy, his gut told him—but he was taking no chances.

"You wanna talk Munn, huh? What's the deal with that POS?"

"Munn gave up one last victim to bypass the death penalty, guess you know his case."

Swisher nodded and waited for him to go on.

"I've given it some thought, and this is only a preliminary working theory." He glanced at Ryder. "And, I haven't told the team my theory yet."

Frankie's brows lift. "Okay, Bergman, spill it, because both the warden and I are all ears." As she crossed her arms, she gave him the sideways cocked head look.

"Sorry, Frankie, I won't keep my thoughts to myself again."

"Sure, fine." She waved him off. "Now, what's this theory of yours, we'd love to hear it?"

"An odd idea occurred to me. We know these letters..."

"Letters, you mean there's more than one?" Aaron frowned.

"Uh-huh, but they're not all from Huntsville. That's another issue. Anyway," Kasper said, not going into further details about the letters, "the cons whose inmate numbers were on the return addresses didn't pen them. So, I wondered if someone was intercepting the mail to find his targets."

A look crossed Frankie's face. "You mean our killer's in lockup, or he *was* and now he's out?"

"Not sure."

"What do you mean, not sure? That's ludicrous, and he must be out to kill. Shit." Now Frankie's miffed, she thought this was stupid.

Warden Swisher frowned. "Lots of guys come and go. Could be your killer's in for something unrelated and is a short-timer; we got lots using the revolving door."

"Not sure. But it's what my instincts are telling me, for the time being."

Swisher tossed in his two cents, "People write to prisoners all the time. You should see the mail room."

"Aaron, we're certain these letters play into this. It's just a matter of fitting it together," Francine clarified. She was not sure about Kasper's theory, but sure the letters meant something.

"I know, Warden, and you're right, there's no absolute proof, just a few letters, a clear shot in the dark." Swisher moved to speak but Kasper raised his hand to silence him, then he added, "Other than the killer's method of murdering each victim."

"Strangulation, possible rape. Our only other link is the letters."

Swisher moved his head slightly in a negative gesture. "I've been the warden for fifteen years, and Munn's been a guest of our fair state for coming on nineteen years. Transferred from the ADX facility in Colorado."

"Yeah, and the guy might be dead if they'd left him here. We read about the other prisoners who beat the absolute shit outta him, but I don't feel sorry for the bastard." Kasper's face twisted up in a sneer.

"Uh-huh, guess him getting locked up here works out for you guys—fewer roads to travel—but it wouldn't hurt my feelings to transfer him out in a pine box, if ya catch my drift. Guys like him make me wanna spew."

"We hear ya, Aaron, and believe me, as a female, I wholeheartedly agree, but as an agent, well, you know?" Frankie was unapologetic.

"Look," Swisher said, "Munn's files say his first five years at ADX he wouldn't speak three words to any shrink, so they stopped coming. He refuses to speak to anyone here as well. This guy acts like he's a monk who swore a vow of silence."

"Do you think he'll refuse to speak with us?" Francine's spirits took a dive.

"No, cuz the douchebag had no female shrinks, as you'd expect. You being a gal might set him off to talking."

"Does he converse with anyone outside of the facility...his attorney?" Kasper asked.

Swisher reclined in his leather executive chair and scratched his nose. "He's your basic loner, has two celly pals next to his cell. After all the beating at ADX, the guy mostly acts like a monk. Only one time I recall when he spoke with outsiders, and it surprised me."

"Is the guy still filing appeal, or taking legal action against the ADX? Was it his attorney?"

"Neither. It was some odd training session involving different law enforcement agencies."

It startled Kasper as he'd never heard of anything like this before. "Oh? Can you give me some details? How long ago was this?"

Warden Swisher scratched the stubble on his jaw, thinking. "Oh, in 2011, I guess late summer, had the company of police officers from other cities, shrinks-in-training, that kinda stuff."

"Shrinks-in-training, really?" Kasper's forehead creased in question. "Like doctors?"

"No, they're called student agents, and we still have them periodically."

"You're telling us, as in trainees from the FBI out of Quantico?"

"Yep, surprised you ain't heard about it, being FBI and crap. But not just them either. We had police detectives and the like from all over Texas."

"Well, guess they don't tell us peons everything." Kasper looked at Frankie, his eyebrows puckered up, and wordlessly she shrugged.

"They interviewed just any inmate?"

"Nah, handpicked five of 'em, and they selected Munn."

"Who were the others?"

"One's in the prison hospital dying; he's eighty. Con's old and beat up. Guy's got Alzheimer's. Dude's been here for forty on a felony murder during a bank heist. Two cons died, killed here—you know prison violence—we know who did it and they're both on death row. They released the fourth con in 2012. Guy was right back eighteen months later, and he got shanked six months in. Then there's Munn, number five, who's still gracing us with his sickening presence."

"You have any information about these sessions? Dates, times, logs, anything?"

"Nah, can't even tell you who to call. It was all randomly done spur-of-the-moment shit. Treated it like it was top secret and we got no details, don't mean Munn can't tell you about it, but only if he wants to. But he doesn't talk to a guard unless it's absolutely necessary." Warden Swisher looked at the time. "If you'll wait here, one of my staff lieutenants can take you to meet the introverted but murderous Mr. Preston Munn." With those words, Swisher left them in his office, closing the door neatly behind him.

Her eyes stared at the closed door, and Frankie asked, "What'd you make of that?"

"Don't have the foggiest idea what he's talking about."

"Never heard of it. Did we miss something at Quantico?"

"Don't think. This is news to me, too. Even if it was FBI, you know we weren't in Quantico in 2011."

Francine Ryder's brows dipped in a pissy way. "Well, if it was a failed training exercise I'm sure the Bureau would never admit to it. Maybe they were testing a new teaching method?"

"Shit, who the fuck knows? If we get the scoop from Munn, then we'll know something. If not we can ask around, uh, quietly, cuz sounds like we weren't supposed to know anything about it." Kasper's brain hunted for a name. The only name popping up was Dan Robbs, a man he trusted.

A huff blew out her nose. "Being FBI doesn't mean we're privy to everything, but I think we should know about this crap, you know?"

"Frankie, you and I can dig and search where others can't and obliterate our footprints." He saw the imaginary lightbulb blink above her and her face lit up.

"Ooh, I love that aspect of the job, almost wish I was CIA. That spy shit's so much fun."

Warden Swisher walked back in. "Sorry, I'll have to escort you guys. I forgot my staff's meeting with their general supervisors. You ready?"

Out of his chair, Kasper said, "Lead the way." He walked out first letting Frankie follow, thinking it best if he took point in a penitentiary full of men. Swisher grabbed keys from his top drawer, the Taser from a coatrack behind him, then looped his Billy club to his belt. He walked out last, shut, and locked the door behind him.

Seated behind a heavy metal door in a windowless room, they waited. Guards led Preston Munn in wearing shackles, waist chains, handcuffs, and ankle chains. His jumpsuit a dank white, stenciled above the upper right pocket was inmate number 10121-013, his main identifier for the BOP.

Guiding him to the opposite side of the table, the guard pushed Munn toward the chair against the wall. The other guard stayed Taser ready. Guard number one uncuffed Munn's hands from the waist chain, then re-cuffed them to the metal loops on top of the table. Squatting, he repeated the process with Munn's feet, reattaching them to loops on the floor. Munn wasn't bound to run anywhere, and as Kasper watched, he thought about Ted Bundy's two escapes. This infuriated him. Bundy made law enforcement officers look like Keystone cops.

Upright, the guard who'd done the uncuffing looked at Munn, giving him a hard but not hateful stare. "Munn, it'd be real nice if you tried to help these folks."

Prisoner number 10121-013 stared ahead, his eyes focused on a spot on the wall, nonresponsive.

The first guard peered at the agents, his facial expression denoting an apology of sorts. "Good luck with this. It's like having a comatose man staring through you. Ma'am, sir, we'll be right outside. Knock when you're ready to leave."

"Thank you, Officer Perez, and you too, Officer James."

"Hope you ain't wasted your time," Officer James uttered backing away from the prisoner. One never turned his back on a prisoner, chained up or not.

They sat, two FBI Special Agents and one heinous killer, eyeing each other.

CHAPTER TWENTY-SEVEN

Ryder placed the small recorder onto the table. There was complete silence. Their plan was for her to get him talking and Kasper would jump in when necessary.

Munn's eyes stared straight ahead, looking beyond her scrutiny as she steadily took in his teenage acne scars, and his blackhead-filled nose before her eyes squared up with his.

Preston Munn, born May 18, 1955, incarcerated at age thirty-six; in lockup almost twenty-five years. At sixty-one, he looked more haggard than a man in his late seventies. Prison life aged you. Wild grayish-black nose hairs protruded from his nostrils, his teeth yellowed, his hair loss significant. Dark circles underneath his hooded eyes—eyes which were lifeless, soulless. No compassion behind his eyes, painting a clear picture of a total sociopath. What made this man tick, she wondered. The bigger question was, would he be of any help?

She switched on the recorder, breaking the all-consuming silence, and Kasper's eyes darted momentarily in her direction, then to the prisoner.

"Almost twenty-five years. We heard the first six were tougher up at Florence, that right?" Silence, as she expected. "Confinement wouldn't have worked for me, but seems it's worked out for you. Except for the beatings you got up in Colorado, you weren't invisible or untouchable anymore, huh? I'm guessing you got touched a lot. The guards acknowledge you but they think you're a bottom-feeder, don't they?"

No answer. Not even a head bob. His eyes glossed over, his body stiff, Munn remained trancelike.

"Huh, well, I get you, I do. Back when I was this gawky, unpolished teenage nerd, hell, I was invisible, too. No one saw me until they wanted to tease or taunt me. You know, the poor geeky ugly girl, the butt-load of jokes, signs taped to my back, tripped in the cafeteria, pushed in the hallway, books flying everywhere. That was just high school, and man, college felt worse. Obnoxious sorority girls and the frat boys...heck, I was another large red target for them. Unlike you, though, I'm a survivor, got stronger for it. You, though, you became a killer, made you feel tough, in control." A despicable laugh burst from her lips. "They broke your sorry ass, big tough man, and this little nerdy girl flourished into an FBI agent." She leaned back, eyeballed him, and asked, "Now, how the hell did that happen?"

Nothing. Munn silently inhaled and exhaled with slow intermittent blinking, sitting ramrod straight, his elbows propped up, his cuffed hands folded as if he were readying to pray. Frankie's eyes narrowed, but she didn't speak.

Kasper moved his chair away, the legs screeching on the cold cement floor, disrupting the silence. Munn's eyes shifted to Kasper, then to the blank wall behind the agents' heads.

"Guess he ain't so tough, Agent Bergman. I'm thinking he's a pussy since he can't get no pussy, means he *is* the pussy on his cell block."

Francie Ryder was laying it on thick. Kasper saw the man's left eye twitch. She was getting to him, so before he went apeshit on her, with a stern tone he said, "Munn, you can choose not to help us, it's up to you. If you won't cooperate, we'll leave."

Only his eyes moved from Kasper back to Ryder, who swore she saw something flicker behind those dark, soulless eyes. She adjusted her position, sitting more upright with her hands pressed onto the table, her gaze fixed on him, moving herself away, her chair rolling back from him. "Might as well leave, he's nothing but a comatose asshole."

Munn spoke, "How about you get me a hooker, then I'll cooperate? Or,"—he looked at Ryder—"how 'bout I do you? Slip off those baggy-ass slacks and I'll fuck you so hard your head will spin." He puckered his lips, sending her an air kiss, watching Bergman from his peripherals. Then, "You wanna watch? Maybe take a turn?" The prisoner rattled his handcuffs, thumping his feet in rapid succession under the table. His eyes bulged and a harsh laugh spewed out while the upper half of his body rose from the chair, leaning toward Ryder menacingly.

She'd already pushed away from him, so she stayed composed, unresponsive to his nastiness.

Kasper reacted instantaneously, shoving Munn back onto his chair. The man hit the seat with a hard thud.

"Sit your sorry ass back or I'll call a guard and have him Taser you and escort you back to your cell. Kasper loomed over him and Munn's top lip wrinkled in disgust.

"Huh. She your girl, Bergman, or you even have a girl?"

"Enough! Shut the fuck up, you prick. Bergman, back off," Ryder's tone rigid.

"Bossy bitch, ain't she?" Munn's face drew up in a gnarly expression.

Kasper kept his cool but stayed silent.

Ryder took over. "Good, you haven't forgotten how to talk. So, talk. Men like you, a fucking sociopath, love recreating your murders. It empowers you, so how about you tell us about yours? Why not show off a bit and allow us to acquaint ourselves with the real you?"

She left her chair at a distance from the table and him. Francie stretched legs out straight and calmly crossed one ankle over the other. She waited.

Munn had a smirk on his face as he stared at her, but didn't speak, so she prodded him.

"Enlighten me about Arizona. What was your first experience like?"

At first, Preston Munn remembered how appalled he'd been, killing another person, and he'd left the state in a panic. Then he told Ryder why he'd snapped. "She laughed."

Agent Ryder shifted, uncrossing her ankles, and asked, "A streetwalker laughed and you killed her?"

Munn's lips settled into a thin line, his face pulled. "The whore laughed, made fun of my Johnson, and shit, I was fucking a load of women, nobody complained."

"You were paying these gals good money, so why would any of 'em complain, cuz I'm betting you were a regular Don Juan, smooth as honey, am I right?"

Munn's gaze shifted to Kasper, a frown creased his face, creating an even uglier look. "This is how you ask for my help, by insulting me?"

Kasper's tone remained level. No matter how he despised this creep, he wanted him to stay calm. "You're not a lover, and boinking a prostitute doesn't make you one, so cut the crap."

Munn semi-slumps in his chair like a gangbanger. "How the devil do you think I can help you?" Hatred directed at Kasper flowed from his dark eyes. "I paid for whores and only killed the ones who laughed. Thing is this. If they hadn't laughed, I wouldn't be here. Look, I never wanted to kill anyone."

"Right, that's why you left a wake of twelve dead women in your travels and it's got me thinking your Johnson must be pretty small, because I'm betting you enjoyed killing, got off on it in fact."

"Why didn't I kill every whore I fucked, then?"

Kasper shrugged his shoulders. "Dunno. Maybe you were picky, or having a male period, but what I do know is you enjoyed killing or you would've stopped."

Munn stayed silent for a moment, then, "You're right, some of 'em I sure as shit enjoyed killing, right after I fucked 'em. Watching the light go out behind their eyes as they breathed their last breath... oh fuck, that much power over a human being, God, it made my Johnson tingle so hard it was a shitload better than the sex."

Bergman bit his nasty retort. Munn was talking, no sense in mucking it up.

"We've got a killer who follows the same pattern as you, allegedly raping them then strangling with their underwear."

"Hey, look here, Agent Smarty Pants, I didn't get a whore planning to kill her."

Kasper's eyes narrowed; he didn't believe him but wasn't gonna argue, so he continued about their suspect. "After he kills them he carts them off and buries them."

"Again, not my MO. I left the dead whores in the rooms, then skipped outta town." His lips wrinkled in a repulsive grimace.

Ryder got into the conversation. "Remember the hitchhiker you confessed to, to get the death penalty off the table? You raped her, strangled her, and buried her body then drove her belongings a few miles away and buried them, too. You forget her, Preston?"

"A fat girl in the wrong place, bad luck for her." Munn was indifferent to the whole thing, his eyes deadpan. Recalling this murder never excited him. Rape hadn't thrilled him, especially with a lard-ass chick.

Recalling this murder pushed him back to a place he didn't like. Her name appeared inside his head. Corrine. He'd treated her like everyone treated him, making fun of her, telling her she was a fat-ass no one wanted. After he'd killed her he'd found the letters. Upon reading them he'd learned there *had* been a man who wanted her, a stupid convict. Her pen pal lover was up for parole and this angered him. Somebody wanted her as an ugly fat-ass yet no one wanted him; no one ever had.

His stare turned colder. "Don't wanna discuss it."

Kasper felt it—killing Corrine was a low point for him. He found it odd because normally the thrill of reliving a kill promoted a euphoric feeling; however, not this time, not this girl, not for Preston Munn.

"Women who fit her profile are being targeted," Kasper shot back, not letting up to spare this slime's feelings.

"So, look here, I ain't killing anybody, why are you badgering me?"

"Do you get letters from anyone on the outside?"

"If I say yeah, what of it, does it make me a killer? Oh, hell's fire, I forgot, I am a killer, ain't I?" Munn attempted to be funny, but no one appreciated his attempt. He had no desire to talk about the girl named Corrine or the letters. They'd badgered him about this a year ago. Young punks asking questions—cops, suits, made no difference—he didn't wanna discuss it.

Francine fed up with this a-hole, said, "Stow it, Munn. You know why he's asking, so answer the question."

Kasper's knuckles rapped the tabletop. "I'm going to ask you again. Do you write to anyone?" He refrained from pigeonholing his question with just women, hell, sometimes men wrote to prisoners; Raymond/Rayna Anderson might have.

Munn's hand rose to scratch the bridge of his nose causing the cuffs on his wrist to jangle. "A few stupid letters, shit, even replied to a few. Y'all gonna toss me in the hole for telling some ugly, lonely, stupid slut some lies in a letter?" Yucking it up, his laugh sputtered out like a frog croak, too many years of smoking.

"You still have the letters?"

"Weren't none worth saving, no naked pictures."

"Communication from nice people and you trashed 'em. Why?"

"Ran out of toilet paper."

Kasper ignored Munn's flippant response, his stare rock hard.

"Anything else you wanna know?" Munn looked between the two agents, smirking.

Bergman replied, "Yeah, the names of persons you might have discussed your murders with and when."

Preston Munn silently contemplated the agent's request. He'd been here for nineteen years. His first six years at ADX Florence, Colorado before this. Confined up in local jails and holding cells. They'd imprisoned him in detention centers and secure holding facilities during his trial. Now here in his cell at Huntsville, his permanent home until he bit the dust or got shanked, whichever came first—and getting shanked was a good bet. Just because he hadn't spoken to any of the prison shrinks didn't mean he'd never spoken to anyone. Didn't they know about the sessions he'd been involved in? FBI: *F*ull of *B*ullshit *I*diots. That's what the initials stood for. Anyway, really, what did it matter what he said and to whom?

"What the fuck do I get if I help you?"

Kasper moved his seat away, propped his right foot on his opposite knee, crossed his arms, and responded with an apathetic gaze boring into the prisoner's eyes.

"Nothing, not a damn thing." He paused for a mere second. "Hell, that's a lie. I'll tell you what happens when you refuse to cooperate."

Munn's glance veered to Ryder, a person whom he felt understood him better and perhaps had more compassion. Nope. The scorch of her stare told him she saw him for what he was. She, like all the others, considered him a pure piece of shit.

Eyes glassed over, the con peered numbly at the wall behind their heads and he let out a lengthy sigh. "Fuck, what more can you do to me? Shit, I'm already trapped like a wild animal and sentenced to life without the possibility of parole. Gonna be here until I'm dead. I ain't got anybody who gives a rat's ass so ain't much more you can do to me."

"Your evaluation reports say you have two buddies, one on each side of your cell, perhaps you should live in solitary."

Munn cocked his head slightly, anger etched his face, but he stayed silent.

Kasper continued, "Your only conversation is with the guards and your shrink daily. Add in no yard time and we do this until you cooperate?"

Munn screwed up his eyes in hate. His two adjoining cellmates were the only family he'd ever had; they were his only friends. He hated the guards. They were assholes. He'd spent the first four years of his sentence in rooms with doctors. Psychotherapists pressing, questioning, and probing. Nah, he didn't want to do a repeat. Not to mention any earned privileges. Even lifers earned privileges. It was like getting Christmas presents. An extra hour outside in the sunshine was an earned privilege.

Seconds ticked by. Not a single word uttered.

"Munn, I'm waiting. We need—"

"Sure," Munn retorted, "but its chow time, and I don't wanna miss supper."

Kasper looked at the time, it was 4:50. "Fine, we'll come back. You break your word, it won't go well for you, got me?"

"Abso-fuckin'lutely, Agent Bergman, count on it. Now, bang on the door. I wanna get back for chow."

A quick rap-rap-rap and the correctional officer unlocked the heavy metal door. Taser in hand, he took a few steps in, and it was the second guard on his heels who spoke, "Ma'am, sir, there's a guard waiting to escort you back."

"See you later, Munn. I'm warning you, don't waste our time."

"Yeah, yeah, deal's a deal." Munn leaned toward Francine, wanting to rattle her chain. "I know how to fuck a gal, so's how about I give you a taste?" He jutted his face sticking his tongue out making a vulgar gesture, but Francie Ryder didn't flinch or blink.

The first guard hit him with his baton. "Sit the fuck back and shut up."

Ryder's hand snaked out shutting off the recorder, and she picked it up slipping it into her pocket. "No need for that, Sergeant." She looked at Munn. "You're nothing but an uneducated man with the IQ of a housefly, a mere maggot who morphed into a dangerous, infested human being contaminating our society with your sickening filth, and I lied. I don't get you, never will." Turning with an abrupt move, Francine exited giving Munn no time to reply. This detestable creep hurled disrespectful remarks at her which would cause most women to blush fire red, but Francine Ryder fired back calmly without hesitation putting him in his deserved place. Kasper's admiration for her grew.

CHAPTER TWENTY-EIGHT

Ryder slammed the car door, huffing. "That piece of dog shit better have something for us cuz I can't wait to return to Dallas."

"You don't like my company?"

"Nah, Bergman, you're decent company, it's just this place." She fixed her eyes on the gate. "From my perspective, profiling isn't my thing."

"Hmm, dunno, Ryder. I mean, you haven't let the bastard rattle you. You've done great."

"Tell my kneecaps so they'll stop trembling in pure terror."

"Hey, it's an experience you can build on no matter your job with the Bureau."

Her shoulders lifted and dropped. "Yeah, I guess, but I think I'd rather interview lady killers."

"How about I go after him? I don't mind, you know?" Kasper didn't want her to give up. He felt Frankie intimidated Munn, her being a female he had no control over, a woman who wasn't a weak prostitute or a young, frightened girl.

"Why don't you start and let me jump in? I'll play the merciless agent because I don't want him to like me."

"Sure." Deep down Kasper felt Frankie had a sleeping tiger waiting to be poked. What he wanted was her fierce tiger unleashed ripping Munn a new asshole.

Three hours later, the guard buzzed them in. Wands, pat downs, and ID checks, then led to the warden's office.

"Glad to have you back, Ryder, Bergman." Warden Swisher proffered his hand for another good-old-boy handshake.

"Hope it's the last. No offense, Warden." Francine Ryder shook his hand.

"None taken, Agent Ryder. Someone mentioned he was a bit of an asswipe, sorry."

"Yep, but it comes with the job. My dealings with asswipes and dickheads are a daily occurrence." Ryder paused briefly. Then, "That's just in DC. Here I am now in a prison dealing with convicts."

Her quick-witted comeback caught Warden Swisher off guard, and he snorted a laugh. Kasper's eyes widened, and he laughed, too. Francine Ryder might not think she could handle this stint interviewing a slime bag convicted rapist killer, but this woman was holding her own and doing it beautifully. When they arrested someone or had a person of interest to interview, Kasper wanted Francine to go for it. He was positive somewhere embedded in her was a vicious lioness waiting to pounce. There was no doubt about one thing. Corneal Sebastian had a lot to handle with Francine Ryder. A chuckle bubbled deep within Kasper's gut but didn't reach his lips.

Munn waited in the interview room chained and seated, his head stooped as he studied an imperfection in the tabletop.

Frankie pulled her chair out, placed the tape recorder on the table, then snapped her fingers to get his attention.

"Wake up!"

Munn's eyes moved upward to meet her gaze as he lifted his head. Frankie apathetic to him, asked, "Who gave you the mouse on your eye?"

"Slipped in my cell, hit the wall. No one came to your defense, in case you're thinking someone gave a shit. Sorry to disappoint you."

"Huh...well, too bad, might've had to give 'em a medal for doing a good deed." Ryder's eyes bore into his, her look unsympathetic.

Tapping the table and pointing to the recorder, Kasper cut his eyes over and she hit "record," not saying another word.

"So, Munn, start."

The prisoner's eyes stayed on Francine Ryder, his brows puckered, as his pockmarked face contorted into a sneer and he answered Bergman with a question of his own. "You read my files?"

"Yeah. So?"

"You read them too, honey? Did ya get a rush, did it turn you on?"

Francine stopped the recorder. "Cut out the sugary bullshit, you miserable waste of space, or I'll ensure you feel more than just the pain of a mouse's eye, hurting you in ways you can't even fathom. We ask questions, you answer them, so stop hedging or I swear you'll regret it."

"Are you intentionally irritating me, Ryder?"

"It's Special Agent Ryder, get it straight, and irritating you is something I'll never worry about. I won't stay another night wasting my time with a man as repulsive as you. Now answer my partner's questions, you repugnant vermin." Her voice was unfluctuating, yet he heard the threat her words didn't convey. Well, this was a first—fear of anyone, especially a girl. Ryder's appearance already cost him a mouse eye along with some bruised ribs from the new correctional officer. He should have kept his mouth shut. Shit, the new cowboys didn't like it when a con disrespected a woman.

"Fine, except you butt out, it's me and him." Preston Munn lifted his cuffs thumbing toward Kasper.

"Super, that works for me."

A small sense of satisfaction filled her. She'd pissed him off enough to have him ignore her. Now his focus would be on giving Kasper information to help them find the sociopath they were hunting.

Preston Munn looked at Kasper. "My records say I never spoke to the therapists or the shrinks, correct?"

"Yep, and?"

"Fuck the system for its record-keeping, huh? Some years back, they had a stupid training experiment. Part of it was interviewing inmates they figured had psycho issues."

"When was this?"

Munn's saggy shoulders twerked upward. "Christ, hell, what do I care about years?"

Frankie's open palm hit the metal table.

"You'd better care, you damn cretin."

The splat of her hand sounded. Munn, not paying attention to her, jumped when the sound echoed off the concrete walls.

His voice tight, "Jesus H. Christ, lady, you think there's a freaking calendar in my cell I'm counting off the days to when I'll be outta here?" His eyes protruded in anger, his composure rattled.

"Take it easy, Munn, give us as close as you can recall. Agent Ryder's not gonna butt in again, right?" Kasper gave her the fake stand-down look. In a planned act she narrowed her eyes, huffing.

Munn bent his head to his cuffed hands scratching his forehead. "Lemme think."

"Think fast, one more night we gotta stay here won't be good for you."

Munn groaned, shaking his head, loosening the cobwebs of being in prison for twenty-five years. Why did he need to remember anything? Every day was a reminder. Every day at Huntsville was the same.

"Munn?" Kasper's finger drummed the table.

With his eyes shut, he recounted, "Maybe it was six years ago, can't remember. Christ, locked up this long, it surprised me to see men who weren't prison shrinks or card-carrying psychoanalysts. All here to talk to us lowly cons. Shit, none of us were big criminal names, making major headlines, or have movies made about us, though they could about me I reckon."

"Stop the drama crap, and just tell me why they were here."

"To interview crazy people like me. Funny, huh, cuz not once did I ever talk with the shrinks and psychiatrists. Fuck, I didn't plan on breaking my streak of twenty-five years of steering clear of these types. Gonna until my last breath," he hooted and coughed yucking it up.

Ryder clapped her hands in a slow hard applause. "Good for you, Munn, way to hang in there and stay true to your repulsive self."

"Ryder." Kasper's voice was low; she shrugged with indifference.

Munn spouted, "You're an asshole, Special Agent Ryder."

A look of satisfaction perched itself on her face as she leaned back, delighted to be a splinter in his ass, aggravating him. Best part, Munn couldn't do anything about it and this gratified her.

"Who did you chat with?" Kasper resumed.

"Funny me telling you, ain't it? We got no names and no IDs. What I can say is, it was cops, or agents, or both."

"Why were they here?"

"How the fuck should I know? I'm a felon, ain't got no smarts—ya know, like Agent Ryder says, I've got the smarts of a fly. So, what do I know? Different men came and went. Some talked to us lowly felons, others interviewed guards. Honestly, I didn't give a rat's ass because it felt bogus. Shit, ain't anything on the up and up, not in our jail system. Don't you live in the real world?"

"What sort of questions? And Munn, don't bullshit me. I'm not in the mood."

"Got no reason to lie to ya, cuz what'd it get me iffin I did? These hard-asses asked the same questions a profiler might ask, I suppose.

Shoot, what'd I care what they asked me, I got out of lockup. Fuck, we even got coffee and donuts for participating, and once we even did what they called a group session. I called it the CA gang."

"CA?"

"Criminals Anonymous."

"How many were in these sessions?"

"Four plus me, sitting in a big room. Us all chained up, shit, buttoned up tight, doing a fun bullshit session."

Kasper's brows knitted. "You do these group sessions often?"

"Only a coupla times, cuz..."—Munn barked out a laugh—"us cons tried outdoing each other, nobody was telling the truth, so these guys decided a group session with liars, cheats, murderers, and rapists wasn't a good plan after all."

Munn found this humorous. Kasper didn't.

"You got the names of the others?"

"Hey, we don't all know each other. Just some other assholes." He stopped to think. "Only knew one dude, my ex-celly. He called it the prison's donut coffee program. What a laugh."

"What's his name?"

"Don't matter, he's dead; shit, his number came up last year. The poor bastard died of cancer. "

"Wow, how fortunate for him. They say they went to other prisons?" This time it was Ryder's voice. Munn abruptly shifted his attention to her.

"I'm not privy to know important stuff, I'm just a stupid con, and fuck all, I never asked." His eyes bore into her with an evil glower. Ryder smirked but stayed silent.

"This went on for how long?"

"Asking me about a timeline again, shit. Like I tole ya, they uncaged me three or four times in the span of, fuck, I dunno, a month. Like I tole ya, I wasn't marking a damn calendar. How can I make that clearer?"

"Alright, fine. What about these sessions?"

"They asked questions about the crimes we committed and chatted about what ifs."

"What do you mean, what ifs?"

Preston Munn's face lit up behind his dead, uncompassionate eyes. An almost dreamy look manifested when he spoke.

"Like what if we hadn't gotten caught? Would we be committing these same crimes? I said, hell, yeah. Maybe I'd have been a model citizen if my life hadn't been shitty growing up."

Kasper didn't care about Munn's shitty life. Lots of people had shitty lives but never resorted to murder.

"So, you cons would still be out there wreaking havoc on people's lives. It was a stupid question."

"I agree, and ain't it funny, *me* agreeing with *you*?"

"Yeah, it's damn hilarious." Kasper was growing perturbed. "Listen, you prick, you'd better give me something useful or we're gonna walk outta here and you get nothing but misery. Got me?"

Munn straightened. He knew by the agent's tone he meant business. "On a couple of occasions, we had faceless one-on-ones, and—"

"Wait. A faceless one-on-one, what the hell's this, for Christ's sake?" Francine's eyes narrowed, her brows came together in a pointed V.

Munn's face pinched. "You're aware I'm not speaking to you, right?"

Ryder glanced at Kasper to signal him she wanted in; he nodded, she continued.

"Let's call a truce. You behave, talk nice to me, and I'll cut you a little slack on my end, It'll go better for you if you act like a normal person. Deal?"

Munn mulled it over, his eyes boring into hers. It'd been twenty-five years since he'd been near a woman, agent or not, she was a female. Hell, even in the infirmary, all he'd gotten were male nurses, men, doctors—every single worker at this prison was a fella. The company of a female FBI agent wasn't ideal, however, it was better than no woman. This was how his brain processed it.

"Deal. But I'll only behave if you stop acting like a ballsy man." He held out his cuffed hand, and she eyed him suspiciously. In her peripheral vision she saw Kasper shake his head, but if she wanted to get anywhere with this shithead convict, she needed to put herself out there. Bringing her right hand up, she grabbed his cuffed hand, their hands squeezed, moving in short bursts before Ryder released his, and Munn played no games at trying to keep her hand in his sweaty palm.

She leaned back, not attempting to wipe her hand off showing him a small nth of respect. "Now, explain a faceless one-on-one."

"The CO takes you to a room with a phone and mirror. Fuck it, we know it's a two-way mirror. So, we sit staring at ourselves and they stare back from the other side. We know because just cuz we're cons, we ain't stupid, ya know."

"Sure, we get it. Tell me about the interview."

"We don't see the guy. We used the phone intercom system, and they asked questions."

"Enlighten us. What questions?" Ryder counted to ten in her head; this was like watching paint dry.

"How we picked our victims. Why we picked 'em. What we did. How we did it, and how we covered our tracks."

"You never planned on killing any of the prostitutes, cuz per you, all you wanted was sex, so how could you answer?"

As he brought his fingers up to his face to itch his blackhead-covered nose, his cuff's jangled, his brows creased in thought.

"Man, the sex was outstanding. I fu...uh, screwed them good, more than once. Hell, I never considered killing them until the one bitch laughed, which changed everything." He inhaled deeply. "The killing, I hafta admit, I liked it. That complete power was almost as good as sex." He watched Ryder's face and saw the tiniest flash of disgust in her stare. "Hey, if you don't wanna hear how I really feel about it, I ain't gonna tell ya being I'm in here for life with no chance of parole, so I got nuttin to lose by being honest."

"If you're worried I might be squeamish, don't."

Kasper shifted his gaze from her to him. "Ryder's right, so talk, and let me remind you, it's being recorded."

The convict shrugged. "Like I told ya, I got nuttin to lose."

"Then talk."

Without question, one thing was certain. They had no desire to visit this asshole again.

CHAPTER TWENTY-NINE

It had been a long day; the ride back to their hotel was quiet, each in their own thoughts.

There was a lot Frankie thought Preston Munn made up when telling his stories, making him sound more monstrous. She wanted to call him out on it, but decided it was best to let him rot in prison with his delusions of grandeur that no one did it better. A sick claim to fame—him, Bundy, Dahmer, Gacy, effing Jack the Ripper.

Kasper drove his thoughts on these unknown men. Who were they? Were there papers being written, lessons to learn, better insights for profilers? Which agencies? Was the FBI involved? Whose brainchild was this? Why did no one talk about it? And what else was Munn hiding? His gut said the convict had more information, but he held back—why and what was in it for him? The bastard was gonna die in a cell, nothing could change that fact. He blinkered taking the exit to the hotel, turned into the parking lot, and cut the engine. Time ticked by before Kasper spoke.

"I can't say for sure, Frankie, but something isn't clicking, you know?"

"Yeah, and I felt Munn was messing with my head. He's a sick person."

Kasper took the keys from the rental's ignition, and an intense look crossed his face.

"What if a con got inside someone's head? Trying to mess with him?"

Frankie unclasped her seat belt and looked at him. "Like mind control?" Sputters of laughter escaped her, but Kasper didn't share her humor.

"I mean, look, people can be susceptible to suggestions."

"You're serious?"

"Yeah, I got a what-if scenario playing in my head. What if a suit interviewing sicko convicts was prone to the dark side?"

"Oh, Lord, really? You think they pulled one of our guys into the vortex of the dark side, like *Star Wars*? Oh, come on, Kasper this is real life, stuff like that doesn't happen."

"You think it doesn't? Frankie, get your head out of your ass. I damn well worked with a DEA agent in Houston when I was working tech, and the man was a cartel hitman, so don't tell me this shit doesn't happen." After flicking his seat belt off he opened the door, got out, and slammed it shut. Walking toward the car, he stood, resting his backside on the trunk. Frankie got out a bit more collectedly. Positioning herself beside him, she said, "Sorry, Kasp, yeah, you're right, money, and glitz could sway a man, I suppose lots of cash can manipulate a decent man, and if money's not the motive, then it's something else entirely, something sick."

Kasper shoved his hands into his pocket, watching the toe of his shoe pat up then down as he thought. Frankie kept quiet knowing he was working something out in his head. She gave him time.

"No, you're right. Money isn't part of it. It isn't what drives our guy, it never was. As far as how this began, I'm only guessing, but for our psycho it was an internal struggle. Then something pushed him over the edge. Our guy thrives on power and not getting caught, and he is far from stupid. I think his personality's been screwed up for years. A man whose been hiding his evil side for a long time so no one suspects he's messed up. He's aggressive, a ticking time bomb, thinks he's in total control, but he's not, he's losing control and quickly. He has a false sense of security, believes he's untouchable, and this will be his undoing."

"Seems like you have this dude figured out, Bergman—in short time, I might add."

"Nah, I'm winging it, just spitballing. "

"What else?"

Kasper pulled his hands out of his pockets, leaning an elbow on the trunk lid of the car. "This man we're looking for, I think something happened which exacerbated his already messed-up personality."

"So, he was born a killer?"

"Uh-uh. I believe he would've been a good man, only something happened, and he felt he had to kill to solve his problem. I imagine he's in his forties, which has me thinking he might've been about eighteen the first time he killed."

"Wow, you've given this a lot of thought, haven't you?" Frankie turned to him and he only nodded. "You wanna tell me what Munn and this clandestine whatever-the-hell-it-was interview session might have to do with our case? You believe a cop or agent could be involved?"

"Not saying it's anyone involved in these secret interviews, but think about it. All kinds of people are lunatics. My thoughts are the man we're looking for has a bad person talking in his ear. Before you say any shit about *Jedi mind control,* just listen."

Frankie leaned against the car looking into the night sky. "Okay, I'll listen, however, I reserve the right to laugh or scoff afterward. Deal?"

"Yeah, sure, do what you hafta do, but here's what I'm saying. We think our guy killed in 2011, or he might've killed before. Now something's happened in his life which has spurred him to kill again.

Can't say why, but I think our killer has a mentor or a hero, or both, but someone is keeping him motivated."

She looked at him dubiously. "So, what you're telling me is the perp would stop killing but someone's been keeping him going? Like what? Someone in prison has him attached to a charging cable, keeping him revved up, really?"

"No, he's not gonna stop killing, because—now, listen, this sounds odd—but he feels killing is necessary for his survival, plus he's enjoying it. Add in the FBI's involved and the cat-and-mouse games are a turn on. Also, since the timelines between murders are getting shorter, he thinks he has it all in check and might feel invincible because he hides with the law in some fashion."

Her arms crossed, she faced him, her brows knitted, not entertained with how his theory was panning out. "You think it might be someone from the FBI, DEA, or even the CIA? Maybe a police department who could be doing this crazy shit? And please tell me, how does our prison pen pal theory fit? Jesus Christ, Bergman, this sounds like a thriller, made-for-TV movie you're writing." Frankie scoffed with more vigor than necessary, putting him a bit on guard.

"Man, Frankie, truth's stranger than fiction, and crud, serials look and seem like normal people, at least most did, and no one suspected them. Damn it!" His foot kicked out at the pebbles as he jerked away from the car, taking a few steps.

Her face softened. "Sorry, I'm just, well, you're right, the good guy could be a bad guy. Certain types of people are susceptible, but all agency personnel get deeply vetted. Police personnel go through vetting and have a psych evaluation to pass. Shit, we did before Quantico. It's hard to believe anyone, male or female, with a personality anomaly wouldn't show up. Plus, this training exercise Munn described was hogwash and lies. Hell, the man's a convicted killer and psychopath. Who's to say he wasn't feeding us as long line of horse manure and he's in his cell laughing his ass off?"

"You're right. Besides, it's a theory, not absolute truth." With a head gesture, he moved forward to the hotel lobby doors. He needed a shower to wash off the prison stench, and a few winks. He'd be ready to drive back to Dallas in the morning. Frankie followed him into the lobby to the elevators. She pushed "up." The doors parted, and he followed her in, pushing "three." At the third floor, the door opened. He let her out, stepping behind her in the hallway, and they stood beside the elevator doors.

"Our victims may not have been born and raised in Texas, but he murdered three of them in my home state, and one is still missing." He put a hand in his pocket and pulled out his door card key.

Her face screwed up in thought. "And four are from Oklahoma originally. Add in one trans woman, which boggles this girl's mind, and then there's the missing Choctaw woman, but we can't say for sure she's involved."

"I'm saying she is because of the letters her sister found. The transgender woman has me scratching my head, though."

Francine's gaze fell on the blue-striped yellow-speckled indoor-outdoor carpeted floor and she asked, "Yeah, why did he kill Anderson? I mean, the victim didn't physically start life as a woman. Not a normal victim. Something about his killing Anderson is off, I gotta say."

Kasper thought a minute before speaking. "Our unsub—Christ, I sound like an actor from the show, *Criminal Minds*, sorry—our suspect has anger issues, like I guess all serials do."

"You mean it pissed off our killer when he discovered Anderson's secret? That he was formerly a man? If he hadn't, you think Anderson would be alive? And hey, even though we don't gotta jet like they do, I liked the show."

Kasper yawned. "Yeppers, would've been nice if we could have jetted here instead of driving five hours, or used the FBI helicopter." They both chuckled, and he continued, "Anderson died cuz our killer can't leave a witness. So he had to kill her."

"Was this pure accident?"

Another yawn escaped Kasper. "Sorry. Yeah, I think Rayna Anderson might've misled our killer. This got him killed because our guy wasn't searching for transgender women, and this was a complete surprise."

"It'd be nice to know why Anderson wanted to meet an ex-convict. She couldn't keep her secret forever. Any man, ex-con or not, was gonna figure it out, right?" Frankie put her fingers to her temples. "I've got headache thinking about all this. "

"So, the guy plans to rape her, and he gets Rayna into a room. Then finds out she used to be a man. I mean, I've never seen it, but they have surgery to change the anatomy. I, uh, mean, he might have had—" Kasper's blush went deep-purple forgoing red altogether, and Frankie doubled over, holding in her amusement, yet laughing so hard she had to catch her breath before she could get the words out.

"Yes, they have a procedure to remove the male parts, inverting it to create a female part. I've never seen it, and don't plan on doing the research either. My best bet is it isn't the same as the real thing. The killer learned this the hard way. Uh, and no pun intended either."

"Jesus, Frankie, stop it." His blush deepened. "So, he finds out. Anyhow, he doesn't want Rayna crying rape to the cops. Plus, she's seen his face, now he has no choice but to kill her."

"It all sounds logical." Frankie shifted her feet, ready to end the conversation and get to her room.

Kasper pulled his key card out of the sleeve. "Our odd victim is Mera Soon-Lee. My gut says we need to learn more about this woman."

"Gut instincts. We heard the detective you worked with in Houston had superb gut instincts. Could be it rubbed off on you."

"Doubtful."

"Look, you just reeled off a theory, a superb theory, Bergman. I'd say your head and your gut instincts are in the game. Remember what instructor Dan Robbs said? He thought you had a profiler's instinct."

"Don't mean he was right."

"It doesn't matter, cuz I think you're onto something. Besides, Robbs has been an instructor at Quantico for years, with good instincts about his students." Frankie covered a deep yawn. "Let's get some shut-eye. I'll see ya bright and early. I'm ready to head back to Dallas." At the door, she turned waving good night.

Kasper turned walking the opposite direction, his mind on something instructor Dan Robbs said five years ago: "*Stay focused and on track. There are several decent people in our organization, Bergman. Some people don't follow the correct path. You're among the good ones. Keep this to yourself, but I'd advise you to exercise caution with your classmates. I won't say anything else. Just use your instincts, kid.*"

An hour later, his room phone rang, and he answered, thinking it was Frankie.

"What, Ryder?" he asked, lying on the queen-sized hotel bed, his arm covering his face.

"Uh, it's not Agent Ryder, Agent Bergman, it's Warden Swisher, Aaron."

Kasper bolted his eyes wide open, fully awake. His first thought was Munn got shanked because they'd been there.

"Warden, I wasn't expecting to hear from you tonight. Is everything okay?"

"Nobody's dead, if that's what you're asking, but I do have someone who wants to speak with you."

"Oh?"

"I'm gonna hand the phone over. It's Smitty, a mail room trustee."

"Okay, then."

"Agent Bergman, I'm Smitty, a lifer, but ain't gotta tell ya what I did."

"Sure, Smitty. What is it you need, then?"

"I work in the mail room, I see the dead letters that comes in, and then I see where they go."

"And? " Kasper stifled a yawn.

"I heard you knowed about the suits who used to come in to gab with the cons. I was one of them six guys."

"Six? I was told there were only five."

"Yes, sir, but no one knowed about me cuz iffin they did and it got out I talked to anybody from the outside, I'd be dead. You understand the way things are, don't you?"

"Smitty, what's your full name?"

"Nope, uh-uh, don't wanna be dead, just go by Smitty. Got me, Agent?"

Bergman got it. He suspected the guy was involved with the mob and keeping his identity hidden. The bigger question was why was he taking this chance right now?

"Alright, Smitty, what's on your mind?"

"A guy told me to write a few letters. Told me to write like I was writing my girl—make 'em sweet, with a little dirty talk, be sexy. Asked him whose name I'm writing to, and he says no names, put Baby Doll, or Sugar, or any other sweet nickname."

"Who was this man?"

"No name and didn't see a face either."

Kasper's steady stare watched his bare feet wiggle. "The other cons do this?"

"I'd guess so. But none of 'em knew I was in on this fucked-up shit."

"Why are you telling me this?

"Trying to get another brick in my house upstairs, I suppose. I was the guy who cleaned house for the boss, but never kilt a woman, ever. One time long ago I was a good man but ain't anymore, except I'm trying to be one again. Look, Agent, my time's up."

Smitty hung without a goodbye, leaving Kasper wondering. He'd mentioned to Frankie the killer might be in law enforcement, only she'd pooh-poohed his idea as nonsense. Bergman knew good men could fall from what's good and right, just like Smitty. Men suddenly turning to a side of themselves they never knew existed, never finding their path back to goodness.

CHAPTER THIRTY

Long banker boxes lined the back wall of the task room, unlabeled. Curious as to the contents, Kasper lifted a lid peering inside. Trinkets, cheap thin photo albums, loose papers, mail, and junk mail, magazines, and scattered photos. Just as his hand reached into the box, his brain went into FBI mode. Reaching over he grabbed a napkin off Lefty's desk then carefully lifted out an envelope holding it by the corner. A past-due notice addressed to Annelle Mackey, 1059 Weave Street, Lot 19, Itasca, Texas. He glimpsed the whiteboard: Annelle Mackey, their most recent victim.

The door hinge sounded, and he turned to see Lefty.

"Morning, bud. Got coffee brewing?" With a full-blown yawn, Lefty set his satchel by his chair heading straight to the coffeepots. No coffee, damn. He filled the empty pots with water from the cooler, grabbed a filter and the grounds, and began dumping.

"Nah, just got here, saw the boxes, and you know me, curious, wanting to see what presents you guys brought in. Where's Frankie? Didn't she ride with you?"

"No, she dropped me off, went to get breakfast. Also, hey, don't blame me. You can thank Harri for the boxes and the critters, if there are any." Lefty poured water into the Mr. Coffee then waited as the smell of fresh coffee filled the air.

A perplexed look crossed Kasper's face. "Critters?"

"After our visit with Mackey's cousin Ernie Gorman, God, his place was a nightmare. Here." He handed Kasper a cup of hot coffee.

Kasper sipped the hot liquid from his coffee-stained, light-blue, unofficial FBI mug. "Hmm, muddy-dark nectar of the Gods, even if it's not Columbian. No other way to make coffee—a pound of grounds to a full pot of water. So, how did..." His words cut off as the door opened and in walked Harlowe, followed by Frankie carrying a box from a local mom-and-pop donut shop.

"Donuts, apple fritters, and Kolaches. Who's hungry?" Frankie sat the box on her desk and they acted like hungry vultures.

Pastries eaten, coffees refilled, Lefty and Harlowe recounted their visit to the Royal Motel and their visit to Annelle Mackey's cousin, Ernie Gorman.

"Anything else?" he asked.

"Sorta, uh, we've been batting around an idea about how our killer got out of town after he dumped her body." Lefty filled them in on their abandoned car concept.

"What about the cars? Did you talk to the DPS? Is it possible to check on all tagged cars over the past few months?" Kasper waved off more coffee when Frankie gestured with an almost empty pot.

Harlowe flipped through her notebook. "We called, but got pretty much nada. There were ten cars tagged within a ten-mile radius. Four cars tagged and never claimed, got sent to auction. One met the criteria of being crushed after not locating the owner. The rest were claimed by rightful titleholders."

Frankie asked, "How can you not find the owner? The car has to be registered, doesn't it?"

"Ya'd think, wouldn't ya?" Harlowe responded. "But they sell cars, I mean older cars, without registrations. People buy cheap-ass cars because they need a sorta reliable ride to get from A to B."

"Harri's right. Most illegals want cars or work trucks and they buy them outright not worrying about taxes or registration. If they need it inspected, they find a shady mechanic who accepts cash only and one who can get inspection stickers. We know this still happens, no matter how the states try to regulate it. These cars are cheap, considering the cost of new ones, and no paper trail since everything is done with cash."

Kasper stared intensely at the wood grain of his desk, his head wrapping around this vehicle theory. "This hypothesis about using old cars and leaving them abandoned is a great idea, one which gives me the impression this person, whoever it is, is smarter than we're giving them credit for."

Lefty looked over his desk at Harlowe, then back to Kasper. "Or there's a pair of killers working together."

Well, this was something neither Kasper nor Frankie had considered.

Frankie's grave look said it all. Hunting for one man was hard. Hunting for two who were working together made this job tougher.

Kasper leaned in resting his elbows on his desk. "Set that aside for now. Let us tell you about our visit with Preston Munn."

Frosty words left Agent Ryder's lips, "What a freaking creep."

"I take it you didn't like the guy?" Harlowe gave her a side glance.

No words were needed once Harlowe saw the darkness fill Frankie's eyes.

"Well, shit! Somebody should've told us about this covert training operation." Lefty hated being treated like a redheaded secondhand agent. Always last to be told.

Harlowe let out a breathy sigh. "Who knows? It could've been a top-secret failure, and if it was, that's why we weren't told."

"Hell, we didn't get asked or included, Harri. Even if it didn't work, we're still in the dark; how's that any good? Shit." Lefty was an unhappy camper.

"We can't change what we didn't know about. Let's move on," Francine Ryder, the voice of reason.

"How about asking a senior agent? But asking someone up higher about a field experiment an effing convict told us about might be one stupid move. We ask them. They know we don't know. I don't know about you three, but I'd like to know. How can we check this out?" Lefty asked.

"Wait, was that a question? All I heard was one damn word."

"What word?" Lefty looked over at Harlowe.

"Really, you don't know, then hell, I don't know either."

"Know what?

A snort came out of Harlowe as Frankie wadded up a piece of paper, throwing it at Lefty's head. "K-n-o-w—the word *know*—you used it four times in one sentence. Now, can we get back on track?"

"Thanks, Frankie, great idea. Back to business. I've got some ideas I've been mulling over. Y'all are going to Tulsa. Harlowe, you and me will head to Austin."

Harlowe looked at him. "Why?"

Let's discuss Soon-Lee and Anderson. These victims have more to tell us. Soon-Lee had four prison pen pal letters, laminated, which tells me she wanted them preserved, plus, she hid them under the lining in her purse. The big question is, if the letters weren't for her, why'd she have them?"

Lefty crossed his arms. "Good question, Bergman. You got an answer?"

"Maybe she was researching somebody, or she was onto something. Only who gave her the letters?"

"You think she knew someone in prison who got them for her? Not talking about a prisoner, but a staff member?" asked Frankie

"Are you saying he killed her to keep her quiet?" Harlowe leaned forward, her heart racing; conspiracy theories excited her inner CIA agent.

Kasper tilted his head in thought, his stare fixed on the whiteboard. Photos of their victims hung next to their names with the dates reported missing, and where the bodies were found.

He eyeballed his fellow agents, one by one. "What I'm saying is, there's more here than meets the eye. More than correspondence from dead prisoners to murdered women, much more. My thoughts are the letters might be a red herring, one we're chasing because we're being led to do so. They're a piece of the puzzle, but it's more complex than just a bunch of sickly love letters written by deranged men."

"Are you saying someone on the outside's making us think the letters are the scheme for killings?" Harlowe fixated on the conspiracy idea.

"What's on your mind, Bergman?" Frankie's face creased with intense curiosity.

"The letters link our killer to our victims, but not directly. None of the prisoners who supposedly wrote the letters are alive or if they're paroled, they have solid alibis. So, I asked myself, why these convicts? Why'd their names pop up? You can't talk to a dead man, and if there's a solid alibi, then the guy's in the clear, so then what?"

Corneal Sebastian spoke, "So, you think our perpetrator has some type of connection with the jail system?"

Kasper's head bobbed a few times. "Yeah, maybe."

No one spoke, letting this idea sink in. It was as if a movie played out in their thoughts, each seeing a different psychological thriller.

CHAPTER THIRTY-ONE

"Man, Kasper, this is hard to believe. I mean, it sounds like a movie plot, doesn't it?" Lefty tried to wrap his head around this idea.

"Yup, it does. Think of it as a storyline created by the criminally distorted mind, you know, sorta like a screenwriter or an author would dream up. People with crazy ideas stuck in their head and they gotta get it out by writing it; but none of 'em is a criminal. They're individuals with wild imaginations who'd never carry out the despicable plots they've dreamed up for our entertainment. Now, the psychotic mind of a killer—a man with no problem carrying out his heinous story or desires—he dreams and fantasizes too, but not for our viewing pleasure. This guy we're hunting is hiding in plain sight, we just gotta pull back his mask."

"I agree, it sounds like a great made-for-TV series plotline. So, now we've created the makings of a good storyline for TV or the cinema, Kasper. And Rayna Anderson, what about her, then?"

Kasper raked his hand across his chin. New razors were in order; his shave not as close as he'd preferred. With the same hand, he ran it around to the back of his neck feeling his hair—he probably needed a haircut. With a slight shake, he cleared thoughts of his personal hygiene to answer her.

"Dig into his life before he became a woman. If memory serves me, he'd officially been a woman for seven years."

Frankie shoved some papers over flipping open a file. "Anderson lived as a woman early on." She thumbed through a few pages. "Yeah, here it is. The reports state in 2002, when he was twenty-four he began being Rayna Anderson full time, then in 2009, he became a bona fide *female*. Afterward, in the latter part of 2013, Rayna Anderson goes missing. Her body resurfaces four years later when a guy bulldozes a washed-out motel he owned.

"Anderson spent twenty-four years of his life living as a man, and if he was living as a woman, he concealed it successfully."

Lefty stood working the kinks out of his back. "You think him being a man in the beginning got him killed? Or because he changed into a woman?"

Kasper pondered his question briefly. What was his honest opinion? Was Raymond/ Rayna Anderson a random victim? Was he/she a target like the rest?

"I'm not sure, could be pointless. But knowing more about the victims helps us learn about our killer."

"I must admit, four dead women of different races, and one dead trans woman. Well, our killer ain't too picky, or he's more deranged than most."

"Yeah, I agree with Frankie because most serials don't have such a variety of victims." Harlowe looked from Frankie to Kasper, then, "Alright, about Mera Soon-Lee. We know she was collaborating with Cal Thompson, an investigative reporter, on a story about a campus rapist when she disappeared. What are we searching for?"

"Was Mera a casualty of a rapist, who committed murder for the very first time?"

"It crossed my mind. As I pointed out earlier, Lefty, laminating those letters, was odd, then hiding them in the lining of a purse, odder. Since the rapist went dormant, never resurfaced, it's still a cold case in Austin."

"Y'all want some fresh coffee?" Francine was brewing a new pot.

Kasper went on while he watched Frankie dump out the old filter full of used coffee grounds, put in a fresh filter, then refill it with enough grounds to make stout coffee.

"After seeing her photo and learning just a little about her personal history, Ms. Soon-Lee wasn't like the other victims. She wasn't our killer's type."

Harlowe agreed. "Yeah, she was thin, probably weighed a buck-ten soaking wet, and years younger than the others."

"She wasn't from a poor neighborhood," Kasper said. "Mera lived in Austin proper, yet they discovered her remains in a grave at the border of Texas and Oklahoma in an old cemetery no one used in years. And what's funny—not ha-ha funny either—is they'd never have found her if they hadn't been transferring two graves to a new larger family plot at Brown Springs Cemetery, which coincidently is near Thackerville, Oklahoma."

"Uh-huh, same place our missing Choctaw woman was from. Good chance they link to the same killer." Harlowe's gaze shifted to the map with the pushpins, noting the locations were awfully close.

Frankie strolled to the whiteboard as the coffee brewed and stared at the DMV photo of Mera Soon-Lee. She would've been thirty-three on her next birthday, had she lived. "She was a beautiful young lady."

Lefty's brows wrinkled. "Was she a victim of something else entirely? I mean, she just doesn't fit the victimology of the others. And look at Anderson, born male and changed into a female in every sense of the word. Add in he was also large, and from what we know being a large woman fits the correct body style. Soon-Lee was small, smaller than the rest of them."

"It's the letters she had," said Kasper. "They don't fit or hold a key to the puzzle, and that's what's been bothering me. Something about her murder seems, well, personal. In my opinion, Soon-Lee posed a danger, but I'm having difficulty comprehending the reason."

"Seems like a fair assumption, thinking her murder was personal, but what about the other ladies without letters? Why are they connected to this case?" Harlowe didn't see the connection, but Frankie did.

"The hitchhiker, raped and strangled by Preston Munn." Frankie held up a finger and Harlowe closed her mouth. "Wait. We know some hookers he didn't kill, but once he got started, he couldn't control his urges. It's clear the hitchhiker wasn't a prostitute, but she set him off, and Munn thought she was lying to him about having a fella. He saw her as fat and not pretty, but he raped her all the same then strangled her. Afterward, he buried her and her belongings in nowhere land, never told anyone until he needed something to use as a bargaining chip to remove his death penalty. That's when he finally disclosed this murder."

"Geeze, Francine, we knew this already." Harlowe huffed.

"What Frankie isn't saying, "Kasper went on, "is Munn never talked about the pen pal letters from the convict she had with her the day he killed her. He'd saved a few letters but later destroyed them, or so he told us. Once they located her body and verified his story, there wasn't any reason to divulge information about the letters, because this correspondence was immaterial, because it had nothing to do with the rape/murder. One thing Munn never mentioned to cops, lawyers, or anyone else was anything about the letters. The man never talked to the shrinks, didn't tell a soul about the letters unless it was another inmate. So, when these asinine secret interviews with faceless men come to pass, Munn suddenly turns into Chatty Cathy once he's stuck in a room behind a two-way mirror, and can't tell us who he was spilling his guts to."

Harlowe tapped the surface of her desk with her pencil, the rubber end bouncing in rapid motion and the soft pitter-patter of the small pink eraser sounded on the cover of a closed notebook. "So, he decides during these hush-hush interviews to spill his guts. Why?

Incarcerated for twenty-four years, he utters not a word. If this was four or five years ago, don't you think it's strange he finally felt like talking about it?"

"Yep, especially since the guy's been harboring this crap for twenty-four years and has the rest of his pathetic life to hold it in. So, why talk now? Maybe these hush-hush sessions opened a can of worms. Hell, Frankie and I heard a firsthand rendition of his crimes, the creep got off reliving it; the shitbag has no conscience and zero remorse."

"Munn's a sick fuck for sure, plus, it felt like he was trying to get onto our heads. And the deal is he's got nothing to gain by telling us, or anyone, his story; it doesn't give him any leverage at all. Who were these mystery interviewers and which guy made such an impression on Munn that he suddenly had loose lips?"

Kasper's head tilted left, then right. "Great question, Ryder, I wish we could find the guy and ask him about Munn." Somewhere deep inside Bergman's gut a voice whispered, *your killer and this guy are the same man.* Wordlessly, he told his gut to keep quiet—for now.

CHAPTER THIRTY-TWO

"We've a lot to do before tomorrow. Lefty and Frankie are leaving for Tulsa in the morning. Their homicide department is expecting y'all around noon, so I got y'all a small SUV. It's in the parking lot on the north side, and here's the hotel information."

Lefty took the paperwork, winking at Kasper. "One room, you want me and Frankie to share?"

A sharp gasp came out of Frankie and she turned pink, looking at Bergman with narrow eyes.

"Come on, Frankie, we know what you and Left do when you're alone. Don't deny it."

"I'm not denying it, Kasper, but, uh, can we just not discuss our private stuff?"

Harlowe jumped into the fun. "What, Frankie, don't you kiss or anything else and tell?"

"Shut up, Bishop, I mean it." Francine Ryder's face turned cherry tomato red.

"Look, we don't give a rat's patootie what y'all do in private. We're happy for you guys."

"Really?"

"Yeah, Frankie, really, now, can we not waste our day talking about your sex life and work our case?"

"I'm all for that, aren't you, Lefty?"

"Absolutely, but I am looking forward to going to Tulsa, especially those Tulsa nights." Lefty did an eyebrow wiggle like Groucho Marx.

"Now, damn it, Corneal, will ya just stop?"

"Sorry, Fran, I'll stop."

Kasper ignored them, thinking they were a pair indeed, and who'd have ever thunk it? He was envious. They had each other and were doing what they loved, working with the FBI.

Harlowe Bishop's face held a wistful look. She might be just a hair jealous but would never admit it.

"Okay, team. Harlowe and I will go through Miss Mackey's boxes, look for any lead, and if there's nothing, we'll return them to her cousin. About the abandoned car theory—Lefty, I want you to dig into the ones tagged *unclaimed,* find out who they're registered to because these vehicles have a backstory. Find any previous titleholders; go as far back as you can. Then look into which auction house they got sent to and include the car they crushed because someone owned it once. Frankie, you take the names of the owners, run them through NCIC, see if anything pops. Also, take the case files for our victims, run them through ViCAP. You never know, another case may link to ours."

They got to work. He and Harlowe dug into boxes with papers in a jumbled mess, combined with junk mail and scraps of paper with grocery lists, to-do lists, and plain out-and-out garbage. Frankie continued to run specific data through ViCAP. Lefty called the DPS and the county motor vehicle registration office.

Lefty stretched, looking at his Fitbit. "Good Lord, it's after one. I'm starved; y'all know I never miss lunch."

"How much paperwork can one person stuff in a few darn boxes, good gravy?" Harlowe plunked another box on her desk, grabbed hand sanitizer, pumped some out, and rubbed it into her palms and over her fingers. "How's about ordering pizza so we can keep working, cuz at this rate I'll be here for another ten hours on one box. I mean, really, I am combing over every single scrap of paper."

"I agree, we need to eat and work, cuz this box is the same, it's a jumbled mess, and look, we've got three more boxes to dig through and I'd rather not take them home tonight." Kasper stood to stretch, cracking his neck left and right and worked out a kink.

"Yeah, let's eat and keep working. Good idea, and listen, I could go for a double meat deep-dish pizza." Frankie leaned back raising her arms over her head to stretch.

"The reason we make a terrific match, Francine, I love me some deep-dish pizza, and none of you better add pineapple or I'll hafta kick some ass." Lefty went online to find a pizza joint that delivered.

"Get salads too, and garlic breadsticks," Frankie requested.

Kasper deposited his Latex gloves into the trash can. They took a free minute to sit quietly, listening to Lefty order the pizza, and after he'd placed the order Kasper called the lobby receptionist.

"Hi, Carole, uh-huh, I'm good, hey, listen, we ordered pizza, be here in about forty, what? Sure, you can have two slices. What? Yes, and two breadsticks." Kasper's eyes rolled up toward the ceiling: "Yes, I know you're half Italian. Goodbye, Carole." He hung up, his shoulder slightly shaking.

The room was hushed and quiet. Had an old-fashioned clock been hanging nearby you would've heard it ticking. They got back to work; they had forty minutes before the pizza arrived so Kasper piled two fistfuls of loose papers on his desk and began sorting. He shut his eyes leaning back in thought. A little over six years ago, working as a tech at the Houston PD, he experienced being stalked via his IP address. Theo Sykes, ex-DEA turned hitman for the Lobos Cartel and Drug Lord Omar Villa Lobos. Sykes was once a trusted member of law enforcement but let money and power turn him. Had someone in law enforcement become a cold-blooded killer like the ex- DEA agent? If it happened once, it could happen again; nothing was impossible. Sykes was still out there on the lam, most likely living in another country. Kasper knew Theo would come for him one day. The big question was when? Kasper grew eyes behind his head and he wasn't afraid. One day he'd meet Theo again and one day...his phone rang, jarring him back to reality.

"Thanks, I'm coming. What? Okay, sure. Diet okay? I know it is, but it's all we've got. I can bring you a bottle of water—okay, fine, diet cola. What? Yeah, sure, I'll ask 'em." He hung up, looking at the others. "Carole wants to know why we're worried about sugar in our soda if we're pounding back pizza and breadsticks." Kasper grabbed his wallet from a drawer, chuckling while he headed to the ground floor to get their late lunch so they could recharge, eating as they worked.

Harlowe started a fresh pot of coffee and gathered empty boxes and salad containers.

Kasper's disappointed. "So far, nothing but junk—bunches of unpaid bills, same as the first box I shuffled through. I've not found any personal correspondence, not even a birthday or Christmas card, nothing."

Lefty tilted in his chair. "Well, I got mostly nothing on the orange tagged cars. They crushed one, leaving the remaining two. They sold these at auction. Looks like the new owners allegedly never registered them, not with their real names, anyway. The names listed on the titles were bogus, and the registration stickers were counterfeit."

"Yeah, heard the Bureau had a couple of undercover stings they've been working on counterfeit registrations. Several U-tote-the-Note places, shady used car dealers, even individuals buying junkers, getting them running good enough to sell, are using fake registration stickers." Kasper felt bad certain people got duped and taken advantage of.

He found nothing in this stack of papers so he lifted the entire pile and dropped it into the box, then picked up the next box, removing the lid. Cheap three-ring notebooks with photo page savers and loose photos of family, he figured, and what looked like school pictures of her son. More were in the last box, in no certain order—stacks and bundles with photo store packets and old albums. Annelle Mackey's life in pictures, fantastic.

"Great, a shitload of photos. Here, Harlowe, help me flip through them, see if anything catches your eye, will ya?" Kasper held up a bundle.

"Fine, hand it over. Just finished an entire box of coupons, junk mail; she never tossed a scrap of paper away, ever."

Lefty stuck his hand out. "Hand me some, I'll help. I'm waiting for a coupla callbacks."

Kasper handed him a stack of Photo Mart, Walgreens, and Walmart Photo Center packets rubber-banded together with a super extra-large rubber band.

"Gee, thanks, buddy."

"Hey, you wanted to help."

"Yeah, flipping through books, not a million loose photos. I'm betting these are photos from when her kid was little. You know, at the zoo, tons of photos of elephants, tigers, and giraffes, oh my. Christmas, Thanksgiving, and a crappola load of birthday parties, yippee."

"Do it and stop bitching, will ya, Lefty? At least you didn't hafta sort through ten years of store coupons and newspaper flyers, holy mackerel. Besides, at least photos have a bit more personality." Harlowe shot him a grin. "One day you and Frankie might be pulling out a wallet showing off your own brats."

Kasper closemouthed chuckled as he watched Lefty flip Harlowe off then glanced at Francine. "Hey, Fran, you gonna help me defend our unborn kids or what? I mean, we ain't gonna have brats, are we?" Lefty swiveled his chair to see if she was even listening since she'd hadn't come back with any retort whatsoever.

Francine Ryder's brows knitted together as she read something on her computer screen, scrolling slowly.

"Fran? Earth to Francine Ryder." Lefty's fingers snapped near her ear getting attention.

"What? Oh, sorry, didn't hear what you said, was reading. What did 'ya say?"

"Nothing, skip it, it ain't important. What's got you so engrossed?" Lefty relaxed into his seat.

"Didn't her cousin Ernie Gorman tell you Annelle was originally from Oklahoma?"

"He did, some little town called Overbrook, but she was born in Ardmore. "

"Huh." It was all she said as she typed into her computer.

"Well? You gonna tell us why you asked or are we suppos'ta guess?"

"Just give me a second."

The three waited as time ticked by then Frankie finally uttered, "That's it, there's the connection."

Kasper stopped flipping through photos. "Wanna share with the class, Francine?"

"Uh-huh. So, Sylvia Amos was from Thackerville but born in Ardmore, just like Annelle Mackey and Rayna Anderson. Amos grew up in Thackerville. Lived in one small town or another as a teen and went to high school but didn't graduate. Same high school as Annelle Mackey and Rayna Anderson; these three were close in age—Anderson born in 1978, Mackey in 1979, and Amos in 1980. Anderson graduated, the two women didn't."

"Is there more?" Kasper asked.

"No, I'm still digging, but this is pretty coincidental, dontcha think?"

"Don't believe in coincidences any more than I believe Tinker Bell can fly; keep digging, Ryder, you might be onto something we can sink our teeth into."

"You think our suspect might be from Oklahoma?"

"Dunno, Lefty, but if he kills across Texas and Oklahoma, who's to say he won't go into another state to kill?"

This wasn't an option. They needed to catch this guy before another woman disappeared or another body surfaced.

CHAPTER THIRTY-THREE

The phone rang at Lefty's desk. "Special Agent Sebastian. Yes, sir, I did. You did? Sure, wait, let me grab a pen." Lefty was writing as his head bobbed with the phone stuck to his ear. "Yep, got it, and thank you. Will you guys keep the area secured until we get there?" Corneal looked at his watch. "With five o'clock traffic, it might be awhile, about an hour and a half. Tell you what, I'll text you when we're about twenty minutes out. What's your cell? Got it, and listen, like I said, secure the scene and touch nothing, got me? Yeah, I know you know your job, but buddy, this case is bigger than you think, and I want nothing compromised. Uh-huh, sorry for barking at you. See you soon." Lefty hung up and looked over at his cohorts. All eyes staring, and Frankie's mouth opened in a small "o".

Lefty saw her face; his brow puckered. "What? Why ya looking at me like that?"

Her head slanted. "Well, I've gotta say, Special Agent Sebastian, you sounded quite impressive, and I've never seen this side of you. You're a real FBI agent. Wow."

"Yeah, Lefty," Harlowe quipped. "None of us has ever seen your serious FBI agent act before, very impressive indeed."

"All joking aside," Kasper piped up, "you sounded quite official. So, about the call, where're we headed? And who are you barking orders to?"

"The Azle Police Department. They found a body—Nora Mendez-Finch."

"How'd they know to call you?" Kasper grabbed his phone and wallet from the top drawer and stood.

"I called them last week, told them to call me in case a body or Mendez-Finch turned up alive. They'll secure the crime scene until we get there."

"Well, we heard you, you commanding beast." A wide grin on her face, Frankie stuck her arm into a heavier jacket, touting the acronym "FBI" in gold lettering.

Harlowe slipped on her lanyard carrying her credentials and then slid on her shoulder holster and her official FBI jacket. "Catch." She tossed Kasper the keys to the Yukon.

His jacket zipped up a fraction; he stuck the keys in the side pocket. "Alrighty, team, let's roll." He looked at his phone. "It's five-fifteen. Get ready to sit in traffic, tollway or not."

"It'll give us some time to bounce around some ideas." Lefty pulled his jacket off the backrest of his chair. The four of them wearing the same FBI jackets always reminded him of the movies, shows with the FBI converging on a scene. His heart sank because this was real life and not a movie.

"Yeah, let's do some theory building. How about it, Harlowe?"

"Absolutely, Frankie, and I call shotgun!"

No one argued, Harlowe called it, and besides, Lefty and Frankie didn't mind sitting in the back. They might sneak holding hands for a bit.

Daylight Savings was coming soon and darkness crept in just a hair sooner as the night air got cooler. The funny thing in Texas—one night there could be north winds up to twenty mph and forty degrees felt like twenty-degree weather, then three nights later it could be sixty-two and balmy at nine p.m. This was one of those cooler nights.

Thank goodness for the lightweight jackets as they rolled up to the address given to Lefty. It was a small frame house on a county road. The Azle Police Department had lights set in place and the area roped off with yellow crime scene tape. Not many onlookers as there weren't many neighbors. Homes were either frame houses or trailers, single- and double-wide, set as far apart as a half-acre, and some further back off the main road. The group headed toward an old barn. Cops and the Azle Fire Department buzzed around the scene.

His badge flipped open as he walked up. "FBI, Special Agent Kasper Bergman, and these folks are Special Agents Sebastian, Bishop, and Ryder."

"Lieutenant Detective Mark Mitcham, Homicide, Azle PD. Nice to make your acquaintance. I'm just sorry about the circumstances."

Lefty stepped in, his hand extended. "We spoke on the phone."

He grabbed Lefty's hand, a good solid Texas handshake. "Yes, sir. Let me get you up to speed. Then see the body, okay with you?"

Lieutenant Detective Mitcham regarded Lefty who turned to Kasper.

"Agent Bergman heads up the team, it's his call."

"Huh. You people really work as a team? Not at all like the movies?" He winked, and then frowned, mad at himself for being flippant in this serious situation. The detective coughed, clearing his throat in embarrassment. "Sorry, it's not the time to joke around. I apologize."

"No worries, Lieutenant Detective Mitcham," Harlowe told him. "We understand. Sometimes humor relieves the stress of the job."

"Mark. Call me Mark."

She took out her notebook and pen. "Sure, Mark. Now, can you lead us through what happened tonight? And why's the fire department here?"

"I called them to set up the lights."

"Good, now will you please take us through what happened?"

"Around three-forty this evening, after the school bus dropped off the kids, a few of the high school boys promised to help Mr. Grantham get his barn ready for winter."

"There are animals in the barn now?"

"No, ma'am, I mean, Agent Ryder. Old Man Grantham's horses and a few heifers and bulls are in his brother's pasture up in Bowie."

"Call me Frankie. Okay, Mark, go on with your story, sorry I interrupted."

"Sure. Anyway, the boys started cleaning out the barn, getting rid of the old hay, sweeping it out including the loft and hosing the place down. Old Man Grantham left more than a hundred bags of cheap dirt. His instructions were for them to dump it in the rear area of the barn to fill a void at the far-right corner, as the drainage in the rear portion of Mr. Grantham's barn is suboptimal and with the rains we've had recently, it's washed away a lot of dirt. The barn's old and he's planning on rebuilding next spring, cuz the current barn ain't set on a concrete slab and he's tired of trying to keep it leveled out." The Azle detective cleared his throat." Sorry, guess y'all don't need to know all this. Anyway,"—the detective thumbed behind him—"one of the boys, they're all three over there waiting. Larry Carter saw part of what he thought was a heavy-duty trash bag under the barn's corner. They were fixing to dump the dirt. So, he and Carrey Bayles tugged at it to pull it out from under the barn, but they ended up pulling up a human leg, which freaked them out."

"And they told Mr. Grantham, and he called you guys?"

"Grantham ain't home. The boy dialed 9-1-1, and we came out."

As the detective spoke, Kasper gazed around and observed the boys huddled together, imagining it scared the holy crap out of them.

"How did you determine you'd found Nora Mendez-Finch?"

"We uncovered her but haven't moved her body; it's wrapped in heavy, thick plastic, like the kind used in flower beds. She's a hefty woman, around 220 pounds, five-foot-nine, wrapped up like a mummy. Not knowing who it was, or if it was human, I mean, Grantham could've buried one of his livestock, he has before." He shook his head and clenched his jaw. "Sorry, not something I've seen before, and won't forget for a while. Homicides are not a common occurrence here. And well, I..." He trailed off, swallowing the urge to upchuck at the recollection of what he'd seen.

"We understand. No one gets used to it, not really. What made you realize it was Nora Finch, Mark?"

"Apart from her being the sole missing person reported in the past two decades, she was wearing her recently acquired Walmart name tag."

"We won't subject you to another look-see. Just point us to where she is."

Mark Mitcham, the Lieutenant Detective, had an apologetic expression. "Thanks, appreciate it. Also, the Tarrant County ME's on the way. I called them almost two hours ago, but an accident on 820 has them sitting still."

"Mark," Kasper addressed him. "Do us another favor. Get one of your patrol officers to rope off a large area, about five hundred yards around where they located her body. Tape it off from north to south and outward from the burial area. Get some guys out here with shovels. Her family notified?"

"No, we haven't gotten to the notification because we called you first. What should we be searching for, Agent Bergman?

"Any personal items she might've had with her...and call me Kasper."

"On it, I'll have some officers handle this immediately."

Frankie walked up to the detective and questioned, "Have those boys' parents been called? They might be worried."

"Yes, we called them, but didn't tell them anything."

"Have one of your officers take the boys home and explain to the parents, enough so they know their kiddos aren't in trouble. Just get full names, phone numbers, and addresses, okay?"

"Absolutely, ma'am, I'll get some uniforms on it. Man, those kids are gonna have nightmares, poor fellas."

Frankie concurred with a wry smile. "Thanks, Mark, you guys are doing a bang-up job."

She left him with that compliment, to catch up with Kasper, Corneal, and Harlowe, and a dead body—her least favorite part of this fucking job!

CHAPTER THIRTY-FOUR

Gloved up, booties on, they stood over the victim.

"Never will get used to this, it sucks." Harlowe covered her mouth with the sleeve of her jacket.

Lefty stepped up next to Harlowe. "Nobody should hafta get used to it."

It was early October and with recent rains, the temps were lower. The body, wrapped in thick black plastic, landscaping liner, deprived of oxygen, and semi-protected from insect activity and other wild animals. As it was, her decomposing body wasn't as bad as it could've been. The Azle detectives had used a sharp knife to slice through some of the plastic, and Kasper noted her killer rolled her body up several times in the black liner. The body was buried in a four-foot-deep trench, which took time to dig. What killer had that kind of time? Was the property owner Grantham out of town when this happened?

Kasper took his phone snapping photos from several angles and the surrounding area. Bending, he photographed her Walmart name badge, a frown creasing his face. She'd just started a new job. He knew she was going through a divorce, and hadn't worked outside the home since her kids were born. She was excited about her new job and starting over, because she'd been the one who had filed for the divorce, not her husband.

"Hey, Kasper, look at this." Frankie squatted near the victim's head. She pointed. "What's wrapped around her neck?"

Squatted on his haunches he shook his head. "It looks like it might be her panties." He pointed out the leg hole, and a part that looked like a thin elastic band wadded next to the same area.

"Looks twisted like someone was wringing water out of them."

Harlowe bent, her sleeve still covering her nose and mouth. Her eyes went left to right, viewing the victim's neck. With her gloved hand, she took a pen from her jacket to lift the item away from the woman's neck bone, away from decomposing flesh.

"Yeah, it's ladies' underwear. By the size, it's hers, which tells me she's probably no longer wearing any."

The sound of footsteps had them turning; the ME had arrived.

Kasper stood, stripping off his right glove.

"Special Agent Kasper Bergman, FBI."

Her outstretched hand clasped his. "Nikki Lam, Deputy Medical Examiner."

"Agents Bishop, Ryder, and Sebastian," Kasper made the introductions.

"Nice to make your acquaintance, too bad it's over death." Donning a pair of gloves, she bent to look, then took out a handheld recorder from her jacket pocket, squatted, and hit "record."

"Adult female; from the details of her missing person's report, her approximate height was five-foot-eight, weight two hundred twenty pounds, missing two months, presumed dead for same time period but will confirm at autopsy." She looked up at Harlowe. "Have you bagged any evidence?"

"No, but the panties twisted around her neck are a sign someone possibly strangled her, but of course you'll have to confirm at the autopsy. Is he your assistant?" Harlowe's head gestured to a young man walking up.

Lam looked at Harlowe, a tiny furrow between her lovely eyes. "Is the FBI working this case, or are we?"

Kasper responded, "We'd like to coordinate with you and your office, Dr. Lam. Is it possible for you to rearrange your schedule to put us at the top? If not, we can have our people move her over to the FBI lab. Right now, our case takes priority."

Still squatted, Nikki Lam, her shoulder-length hair pulled back in a ponytail, looked at Kasper with her almond-shaped exquisite amber eyes, her frown line more distinct. "Special Agent Bergman, the FBI doesn't work local homicide cases, and this is not federal property, plus, this victim isn't a political or prominent figure. I'm thinking you've caught a serial case, not just in Texas either. Tell me, Agent Bergman, how many more victims and what other states are involved?"

Kasper suppressed his grin. She was not only attractive, she was smart, too.

"Mrs. Nora Mendez-Finch here makes six, and one missing Oklahoma woman, presumed dead."

She stood to face him. "Are you telling me the FBI wants to work with the Tarrant County ME's office and not with your own lab?"

"Unless you think you can't handle it," he challenged her.

Dr. Lam stripped off one latex glove and stuck her hand out. "Okay, call me Nikki, since we're gonna be working together."

"Excellent. Call me Kasper."

They shook hands, and after that she tugged on another glove, resumed her squat, and turned her attention to the body. She hit the "record" button and picked up where she'd left off. "The victim wrapped in landscaping liner, appears rolled up in this liner several times; once we get her to the lab, we'll have more details. She's buried"—she paused, took out a folding ruler from her pocket, measuring the depth of the hole—"in a four-foot-deep grave, approximately." She stood and clicked off the recorder.

"You always carry a folding ruler?"

"Here, in the middle of nowhere, I don't need to use fancy tools to do a good job, Special Agent Bergman, but we do have a state-of-the-art lab, so don't worry." Her eyes held a glint of laughter.

"Not worried at all."

She gestured toward the remains. "Let's continue with her, okay?"

"Of course, Doctor." He liked this woman; his stomach did a flip-flop.

The ME went on, "A larger body mass decomposes quicker because fats liquefy at a more rapid rate. Buried four feet behind this barn, and with no direct sunlight."

"Well, our killer had one thing going for him."

Harlowe glanced between Nikki Lam and Kasper. "What's that, Bergman?"

"He had time to dig this out. Nora was a big gal and Texas ground is dry and hard because of heat, but we've had heavy rains off and on over the last few months. So I'm thinking we should review the weather forecasts from the past three months, might give us a better timeline of when he dug this hole out to bury her, and we're gonna need to have a chat with Mr. Grantham, the property owner."

Frankie waved at Detective Mitcham motioning for him to come over.

"Yes, ma'am?"

"Mark, is Mr. Grantham gonna be home tonight?"

"No, he's not. The old guy's got a travel trailer up in Bowie, and one of the young boys said he was gonna visit his brother in Decatur before rounding up his livestock to transport back. Cary Bayless said he told 'em he'd be gone until Sunday evening. Sorry."

"Not a problem, but we're gonna need to speak with him, so if you'll corral him for us, no pun intended." Frankie shrugged.

Mark Mitcham chuckled a little. "Yeah, well, it's Texas, so it fits. I'll call him, because if he comes home and sees the crime scene tape, he'll freak out."

Nikki Lam stood, waving over two men toting the gurney and

body bag. She instructed them to deliver the body to the morgue, then slipped off her latex gloves, facing the FBI agents.

"I'll get her autopsy started tomorrow, but I've got one on my table to finish tonight, then I'm going home. My apologies if you thought I'd work through the night, but I've been up to my armpits in dead bodies since three a.m. this morning."

Harlowe frowned. "You have? Gosh, sorry to hear that."

Nikki heaved a sigh. "Yeah, a shooting at the Stockyards killed two, and I already had two other autopsies waiting from the hospital, one a possible suspicious death and another requested by a family."

"I hate to add to your work schedule." Kasper looked at her tired face.

"The Chief Medical Examiner and I will work this out, no worries; besides, working with you guys is sorta my dream. Don't piss on my dream, okay?"

Bergman grinned. "Hey, I'd never piss on anyone's dream. Here's my card with my cell number. When you've got the autopsy done, call me. If you find something we need to know beforehand, call me. Oh, yeah, also, if you need us to do anything like get the FBI lab involved, just call me."

The others watched as Kasper turned into a blathering idiot.

"You got it." She turned to leave, but he called her back.

"Nikki, you have a card, uh, with your number?"

"Sure, almost forgot, it's been a long damn day." She pulled a card from her jacket pocket. "See you later." She shifted her attention to the others. "Good to meet you."

They watched Nikki Lam head to the coroner's car to ride to the morgue and log the body of Nora Mendez-Finch into the system, and get her refrigerated.

Harlowe, Frankie, and Lefty eyeballed Kasper, as he eyeballed Nikki Lam, watching her walk away, a silly grin flitting across his face.

"A little starstruck, Bergman?"

Kasper's head swiveled. "What are you jabbering about, Bishop?"

Frankie hooted. "Oh my Lord, Bergman! Why didn't you just ask her if she'd like to meet you for lunch to discuss the case?"

"Cuz I'll talk to her tomorrow, before lunch I reckon."

Harlowe let loose a laugh.

"Don't know why you find that funny, Bishop."

Lefty walked up to Kasper and slung his arm over his friend's shoulder. "Dr. Lam's a nice-looking gal, isn't she?"

"Yeah, she is, I—" He looked at Lefty, then the girls, and scowled. "Oh, I see, I see. You guys think I've got a thing for the Deputy Medical Examiner?"

Lefty cracked up. "By damn, yeah, we do, and I gotta tell you, if I saw it, then it was freaking pretty obvious because I'm not Captain Obvious about this kinda crap."

Kasper's face grew ten shades of red. He'd found Nikki Lam lovely, with her amber eyes, eyes he could melt in. Flirting was not something he was proficient at, nor, so it seemed, was hiding his attraction to the woman.

He huffed off toward the Yukon, leaving them all laughing, following behind.

CHAPTER THIRTY-FIVE

Kasper's arms came up over his head, stretching. The time in the lower right-hand corner of his monitor blinked six a.m. He'd been at it for about two hours, finding nothing, absolutely nothing. *Nada, nada, nada...* he sang these words to a tune he made up in his head. He was getting punchy with little sleep.

This was the second go-round searching through Annelle Mackey's boxes of papers and photos. He and Harlowe had gone through these boxes, but this morning he'd decided they needed another look-see, and he took the boxes she'd dug through to follow up. Each scrap of paper, front, back, and sideways—they had to find something.

His eyes were blurry, so he took off the latex gloves, resting back in thought. Harlowe would be getting up about now. He'd left a pot of coffee ready to start and a note with the number to call a trusted Uber driver, one he used from time to time.

He closed his eyes and the Azle crime scene flashed in his head. Granted, not in the way an FBI agent usually re-sees a crime scene, which was a gruesome picture, one you could never unsee. No, he didn't see the crime scene; what he saw was the face of Tarrant

County's Deputy Medical Examiner, Nikki Lam. His eyes still closed, he relaxed deeper into his chair.

She wore minimal makeup and her skin was smooth and clear. What had him mesmerized were her eyes, not brown nor hazel, but liquid amber, beautiful, yet tired eyes, eyes he could melt into—crap, he wasn't a lovesick idiot. What was he doing? He shook himself out of his foolish reverie. Here was the plain absolute fact: Dr. Lam was attractive, and he wanted to get to know her. Meeting women at a crime scene, how ghoulish, he thought. Funny, the last woman he'd dated was one he'd met at an FBI conference for academic institutions. He'd met Erin Halco, recipient of the National Science Foundation's Graduate Research Fellowship (GRFP) award, three years ago. At first it was great—a new relationship begins, the heart-pounding feeling when you see each other after being apart.

Erin was lovely and so damn smart it blew him away, but she'd become needy. Not girlfriend needy, but colleague needy. Constantly in work or school mode, never in relationship mode, and after ten months of trying to work it out, he gave up.

He had thrown himself into his work with the FBI and stopped thinking about women or love; it suited him. He'd had nothing lasting since he wasn't looking for lasting. All he'd need was a simple short fling, and he could count those on two whole fingers. Kasper Andrew Bergman wasn't a sleep-around kinda guy, he was an all-or-nothing sort of fella, and since he wasn't finding a long-term, lasting relationship, he decided he'd settle for nothing. He had his work and just enough social life to sustain him. Hanging out with his coworkers at company events, birthdays, or just to chew the fat. Or just sitting at the bar at A Bit O' Dublin, people-watching while he drank a cold one or chatting with Becky about nothing in particular.

Nikki Lam. He wondered if she'd like his favorite little pub. What the fuck was wrong with him? It was 6:20, and he'd been reminiscing about his past love life, his lack of love life, and a possible new love life for the last twenty minutes.

Under his breath, he whispered to himself as he slipped on a second pair of gloves. "Pull your head out, dork." He plucked the lid off another box, pulled out a pile of papers, and put them on his desk. He flexed his fingers and dug into the stack.

Two-year-old credit card bills and past-due notices. Did this woman ever toss anything? The next few pieces of mail were postmarked from four months ago. At least this was more recent. He slogged through more years of old mail with nothing to show for his efforts until he caught the edge of an oversized plain white envelope peeking out from between two newspaper advertisements. It was addressed to Annelle Mackey, Lavender Street, Overbrook, Oklahoma, but forwarded to her address in Itasca, Texas. Harlowe must've missed this, he figured, or she saw it and dismissed it.

It was postmarked 2004, twelve years ago. Kasper pulled out a birthday card and when he opened it a very faded Polaroid of six kids, all of whom looked to be in their early to mid-teens, slipped out. Flipping the photo over, he read in faded red ink: *J, Gloria, Den, Annie, Matty, and RA*. Well, a fat lot of good that did, except he figured Annie was Annelle Mackey—she would've been around fourteen or fifteen, the picture taken before she moved to Texas.

Kasper studied the faces; they seemed normal enough. He studied the order in which they stood, and it would seem whoever J and Gloria were they were a couple, his arms around her waist. A more slender version of Annelle stood between Den and Matty, her arms around their shoulders, and RA, a rather goofy and chubby boy, stood by himself, smiling. She got this card on her twenty-fifth birthday, a milestone birthday. He looked for signatures and found none. It simply read, *Happy Birthday, Annie, remember the gang?*

Hmmm, he thought. *Who took the picture?* His stomach rumbled as the door creaked opened and Harlowe walked in.

"For God's sake, Bergman, are you a man or a machine? Oh, and thanks for the Uber driver. He was a hoot; oh, and for setting up the coffeepot, I really needed a cup of stout java this morning." She pulled out her chair and booted up her laptop, then entered her password, still shooting question after question. "What the heck ungodly hour did you get here? Why didn't you wake me? Aren't you gonna be toast later?"

"Slow down, holy moly, did you spike your coffee with Red Bull or what? I got here around four. Glove up, I want you to look at something."

She slipped on gloves and he handed her the snapshot.

Harlowe looked at the faces.

"Turn it over."

Reading the back, she nodded. "Guessing Ann is Annelle Mackey. Boy, look at her, all skinny and smiles."

"Look at the postmark."

"A twelve-year-old birthday card. My goodness, the woman saved everything."

The door swung open and Frankie strolled in followed by Lefty who carried a brown paper bag of something smelling delicious, catching the tail end of the conversation. "Who got a birthday card?"

Kasper informed them of what he'd found while Lefty pulled out hot, homemade breakfast burritos, handing them all one.

"Where did you get these, the hotel?" Harlowe brought hers up to her nose.

"Nah, yesterday I saw the breakfast food truck at a construction site a few blocks from the hotel, so I thought I'd try 'em out."

"Thanks, I'm starved." Kasper bit into his. "Mmm, good stuff." Just as he swallowed the last bite, his phone rang. "FBI, Bergman. Uh, well, good morning to you too. How are you?" He listened, then, "Around two? Great, see you then." He hung up, a silly grin plastered on his unshaven face.

"So? What'd Dr. Lam say?" Harlowe almost sung the words.

"How'd you—"

"The sappy look on your face."

"She's starting the autopsy in twenty minutes. I'm gonna go to Fort Worth to talk to her later."

Lefty garbled with burrito in his mouth, "Why can't she just call?

We've got other fish to fry, and Frankie and I are leaving for Tulsa, aren't we?"

Slightly sleep-deprived and anxious at seeing Nikki again, Kasper was in a mannequin state when Lefty tapped the desktop to get his attention. "Hey, dude, earth to Special Agent in Charge, Bergman."

"What?"

"You still want Frankie and me to head to Tulsa, or should we postpone?"

"No, call 'em, tell 'em we'll be in touch. Oh, call the hotel and cancel the reservations." He looked over at Harlowe. "We're not headed to Austin either, we need to stay here and process the newest victim. Also, the photo in the birthday card is niggling at me. Something doesn't seem right, so let's take all the loose photos and her albums, look through them again and do it with a fine-tooth comb. Search for photos from her past, twenty-plus years ago, when she was ages fourteen to seventeen. Harlowe, call Ernie Gorman, have him look for any school annuals Mackey might have had, and if he finds any, send a courier to pick them up. Got it?"

Heads nod as they got to work. Kasper's inner kid was giddy. He was gonna see Nikki today, this afternoon—suddenly he was worried about shaving and a haircut.

CHAPTER THIRTY-SIX

"So far, this has been a bust." Lefty rubber-banded another stack of photos together he'd finished looking through.

"Well, you know what they say. Ya gotta kiss a ton of frogs..." Harlowe grumbled. "Oh, and Mr. Gorman wasn't home. I'll call again later to ask about the school annuals."

"Uh-huh, I'd rather kiss a frog or two than go through any more zoo and Christmas pictures with her and her kid. Lord. Why isn't Frankie helping us? What's she doing?" Lefty stood to stretch and noted she had zero packages of Walmart or Walgreen photo packets on her desk. "I thought the plan was we all hafta look at this crap? Man, we haven't even started on the ton of photo albums which are every size, shape, and thickness. What gives?"

"She's working on something else."

"Wanna clue us in? Maybe we've got some ideas, too." Harlowe reached for an empty coffee mug and stood.

"I will if you'll put on a pot of coffee and be nice," Kasper said.

With an affirmative jerk of her head, Harlowe got up to make fresh coffee. It was only ten and Kasper having been up since three a.m. felt himself sinking.

"After seeing that photo a theory popped into my head regarding the individuals from Oklahoma. I've got Frankie digging on connections between Amos, Anderson, and Mackey. They lived within minutes of each other off Interstate 35 in Oklahoma. That can't be a coincidence. Can it?"

"Awe, come on, sure it can. Just cuz they were from the area doesn't mean they knew each other. Also, only one person got murdered in Oklahoma and the other one's still missing."

"Well, let's see. Unaccounted for what, seven years now, I'd venture a guess she's not just missing, she's dead. How about it, girls?" Kasper asked.

"Dead," they said in unison.

"I'm sure y'all are right. Hell, just once I'd like to find our missing person still alive," Lefty spouted.

They all felt the same way, but reality was—well, reality.

An Hour Later

"Got something, guys," Francine announced.

"Me, too," Harlowe followed. "Interesting picture. Tell me what you see." She passed the photo across the table to Lefty.

"Looks like a summer camp in the background, can't make out the name, though. A group of teenagers and looks like a camp counselor." He passed the photo to Frankie, who agreed.

"That's it, really? Give it to Kasper. Let him look."

He looked shaking his head, asking, "What are we missing?"

"Not what, *who*. Do we have an overhead projector in the building somewhere?"

"Call Tech, someone can get one for us, but why dontcha just tell us?"

"Better you see it for yourselves, not have me put any ideas in your heads. I mean, I could be wrong, but this way I'll know."

Harlowe called and requested an overhead projector, and then she turned to Frankie. "Sorry, Frankie, what did you find?"

"It's okay. I've been trying to connect our victims, particularly those from Oklahoma, and I found something. Amos, Mackey, and Anderson went to the same junior high near Marietta, and they rode the same school bus, which doesn't make them friends but it's a connection. I'm gonna venture a guess since it was a small school they *did* know each other; I mean, it's a reasonable assumption. These three were also close in age, born in 1978, '79, and '80. I checked on the junior high they attended, but it's no longer there because in April of '82, a tornado damaged a significant portion of the school. Seems they hadn't moved into the computer generation. Another interesting tidbit is while I was digging into the victims, we'd heard Trina Robinson was from Louisiana, but she wasn't from Louisiana originally."

Lefty frowned, asking, "And how does this tie into our case?"

Frankie tilted her head back to see him. "Would it interest you to know her parents lived on a farm a few miles outside of Marietta, Oklahoma?"

Kasper rocked back in his chair. "Well, I'll be damned. Ha! Maybe the Bureau should've passed this case to the Okie Feebies."

"Robinson lived in the same school district. It's probable she attended the same school. The summer before she turned sixteen, she ended up pregnant and they up and moved to Louisiana; seems her mom had family in Buras Triumph, Louisiana, and she was there until Katrina hit in 2005," Frankie explained.

"She was born in Oklahoma then?" asked Harlowe.

"No, they moved there when she was ten. Trina was born in Arkansas. Her mom met her dad when she was visiting friends for the summer. How she got to Oklahoma isn't the point; the point is she lived there, along with three of our other victims, that's the point."

"Not to sound repetitive by using the word *point*, Frankie, but that's an excellent point, "Kasper expressed.

"Knock–knock," a voice called as he stuck his head in the doorway. "Did someone request an overhead projector?" Tad from research wheeled in a cart.

"I did. Can you put it behind the table, over there?"

"You bet, Agent Bishop. Call when you're done and I'll come get it."

"Thanks Tad, I will." Harlowe waved with a brilliant smile and the young man blushed, waving back.

"Okay, Harlowe, the floor's yours." Kasper stretched out his arms, his eyes cut to the wall clock. If he got outta here soon, he'd have time for a quick shower and shave before heading to Fort Worth.

Bishop snapped off the overhead lights, walked to the projector, plugged it in, and placed the photo down. "Here goes nothing." She flipped the switch and on the white wall a photograph illumined enlarged as she fiddled with the knobs, adjusting the clarity as much as she could since the picture was old and worn. She tapped the last two faces with the end of the ruler. "Who does this look like?"

Lefty's eyes scrunched up and his shoulders heaved up then down. "Nobody I know, what about you guys?" He looked at Kasper then Frankie.

"Here, try this." Harlowe scooted the picture over. One side showed on the wall. She enlarged again as much as she could without distorting the faces.

"Well?"

Francine Ryder inhaled sharply. "I'll be damned."

"Okay, I give up. What are Left and I missing?"

"Look." Harlowe drew attention to the person on the end. "Does this face remind you of anyone? Like a fellow NAT from Quantico?"

Kasper walked up closer to scrutinize the face. "Huh, I'll be damned. Hello, Jay Greenberg, camp counselor at"—he moved the picture over to see the sign in the background—"Camp Dove Tail."

Lefty got a closer look. "So what? Everyone has a twin, and kids, especially teenagers, shit, we all look alike—tall, gangly, and goofy looking."

Harlowe's brows knitted. "Kasper, you think a man in law enforcement's involved with these murders?"

Bergman shrugged a blank look on his face. He needed to make a call, but wasn't gonna share his theory yet, so he asked, "Can you magnify the name tag?"

Harlowe tried. "No, it's too distorted."

"See if someone in Tech can work their magic."

"I'll check facial recognition too, see if we get a hit."

Lefty turned facing them. "A picture from what, twenty years ago, you know people change."

"He's right, Harlowe. Take it to the forensic artist, have him do an age enhancement," Frankie proposed.

"Push it to the top," said Kasper. "We need this shit sooner than later. It's a lot to ask, but let's go through all the photos again. This time, focus on older group pictures, set them aside and let's keep trying to reach Ernie Gorman."

"Yep, we're on it, no worries," Harlowe said, then, "Can you do something for me, Special Agent in Charge?"

Kasper looked her way. "What?"

"Call ahead, ask Dr. Lam if she's had lunch and if she hasn't eaten, take her somewhere because you need to eat. Go home first, shower, and shave; you look like hammered dog shit." A mischievous smile tugged at the corners of her mouth as she pulled at his arm to get him off his chair.

Kasper stood, stretched, and looked at his phone. If lunch was in the works he needed to hustle or he'd miss his window of opportunity.

Harlowe looked at the other two. "What did you guys make of that?"

"Make of what?" Lefty asked her.

"I asked Kasper a question, and he didn't respond."

"You mean if he thought our suspect worked in law enforcement?" Frankie stopped writing for a second to look at her.

"Yeah, and he didn't answer."

"Good gravy, you girls, he did to answer. He shrugged, to say he didn't know."

"That's not an answer, it a gesture, an answer's verbalized, and I know Kasper, he's got something on his mind and he isn't sharing."

"Come on, Harri, the guy's sleep-deprived and lovesick, cut him a break for not using his freaking words and using his shoulders instead."

"Hey," Frankie said, "let's let the guy do his thing. Whatever it is, I trust him.

Nikki Lam. He was going to see her again; this made him nervous and excited. Kasper wondered if she might even want to see him outside of a case. Or would she just like the idea of dating an FBI agent? Shit, he was a little paranoid, and he lacked the self-assurance of the average man. As an FBI agent he was confident as hell. Asking out an attractive woman triggered a nosedive in his self-confidence. Kasper shook it off. He was an FBI agent first, lovesick man second. Love and/or attraction needed to take the back seat. It'd all work out, or it wouldn't. These were the only two absolute truths.

Yukon in "reverse," he pulled out of the parking space and drove out of the gate, waving at the security officer as he made his turn onto Justice Way. He sped up while driving on Storey Lane, curving around to Loop 12, hitting Interstate 635 which was a direct shot to his apartment in Coppell.

The headlights came on as darker clouds gathered ahead of him. Eyes over the dash he stared at the skies, his hands resting on the steering wheel. Rain. It looked like rain or a solid storm. His gut clinched. Another storm he felt deep within—bad news, good news. It was an odd mixed feeling.

CHAPTER THIRTY-SEVEN

The hot shower was invigorating, and he felt better. Dark slacks, a light-gray pin-striped shirt, his official FBI jacket, keys, and phone in his pocket, and he was out the door.

In the Yukon, he made a corporate decision, and he sent a text to Nikki Lam's cell:

> Headed your way; if you haven't had lunch yet, can you wait? I'd like to buy you a burger before we get into the autopsy.

Best to ask now and if she's had lunch he'd wait and ask her another time, maybe to dinner. He waited with the Yukon's engine humming, expecting a response, hoping she wasn't knee-deep into the dead body and unable to respond. Two minutes...four minutes... hell, he should just go. Sitting here waiting was dumb. He needed to be on the road, even if she answered.

He backed out of his parking spot, put the Yukon in "drive" and just as he turned the steering wheel a message popped up on his dash. A text from Nikki Lam. Kasper grinned. He'd set her up as a contact so he'd know when this number popped up it was her. He hit the message box to read her text.

I'm starving, haven't stopped for lunch—got delayed and just started your autopsy. A burger sounds great. How long?

Forty-five minutes if traffic doesn't bottle up; looks like rain.

Drive careful, see you soon—Nik

Two things made his day. Both caused him to smile. She was gonna have lunch with him and she'd ended her text with Nik. Not Nikki or Dr. Lam, but a shortened version of her name. This was a promising sign. You had to begin as friends, right?

He made his way over to State Highway 121, hit the 183 Freeway and the TEXpress directly into Fort Worth. Traffic could've been worse since rain loomed ahead; he got lucky. Droplets hit every few minutes, less than a steady drizzle. It was a teasing rain, however, all the clouds in front of him said they weren't messing around. The bottom would fall out of the sky soon.

He'd made good time as his tires hit Rosedale Street heading toward South Main Street. It was almost two. The County Medical Examiner's Office was on 200 Feliks Gwozdz Place in the medical district of John Peter Smith Hospital. JPS, a county hospital, and the only Level One Trauma Center in Tarrant County at 1500 South Main Street, Fort Worth, Texas, had been operating since 1906.

Kasper turned off South Main on to Feliks Gwozdz and found a parking spot in front of the building, thankful parking was available. He inspected his face in the rearview and laughed at himself for acting like a girl. After checking the chamber of his Glock 17, he re-holstered, slipped on his jacket, and zipped it halfway. He took a deep breath, opened the door, stepped out onto the asphalt, hit the "lock" button on the fob, and walked to the front doors of the Tarrant County Examiner's office.

"Good afternoon. May I help you?" the receptionist asked.

"Dr. Lam's expecting me." He flipped open his badge, and with his boyish smile said, "I'm FBI Special Agent Kasper Bergman."

Her name tag read *Martha*. She looked at the blotter on her desk, tapping a short pink fingernail on today's date and a note written in the margin of her calendar.

"Well, yes, she is, Special Agent Bergman. Let me ring to the back." Martha made the call hanging up with a smile. "Grayson will be here in a minute. Would you like a coffee or water?"

"Thank you, Martha," he called her by name, "but no, nothing for me right now."

The doors behind the reception area opened and a young man wearing faded light-green scrubs, a surgical cap, and shoe booties over his tennis shoes walked in.

"Special Agent Bergman, I'm Grayson." He held out his hand. "Nice to meet you."

Kasper reciprocated. "You, too."

Kasper looked pointedly at Martha. "Thank you, Martha." Then, "Grayson, lead the way."

The autopsy technician's tennis shoes made a soft padded sound, as did the bottoms of Kasper's rubber-soled dress shoes on the tiled corridor. The hallway was longer than one might imagine. He followed the technician past offices and rooms where people were silently eating and working to keep up the pace of the job. Death didn't take a vacation or holiday. Nor did it sleep. Dealing with death was a never- ending business.

The hallway led to a block of offices toward the back. Just past the first door, Kasper saw the plaque on the wall next to the door:

Hiram Sinclair, Chief Medical Examiner, Tarrant County: 30 *Years of Service*

He'd heard Sinclair was planning to retire in five years. Hiram Sinclair was an older gent and after thirty years, why add another five, unless it was a financial issue? Kasper hoped his retirement plan kept him from chasing the bad guys on foot into his sixties! Another question popped in his head. Was Nikki in line to be the next duly appointed Chief Medical Examiner after Sinclair finally retired? Good for her, if so. Dr. Lam was a reasonably young woman in the position she now held and women made outstanding leaders, so why not a female Chief Medical Examiner? Television and books had women in these positions, why not in real life? Women in power never scared him. They were exciting.

Her office was two doors down. Grayson lightly rapped on the door. "Dr. Lam?"

"Come in, Grayson, is Agent Bergman with you?"

Kasper walked around the tech and into her office.

"Great to see you again, Dr. Lam, and I hope this is a proper greeting given the reasons I'm here." Kasper held out a hand, and she grabbed it firmly. His heart skipped a beat, and he hoped he didn't have a sappy look on his face.

"Of course." She chuckled. "Don't want people unhappy to see me." She waved a hand to encompass her office. "This *is* the morgue. It's understandable why most people aren't happy when they come to see me." Her eyes went to her autopsy tech. "Thanks for escorting Agent Bergman back, Grayson. Have you had lunch?"

"Yes, ma'am, took an early lunch. Want to get the reports on Ms. Hopkins finished, so I can call the mortuary to pick up her body—the family called again."

"Yep, another body out the door," Dr. Lam began and Grayson finished it for her, "Makes room for one more."

"Glad to hear you guys have a sense of humor."

"Gotta get back to work, Special Agent, it was nice meeting you. See ya later."

"You too, Grayson," Kasper uttered with an upward jerk of his head.

"Put a copy of the report on my desk, will ya, Gray?"

Grayson left, with a, "Yes, ma'am, soon as I'm done."

The duo was alone.

"Please, sit, Agent Bergman." Nikki dropped into her chair.

Kasper watched her from across her desk. Dr. Lam's slim shoulders, brows, and eyes lifted simultaneously. Her expression became melancholy. "It took me a while to laugh or smile when I started working in the ME's office because there was so much sadness and grief, not to mention the waste of lives taken unnaturally. One day, though, it fell into place and I understood I was here to speak for those who can no longer speak for themselves." She put up a small hand. "Yeah, I know all medical examiners quote this in movies and television, however, I believe it's the mantra of a medical examiner—we're the voice of the dead."

"Sounds like a book title or movie."

"What does?"

"The Voice of the Dead."

"Yeah, I guess it does. You gonna call Hollywood? You have connections?" she kidded him.

"Nah, amongst the sea of us unknowns, I'm a big fat nobody."

"We're nobody to most people, and somebody to a few. Everyone has someone who cares about them. This is where I feel I do my best, getting closure for those who lose a loved one. People get murdered in our city and the world couldn't care less. The people who care are my focus. It's my job to ease as much pain for them as I can."

"I love your dedication and drive. Reminds me of someone I know."

"Oh, really, who'd that be?" Nikki winked and somewhere deep inside his gut a few butterflies fluttered again.

He winked back when he answered, "Me. Now tell me, you got a good burger joint nearby, and please don't pick a fast-food place? I'm looking for a hole-in-the-wall place, serving greasy, fat cheeseburgers with all the fixings."

A smile flitted on her attractive face. "Yeah, there's a place, five or six miles off Granbury Road called Charley's Old-Fashioned Hamburgers. They make French fries, with the potato skin still on and hand-battered onion rings. The place is small. It reminds me of something out of the 50s sort of Al's Diner like in *Happy Days*."

Kasper stood laughing. "Sounds like what I'm looking for. Come on, I'm driving."

Dr. Lam grabbed her phone and purse. Trailing him out, she locked her door, and they walked through the hallway discussing the merits of fries opposed to onion rings and mustard versus mayo.

Over lunch, they talked about how they'd grown up and what schools they attended, odd jobs as teenagers, embarrassing moments in school, and their parents. Dr. Lam's grandparents were from Vietnam, her parents both young when they came to the United States, met while in college. She was a first generation Vietnamese American.

"They stationed my Pop in the United Kingdom, Guam, Italy, Bahrain, and he even did a short stint in Turkey. I don't remember these places because I was too young, so all I've got are vague memories of Guam and Bahrain. And to boot, I was only in elementary school so I went to school on base with the other army brats."

"A well-traveled man, hmm. Vietnam's a beautiful country and I've been there several times, as well as Mexico, Cabo, and Cancun during my college years, oh boy."

"I visited Mexico twice during college." Mexico. He considered Theo Sykes for a split-second. It was pointless to discuss Theo. He wouldn't put Nikki in the crosshairs of anything bad. He'd worried about this when he was with Erin. Was that the reason he wasn't in a steady relationship? It'd been two years since he'd broken it off with Erin. Could Theo Sykes be controlling this aspect of his life? He shrugged it off. This was worry for another time.

"How about we hash the good old days later? I gotta get back; you ready?"

"Yes, ma'am, I am."

"Agent, do you have a strong stomache?"

"Yeah, I promise I won't lose my lunch. Already been there and done that."

Nikki's brows rose in amusement. "Bet that was fun, puking right in front of your colleagues."

She thought he'd seemed fine last night, however, in the morgue, it was different. Who knew?

"Too many newbies upchucking, no one cared what the other guy was doing, much less was watching."

A solid laugh rumbled out of Nikki.

CHAPTER THIRTY-EIGHT

Gowned, masked, gloves on, shoe booties covering their shoes, Dr. Lam led Kasper into the autopsy room where Nora Mendez-Finch's body lay fully covered with a sheet and the Y-incision cut and sewn up before he arrived.

"She's been dead for at least eight weeks. How long was she reportedly missing?"

"Two months, so she died shortly after he abducted her, I take it."

"Here's where it gets real. You ready?"

He took a deep breath. "As I'll ever be."

Dr. Lam uncovered the upper section of the victim's body. Decomp was never attractive, no death was a pleasing sight, but without preamble Dr. Lam hit "record" and went into her monologue.

"White female, age thirty-two, height five-four and three inches, weight two hundred sixteen pounds. Body found wrapped five times over in thick landscaping sheeting, buried approximately four-feet deep in a shaded area. The body's putrefaction slowed only slightly. My best estimate of how long she has been dead would be approximately six to seven weeks. Can the FBI get me a forensic entomologist? The techs collected larvae, which can help determine a more exact time of death."

"I'll make a call."

She pointed to the victims' neck. "Upon examination I found a pair of undergarments, unknown but thought to belong to the decedent, twisted around the neck: cause of death, strangulation. She had a fractured hyoid, and upon closer examination of the undergarment, I discovered fiber particles consistent with tree bark. My conclusion is our killer used the underwear like a garrote and with the help of a tree branch or short limb he placed through the leg holes, the perpetrator twisted them with so much force it broke her hyoid." Dr. Lam stopped the recorder to look at Kasper. "Did you find a limb nearby? One he could've used to tighten the panties around her neck?"

"We didn't know to look, so I'll alert the Azle PD, ask them to go out and search. I'm thinking our killer's not just strong, but a good-sized man, don't you agree?"

A pensive look crossed her face. "Yes, I do." Her thumb pressed the record button, and she went on with her autopsy monologue. "From what I note, there appear to be what look like defensive wounds on her hands and face, which likely occurred while she tried to fight off her attacker during her strangulation. Her nails were short, either she bit her nails, or her killer cut them postmortem, thus removing any skin cells or other DNA we could've gotten. Cannot rule out conjunctival or facial petechial hemorrhaging as the decomposition stage is too far in its process to be definitive." She stopped recording again.

"I wanna do a look-see in her throat. You gonna be okay?"

He swallowed hard. "Yeah, but I see where your sink is."

Dr. Lam's shoulders shook as she held in her laughter as she went about doing her job. She placed the recorder on the table edge then hit "record," noting the victim's tongue size and the teeth either missing or decayed. With a light, she examined the inside of the mouth, swabbing the victim's inner cheek first, and then her nose. Nikki fed a tiny camera into the deceased's throat.

"On examination of the pharynx, I see no foreign bodies, just old blood, and possible vomit." She pulled the camera out setting it aside. "Not a real conclusion, but I think our victim was so sacred she got sick, but him choking her kept her from being able to vomit, thus, why there's vomit lodged in her throat—again, my guess only."

Pulling the sheet past the victim's navel and without preamble, she cut into the abdomen, flaying the back of the skin, readying to get to her stomach to collect the contents. Dr. Lam looked up. Kasper was a few shades of pale green and she stopped and repositioned the sheet to cover the entire body.

"What?" he asked.

"Your face, it's green, and I don't feel like seeing your burger for the second time."

"Whew, yeah, I agree, don't want you seeing it either. Be best if I leave you to it."

"I had her medical records sent over. Let's go to my office and discuss the findings. I'll finish the autopsy after you leave."

This suited him and he led them out into the hallway. He stripped off the gown, mask, booties, and hair covering, tossing them into the receptacle outside the doorway.

Hands washed and sanitized, Nikki took her place behind her desk motioning for Kasper to take a chair as she sifted through folders to find the one she needed.

"Nora Mendez-Finch's medical records—got 'em sent over this morning. I'm betting you didn't know she'd lost thirty-two pounds. Three months ago she weighed two-fifty-two."

"Diet pills?"

"Not prescription, over-the-counter diet supplements, think the divorce and the added stress caused most of her weight loss. Per her

OBGYN records, she and her husband had abstained from sex several years back."

"Are there signs of sexual activity? We think they're raped before he kills them."

"You have proof, DNA, sperm, anything on your other victims?"

He stopped to think, his eyes narrowed. Nora Mendez-Finch and Annelle Mackey were the only two victims that weren't just bones. Mackey's autopsy reported a rape swab was done, but it was inconclusive, and the others, well, how does one check for rape on bones? You don't or can't.

"They checked for rape on the Itasca woman and found trace amounts of semen, so it's hard to know if a rape occurred; it could have been consensual sex. We've been assuming sexual assault was involved, although this rings true most times."

She shrugged her slim shoulders. "Why do y'all assume this? Are all men who kill women considered rapists?"

Kasper thought for a second. She was right.

"No, you're right, they're not. Could be we're looking at it all wrong. I mean, we've been focusing on the letters as the means for our killer to find his victims, and—"

"Letters, what letters?"

Damn, she hadn't gotten the entire story, so he briefly clued her in.

"Makes sense, if they were love letters, I suppose." Her lips pressed in thought.

"Yes, so yeah, the letters mean something, but you're right, it doesn't mean our killer raped them."

"DNA found on the other victims?"

"Only on one victim, Trina Robinson. They discovered her locket, and we got hairs, but no hits in CODIS. Since they found our victims in a state where DNA was hard to collect, we have limited evidence to work with."

"Yeah," she stated, "bones don't give off much DNA other than the victim's. I did a scraping under Nora's nails, but I'm not hopeful."

"Was she raped?" he asked again.

Nikki's head moved in a small shake and tilted just a hair. "We'll do a rape kit, but without evidence of vaginal trauma it could've been consensual sex. Her health records state she was gravida two para two, meaning pregnant twice with two live births. Her records state both times she'd experienced substantial tearing during delivery, so there was scarring, but with the condition they found her body, no way to say for certain a rape took place. Wish I could give you more, but can't right now."

"What about her clothing? Find any foreign hairs, carpet fibers, anything?"

"Just started her autopsy and haven't had time to go over her clothing. I'll get it done and run a fine-tooth comb through it all. How about I call you later? I know you need to get back to your team and promise if I find something important, I'll call you. Right now, I'm obligated to finish Miss Nora so I can release her body tomorrow, and they're piling up in the cadaver fridge."

"Of course, and I appreciate your help on this." He again proffered his hand, and she took it with a twinkle in her eyes.

"Thanks for lunch and the good company. I thoroughly enjoyed it and hope we get to do it again."

"Me too, only let's make it dinner, okay?"

"I'd love to. Can you find your way out?"

"Yup, I think so, talk to you later."

Kasper waved goodbye, then turned to leave. Nikki walked back into the autopsy room. Both had silly little grins on their faces.

CHAPTER THIRTY-NINE

In the parking lot, leaning against his ride, Kasper dialed the Azle Police Department.

"Homicide, Mitcham."

"Hello, Detective, this is Agent Bergman."

"Hi, Agent Bergman, what can I do ya for today?"

He listened, his head nodding. "Sure, sure, I'll send patrol, get them to cover the area. What? Oh, no, Old Man, uh, Mr. Grantham's still in Bowie. I called him. He's staying in Bowie for a few more days. Gotta tell ya, he's wigged out with this entire ordeal. He gave me carte blanche to do whatever needs to be done, promised to drop by the station when he gets back."

Again, he listened. "Yes, absolutely, the man's a pillar of our community, I mean, I know it takes all kinds, but Mr. Grantham as a suspect, don't see it, but I'll get his statement and do it by the book."

"Thanks, Mark. If you find anything, get it over to Dr. Lam pronto, will ya?"

"Sure thing. Hope we catch this son of a bitch, uh, sorry."

"Yeah, well, I feel the same way, Detective. You nailed it the first time—he's a son of a bitch." Kasper clicked off unlocking the Yukon.

Once he started the engine and shut the door, his FBI brain went into thinking mode. His and Dr. Lam's discussion about rape echoed in his head.

Were these women raped, including Rayna Anderson? There was no definitive proof with zero DNA recovered since they had mostly skeletal remains of the others, making it impossible to pinpoint rape. He assumed the correspondence was a deliberate misdirection. Letters written by dead men or freed convicts with solid alibies. Was this a wild goose chase, and where would it end?

The connection to four of their victims was odd, but for it to fit together, all their victims had to connect somehow. They needed the connection each had to Mera Soon-Lee, if there was one. How did Nora Mendez-Finch, the Azle victim, connect to the others?

Kasper reflected on the letters uncovered in Mendez-Finch's car after she vanished. Upon reading them, he'd found nothing significant, just a meaningless exchange between two people with no relevance to the case. The letters uncovered with Mera Soon-Lee seemed unusual. Why her? Why did she have these letters? Was it a ruse? They needed to dig deeper into Miss Soon-Lee's past.

Kasper's theory: these letters were significant but only to the killer, not to their case. Was this perpetrator playing them, running them around in circles to make them look like fools? Did FBI stand for Foolish Bureaucratic Imbeciles?

The trip back to Dallas was taking longer because of the rainstorm. Thankfully, he'd been on the TEXpress lanes when the torrential waters poured from the sky. Hitting his hands free, he called Harlowe's cell.

"Hiya, Bergman, you still in Fort Worth?"

"No, driving in this crappy rain, headed back."

"Did you take Dr. Lam to lunch?"

Kasper could hear the smile on Harlowe's face.

"Yes, I did, it was very nice. And no, in case your next question is did we talk about work, we didn't, so there."

A laugh sounded on the other end, then, "Good for you, damn it! Will there be another meal?"

Thankfully, she couldn't see him blushing. "I told her we should do lunch again, only make it dinner, and she said okay, so yeah, I'm gonna see her again."

"Marvelous, you needed this, make you feel human again, not like a robot FBI agent."

"Yep, and you need to practice what you preach." Another call beeped in; it was Nikki Lam. "Hey, gotta call you back, Dr. Lam's calling."

"Uh-huh, she misses you already. See ya." With a tiny giggle, Harlowe hung up before he could respond.

"FBI, Bergman."

"Agent Bergman, Dr. Lam. Have you made it back to Dallas?"

"No, I haven't. Traffic's slowed because of a short monsoon, which turned into steady rain, and now there's a fender-bender on 635, and I'm stuck in a turtle crawl. You find something?"

"I've been processing the other items found with our victim; oh, and before I forget, Detective Mitcham called. They found two limbs and someone's bringing them in for me to process. We'll check for fibers to match to the undergarment and I'll see if the lab can get prints, but wood is porous. See if they can superglue fumes but don't hold your breath."

"That was quick. I'll have to thank Detective Mitcham for being so fast. As far as holding my breath, I won't, and thanks for asking them to try. Did you find anything else?"

He hadn't been gone but about thirty minutes, but hey, an FBI agent could dream.

"Yes."

"You did, really? I'm impressed. That didn't take you long."

"No distractions."

Kasper heard the smile in her words and his face flushed pink.

"Oh, well I, uh, okay, then. Tell me whatcha found."

"Well, for starters, I found a few hairs which weren't Ms. Mendez-Finch's on her shirt; two have roots intact. That's good news. Here's a kicker for you, though—I also found semen."

Kasper's brow dipped in question, but he was quiet.

"Agent Bergman? You still there?"

"Yeah, sorry. Guess I'm a little stunned. You found it on her, physically?"

"Yes, just not in the conventional place you'd normally get semen."

"Where exactly did you find it?"

"Behind her right ear. I've sent a sample to our lab, along with the hairs."

"How did you discover it behind her ear?"

"When you mentioned rape was a likely scenario, I did some reading about serials and their victims, how men like Kemper, Luis Garavito, Dahmer, and the Green River Killer, Gary Ridgway, and they all confessed to necrophilia of some fashion. Made me wonder if your guy would ejaculate on his victim, inciting another sexual release after the murder. I got my Wood light out and checked her clothing and found some at the edge of her shirt collar. Then I examined the flesh at the nape. Found it around her earlobe, of all places, and several hairs on her shirt. Likely hers, by the color, but I'll test to be certain."

"You think she was dead when he did this?"

"Yes, I think so. There were postmortem bruises on her chest. My opinion only is he kneeled on her chest while he did his deed on her face. Not a fact, just what I think."

"This is the first good news we've had. I could kiss you." The words popped out and his face reddened. "Dr. Lam, I, uh, well—"

"Agent Bergman, I might need to give you the news next time in person if I'm gonna hold you to any kissing." There was a bright smile in her voice.

Silence again, but short-lived. They laughed in unison.

"Sounds like a plan. Finally, we've got something to tell the team...uh, not about the kissing stuff," he jabbered embarrassingly. "Hey, uh, listen, can I call you later?"

"I'd like that."

"Me too, so see ya later, or talk to you sooner, whichever happens first, Nikki."

"You got it, Kasper, and if anything new pops up, I'll call. Bye." Dr. Lam hung up, grinning. Kasper's own smile was from ear-to-ear as he clicked auto call. "Call Task Force Room."

"FBI, Bishop."

"It's Bergman."

"So, how's Dr. Lam?"

"Fantastic and finding evidence."

"Great to hear, what'd she find?"

"Detective Mitcham found two limbs which could've been used to tighten the underwear around the victim's neck, like a garrote. He's taken both limbs to the lab and Nikki's gonna match fibers from the underwear for comparison, get the lab to superglue both limbs, see if they can get prints, and there were hairs not belonging to Mrs. Mendez-Finch found, two with roots intact."

"What else? There's more, isn't there? Spill."

"Dr. Lam found semen."

"He raped her, then?" Harlowe frowned.

"No." Then he replayed Dr. Lam's story, blushing a tad when he repeated the part about the suspect jacking off on the victim's face and it streaming behind her ear.

"Interesting."

He was quiet.

Harlowe tapped the mouthpiece of the landline. "Kasper?"

"Uh-huh, I'm here."

It was then she realized this might've embarrassed him, telling her some man jacked off spewing semen on a dead woman's face.

"Hey, buddy, I've worked cases where they've found evidence in weirder places. Did I ever enlighten you about the time we found some se—"

"Okay, okay, stop it! I've never discussed this stuff with a woman."

"Hey, this stuff's old hat, you know. Since I've been in the sex trade, I've seen it all."

"Damn it, Harlowe! Good grief." Kasper was happy to hear humor in her tone, a good sign she was overcoming her sorrow—joking about the sex trade without crumpling into tears.

CHAPTER FORTY

"What I'm saying is even if Dr. Lam tries pushing the DNA and hairs to the head of the line, we won't get results any faster. Shit, this ain't like TV and a forty-five-minute crime drama."

"Lord, Lefty, you're preaching to the entire Tabernacle Choir. We know how it works, crud." Harlowe tucked her hair behind her ears, stretched her arms outward, and wriggled her fingers to get the blood flowing again.

Frankie went to the whiteboard rolling it closer to her desk, sitting with her butt against the edge of the desk. "So, here's what we have: four victims—Anderson, Mackey, Amos, and Robinson. They could've known each other. I'm going out on a limb to say their paths have crossed. Think about it. Marietta, Oklahoma, has a population of less than three-thousand, Ardmore with around twenty-four-thousand, is also a reasonably small town."

Lefty rolled his chair back, swiveling around to face Frankie, crossing his arms over his chest. "Here's a major oddity. I can't find any social media for them. No Facebook, not even a Myspace. Any emails I've found were either work-related or nothing leading us to anything usable. Seems there's no one to ask. Family members apparently know diddly-squat, so this makes me feel like we've hit a brick wall."

"So, somehow Oklahoma connects these four victims. Soon-Lee and Mendez-Finch don't seem to have an Oklahoma connection. Makes them the odd men out," Kasper said. Then, "I think we've got to take these two women and a huge shovel, dig to China to find anything connecting them to the others."

"Alright, Big Kahuna," Lefty wisecracked, "dole out assignments. We need to get to work."

"Work Soon-Lee's financials from her first credit card to her last. Look into her checking and savings, see if she had a 401K. Call the Social Security office, check out every job she ever had, then what bills she had. Look into where she spent her money, did she travel? Did she have any hobbies?"

Lefty answered, "I'm on it."

"Frankie, dig into her school life from kindergarten to college degree. Search family vacations and girls' trips. See if you can locate her sorority sisters, and keep trying Cal Thompson, the investigative reporter."

Frankie jotted notes. "You got it, Kasper, I'll dig."

"Okay, Bergman, whatcha want me to dig into?"

"Harlowe, dig into Nora Mendez-Finch, her financials, then up to her last year as a high school junior. She didn't work many jobs because she was a stay-at-home mom. Dig into her marriage and into Stanley Finch. He could be a link somehow. Who knows?"

"Got it." Then she asked, "Kasper, what are *you* gonna dig into?"

"Mera Soon-Lee's life, see if I can locate her father...was told he moved back to Korea."

Harlowe shifted in her chair. "Her mother's ill, that's the story I heard."

"Mera's disappearance had a severe impact on her health, resulting in a prolonged period of depression which lasted three years. After discovering her remains, Mrs. Soon-Lee fell to pieces completely. She was never herself again." This was something Bergman found heartbreaking.

Frankie glanced at them. "Were her parents still together until then?"

Kasper's head shook. "They'd separated a year after Mera vanished but Mr. Soon-Lee stayed in Austin, put all his stuff into storage, and then he rented a small apartment. Her mother, Gladys's, mental state deteriorated after the funeral. Mera was their only child."

"Sad business when a child doesn't outlive a parent." Harlowe thought about Monica. Her cousin was in the afterlife with her own mother; it was the only comforting thought she could muster.

"Do you think it's worth trying to talk to Mera's mom? I'll make the call, seems these days bad news is what I deal with." Sadness clouded Harlowe's eyes.

Bergman rubbed the back of his neck. "Anything is worth a shot I suppose, but use your best kid gloves, got me?" Kasper locked eyes with her. "I'd hate to be the one who pushes her over the edge, know what I mean?"

"Yes, I know what you mean, and I'll be sympathetic. After what I've just gone through, I have that empathy."

To most it was tedious work, but because this was what they did, they loved it. It was challenging research and putting puzzle pieces together, albeit they hated the reasons they had to do it. Financials—your typical spending, small paychecks, large credit card bills, borrowing from Peter to pay Paul, and not having two Buffalo head nickels to rub together, much less two cents to save in an old-fashioned piggy bank.

From grammar school to high school graduation, for those who graduated, it was the same-ole-same-ole. Minor school infractions from cutting class to being caught up in a cafeteria food fight, which was what got Nora Mendez-Finch suspended from school for a week. Soon-Lee, an Honor Roll student, worked on the school paper, had geeky friends, voted Most Beautiful Girl in high school. She'd been to Korea several times since her father was a native and got his US citizenship before she had turned five. Both women had semi-normal lives. Frankie, Lefty, and Harlowe were exasperated at not finding anything to connect them to the victims in the State of Oklahoma.

Papers in hand, Harlowe went to make a fourth pot of coffee. It was three o'clock and the end-of-day sinking sensation kicked in, so she made their java stouter. She read as the coffee brewed, tapping her foot on the carpet nervously, shuffling the first page to the back, reading the second page, her brows crinkling up. "Hey, how about this? Nora Mendez-Finch had a great-great uncle, and guys, listen: he was a Choctaw Indian, on her mother's side, plus, guess where he's buried?"

Lefty's eyes were glued to his computer. "Choctaw, huh? Is he buried in Ardmore, Oklahoma?"

"In Marietta, but that's close enough, dontcha think? "

Kasper's eyes rolled up to see her. "Bring me a cup of Joe, will ya, please? Her great-great-uncle's funeral was when?"

"Nineteen-ninety-five; Nora was fourteen. "

"Is this our connection? Nora met these other victims at a frigging funeral? It seems absurd," Frankie commented.

"Harlowe," Kasper addressed her. "How did you come by this information?"

"There are a few websites we can use without a warrant. Three I looked at were GED Match, Family Tree DNA, and Family Search. I found this on Family Search. Do you believe it?" This amused her.

"Gotta love it, plus, no hassle getting a warrant, like with Twenty-Three and Me, or Ancestry.com, makes this perfect." Lefty shoved his chair back and stood up to stretch out his kinked-up legs.

"Tons of ways for people to trace things these days if you're willing to pay the fee. You can get background checks on a date or an evil neighbor."

"Good job, Harlowe," said Frankie, then, "At least we've got Nora in the same state as the others. We just gotta connect them." She looked at Kasper. "I've got a question."

"What?"

"This crap with Preston Munn and the pen pal stuff, you think it has anything do with our case?"

Bergman focused on the back wall thinking about how to respond.

"These letters are important, but only to our killer. But it's the *why* I haven't figured out yet."

Lefty let out a wide yawn. "So, whoever wrote the letters didn't directly address the victims by name. Means nobody was writing letters to anyone and all this pen pal shit was just a ruse?"

"Think about it," Kasper stated. "Each letter was associated with a convict who is dead, illiterate, or paroled with a rock-solid alibi. The letters found with Mera Soon-Lee weren't written to her directly, but she had them in her possession—it's the *why* I can't wrap my head around unless she was researching a story, and even then I can't confirm that's the reason she had them. The convicts that allegedly wrote the letters were old men. She'd never been interested in them romantically, or as friends. Every bone in my body is telling me these letters only mean something to the killer, absolutely squat to our cases, just a bogus lead."

"I guess we wasted our time talking to Munn, and I'm also assuming we don't need to worry about the hush-hush shit going on in the prisons."

"Oh, I still want to know, Frankie. I'd like to know if it's helped the Bureau, and how."

Harlowe retorted, "Good luck with that, because there's no one to ask."

Kasper didn't comment, although he had one person he wanted

to ask. If he was told it was none of their business, then sure, they didn't need to know. Instead, he said, "How about we call it a day?"

It wasn't five o'clock yet, and they had no specific quitting time, but his team needed to relax their brains and recharge their bodies.

"You gotta date tonight?" Harlowe harassed him about Dr. Lam again.

"Nah, just need to take a break, eat, and recharge. Start over in the morning. Harlowe, I have some personal errands to run. Can you Uber back to my apartment?"

Her eyes widened in question. What did Bergman have up his sleeve?

"Yep, no prob, and hey, should I check into getting a hotel and a rental? Don't want to cramp your style, Bergman."

"I'll see about getting you a rental. Then you can stop Ubering, but as far as cramping my style, Bishop, I'm not a sleep-around kinda guy. I just met Dr. Lam, and anyway, we're working a case. So stop, okay?"

"Fine, I'm just saying."

"Super, now that's settled, see y'all tomorrow."

Frankie and Lefty didn't dawdle. They were on their feet, Harlowe on their heels. She looked back. "You coming, Kasper, I'll hold the elevator?"

"Nah, y'all go on, I'm gonna dump the coffee, clean up a bit. See you later."

"Right, see ya later." Harlowe was smarter than he gave her credit for. He was gonna stay and work, and he wanted to do it alone. His working all the time drove her nuts, but it was how he'd worked in Houston with the HPD too. Technical people did their best work alone and Kasper was at heart still a tech geek.

CHAPTER FORTY-ONE

No one to distract him, Kasper dug more into the life of Mera Soon-Lee. Her medical records showed a healthy twenty-six-year-old, on the pill, sexually active he guessed. Next, her phone records for the last year she was alive. No anomalies jumped out and since she researched for an investigative reporter, no telling who she might've called. *Reverse Number Lookup.* The thought ran through his mind.

Off his chair, he wriggled his arms, stretching them overhead. He interlaced his fingers, popping his arms from left to right, and rolled his neck. His legs were stiff, and he squatted, placing his hands on his upper thighs, doing it a few times to get the kinks out, and then he did a full body stretch which brought on a full-on yawn.

He walked around the desks three or four times just to be moving. He needed to get to the gym. Or go jogging. Work at keeping in shape. He'd failed miserably at keeping a routine. He stopped at Lefty's desk, pulled out the chair and scanned the papers his fellow agent had left strewn over his desk—Mera Soon-Lee's bank records and credit card charges. Agent Sebastian had been combing through these accounts and each page he'd completed he'd marked with an X in red Sharpie at the top and placed it facedown in a pile just to his left. Kasper turned over the top page. Lefty highlighted items putting them in categories: general merchandise, fuel, food, bills, car payment, school loans. Normal purchases—nothing shocking. He scanned the last few pages Lefty had examined; nothing popped. Kasper took the stack, thumbing through, looking at dates and charges on her bank card for a trip to Oklahoma, Ardmore to be exact. Again, it didn't connect her to the others in their youth. Why was she in Ardmore, Oklahoma? There was a notation to the side: *Contacted the Austin American Statesman; was not working a new story with Cal Thompson—still working the serial rapist story.*

Kasper pondered the idea that perhaps her trip was a vacation. But a vacation alone to Ardmore, Oklahoma, not knowing anyone, didn't seem right. Ardmore wasn't the single person's hot vacation spot, unless she was hitting the casinos from Thackerville to Ardmore, but nothing in her personal history said she was an ardent gambler. Mera hadn't known Mackey, Amos, Anderson, or Robinson back in her youth. She lived in Austin with her parents and went to school in Austin, including college. A visit to Oklahoma in her late twenties didn't connect her to the others; it was pure coincidence. Or was it?

He kept digging, this time into her love life. Reports stated she'd been dating Jason Wallen, a vice detective with the Austin PD when she'd gone missing and it had devastated him. He went through grief counseling and because he was so emotional, he missed taking his Sergeant's exam.

Kasper dug into the officer's background and personnel jacket, but found he'd left the Force with no forwarding information. The man dropped out of society without a trace. It was a shame since the officer had a stellar police service record and a few accommodations to his name. Sometimes he wondered how Detective West, his mentor, coped with losing a loved one. His girlfriend of two years got raped, then murdered. It took an especially strong individual to face that kind of tragedy; however, with some people like Mera's mom, heartbreak of this nature put them in a six-foot grave with their eyes still open and them still breathing. No life left for the living.

After all these years, where did Austin Vice Detective Jason Wallen end up? Kasper knew Wallen wasn't still on the Force in Austin. So, where was he? What had happened to him? No one, not his commanding officer nor his fellow vice detectives, and nobody in Human Resources knew where he was. Wallen's 401 monies were cashed out, taxes and early withdrawal fees paid, checking accounts closed, no credit cards or credit card bills, utility bills, or any bills in Wallen's name. No rentals or cars, nor car insurance either. No traces the man ever existed. This was odd, but loss and grief sent a person over the top. Feasibly he could be living on a beach or another continent these days. Digging into his family history, or what he could find, Kasper learned the guy had two brothers and their father died of cirrhosis of the liver.

Matthew Wallen's whereabouts—no known address, only a PO Box, and he was supposedly on disability from a work injury, and Dennis Wallen deceased. It was a sad state of family affairs concerning these brothers and their father with no mention of their mother—another oddity. Kasper wanted to talk to Jason since he'd been dating Mera before she went missing then found dead. Drumming his fingers on the desk, he wondered how he might find this man. Pages and pages of Mera's phone numbers stared him in the face; one had to be Jason's number. There was a cell number listed in the HR records for the Austin Police Department. After two minutes, an elderly woman answered. She'd never heard of Jason Wallen, another dead end.

Kasper picked up a stack of photos Lefty was searching through. After he straightened the stack, he shuffled through them again. Something was nagging at him—the photo from Camp Dove Tail and the question, *who took the photo*? With his foot propped on Lefty's desk, he leaned back looking at each picture, paying close attention to all group photos.

He found more photos. Summer pictures taken in a backyard,

pictures at the lake, pictures of them sitting on the tailgate of an old faded blue Ford pickup and...Kasper's leg slid off the corner and he leaned forward staring at the photo. The license plate on the back of the truck glared at him. Who owned this truck?

After typing the plate number into the Oklahoma DMV, he hit "enter," and it popped up quickly. The truck registered to Theodore Robinson back then. Robinson, as in Trina Robinson? It must've been her who took the Polaroids. According to Frankie's research, she moved to Oklahoma at ten years old. So, was this the connection? He returned to his desk with the files on Trina Robinson and started searching the computer database for birth records in Arkansas. Keying in her information, it didn't take long to find out Trina's father was Theodore Cleveland Robinson, and her mother, Elbie Ann Robinson. Frankie said they lived on a farm after moving to Oklahoma. He looked at the picture again. Yes, there was farmland in the background. Trina Robinson was definitely part of this little group of kids.

Robinson conceived her son while living in Oklahoma right before she turned sixteen. She didn't get married until she was twenty-two and never had more children. Who was Tobias's father? His biological father was in Oklahoma, and the kid's last name was Robinson, like his mother and grandfather. He dug through Trina Robinson's file and pulled out the info on her son, looking for a phone number. He dialed the number listed and got a message that the number was no longer in service. Shit. He tapped his foot on the floor under the desk as he thought. Okay, her parents moved them to Buras Triumph, Louisiana, and she'd been pregnant, so chances are her son was born there. It only took him five minutes to pull up a birth certificate for one Tobias Robinson, born in Buras Triumph, Louisiana, mother Trina Elbie Robinson, father unknown. Well, shit. Another ball of string to untangle; he needed to talk to this kid.

They'd finished with Annelle's photo albums, family photos, and school photos of her son, and they were of no use to them. Time to re-box the crap and take it back to Ernie Gorman. Kasper lifted the empty box to put stuff back and as he upended it, a yellowed envelope slid out from under the flap of the box. Inside were six old photos. One kid stood in the back of the blue Ford pickup. He flipped the photo looking for names written on the back. He was in luck. In faded blue ink were the names: *J, Gloria, Den, RJ, Matty and me, but no RJ*. He must have been taking the picture this time, because the person titled as "me" was Trina Robinson. Kasper looked at the next photo. This time Annie was missing and RJ, Den, Matty, Trina, Gloria, and another girl called Silly. Who the heck was Silly? Whoever she was, she was Hispanic with light-brown skin, dark hair, and dark eyes. She wasn't in any other photos they'd seen. Was she new to their group?

The next picture was just the boys—Den, J, Matty, RJ. Okay, not too hard to figure out, and one of the girls was taking the shot. Picture number four was of six kids, coupled up, lounging on the wraparound porch of the old farmhouse. Kasper leaned in, squinting. It was J, with his arm around Gloria, Den with his arm around Trina, and RJ next to the Hispanic girl they called Silly. He turned it over to see if he'd gotten it right. Shit, he had, and shit, Silly wasn't Hispanic. She was Indian, Choctaw to be exact, and her name was Sylvia. Her nickname was Silly. The fifth photo was of just the girls—Annie, Gloria, Silly AKA Sylvia, and Trina. What's the story behind these kids?

Kasper lifted the Polaroid from Camp Dove Tail, whispering, "So, Trina, you're the photographer, aren't you? And who was your baby's father? What secrets did you take to your grave? Is this why someone killed you?"

He lifted the group photo from the campgrounds again, staring hard at the name tag on the youth counselor's shirt, and hoped Tech could enhance it because the age-enhanced drawing got them squat—just an older version of someone who looked familiar, nothing solid. The picture old and distorted, the color fading, it could have been any teenage boy. Yet this bugged him. The camp closed years later, then turned into a water park, mini-golf and arcade center now named Fun-N-Sun. Who'd owned Camp Dove Tail back then? He got busy with Internet searching, Better Business Bureau, old business archive, county, and state property tax sites. He looked up Camp Dove Tail, which had no active website. Then he researched the sale of land in the area and got lucky. Camp Dove Tail's last adventure was in 1994. Its owner got sick in 1996 and the place closed for good. After his passing, in 1999, they sold the land to a developer. Great, he had a starting point—the realtor's name who listed the property. Kasper prayed the realtors were still active. After dialing the number, he got voicemail: "*You've reached the real-estate office of Tim and Natalie Clark. Leave your number we'll get back to you. If this is about the acreage for sale near Leeper Lake, please call Terry Stone's office at...*"

Kasper left his name and cell number but not the fact he was FBI.

It was almost eight. Crud, he'd hoped the realtor would call back, but who was he kidding? Shit, people worked lots of hours these days, but they also had lives. These days, all he did was work. It'd been that way since he and Erin broke it off. Once the relationship newness wore off, all they'd had was work. He wondered if it might end up the same with Nikki.

With closed eyes, he ran his fingers through his hair popping his neck from side to side, feeling ten years older than he actually was, wondering if this job was going to age him and turn him into a tired, worn-out, old man before he hit forty. A sigh blew out between his partially opened lips, and he let his body go slack. It was time to go home; he'd done all he could and needed to follow the advice he'd given his team—take a break, eat, recharge, start over tomorrow, bright and early.

CHAPTER FORTY-TWO

Lights out, Kasper stood facing the task room. The softer lights illuminated the room, casting a soft shadow over the whiteboard. The pictures of the victims' faces were barely discernible and as in death, soon their images would disappear, but somehow, not for him. Deep in the recesses of his memories he knew he'd be able to conjure each victim's image as the years passed. It was a talent he wished he didn't have.

As he turned the doorknob, the landline rang. Who'd be calling at this hour? He stepped to his desk, noting the extension was from within the building. Who the hell was still working?

"Bergman."

"Hi, Bergman, it's Fitzhugh in Tech. Hey, I wasn't sure anyone would be here."

"Hey, Fitz, what's up? Why you still here, man?"

"My wife's outta town and I got nuttin to go home to except a house that echoes and a Hungry Man TV dinner. Listen, you headed out, or you got a few?"

"Whatcha got?"

"You know the old photo you're working with?"

"Yeah, why?"

"I did some more work on it. Can I come up and show ya?"

"Well, if you don't, I'm gonna hafta hunt ya down. Yeah, I'll be here."

"Cool." Fitz hung up. Kasper turned the overhead lights back on and waited.

The door opened softly and Leland Fitzhugh stuck his head in. "Bergman?"

With a wave of his hand, Kasper beckoned him to come in.

"Hey, Fitz, nice to see ya," Kasper said and offered his hand.

"You too, Agent Bergman, and I gotta ask, why are you here so late? Don't you have a life either?"

"Hey, you gotta life. I mean a wife-life. Hell, I ain't even got a girlfriend."

"Yeah, and did I mention we're expecting our first baby?"

"That's great, Fitz, congratulations."

"Yeah, we're super excited."

"So, what's up with the photo?" Kasper got back to business.

"The color was super faded and the picture so old it was hard to enhance as it was. You know how they colorize old black-and-white films?"

"Yeah, I know the concept."

"It's already a color photograph, so I tried tinting each part with the color it appeared to be, and I did this after enlarging the photo five times. It was too much, so I decreased, then gradually began increasing. Each time I re-tinted color I enlarged the photo, then I took the section with the dude wearing the name tag, which was what you needed and I cropped it out, to keep working that area."

Fitz pulled the photo out of a folder, handing it to him. "Does this help?"

Enlarged, the colors were not vibrant but unquestionably clearer and more defined. Kasper's eyes widened. In the cropped photo stood a younger and much thinner Annelle Mackey, next to her, RJ, the former Ray Anderson, but it was the teenager next to Annelle that grabbed his attention—that and his name tag: *Jason Wallen, Teen Counselor*.

"Is this my copy, Fitz?"

"Yeah, and I can make more. Does this name tag help? If you want me to improve his face, I can work on it further."

Kasper clapped Fitz on the shoulder. "This is perfect, Fitz. You do great work, man, and yeah, the name helps a lot."

A smile crossed Leland's face. "Thanks, I'm happy I could help; seems sometimes us tech guys don't get to help like we want, but I imagine you understand, since you were a tech on the Houston Police Force back in the day, right?"

"Once a geek, always a geek, I'm afraid. You're right, techs work behind the scene so much no one knows we're there. Sometimes anonymity is good, though, especially if the bad guy's still out there." Theo Sykes crossed his mind for a nanosecond. No sense dwelling on this, nothing he could do about it.

"Thanks, man, appreciate you. I believe it's about time for me to go home and have a TV dinner, a few cold beers, and catch the highlights of the hockey game." They shook hands and Leland Fitzhugh left, satisfied he'd helped the team.

Kasper stared intently at the person's face and name tag. Was it possible? This photo was taken around 1997, twenty-one years ago; these kids would have been in their mid-teens, maybe older. He scrutinized the face closely, squinting. The resemblance was uncanny, so perhaps there was a twin for everybody.

His cell rang. Clark Realty popped up on the ID.

"Hello."

"Kasper Bergman?"

"This is he."

"Tim Clark. You called?"

"Yes, I did, I'm FBI Special Agent Kasper Bergman—"

"Oh, man, am I in trouble?"

Kasper jumped to the purpose of his call, squelching the realtor's fears, and went into his questions. Tim Clark gave him what he could, which wasn't much.

"I'm sorry I couldn't be of more help, Agent Bergman, but there was no need to keep any of Camp Dove Tail's records after it closed." Tim Clark kept talking. "Not like the incident at the cabin...stuff like that has to be disclosed legally."

"What incident was this?"

"This happened at Leeper Lake, a suicide. Young man shot himself in the head. Sad thing was he did it in front of his brother and the place stayed vacant. Afterward, only the owner used the cabin, but he died this past spring, and his widow wants to sell the place."

"That's terrible," Kasper responded.

Mr. Clark, the talkative type, went on. "Yep, his brother was a cop, a detective, or something from the Austin area. Oh, lemme see, this was back in, uh, 2011. Seems this brother had some mental issues or depression, least it's what I'd heard. Oops, listen, that's my other line, gotta catch this call, but hey, if you're looking to buy, gimme a call anytime." Clark clicked off, and a dial tone rang in Bergman's ear.

He picked up the photo. Could this be happening? Jason Wallen and Jay Greenberg were the same person? "Okay, okay, okay," he muttered under his breath, "one step at a time."

On a piece of paper he wrote *Jason Wallen*, then the names connected to him: Mera Soon-Lee, Rayna Anderson, Trina Robinson, Annelle Mackey, Sylvia Amos, and Nora Mendez-Finch, although Nora was not directly linked to him. She'd been in Marietta, Oklahoma, at the same he'd lived there. It meant nothing, though, or did it? His brows dipped. How would Wallen connect to these deaths? It made no sense. He had no grievances with these kids, they were friends, and Mera, heck, he was dating her and they were supposedly in love.

As he fixated on the names, Mera's rang out in his head, and he went to her files. He flipped to her missing person's report three days after no one had heard from her, then to the interviews. He hunted for Jason Wallen's statement and as his fingers slid over the page, he stopped on two words: Huntsville Prison. In Jason's interview, he'd said he'd been out of town for work. Kasper read, *Detective Wallen's statement confirmed by his commander, Det. Wallen was in Huntsville Texas at the State Penitentiary at the time of Ms. Soon-Lee's alleged abduction. Wallen was attending a new training program being launched by the FB, and he was there for four days. The Bureau confirmed this.*

Kasper dug extensively into Jason Wallen. The guy had vanished completely, and now he knew why, or suspected why. It was because Wallen was Greenberg, but why'd he change his name? Made no sense, and hadn't the Bureau done its due diligence when vetting him before Quantico? No way could Jason Wallen or Jay Greenberg have pulled one over on them—or could he? No human was infallible. People got duped every day. On the hour or the minute, every second —paperwork forged, misplaced, or misfiled; people lied, or lied for each other—this crap happened constantly. Government employees, DEA, CIA, political staff, law officers, lawyers, prison guards or even wardens. Bad eggs of all kinds in every walk of life, every corner of the world, there was someone who lied to you, for you, or about you. He had proof of this in his own past. Theo Sykes, a lawman, had been a good guy turned into a murderous hitman. In some ways, Jason Wallen, AKA Jay Greenberg, was like Theo Sykes. Kasper knew he was dealing with a sociopath.

"Exercise caution with some of your classmates." Had Dan Robbs suspected something was off with Greenberg?

He had to talk to Dan and needed the help of one other man, but it'd have to wait until tomorrow. Both men were an hour ahead, and it was late.

CHAPTER FORTY-THREE

FBI Building, One Justice Way, 6:30 am.

Bergman never figured he'd be calling the guy, not after Quantico. He hoped the man had gotten over whatever bug he had up his ass and wouldn't act like a complete dickwad. Hell, he didn't even know which field office they assigned the guy to. Alone in the office, he waited while his computer came to life. He entered his password and as soon as the FBI seal popped up, he began clicking.

On the drop-down menu, he clicked on "Field Agent Directory," and watched the screen flicker, change to a directory of agents by last name, and then he typed in "Townsend." The screen jumped to Townsend, Michael B., current location: satellite office in London, Kentucky, personal cell number, and office information, 312 area code. Mick kept his Chicago number, no reason to change a cell number these days.

London, Kentucky.

Typing in London, Kentucky, he held in a laugh. The population was just over eight thousand; Mick was probably going batshit crazy there. He read on. London, Kentucky, was a small town located two hours from the bustling metropolis of Louisville, and two hours from Butcher Hollow, the birthplace of Loretta Lyn, the First Lady of country music. In addition, it's two hours away from the smallest town in Kentucky—South Park View—which had a whopping population of only seven residents. These were Bluegrass Country towns, near the Appalachians, not at all a Mick Townsend type of environment, unless he was dealing with any types like, oh, the movie *Deliverance.* He was probably bored out of his mind, but hell, these days, who knew? Was Agent Townsend breaking down illegal whiskey stills?

He scrolled to his contacts and clicked on Dan Robbs' number. On the fifth ring, voicemail kicked in. *"Hey, this is Dan Robbs. Leave a name a number and a brief message; I'll get back to you when I can."*

"Dan, Kasper Bergman. Got an issue I'd like to discuss. Call me."

Tapping his foot on the carpet, he contemplated his next call, thinking about the Blue Wall. How would Mick react to him asking about his ex-roommate along with the supposition he was possibly involved in murder? It had been close to five years since he'd had any dealings with either man. Had Mick and Greenberg stayed close? He had to give this some thought and not jump to any conclusions.

London, Kentucky was a small town. How long had Townsend been there? Back into the files, he scrolled through Mick's field office locations. He'd started in Marion, Arkansas, was there for two and a half years before they moved him to Selma, Alabama, and he spent two years there until they moved him to Pikeville, Kentucky, six months ago. None of these offices were the metropolitan type Mick had always hoped for. Mick wanted to be in either Washington or his hometown of Chicago. Kasper wondered what happened causing them to move the guy from not one but two small resident agencies to an even smaller one. Might be a touchy subject, could be it would embarrass Mick. It was none of his business if the guy was less than stellar. If Dan called back, he was gonna ask him first. Then he'd call Townsend. Dan had yet to return his call, and his stomach growled. It was ten till eight and the team should be strolling in, and he needed food.

"You're leaving already?" Harlowe met Kasper as the door to the elevator slid open.

"I'll be back, gotta get, uh, food."

"Great! Bring back some blueberry muffins, I'm starved, and you don't have bread for toast or not one damn egg to scramble in your fridge. When the heck you gonna go buy food?"

"Uber your ass to the store, Bishop, we're working the same hours, oops, scratch that, I'm working OT, you're an eight to fiver."

"Fine, then, I will. Why don't you try sleeping so you can be in a better mood?"

The two glared at each other before Kasper smiled, shaking his head. "I'm not tired, really, but I am hungry. Be back shortly."

"Blueberry muffins, don't forget." She punched the elevator button, and as the doors began closing, she mouthed the words *bye-bye* waving at him like a little kid.

A Kroger bag with blueberry muffins and hot apple turnovers from their bakery lay on the seat next to him. Traffic sucked. No way was he getting in the long-ass line at Starbucks for muffins, even if they were delicious. Kroger was not only closer, less crowded but also easier on his wallet.

"Well, about time, I'm half starved."

"Knock yourself out, muffins and hot apple turnovers." Kasper handed Harlowe the Kroger bag.

"Thanks, I guess. It's better than a poke in the eye, and it's edible." She eyed the Kroger bag wishing it were a box from a real bakery, or a bag from Starbucks. "Oh, and call Dr. Lam. She left a message for you and only you." Plastic Kroger bag in hand, she frowned. "And why just you? Me and them..."—she thumbed over to Lefty and Frankie—"we're FBI too, not flunky agents."

"Can I help it if I'm irresistible?"

"Bergman, you're irra-alright, irritating. Call Dr. Lam back so we can work. And Harlowe, share the goodies." Lefty's hand went out for his share of muffins or apple turnovers.

Kasper gave Lefty the finger then dialed the Tarrant County Forensic Lab, asking for Dr. Lam. They heard his side of the call since he didn't offer to put her on speaker.

Kasper's side: "You did, and the prints? I see, who knows, huh? Oh yeah, you sure? Uh, can I call you back later? Me, too." He hung up and then clicked on his laptop, entering his password with three pairs of eyes staring at him.

"Okay, Special Agent in Charge, enlighten us. What'd Dr. Lam have?"

"The fibers from the panties match one of the limbs our killer used as the garrote. So far, the superglue fuming hasn't picked up any prints."

With a napkin, Harlowe wiped apple turnover from her lip. "What was Dr. Lam sure about?"

"The limb, I guess."

"Bergman? What the hell?"

Frankie got into the conversation. "Yeah, I agree with Bishop. So, Bergman, what the hell's up? You're acting funny, I don't like it."

Blueberry muffin wrapper wadded in a tight ball, Lefty tossed it over the side and into his trash can, and then looked up. "Girls are right, Bergman. Even me, you know, Captain *not* Obvious, can feel you're holding back. Well?" Lefty asked, unwrapping another muffin.

"Okay, fine. She suggested we have dinner together sometime

and mentioned that she enjoyed our lunch. Shit, you guys think y'all gotta know everything."

"And about the effing case, she got anything else?" Harlowe was sick of his evasive answers.

"Nothing yet. But I found a few new things last night."

Kasper pulled out the photos he'd found and let them all look.

Frankie turned the photo over. "Are you saying this other gal is Sylvia Amos, as in the missing Choctaw woman, Sylvia Amos?"

"What the fuck, she was part of this group, this is the reason she's missing, and probably dead?" Even Harlowe was finding this hard to swallow.

Lefty was shaking his head in disbelief as well. "People in Hollywood make this shit up all the time. But never in my wildest would I believe it could be true; it's like melodrama playing out in real life."

"Uh-huh," said Frankie, "and after this is all over, Hollywood's gonna be pouncing on the story."

"Got more for y'all to add to this nonfictional, stranger-than-stranger tale."

Kasper pulled the file from his desk. "Leland Fitzhugh brought this to me last night. It amazed me at how clear the name tag is. Who does it look like?"

Frankie frowned. "Won't it look like who it is? I'm not following you."

"I want you to think ahead. Add years to the face. Who does it look like? Write the name on a sticky note."

"Alright, hand it here then." Frankie was first saying nothing, and then passing it to Lefty who passed it to Harlowe, and each of them handed Kasper a folded sticky note. Harlowe handed him back the photo. "Bergman, what the fuck's going on?"

Kasper inserted the enlarged photo into the file, taking each Post-it and reading what they'd written, his head nodding each time. "I thought it looked like Greenberg, too." Kasper then explained the call to Clark Real Estate and the realtor's story. Then, he informed them about leaving a message for Dan Robbs.

"You think Greenberg's connected to these murders somehow? You're out of your mind." This idea appalled Lefty, but he knew this crap could happen. Corneal Sebastian was aware of an FBI agent found guilty of murder. He'd read the story about an agent named Mark Putman, happened in Pikeville, Kentucky, June 1989. Married man Putman killed his confidential informant, who was also his lover. A departmental tragedy, they said.

"I'm not accusing. I'm collecting information, so we can make an informed decision." He raked his hands through his hair, his head pounding at the implications this meant for the Bureau, causing his blood pressure to rise. This early in the morning, and he needed a stiff drink.

"Can't you just quietly pull his files? And I promise not to leave a smidge of a footprint." The words were spoken out of Frankie's mouth sideways, like she was keeping it on the sly.

Kasper snorted, then resorted to his best 40s gangster voice. "Nah, Mugsy, and why ya whispering outta the sides of your lips?"

This broke them up and gave Kasper a healthy release of endorphins, and he relaxed. Then, he shared with them another idea involving Mick Townsend.

"Ah, shit, Mick Townsend?" Francine Ryder's face fell.

A sigh escaped Harlowe's semi-parted lips as her shoulders sagged. "Oh, fucking great, Mick, the misogynistic dick, Townsend. Why, Kasp, tell us why?"

Lefty looked from Francine to Harlowe, frowning. "That day on the mats, Harlowe, when you beat him, he gained respect for you." Then he turned to Frankie. "And you tutored the guy in computer class or he wouldn't've passed. Working with him he had to have acted civilized. I mean, you didn't have to help the guy."

"So what, I might have taken him on the mats, but none of you saw the crap in the background, especially how the male instructors acted toward us girls. The female NATs worked harder to make zero mistakes, because if we did we got booted out or written up, and Jesus, it was hard to keep our spirits up. I gotta tell you, it was tough going. I bet y'all never heard about the complaints Frankie, Karney Logan, Missy Short, Laurie Bassett, and I put in against a few of the male students. This includes Townsend."

"What happened afterward?"

"Not much, Lefty, not much. A slight slap on the wrist, they had to attend a few sessions of sensitivity counseling." She stopped talking, focusing on her hands, not them.

"Go on, Harlowe, tell them," Frankie urged her.

Harlowe looked up with a pained expression. "You guys remember Missy Short had a thing for Townsend, dontcha?"

They nodded they remembered; she went on. "One Saturday night, Missy, and the girls went out drinking. They dared her to go to Mick's room, so she did. Stovall was there, so was Greenberg, Spokane, and North, but Townsend wasn't. Missy was drunk, pissed because Mick wasn't even there."

"Hell, if one drunken night was a reason to quit, we'd all be gone, right?" Corneal Sebastian had his share of too much alcohol a few weekends into Quantico.

"No, it's not that cut and dried, Lefty. Someone took photos then showed them to a male instructor. He had Missy in his office forthwith, and she dropped out right after. We tried to get her to talk about it, but she said she'd rather try her hand at investigating in the private sector."

"Did they really have photos?" This angered Kasper because Missy Short had the aptitude to make an outstanding agent.

Harlowe shrugged. "I'm guessing so or Missy would've fought back. We heard Greenberg took the photos, and the others denied they knew about it."

Franke jumped in. "Y'all remember Lynn Dresher, our investigative slash ethics instructor? Well, anyway, a lot of the guys were harping on a rumor she was a lesbian, not that it even matters because the woman's married with four kids and her husband works for a law firm as a civil attorney. All the shit they gave her could've gotten them booted, but as an instructor, she tried to see past the naïve attitudes of mere boys in men's bodies. Shit, as it was, I think Greenberg was older than the rest of us and..." Her mouth stopped moving, her brain working instead.

"What, Frankie?"

"Did you just hear what I said?"

Lefty said, "Uh-huh, and we're waiting for you to finish your thought."

"I heard you, Francine," said Kasper. "Greenberg was at least ten years older than us, so why didn't he act like a mature adult? Add in why was he such a late bloomer in the program?"

Lefty was not worried about age because Quantico had all types as well as ages, but the photo was bothering him. "Can we talk about this photo? Do we think Jay Greenberg and Jason Wallen are the same man? I dunno, could be. This face might resemble the guy, but we can't prove it's him. The name ain't even close either. We have a twin somewhere, maybe two or three. Man, the world's a big place."

Kasper's brows crunched in thought. "We've got pieces to a jigsaw puzzle even though I don't think they belong to the same puzzle."

Frankie's eyes narrowed. "Yeah, cuz from what you're telling us, Wallen's not connected to Mera-Soon-Lee's death. And I don't see any reason he had to kill the others. But he is the one constant in this entire mess if you go by his relationship to everyone else."

"The second common element in this, what Frankie calls a mess and what I'm itching to understand, is how these damn letters fit. Do they fit at all?" Harlowe asked.

Kasper pulled a face. "Well, not the physical letters. But our focus needs to be on letters all the same. Three letters of the alphabet —F-B-I—and one of our own."

The ambiance in the room grew somber.

CHAPTER FORTY-FOUR

Kasper's cell phone rang startling them. Looking at the screen he saw *Dan Robbs* pop up; he answered immediately.

"Hi, Dan, oh, I'm great, thanks, and you?"

"Good, never better."

"Dan, I'm gonna put you on speaker. I've got Agents Sebastian, Ryder, and Bishop here with me."

"Sure. Hi, everyone, it's been a minute, hasn't it? Hey, Bishop, you still kicking ass or what?"

"Not like I did at the Academy. Townsend was my coupe de grace, but looks like I might get a chance for a repeat."

"Hmm, wouldn't mind seeing that happen again." He snickered on his end, then, "Bergman, you left a message; is this about the Texas-Oklahoma serial you're working? I heard about it through the grapevine."

"Sorta." Kasper recounted their visit to Huntsville and what they'd learned about the secret interview project a few years back.

"Oh, yeah, it didn't work out like we planned. There were several groups involved, guess it was five years ago, in 2011."

"FBI put this on?"

"Yes, a select few new trainees at the Academy, and we invited officers from the Houston, Austin, and Dallas police departments to join in."

"Francine Ryder here, Mr. Robbs."

"Frankie, call me Dan. How's the cyber stuff coming in DC?"

"Oh, I love it, still hoping for an overseas gig. Thanks for remembering, Dan. Uh, question. Why'd the Bureau invite police detectives to take part? I don't understand how it would help the FBI."

"We invited men, and, uh, Bishop, women too, just so you know."

He heard Harlowe huff a sigh. "I wasn't gonna say an effing word, I swear."

Robbs let out a belly laugh. "I know, I know, but you were thinking it, so I thought I'd squelch your being pissy later. Men outnumber women three-to-one at least. Women who make the grade, like you and Ryder, are in immense demand. Y'all are exceptional agents; I'd work you any day of the week. Got me, Bishop, Ryder?"

"Yes, sir," they out called in unison.

"Let's get back to the experiment we ran. We invited candidates from detective squads, the sheriff's office, border patrol, and a smattering of patrol officers. All interested applicants got vetted and were hand-picked by their Chief of Police."

"Did this serve a purpose for the FBI?" Kasper was a member of the police force in Houston and heard nothing about this.

Robbs' enormous sigh sounded through the speaker before he spoke. "The officers involved were potential candidates being screened for Quantico. We were employing a recently developed method to assess abilities for the agency, among other things."

"Dan, I assisted the Houston PD, even though I was just a tech guy. I worked with detectives and hell, I even went undercover once. Why did I not hear about this?"

"Bergman, you'd have to ask your direct supervisor, that's not a question I can answer."

Lefty joined the conversation. "Why'd the program end?"

"Not enough interest. Most of the applicants' test scores weren't what they'd figured, so they stopped the program. Anything else, cuz I gotta jump off here?"

"Hey, Dan, you got five more minutes for me?" Kasper asked, eyeing the others.

"Not much more. I've got a meeting to prepare for."

Taking his phone off speaker, Kasper pointed to the hallway. "Give me five, guys." Kasper stepped into the hallway out of earshot of the others. "Dan, you remember a conversation we had the last night at Quantico? You said—"

The door opened and Kasper walked back in.

"Bergman, you discussing the case with Robbs, or is it personal business, because you'd better not be holding shit back." Hands on her hips, Harlowe gave him the girlie stink-eye.

Kasper took a seat at his desk. "The night at Quantico, we had a few beers, chewed the fat, told him the story of me and the DEA agent/hitman, Theo Sykes, and working with Homicide Detective Jack West. Same story I finally told y'all about to dispel the rumor mill I was hiding in the FBI because I was a pussy, or Townsend's version where I thought I was a superhero."

"Yeah, we know the real skinny. I'm honored to be in your presence." Lefty did the old kingly hand gesture, Bergman did the bird gesture; they laughed.

"For real, though, I just did my job, and now I worry a little."

"About Sykes hunting you?" Lefty knew Kasper could defend himself; hell, he'd taken Townsend even when the entire class thought he was a cream puff. Bergman surprised them by dropping Mick in no short order either, and the only black belt he had held up his pants.

Kasper shrugged vaguely. "Yeah, a little cuz the guy's crazy, but who knows?"

Bergman's biggest fear was Sykes hurting him by hurting ones he cared for—his fellow agents, his parents, even Nikki, but he didn't dwell on this, he didn't have time. They needed to find this serial, and in his head, he knew they'd already found him—Jason Wallen, AKA Jay Greenberg. They had the man, now they needed the proof.

The girls were quiet, and Kasper looked over to see Harlowe frowning with steely eyes, arms crossed, and he imagined her toe was tapping the carpet irritably.

"Now what, Bishop?" he asked.

"You've not answered the question about why you wanted to talk to Robbs privately, and Frankie and I are waiting. Lefty might not care, but we do."

"Ah, right, my conversation. Robbs said something, and it stuck with me."

"What, pray tell?" Frankie spouted with an attitude.

"God Almighty, you two, keep your panties out of a wad, I'm sure Kasper's gonna tell us." Lefty let out a good grief sigh, rolling his eyes.

"I am, thanks, Left. The Bureau's got a lot of talented agents. But his advice was to be careful with certain classmates and trust my gut."

Her eyes widened. Frankie asked, "You ask him who he was talking about, did he say?"

"That's why I spoke to him in private."

"Well," Harlowe asked, "did he say, or are you gonna keep it to yourself?"

"Harlowe, come on, I'm not keeping it to myself. I'm telling ya if you'll give me a chance."

Lefty stood, went to the coffeepot, and poured a cup. Then he gestured, asking them, "Coffee?"

"Is there any bourbon to mix with it?" Kasper kidded.

"There's a small bottle of airport booze in my purse, Bergman, if you need a small belt," Frankie teased.

"Nah, but tonight we should go for drinks. Think I'm gonna need one, or twenty. Anyway, back to my conversation. I explained the photo, mentioned our suspicions. And his recommendation was to take it slow, be meticulous, and gather some damn compelling evidence."

"Dan thinks we have something? Or are we running backward in a 10K?" A worried look crossed Harlowe's face.

"Yeah, what'd he say?" Lefty handed him hot coffee.

"Said do our jobs no matter who might be involved, fellow agent or not. And he repeated what he told me that night. Trust my gut. "

Frankie asked, "Anything else?"

"Yep, we should call Mick Townsend."

"For the fuck all love of Peter Pan! Not one of us has spoken to him since Quantico, and besides, how the hell could he help us if he's not even in contact with Greenberg? Harlowe's not a fan, Townsend was in the top ten of her 'what I hate' list, right there in line with Kevin Eastman."

"Dunno. He just said call Townsend, get him onboard."

"You're actually gonna call him?" Harlowe couldn't believe they were bringing Mick Townsend into their inner circle. It made her ill.

"Townsend roomed with Greenberg. I'm sure that's why Dan suggested it, and it's been almost four years since Quantico and hopefully Mick's matured." Kasper would let bygones be bygones, not harbor grudges.

Frankie's tone was hostile, "Men like him don't mature, they age, but their brains never grow up, just like Preston Munn."

"Ah, come on, girls, let's hope he's grown up and if nothing else, can help us cross Greenberg off our suspect list. "

Harlowe whipped her head around. "So, you think Greenberg's involved?"

Lefty shrugged. "The dude exhibits that personality type, but a murderer? A jackass, yes, a killer—don't see it, but hey, I've been wrong, once."

Frankie sipped her lukewarm coffee and asked, "By the way, where'd Townsend end up?"

"London—"

Frankie jumped off her chair not giving Kasper time to complete his sentence. "London, oh my God, he gets a gig overseas and I sit here, no offense to you guys, but in Dallas, Texas, are you kidding me?"

"Kentucky! London, Kentucky. For Christ's sake, if you'd let me finish. Population about eight thousand, so I'm sure he's not a happy agent up in them there hills." Kasper's brows wiggled in fun.

"Uh, yeah, I'm betting not, and it sorta thrills the piss outta me," Harlowe expressed with glee.

"Want me to get Mick's number for us?" Frankie clicked on her keyboard.

"I looked him up this morning, got his cell. We might as well get it over with, invite him to Dallas."

"Shit, just freaking Zoom with the guy. Frankie and I don't wanna hafta see him in person."

"Agent Bishop, act like an agent and stop behaving like a mad little girl."

Her eyes narrowed; she pursed her lips in a tight thin line, her brain thinking about what he'd just said, and he was right.

She closed her eyes as her cheeks puffed out and a thick pent-up breath blew out her mouth. "Right, I'm acting like a girl. I mean, I am a girl, but I'm an agent first. You want me to call him and extend the invitation?" Her voice level implied she was serious, not being facetious.

Kasper handed her the number. "Great idea, Bishop. Just invite him to Dallas to help our task force on a case we're working. Tell him we'll update him when he gets here."

"Fine, I'll call him. I'll do it in private, not with you guys staring a hole in me, otherwise I might choke up." Harlowe stepped into the hallway to make the call. She glanced back. "And don't listen at the keyhole either." She shut the door behind her.

CHAPTER FORTY-FIVE

"Well? How'd he sound? Is he coming to Dallas? How'd he treat you? Was he mean? Did he act like his normal a-hole self?" Frankie pressed her.

"Uh, color me stunned. He sounded human, like an actual professional agent. No snide remarks about girls, or me being a secretary making a call for real agents, gotta say it surprised the hell outta me."

"When's he coming?" Frankie was gearing up her moxie; she'd much rather spend time with Preston Munn. As sleazy as he was, she could handle him. Townsend, though, was a threat to her self-confidence and scared her a little.

"He's gonna take the red-eye tomorrow night."

Lefty snorted. "Why? He too cheap to fly in the daytime?"

Kasper pushed his chair back to prop his feet on the desk. "We heard you tell him we needed him here sooner than later, so what'd he say?"

"You guys were listening when I told y'all not to? You motherfuckers."

"Sue us," Lefty said. "And, Harlowe, you actually sounded nice to him, too."

"I am nice, Lefty, you shit. Anyway, he just wrapped up an auto theft case. His office is getting the paperwork to the Justice Department. It was a big case, so lots of paperwork, wiretaps to transcribe with audio playbacks, and a ton of photos they gotta copy and have ready for both sides."

Kasper's brows dipped. "We heard you asking him if he had another agent in his office to help...does he?"

"Yeah, four civilians work in his satellite office and he was the only agent, but since this case got bigger than expected, he needed more Bureau manpower, so they sent him another special agent to join the team." A smile tugged at her lips, but she held it back.

"Well, damn it, Harlowe, who'd they send to help him, just effing tell us? Do we know him?" Frankie was tired of all the hem-hawing around crap.

"Oh, yeah, we know 'em." She paused, the corners of her mouth lifted. "They sent him Agent Karney Logan."

The quiet was short-lived, their laughter not able to be contained. Mick Townsend, the rough misogynistic bully who had a mouth to fit his demeanor, partnered with clean-cut, prudish Karney Logan, whose vulgar language composed of words like "oh, darn," "flaming," and "golly, heck"; this was hilarious!

"Can you say fly on the wall? God, I'd love to be that fly." Frankie wiped tears of laughter from her eyes.

"Me, too," Kasper's deep belly laugh echoed the same sentiments. "Me, too." As the hilarity faded, Kasper went on. "Look, team, we're not gonna talk about Greenberg, or Wallen or whoever the hell he calls himself, not right off. We're going to discuss each individual case, and how they're connected to one another by Oklahoma. Not a word about Wallen or Greenberg until it's time, everyone agree?" Kasper went from person to person getting affirmative nods from his team. No one would tip the scales.

Tomorrow was now today, Mick Townsend was in town, and although he'd seemed nice over the phone, no one was sure how he'd act in person.

Lefty waltzed in and seeing Harlowe, his brows arched and he whistled.

"You look nice today and very female FBI-ish in your dark suit and nice makeup. You dress up for Mick today?"

"Fuck you, Lefty, I always look nice." Harlowe's nerves on edge, she hadn't seen Mick since Quantico and wondered if he'd still held a grudge against her for beating him on the mats in front of his peers. She looked past him, expecting to see Ryder on his heels. "Where's Frankie? Calling in sick today? She scared to see Mick?"

"No, she ain't scared; she dropped me off and went to get breakfast for us."

"Lord, I hope she doesn't bring back donuts. I'm gonna be an oinker if I don't start eating better food."

"Where's Kasper? Didn't you ride in together?"

"No, I Ubered here, he's running late, poor guy's been working so many hours, and he slept through his alarm. I'll get a couple pots of coffee going." Harlowe's nerves were on edge. She wasn't looking forward to this semi class reunion.

The door creaked open twenty minutes later and in walked Frankie, carrying two boxes from a Dallas bakery.

"Please tell me you didn't get donuts." Harlowe's grimace was real.

"No, I got scones."

"Would any of them be healthy?"

Frankie wrinkled her nose. "Healthy scones, are you kidding?"

"I'll just have coffee then. "

"Harlowe, eat a damn scone. Later, run around the building a few times this afternoon and work it off." Lefty went for a scone and Frankie rapped him on the knuckles.

"Ouch! What the hell, I can't have a scone?"

"Can't you wait till everyone gets here? You gotta be a pig?"

"You two, Jesus, get over your nerves. It's only Mick Townsend, for Christ's sake. You, getting all dolled up, nice makeup, and you,"—he turned to Frankie—"getting all fancy with scones. Shit, the guy ain't royalty, he's only a regular—" Lefty's words cut off when he heard someone pushing the door open, and a voice rang out.

"Morning, guys, look who I met in the lobby."

Walking in behind Kasper was Mick Townsend wearing a dark suit, dark striped tie, spit-shined shoes, and a sheepish grin.

"Hey," "hi," and a "good morning" were muttered as Kasper and their new guest walked in.

"Been a few minutes, hasn't it? Corneal, you look fit." Townsend extended his hand.

"Yeah, several million minutes, and call me Lefty."

"Oh, right, they still call you that?"

Lefty shrugged. "Some things never change."

"Uh, Mick, you remember Francine, she—"

"I do," he said, cutting Kasper off and stepping up to Frankie. "Agent Ryder was a lifesaver or I wouldn't have passed one of my computer courses. Did I ever thank you, Francine?"

"Uh, I don't remember," she lied, knowing full well he never once uttered a thank you.

"I know I never said thank you. All I did was act like a fat turd. But I'm saying it now. Thank you, Francine, you saved my butt. Also, wanna apologize for being such a jerk to you back then."

His words were sincere and hers eyes softened. "You're welcome, Mick. Glad to have you onboard."

Mick turned to Harlowe, his brows raised, and a grin played on his lips. "I'm not gonna ask for a rematch, cuz I know you can kick my fat butt anytime you want. I'd like to apologize to you too for my backward thinking about women in the Agency. Recently, I've learned several valuable lessons about not being a narrow-minded male in a world of what should be equality." Mick stuck out his huge hand. "Are we good?"

"See, there I'm all ready to keep hating you and you go on and ruin it, damn it." She grabbed his outstretched hand with a laugh. "You bet, and boy, am I relieved, cuz I really didn't wanna have to kick your ass again."

They all hooted, Mick the loudest.

Three hours and two pots of coffee later, they'd caught Mick up-to-date on most of the cases except for letting him know Jay Greenberg was their target and the part he may or may not have played, or how he might connect to the victims. They also left the enlarged Camp Dove Tail photo undisclosed, for now.

"That's incredible. Who would've figured your victims would link up the way they have? Great job, I gotta say."

"Thanks. We've caught a few breaks here and there."

"Hey, Frankie, I'm betting you'd do alright in an interrogation room. Sounds like you held your own with the creep Preston Munn. I'd heard he was a real piece of work," Mick complimented her.

Kasper didn't miss the past tense, Mick *had heard*, and he jumped on it.

"You said you *heard* Munn was a real piece of work. You know someone who knows him or talked to him?"

Townsend nodded. "Yeah, my ex-roommate at Quantico told me about the dirtbag when we were hitting the books, learning about the profiling stuff. Afterward I did some not-so-light reading on Munn's case."

No one spoke. Not a look, not a sound, each of them knowing Mick's roommate had been Jay Greenberg, also known as Jason Wallen.

Kasper began, "So, Mick, what's your take on Mera Soon-Lee? How would you connect her to this case?"

"I'm not a great profiler, still trying to get that part of my brain wired, but she doesn't seem to fit—not because she wasn't heavy or poor—she just doesn't fit. She never lived in Oklahoma but visited once when she was in her twenties. The others went to high school together, a school Mera didn't attend."

"Yeah, so," Lefty responded, "whatcha thinking?"

Mick's shoulders twerked a tad. "Dunno, but I'd ask if she was dating anyone. You guys know the odds of it being a person they knew are ten to one, like the percentage of noncustodial parents involved in child abductions these days. So, was she dating anyone?"

Tough question to answer since they thought Jason Wallen and Jay Greenberg were the same man.

"Yeah, but he had a rock-solid alibi, unbreakable, so they cleared him."

"She have any bad blood with a coworker, or a stalker, anything like that?" Mick was reaching.

Kasper shook his head. "No, and the coed rapist they were doing a story about fell off the grid. No more incidents after she went missing."

Mick's face softened into an apologetic expression. "Speaking of falling off the grid, listen, Bergman, I was a real shit back at Quantico, you know, about your dealing with the DEA hitman crap. Look, I admire you, you ain't hiding or running, it takes guts, man, real guts."

"Yeah, Mick, and it takes guts to apologize, so thanks."

There was moment of silence, and Lefty, smart-ass he was, began singing "Kumbaya," and Frankie punched him in the arm. The others laughed.

CHAPTER FORTY-SIX

They spent the remaining part of the morning analyzing the separate cases, getting Mick Townsend's feedback, and learning about some of his cases and how they'd worked out.

While telling a story unrelated to their case, but related to one of Mick's past cases involving a botched bank robbery in a small rural area of Kentucky, Harlowe interrupted. "Hey, Mick, can I ask you something?"

"Sure, don't see why not, anyway, could I stop you?" Mick grinned, and Harlowe found his boyish grin sort of appealing. "I've noticed you've cleaned up your language."

His forehead crinkled. "Oh?"

"Yeah, like instead of *hell*, you say *heck*, you say *jerk-wad* instead of what you used to say, which was *fuck-wad*, or *turd-head* instead of *shithead.* When did you clean up your potty mouth?" She rested her chin on her propped-up fist, eyeing him with a quizzical look.

"I might ask you the same thing, you know? Like, when are you gonna clean up *your* potty mouth?" His eyes challenged her.

It was quiet, everyone waiting to hear what she'd say as she stared at him, steely-eyed then laughed. "Probably never fucking will, that's when."

Mick's laugh boomed. "Oh, I can still cuss like a sailor when I'm mad enough, but since Karney and I teamed up, I promised to clean it up, as long as she promises to curse every so often."

"How's that working out?" Kasper wanted to know.

"Well, for the better part, pretty dad-gummed good, but then there are those fucking days I fucking fall off the fucking wagon and she's not one fucking bit happy with me." With a teensy grin, he shrugged.

Left responded first, "Well, guess that answers Bishop's question, doesn't it?"

"Yeah, and I wonder what Karney would say?" asked Frankie.

"She'd tell y'all to go take a flying fuck, cuz this would really piss her off." Mick cracked up.

"Good to know Karney's not a complete pushover. Back to the case." Kasper got them back on track.

"Sure, and I'll stop with the Kentucky tall tales. So, have you got anyone you're looking at?" Mick asked.

No one spoke. Lefty, Harlowe, and Frankie said nothing because it was Kasper's call. Townsend's gaze moved from one face to another, and he saw something he didn't like. Mick moved his chair away, extended his long legs out, and crossed his ankles. He looked away, then back at Kasper, his eyes intense. "You ain't looking at me, are ya, cuz it feels as if you're fixing to question me, and I'm not liking the way I feel right now." His arms crossed in a closed-off reaction, his glare deepened as he waited.

"No, Mick, we aren't looking at you. There's no way you could've been involved. However, we are looking for your help. You might not like or believe what we think but you need to be open-minded. With that I've got to ask some personal questions."

"Alright." Mick uncrossed his ankles, brought his legs up and sat straighter, his arms resting on either armrest, his posture much less closed off. "I'll answer questions you have, but not about my sex life, which is off limits." It was a joke, but his smile didn't reach his face.

"Hey," Kasper put his hands up in effort to stave off his anger, " not gonna get that personal, I promise."

Lefty jumped into the conversation, a planned move. "I heard Greg Spokane is up in the Arizona area. Poor bastard got sent to hell. Jesus, it gets so damn hot up there."

"Yep, Spokane's gotta be bitching in the summer, alright." Frankie smirked.

"I heard they assigned Ned Stovall to the marshlands in Florida, up near the Everglades, with the crocks and gators. I'd love to have seen him with his first cranky gator, shitting himself. He's a bastard and a horrible date." Anger sparked from Harlowe's eyes.

Mick thought back, recalling Harlowe being the subject of conversation after Ned took her on a date and he'd tried to get friendly, but decided he would not mention it. Why stir up that cauldron?

"While we're reminiscing about classmates, anyone heard from Greenberg? Mick, you and he roomed together, so guess you'd know, right?" Kasper tossed out the casual question.

"Nah, we aren't close, never were, but last I heard he was an acting liaison for the Bureau. He was up in Wisconsin, but, and hey, "Mick held his palms up. "I'm not saying it's true, but heard he had issues with one of the female staffers, so they had to get him out before they were gonna hafta kick him out. I hear tell he's an okay agent, and they didn't wanna lose him."

"So, a man helped him keep his job, is that it?" Harlowe, pissed off, saw Frankie's face go dark as well.

"No, actually, it wasn't."

"Oh," said Frankie, "a woman did?"

"Yeah, and y'all know her, she was an instructor at Quantico, but two years ago she moved over to the Wisconsin office. Lynn Dresher."

"She got Greenberg out of hot water? What could have

compelled her to help that motherfucking prick?" Harlowe's ire increased, her language more colorful, her words louder.

"Hey, it might not be true. It's just what I heard. I wasn't there, goddammit, why ya getting pissed at me?"

"Not pissed at you, Townsend, just fucking pissed, and don't even know why I'm yelling either."

The room was quiet for a split-second and they burst into laughter.

"Great tension relief there, Bishop." Kasper looked at her, then at Mick. "It's best to blurt this out, Mick, and tell you who we *are* looking at."

"Well, spit it out, will you? Jesus!"

"Your old roommate."

"Greenberg? Really? Why would you look at him?" You could see the real surprise written all over his face. Mick was stunned.

Frankie pulled out the enlarged photo and handed it to him. "Look, then tell us what you think?"

Mick Townsend studied it, and with his arms like a slide trombone, he held it out then back up close, scrutinizing the face before finally saying, "Yeah, might be him, but you guys know our faces change sometimes when we age, so it might just be a look-alike. But, I've seen pictures of old classmates from high school and they don't even look like themselves."

"The others in the photo...look at them, Mick. One is Annelle Mackey, the other is Rayna Anderson, and we believe the one taking the photo is Trina Robinson." Kasper pointed out.

Mick shook his head. "I can't believe this. I mean, I'm...well, was sorta friends with him. You find out who Gloria is?"

"No, we don't have a last name and anyone we could ask, well, they're dead," Harlowe supplied.

"I—" He stopped, his mind clicking on something.

Kasper saw his expression. "What is it, Mick?"

"Let me think on this a second."

They waited while he thought, then he said, "Jay told me a lot about Preston Munn, said he followed the story when he was about fourteen, I think. Anyway, I thought it was creepy a kid so interested in a sicko killer, but when I think back, he actually hailed that fucker a hero. Oh, my bad, sorry, Karney, wherever you are." A sheepish grin crossed his face. "She'd make me put money in the swear jar for my language."

A lightbulb went on over Lefty's head, metaphorically speaking. "Oh, now it makes sense. Cursing was breaking your wallet!"

Mick grinned. "A little, maybe. Seriously, though, back to this Munn dude. Jay thought this guy was a genius."

Frankie's scowl deepened. "The fucker, and I ain't putting any money into a swear jar, but that motherfucker is a low-life piece of shit, he's got the IQ of a...a...a..."

She was so mad she couldn't think, so Kasper filled it in for her. "A housefly?"

"Yes!" she yelled.

"Not that sort of mastermind," Mick clarified. "Jay said the man provided him with helpful hints on how to overcome obstacles, and I never asked him what he meant. I thought he was talking about profiling. Shit."

Harlowe stuck out a Styrofoam cup. "Put a quarter in the swear cup. We'll all do it every time we swear, be enough to buy five steak dinners in about two hours!"

"Here," Kasper took out a ten-dollar bill. "I'll pay in advance." He dropped the money into the cup then looked back at Mick. "If he wasn't talking about profiling, then what was he talking about?"

"I think his own problems, when he was younger."

Kasper frowned. "If it goes back that far, then it isn't good, not good at all."

"What's that mean, Bergman?" Lefty asked.

"Means Mera Soon-Lee might not have been the first victim." Kasper looked at each of them.

"Holy fucking shit."

Harlowe passed the swear cup across her desk to Lefty.

CHAPTER FORTY-SEVEN

"Where's Greenberg officing?"

Mick scratched his head, thinking. "Not sure, Bergman, cuz from what I know he travels a lot, goes from state to state wherever he's needed. Wait, let me rephrase. He goes to certain states, not all of 'em, the guy ain't Superman."

"When did you last talk to Greenberg?" Frankie asked.

"Eight or nine months ago, I think." Mick frowned. "I ain't got anything to hide. He called me, wanting to know if I remembered a chick named Loretta, some gal he met at a bar when we were at the Academy."

Kasper asked, "Well, did you remember this girl?"

Mick's shoulder's twerked up quickly, and he frowned. "No, she was just a gal at a bar we drank at. Gawd, that was four years ago, lots happened since."

Harlowe looked at him. "He say why he wanted to get in touch with this girl? You ask?"

A sigh blew out of Mick's mouth. "He wanted to talk to her brother, or cousin. About a case he said he was working. Hell, I had too much on my plate to dick around with him and his issues, or his skirt-chasing shit." Mick pulled out a twenty, looking at Harlowe. "You'd better go get a box. That cup ain't gonna be big enough!" He dropped the twenty sitting back with a resounding growl.

"Take it easy, man, you're not on trial here."

"Lefty's right, Townsend, so stop acting like you're a victim." Kasper moved his chair back so he could stretch his legs out. "So, where was he when he called you?"

Townsend thought back and his eyes widened. "He was here, I mean, in Fort Worth, I think."

"He say why he was here, because if Greenberg was here nine months ago this corresponds with Annelle Mackey's murder." Kasper's interest rose.

"No, and I didn't ask. Crap, I was dealing with my shitstorm in Kentucky."

Kasper peered at Frankie. "Do your magic and pull up cases with his name connected. Uh, keep it on the cuff, though."

"Francine, can you really do that?" Townsend is either worried or impressed by the tone of his voice.

She smiled, typing. "Remember when I was tutoring your ignorant ass, and I told you there were ways to make invisible footprints in the snow and you told me no way? Then I showed you a few of my tricks?"

Townsend grinned. "Yeah, I do, and I may need a refresher course."

"Frankie is one of the best—"

"Okay, got it."

"See what I mean," Kasper said, then, "Whatcha got, Frankie?"

"Greenberg was liaising with the Hill County Sheriff's Department on a counterfeiting case with similarities to a fresh case up near Hillsboro. However, they handed it to off to the Secret Service."

"It say how long he was here?"

"Gotta look somewhere else, so give me a minute."

Townsend's brows dipped as he asked, "What other place?"

"Staff files for hours worked, daily, weekly mileage, per diem, hotels, and crap." Kasper watched Frankie type and click with purpose.

Mick looked at her. "Can't hide much from you, can we?"

Frankie shrugged. "You gotta be good at hiding stuff from me. But yeah, I see stuff I shouldn't be seeing. I don't brag about it and keep a low profile, which brings me to this. Mick, you'd better know how to keep a secret, cuz if you don't, I can make your life hell and keep it coming for years. Got me?" She shot him a venomous look, and he nodded, swallowing hard.

"Yeah, of course, I sure as shit don't wanna be on your bad side, Agent Ryder. Mum's the word, or better yet, what happens in Dallas stays in Dallas. Does that work for you?"

Frankie stuck out her hand. "Deal. Now, let me tell ya what I've got. First, Greenberg *was* here nine months ago, stayed for three weeks—two weeks in Hillsboro, a week in Waco. Afterward, he headed to Louisiana, where he still is. So, he was definitely in the area within the time of Mackey's murder. Itasca is around twelve miles from Hillsboro. He could've easily scooted over there, done the deed, and gotten back. Second, this wasn't his first trip to the area. Greenberg was in Fort Worth on a tip called in about a suspected wire fraud scheme which was bogus, and guys, this was only four months ago and within the timeframe of Nora Mendez-Finch's disappearance and murder."

The room became eerily silent, as they considered one of their own capable of such heinous crimes. They had convicted only one FBI agent of murder. If convicted, Greenberg would be the first FBI agent serial killer in history. A tragic way to leave your worldly mark.

Kasper broke the eerie silence shrouding the room. "We can't prove any of this. It's all conjecture, we need solid proof before we rush the gates."

Harlowe's brows dipped. "We've got no DNA, no concrete proof.

All we've got is if he is Jason Wallen, how he's connected to the victims. Other than that, we got *nada*."

"Tell him about our case, maybe he'll slip up, say something we can use," Lefty proposed.

Frankie's head shook. "Shit! Bring him in on the case? Do we really wanna do that?"

Kasper raked his hand over his head, blowing out a long puff of wind before speaking. "It'd be a tremendous gamble to bring him in on these cases. He'd know what we know. He's already been twenty steps ahead of us, has been for the last five years."

Elbows propped up on her desk, she had a dejected look on her face. "Okay, how, for fuck's sake, do we bridge this twenty-step gap?" Closing her eyes, Harlowe opened the drawer to her desk, reached in, and pulled out four quarters then repeated one word before dropping them into the swear cup. "Fuck."

It'd been a long day and a weird reunion with Mick Townsend. The outcome had been great; no one had a fat lip or a black eye, and no female was ready to press sexual harassment charges. So, yep, it'd been a successful day.

"How about we break for dinner? At a decent restaurant, get food and unwind, then come back and see what we come up with?" Kasper was ready for a break.

Standing to get the blood flowing back in her legs, Frankie glanced over at Townsend, staring at Bishop with a lovesick schoolboy's crush expression, and she kept her grin in check. Clearing her throat she said, "How about letting Mick choose the place, it's his first night here? Got a preference, Mick?"

"Yeah. A place loud enough to not talk shop but still talk. Got any suggestions?" Mick asked them.

Kasper smiled. "Texas Road House, they've got great food, and we can have a few beers and chill, sound good?"

A break for an hour or two would do them a world of good.

Photos, murder books, reports, notes, and general chaos covered their desks as they talked it out, trying to connect Jason Wallen to Jay Greenberg. Problem: Jason Wallen disappeared and Jay Greenberg had a file—prints, photos, and a history they couldn't disprove—hell, the FBI had this file. They vetted him, gathered his history, talked to his coworkers in the Bastrop County's Sheriff's office. The strange thing was there was nothing before then they could find. Why and how did the man get into the FBI if he had no past to vet?

Harlowe's fingers drummed her desktop. "It's like the guy never existed before his time in Bastrop, so what the fuck is the deal? I mean, the Bureau vets us from being an egg and a sperm...why not him?"

"Yeah, I find it unsettling that we can't get more than we have. I mean, I'm good at finding crap, but this is ridiculous." This frustrated Frankie.

Bergman's foot tapped the carpet as his brows crunched up in thought and his eyes stared at the whiteboard. What were they missing? Why was there nothing on Jay Greenberg...Jay, J...Jason? His eyes lit up, and he knocked his knuckles against his desk. "Frankie, can you get into the NVSS?"

"The what?" Mick asked him.

"National Vital Statistics System."

"Okay. I'm in, Kasper, what next?"

"Look up the birth of any Jason Wallen, narrow the field by using the name Stanley Wallen, birth father."

No one spoke, only the slight noise of Frankie's fingers clicking on her wireless keyboard. They all watched as she scrolled the page.

Her brows knitted as she skimmed through every Jason Wallen born since time began, finally coming across father, Stanley Lee Wallen. "Got it," she responded.

"What was his mother's maiden name?"

"I'll be damned, it was Greenberg."

"So, this is how he became Greenberg, taking his mother's last name...not illegal to change your name," Lefty remarked.

"No, it's not. However, there's a two-year time gap in his work records from being Jason Wallen to becoming Jay Greenberg. Why? Where was he in that two-year gap?"

"What about his visits to Huntsville when he was on the Austin PD? We gonna check into that?"

"I'll be damned, Frankie." Kasper looked at her, then, "Look at the dates Soon-Lee disappeared...do they match up with the dates that failed new technique to evaluate aptitudes for contenders' applying to Quantico was going on?"

"His alibi was he was at Huntsville?" Townsend pulled a face.

Kasper responded, "Yeah, he got an invitation when he was Vice in Austin."

Townsend mumbled under his breath and Harlowe's eyes narrowed. "What did you say, Mick?"

"That's how the bastard knew Munn. It's how he got the letters."

Four heads popped up once Mick uttered one word—*letters*.

"Alright, Mick, what about these letters? Start talking," Kasper pushed himself back from his desk, his eyes glued on Mick's face.

Townsend cleared his throat. "Well, first, let me say I had no idea he was part of a stupid failed Bureau exercise; all I knew was he said he'd followed the Munn story when he was a kid. It was the key to his career choice, and I thought it'd be an exemplary case for learning to profile. He said he had letters written by cons, of course I thought he was joshing and never called him on it. Knowing now he was in fact at the prison, well, maybe he did have letters, real letters."

"Why in the fuck would he want letters con's wrote, anyway?" This wasn't making sense to Harlowe.

"Uh, well, now it makes sense."

"How does it make sense, Bergman?" Frankie asked.

"I got a call from the warden after we'd talked to Munn."

"Oh, well, guess you failed to mention it to me, or you have brain damage?" Frankie remarked, now annoyed.

Kasper enlightened them about the so-called "Smitty"—not his real name—the call, and how the guy seemed to be mobbed up, and wasn't asking to get his death warrant signed.

"Look, I'm sorry. I didn't dig into this. Since we'd connected our victims to who we think our suspect is, I figured the letters were a red herring, fodder just to mess up our case. That's why I didn't mention it."

Frankie crossed her arms and her eyes widened. "And now, now what do you think, oh high and mighty leader?"

"Stop it. I said I was sorry. The letters have nothing to do with these victims and they mean nothing to our case. Only four of the letters are relevant."

Harlowe narrowed her eyes. "What makes you so sure? They could be some type of message. And what four letters are you choosing? Are you tossing them into a hat and pulling blindfolded?"

Kasper shook his head. "No, I'm not doing this blindly, damn it! Out of the letters mailed, the four found with the victim, Soon-Lee, meant something to our killer, or that's what I think. Our visit to Munn and these four letters are significant."

Lefty jumped in. "Why, Bergman, you gotta have a reason?"

Townsend's hand goes up. "I know."

"Okay, Mick, I'm on pins and needles here, tell us why." Frankie was still mad.

"Munn's story happened when Jason Wallen was fourteen, the guy's pushing forty, and calls himself Jay Greenberg."

"So what? What's one thing have to do with the other?" Harlowe wondered what he was getting at.

"He was fourteen. What fourteen-year-old cares about a serial killer and the case, or later in life goes to visit the sicko, or hails him a genius?"

Lefty reacted, "A fourteen-year-old boy who's already messed up?"

"Yeah, "Kasper rejoined, "so we look into Jason Wallen, the boy, and see what happened to him."

"Could something have happened to him as a boy turning him into a killer?" Harlowe's forehead inched up.

Kasper shrugged. "Isn't that how all killers say they got started, a traumatic experience when they were young, and it messed them up?"

"Well," Harlowe quipped. "He was just an effing kid and wasn't writing love letters to convicts. So, where did these letters come from?"

"Let's dig into his life, going backward." Frankie dug through notes and said, "His dad died in November, 2015, from cirrhosis of the liver; his brother Dennis committed suicide in 2011; and the youngest, Matthew Wallen's, whereabouts are unknown. Only living relative we know about."

"Yup," said Lefty, "and all we have is a PO Box, and we know he's on disability."

"Bishop, get a warrant for the PO Box. Let's start there. He might not even have a physical address," Kasper said. "Frankie, get a warrant for the SSA. See if we can't find out why he's disabled. Search for his medical records."

"How about we try looking for Matthew Wallen's old classmates or teachers? He was the youngest, so he might have had different friends, you know, his age?" Mick said.

"Yeah, good idea, Mick, call the Marietta High School. See what you can find. Lefty, dig up everything you can about Gloria—shit, we don't have her last name."

"Hey, Mick," Lefty called over the desk, "let's work together on this. She went to the identical high school, and I'll give Rayna's cousin a call."

Frankie's hand rose. "Kasper, what about Wallen's stepmother, no one's mentioned her. Think she has answers?"

"I'm gonna search birth records after I get Dennis Wallen's obit, see if I can locate her. Afterward I'll try to locate Tobias Robinson. I wanna see what he knows about his biological father."

"Hey, Kasp," Harlowe said, "what about Mr. Soon-Lee?"

Kasper's lips formed a straight line, and he said, "I think it's time to call the American Consult in Korea, see about locating him."

Without further ado, they went to work.

CHAPTER FORTY-EIGHT

In sections of the task room, low voices spoke into phones, fingers clacked on keyboards, and aggravated moans were heard as they worked, getting what they could and frustrated at what they couldn't.

Frankie slammed her phone with a resounding thud. "Damn it, that's the third judge who's denied me! Anybody have a judge who owes you a favor?" She felt a bit beat down.

Kasper stood, stretched, and then went to put on a fresh pot of coffee. "Trouble with the Social Security office, Frankie, no help, huh?"

"Those hard-asses, and hell no, no freaking favors for the FBI, no matter how nice I ask. Since his birthday is on the fifteenth of the month Wallen gets his check every third Wednesday, and we know his PO Box is in Ardmore, Oklahoma. I'll call in a favor to the Ardmore PD. Ask if they can get someone to stake it out on the third Wednesday, get eyes on him, see where he goes."

"Guess no medical records either. HIPPA will stop us without a written authorization." Harlowe clicked her pen open-shut, open-shut.

"Kasp, you get the obituary on Dennis yet?"

"Yeah, Frankie, why?"

"Let me have it. I'll find the funeral home, call them. Someone had to pay for the funeral, and his father was still alive then. Greenberg was Jason Wallen then, too. See what I can dig up."

"Just don't dig up the body," Lefty quipped.

"Yeah, like we need another body to mess with." Harlowe tossed a wadded ball of paper at his head, missing, and Frankie tossed another, hitting him square between the eyes.

"Manchester," Mick called out.

"What?"

"Gloria's last name is Manchester, and here..." He handed Lefty paper with his chicken-scratch. "The retired high school principal remembered her."

"Great work, Mick," Kasper complimented him.

"I asked him about the family; the dynamics weren't so great. The dad worked long hours, also worked part-time, and the mother was a piece of real work, he said. Oh, and he also told me Matt Wallen was a victim of parental abuse. Although no one pressed charges, the signs were there, he said."

Harlowe's face broke out into a huge grin. "Well, damn the torpedoes, Mick. You're not a terrible agent after all. I swear, I'm impressed as hell."

Everyone witnessed a bashful Mick, with a pink blush on his face. Suddenly Harlowe was seeing him in a completely new light.

"Thanks, Bishop. I guess I meet your approval. Uh, being here, I mean."

It was her turn to blush, and this was alien to her. Bishop was a hard-as-nails type of woman. Shrugging it off she said, "Well, you dorks, let's get to work, we've got to catch up with Mick."

The other three sat, stupefied. Harlowe and Townsend? Hmmm.

Nearly three hours later, everyone heard an, "Ah, shit!"

"What, Lefty, what's the matter?" Francine was genuinely concerned.

"I cannot believe it happened again. I'm gonna hafta fire my stomach."

Harlowe asked, "Lunch? We missed lunch, right?"

The clock said it was two-thirty. Between cups of coffee and bottled water, they'd snacked and eaten all the pastries and emptied a box of Cheese Nips. No one had bothered about lunch as they dug into work, phone calls, records, and newspaper clippings.

"Lefty and I are gonna go get burgers and fries. Any good joint that makes greasy cheeseburgers?"

"Yup, there's a place off of Harry Hines. They've got crispy garlic fries too if none of ya mind garlic breath." Kasper winked, first at Frankie, then at Harlowe, who opened her mouth, thought about it a second, and closed her mouth. He held his laughter in, and everyone gave up money for food.

Kasper picked up the phone, punched in the numbers, propped his elbow up, and waited.

"Hello?"

"May I speak to Tobias Robinson?"

"Who's calling?"

"Kasper Bergman." He didn't say FBI to keep from scaring the kid, and being hung up on.

"Why you wanna talk to Toby?"

Good sign—this person was familiar with Tobias calling him Toby.

"This is about his mother's, uh, death." Again, not wanting to scare whomever he was talking to, he didn't mention the word *murder*.

"You mean her murder, don't you? This is Tobias Robinson. Who are you? What do you want?"

Alright, no more games, Kasper thought. "Mr. Robinson–"

"Toby, please, don't like that Mister crap."

"Sure. Toby, I'm Kasper Bergman, Special Agent with the FBI. We've been looking into your mother's case, and–"

"Wait, FBI? Why are you looking at my mom's case? Was she in trouble or was she offed because she squealed on somebody?"

"Neither. Let me explain what I can, and then I need to ask you some personal questions, okay?"

The silence was longer than necessary.

"Toby, you still with me?"

"Whatcha wanna know, Mr. G-Man?"

Kasper expressed his amusement. "G-Man? You watch a lot of old TV shows, do you?"

An aggravated sigh sounded from the opposite end.

"Look, Mr., uh, Toby. I can't tell you everything because we don't want certain information to get out. Understand?"

"Sure, but what personal information about me can help you?"

"Not sure it will help. What we're doing is learning everything we can about our Vic–uh, about each deceased person. Sometimes this helps in finding a suspect. Toby, your mom ever talk to you about her time in Oklahoma?"

"Yeah, all the time. Mom had good stories. It was the best time of her life, she said, and she'd met her soulmate. She hated she had to move, but my grandpa said they had to."

"Did she ever say why?"

"Don't blow smoke up my ass, Agent Bergman, you know why. She was pregnant with me and barely sixteen."

Kasper was silent, not wanting to verbalize the next question. Thankfully, Toby supplied him with the answer.

"And no, she wasn't raped. He didn't rape her. It was consensual sex. She told me they were in love."

Bergman heard the sadness in his voice and stayed quiet.

"Mom talked about it after I turned eight."

"Why then?"

"I looked nothing like my supposedly biological dad. So I asked why. Mom made me promise not to tell anyone I knew the truth—that her husband wasn't my dad, and my real father was white. Said I didn't need to know who he was, just that he would have loved me."

Kasper let him talk.

"You know, until today, I ain't ever said a word to a soul." Toby paused for nanoseconds then asked, "You think my biological father did this? Man, I can't—"

"No, no, I don't. But the more we know about your mom, well, it's how we work. We dig, Toby, and I need your help, please."

On the other end, Toby sat, phone pressed to his ear, his eyes closed, and he thought and wondered if it would matter to his friends and his girlfriend that his father was a white man.

"Agent Bergman, I can't tell you much. My birth certificate has no name and says 'father unknown'. My granny knew who but wouldn't say and she passed last year, and Grandpa is in a State nursing home in Lancaster, Texas. No use in asking him cuz he's got end-stage Alzheimer's."

"It's not your fault if you can't tell me anything, Toby, I—"

"Agent Bergman," he cut him off, "I didn't say I couldn't tell you anything. Mom told me a first name, but that's it." He was apologetic, Kasper was excited.

"What was it?" He held his breath.

"She called him Matty, but his name was Matthew."

The breath Kasper was holding expelled, and his eyes widened. Matthew Wallen?

"Does that help you?"

"Actually, Toby, it might. I have to ask you another question."

"I'm listening."

"Actually, two questions. Would you be willing to submit DNA for a paternity test? And, if I find your biological father, do you want to meet him?"

Other than their breathing, the silence was earsplitting for those few seconds as Kasper waited for Toby's answer.

As if on pause, the button released, and Toby's voice sounded. "Yes, to the DNA. And yes, I'd like to meet my biological father. My mom loved him. Even after she married the man I called Dad, she still carried Matthew in her heart."

"You sure?"

"Uh-huh, if he wants to meet me, too."

"Good. I'll keep you posted. Call this number, set up a time to meet Agent Cossen in the Beaumont office, he'll be expecting your call. His office will take care of the lab work, and..." Kasper gave Tobias Robinson instructions, and lastly his contact info before ending the call.

"No joking, Matthew Wallen and Trina Robinson. Wow, who'd ever put them together?" This was a shock. Then Harlowe's eyes narrowed into slits. "Hey, you think Toby could be in danger?"

"Well, shit, that's a possibility, isn't it?" Frankie's face crumpled up.

"Nah, I don't think so, but I told him if anything odd happened, he was to call me or go straight to Agent Cossen."

Kasper hoped his gut was right and Tobias wasn't in any danger.

CHAPTER FORTY-NINE

Mentally exhausted, they needed a jump start, news to rev them up and stoke the fires of their investigation. Frankie gave it to them.

"Hey! Okay, finally!"

Four sets of tired eyes looked her way.

Kasper rolled his tired shoulders. "Finally what?"

"I've got two names—Clara Wallen and Lydia Wallen—both Jason's mothers."

"Was his father a bigamist, Frankie?" Lefty joshed.

"No, you dork, Lydia was his stepmom. When Dennis committed suicide, they kept it low profile, probably because Jason Wallen was on the police force and a witness to his brother's death, they wanted to keep it low key. Anyway, there was an investigation, and the coroner ruled it a suicide, just so's ya know. Then Stan Wallen passed away, and no one said diddly about his wife, Lydia."

Kasper stood. "Clara Wallen, his biological mom, passed when he was three. So where's Lydia Wallen, then?"

"Great, I mean, great question, Boss."

"Come on, Ryder, what, she disappear, too?" Mick sounded amused.

"Matter of fact, yes. She went missing in 1994." A smug look covered Frankie's face. "I found a newspaper clipping about this."

"Uh, from what paper, may I ask?" Bishop was a little thrown off with this news.

"*The Mariette Gazette*, no longer in publication."

This impressed Kasper, who said, "You can tell us later how you figured it out, smarty pants; right now, what about the article?"

Frankie went into the news stories regarding Lydia Wallen's disappearance. As her story went on, the pen pal letters fell in place.

"The letters Mera had laminated are from Lydia Wallen? Is that what we're thinking?"

Kasper nodded. "It'd be my best guess, and—"

Mick interrupted, "Do we think he killed his stepmother, too?" He stood, jamming his fist into his pockets. "This is ludicrous."

"Well, Mick," Harlowe's eyes sought his, "fact has always been weirder than fiction. The last article closed the case. They believed she'd run off with some convict, never to be heard from again."

"He used these letters giving her a motive to leave, but she didn't leave, and it handed him a motive for her disappearance. Brilliant, if you ask me."

"What the fuck, Mick?" Lefty grumbled loudly.

"Not condoning murder, just saying he took Munn's story and used it for his nefarious deed, but for a seventeen-year-old kid, he was damn smart."

"Uh-huh, and now we've got another body to locate," Frankie popped off.

"Nope, three more bodies. Two killers."

"Three? And two killers, really?" Lefty looked at Frankie then Kasper.

Kasper held up one hand, raising one finger at a time. "One, Lydia Wallen. Two, Sylvia Amos. Three, Gloria Manchester. Yes, two killers. Jason—or Jay, whoever the fuck he is today—didn't kill

Mera Soon-Lee. His alibi is rock solid. So, who killed her and why? Alright, people, keep digging, and Mick, dig hard into Gloria Manchester, find us something."

Sighs went around the room. The story was getting more complicated. Two killers, bodies still missing, skeletons in family closets were rattling louder, but not loud enough.

"I need a break, think I'll walk outside, around the building, legs are cramping up, need to stretch them."

"Yeah, we've been at it for the past three hours nonstop, think I'll join you, Mick." Bishop popped up out of her chair, not noticing the others eyeballing her. *She was going to walk outside with Mick? What was this? Was Bishop taking a liking to their buddy Mick? This was interesting indeed.*

"Yeah, and I'm sick-sick-sick of this burned nasty coffee. Lefty, you wanna take a drive with me to Starbucks, I'm gonna buy everyone a better cup of java. Who wants what?"

Frankie took orders, and they left, followed by Bishop and Townsend who needed to stretch their legs. Kasper was alone in the task force room. He strolled over to the whiteboard and added, *"Missing: Lydia Wallen and Gloria Manchester."* Jesus, two more bodies brings the count up to eight. Would it end there? Could more be involved in this horror story? The word *rape* came to mind. Somehow, rape didn't fit, even though it was an absolute possibility. This was something they might never prove, other than on Nora Mendez-Finch. He looked at the time: four-forty-five. Swooping up his cell, he scrolled to Nikki Lam's number and pushed "call."

"Kasper, how are you?" was how she answered.

"Tired, but good, and you?"

"It's the same for me. I'm up to my armpits in bodies. It never stops. Some days I've got end-to-end bodies, and sometimes I admit, I sit twiddling my thumbs, wishing work would come in. I'm awful, aren't I?"

She was a breath of fresh air, honest and funny. "No, you just like staying busy. Problem with this busy is I haven't had time to ask you out for dinner."

"In our line of work, we've got to squeeze in time. I mean, we do hafta eat, right? Why not do it together?"

"Yep, so how about it? Dinner tomorrow night?"

His fingers mentally crossed, waiting for her answer.

"Love to, and pray nothing comes in cutting dinner short, or out."

"I can meet you somewhere, or I can—"

Her laugh cut him off. "Better if we meet in the middle. You're in Dallas and I'm in Fort Worth, so what about meeting in the middle?"

"Okay. Steak, burgers, seafood, what's your pleasure, you pick a place."

"How about Mexican, there's a *Mi Hacienda* in Colleyville?"

"Perfect. We'll meet at eight. Now, can we talk shop a minute?"

"Eight it is, now, what's on your mind?"

"Uh, you can say no. I don't want you to feel obligated. But..." He went into his request.

"Getting medical records without consent—nope, same with the autopsy report. Sorry, Kasper, I can't risk a lawsuit for the city."

"I understand, and I wouldn't want you to—"

"Wait," she cut him off. "I didn't mean I couldn't help you."

"Oh?"

"I can make a few calls. I do have friends in the industry, all over Texas, actually."

Kasper's grin broadened. "Sounds good, whatever you can find out, I mean it, Nikki." His voice was more FBI'ish when he said, "Anything is better than nothing. Only don't compromise yourself or your job. Got me?"

"Yes, sir, and I know you can't see me, but I just saluted you. Now, I gotta get to work."

"Me too, so talk to you tomorrow." He ended the call.

Reaching for her Rolodex, she flipped through and found the number she needed. She picked up her desk phone, punched in the numbers, and listened to the rings before someone finally answered.

"Austin City Morgue, Medical Examiner Cindy Graham."

"Cindy, this is Nikki, Nikki Lam, and don't you have a receptionist?"

"Nikki, well, Good Lord, it's been a long time, girl. How are you? Oh, and I do, but she's out of the office today."

"Ah, I thought perhaps you got demoted." Nikki snickered into the phone. "And I'm doing good these days."

"Okay, so you calling for personal reasons, or is this business?"

"A little of both. First, I met a man, and, uh, he's an FBI agent." She paused waiting for Cindy's response, good or bad.

"Nik, are you sure? You and law enforcement men haven't worked out so well, a patrol cop and a deputy sheriff. I mean, haven't you learned your lesson?"

Nikki heaved a sigh. "Cindy, it's been ten years and I already know some of the pitfalls, I can be ready. Besides, we just met, had lunch once, and I don't know what's gonna happen. We might learn that we detest each other."

"Okay, and when it goes to shit, I have two shoulders for ya. Now, what's the business end of your call, and am I gonna get in trouble?"

"I need you to look into a suicide case, get DNA results on the victim, and prints."

"Sure, who?"

"Dennis Wallen, back in 2011, only his brother was a vice detective on the force back then, so keep this hush-hush, okay?"

Cindy's forehead creased when she asked, "Is this part of your new FBI fella's case?"

"What part of hush-hush don't you understand?" Nikki asked. " Also, can you look for all the next-of-kin, see if there are phone numbers listed back then, too?"

"Alright, I'll look, and uh, if I get any info, where do you want me to send it?"

"Here's an email address. It's a secure address, not mine, but very secure, and after they see the information, they will obliterate it."

"What, you know someone who is gonna explode a computer?"

"Nah, my FBI guy knows a girl who's the bomb with computers. And Cin, thanks, I owe you."

"Yeah-yeah-yeah, next time you're in Austin, drinks are on you, oh, and so are the steaks. Later, and don't be a stranger."

Nikki knew Cindy would follow through, but her face crumpled in concern as they ended the call. Kasper was walking a tightrope with this case. If he called out one of his own and couldn't get the proof he needed, what would happen to his career?

Kasper stared at the top of his desk, thinking about all the information they needed. DNA and prints for Dennis Wallen, the DNA to prove Jay Greenberg was actually Jason Wallen, his half-brother. That was about it. Again, not illegal to change your name, look at all the movie stars and ballplayers, even champion boxers who'd changed their names legally. What was Wallen's reason for the name change, though? What purpose did it serve? The name was effective when signed on to the sheriff's department in 2012, and his entire persona as Jason Wallen disappeared. This happened not long after Dennis's suicide, which consequently was only a month after Mera Soon-Lee went missing, and one day after Sylvia Amos went missing. Coincidental? Kasper didn't think so, but how the hell did it fit together?

CHAPTER FIFTY

The ping signaled an email in the box she had set up more securely than Fort Knox. Frankie opened it, motioning for Kasper to come to her desk. "The message you've been looking for popped up. It was from CindyG@aol.net."

"Nikki told me last night her friend's name is Cindy Graham, must be her. Open it, then print it, and erase, expunge, and eradicate any footprint. Got me, Frankie?"

"Yeah, and you know all those words mean the same thing, dontcha?"

He rolled his eyes upward. "Yes, I know. I'm making a strong point, okay?"

"Yes, sir, Boss, your wish is my command. Go to the back printer. " Frankie counted. "There are twelve pages."

The printer started, and he headed back just as Frankie called over her shoulder, "Oh my goodness, I've lost the file foreverrr..." dragging out the word *forever* in a long drawl.

Kasper had capabilities, but Ryder was better, faster, and more efficient; he envied her talent just a wee bit.

Mick and Bishop walked in laughing, but stopped short when

two pairs of eyeballs regarded them in question. Harlowe rushed her words knowing it looked fishy them walking in together.

"Hiya, guys, sorry we're late. We met for breakfast this morning and Mick's been keeping me laughing with amusing stories about the Kentuckians."

"Bishop's such a city girl. I didn't think she'd last two seconds, but with her mouth and brassiness, she'd fit right in." Mick took his chair, as Harlowe took hers and acted as if this was all normal. Kasper looked at Frankie knowingly. Would this blossom into an intimate relationship?

"Where's Sebastian?" Mick asked.

"On his way. He stopped to get us breakfast, but since y'all have eaten, more for us, I guess," Kasper quipped.

Harlowe stayed quiet slanting a look at Kasper that said, *Sorry, and don't ask questions, not now.* Aloud she asked him, "What's all that?"

Kasper held up the pages. "Autopsy report on Dennis Wallen; one was required after his suicide. It has his blood type, DNA, the whole shebang."

"So what?" Bishop crossed her arms, wondering why Kasper thought this was so great.

"I've got Tobias Robinson inquiring about his birth father, and since no one knows where Matthew Wallen is—and that's who I think his father is—we'll do a test for mitochondrial DNA."

"Hold on a gosh darn second. I thought we used mtDNA for the maternal side?"

"Gosh darn? Really, Mick, you don't wanna fill my swear jar?" Harlowe kidded Townsend, who grinned giving her the finger, then laughed.

Kasper went into his explanation. "A father can pass mtDNA to his kids. Siblings with the same mother share mtDNA. Any two people related on the mother's side have identical mitochondrial DNA sequences as long as the maternal lineage doesn't have a break.

Dennis and Matt have the same mother, and Toby is Matt's son, and their mom is his grandmother."

"It sounds complicated." Mick shook his head trying to keep up.

"The effing point here is we want Jason Wallen's DNA, mtDNA, whatever we can get, so we're just playing an angle by getting Matt's DNA to compare. Wallen might've changed his name to Greenberg, but he can never change his DNA."

"What are we comparing it to? We have zero DNA from any victim, not one," a riled-up Harlowe spouted. "We are on a goose chase, just running in fucking circles."

The door opened. "Hiya, guys, apple fritters, still a little warm, help yourselves." Lefty strolled in with a box from a bakery, set it by the coffeepot, poured a cup for himself, and headed to his desk. As he booted up his system, Kasper got him up to speed.

He sipped his coffee, his lips pursed in thought about this DNA crap. "Hey," he said, "didn't one report in Trina Robinson's case have potential evidence for DNA?"

Kasper grabbed the murder book and brought it to his desk. "Okay, what are we looking for, Lefty?"

"Under evidence collected, about finding her locket. There were several reports with different DNA. The room wasn't too clean, I mean, it was a use-by-the-hour kinda room. CSU found prints, not matching anyone in the system. They found Robinson's prints, confirming she'd been there. What about the other stuff? Hairs? Any foreign substances on the nasty sheets, the towels, or in the sink? We know a maid hadn't cleaned the room, probably in decades, but the reports stated they got a ton of swabs. Can we get it tested? See if any of it matches Wallen's DNA?"

Frankie's jaw dropped. Bishop was slack-jawed, too.

"Corneal, what a fantastic idea, shit, can't believe I didn't think of it myself." Kasper beamed. "It might take a century, but who knows, it might give us just want we need, I mean, we're already waiting on DNA results, and crap, might as well throw this in the hopper for safe measure."

Mick slapped him on the back. "Way to go, Lefty, you're smarter than I ever gave you credit for."

"Yeah, thanks, Mick, coming from you it's sorta an insult, since I always thought you were nothing but a large pulsing muscle with eyeballs and wouldn't know smart if it poked you in the ass." The words came out before Lefty could stop them. He made a *yikes* face with a half-apologetic look to follow, but shut his mouth.

Mick frowned, but then got a picture in his head and chuckled. "That'd make a great cartoon character–giant biceps with eyeballs and skinny legs."

"God, Townsend, you really have changed. In the Academy, you would've socked me in the mug for that comment."

"Yep, I'm a new man, believe it, Corneal" His glance veered toward Bishop and a tiny wink ensued.

FBI Resident Agency–Lake Charles, Louisiana

Jay's eye narrowed as he looked around the room. No one paid him any attention; no one cared what other agents were doing unless they were on a case together. His fingers drummed the armrest while his toe tapped impatiently in a nervous gesture. Fingers on his keyboard, he inhaled softy as he typed in a complicated series of keystrokes. If anyone even got close to his private files, even a quick peek, it would ruin him. They were macabre, they were proof–pictures that would have him tossed into a deep dark hole forever–but he thrived on these photos and could never completely erase them. The file popped up, he minimized the screen, the jpg's were tiny, but he knew what they were.

Selfies of him and each victim, alive and together acting like two long-lost old friends arm-in-arm, smiling. Next, a picture of them gagged and bound, eyes wild and scared. RJ, the bastard tranny, he'd beat the living shit out of him. Trina had been harder to overcome, she'd fought like a wildcat in the motel room, swearing like a sailor, and he wondered what Matt saw in her. Jay looked at his hand—scars from the bites she'd inflicted on him were still there, crazy bitch whore.

The other two, Annie and Nora, Jesus, they really thought he was interested. Both so damn gullible, nothing had changed since high school with them. They still had crushes on him. Jay bit his bottom lip to keep from laughing aloud. He'd used their high school crushes back then to get them to do his bidding.

Clicking through the images, he looked up every few seconds making sure no one was watching. Seeing each photo gave him instant gratification. He was eradicating his past. One person left to deal with. His heart sank. He knew he had to, no, he *must*. Then afterward, he would disappear again, this time for good.

"Hey, Greenberg," Jerry called out, his hand waving him over, "get over here, I need your help with a case file, and got a new assignment for you."

Back to work. He clicked the file off, went into his search engines, cleared the cache, and deleted all searches, wiping out any footprint. He did it quickly and efficiently, as he smiled thinking no one would ever know, no one would ever see; well, almost no one. There was one person who possessed the talent to break his code, but Jay wasn't aware of her, or didn't remember her from his past.

Back at One Justice Way — Dallas FBI Office

"All this lab work is going to take weeks, months, shit!" Harlowe carped.

"Yeah, I know, and I'll push as hard as I can, try to take it up to a higher level." Kasper tried to squelch the depression looming over them.

Waiting on labs, the mammoth hindrance for law enforcement

and any prosecuting attorney's office. The perpetrator could kill a dozen more times before the results were in.

"How many more is he gonna kill, ya think? Or is he done?" Mick asked the team, but Kasper replied.

"Two people come to mind."

Lefty looked at Kasper. "Which two?"

"Matt Wallen and Tobias Robinson."

Bishop asked him, "You think he'd kill his own brother? Even if he knows about the kid, how would Tobias be a threat?"

"I'm thinking he spent more time with Trina. Hashing over old times, telling her how bad he felt for her parents yanked her away from his little brother. I also think she told him Tobias never knew much about his biological father," Kasper expounded.

"But why go after the kid if he's oblivious to his real father? It ain't like there's a huge inheritance or anything."

"I can only speculate. The kid knows nothing about him as Jay Greenberg, but his mom might've talked about her childhood friends, Annie, RJ, Nora, and he thinks Toby will one day put two-and-two together so he's thinking it'd be best to put the kid away for good." Kasper shrugged, not sure what he really believed.

Frankie piped up, "It's only a theory, guys. He might not even care about Toby Robinson. The kid doesn't seem like much of a threat to me. The one I'd worry about is Matt Wallen. We don't know what he knows or if he was involved in any of it back then."

"Yeah, that's who I am worried about and why it's so important we find him." Kasper's frown deepened. "And I called the South Korean American Consulate to see if we could get their help with Mr. Soon-Lee."

"They gonna help us, or what?" Harlowe asked.

"Oh, they said they'd look into it, but the vibe I got was they weren't too concerned about speeding up my request." Kasper wasn't hopeful.

Here's where they were:

- Searching for Lydia Wallen, who was completely off the grid.
- Still not able to locate Matthew Wallen and awaiting paternity testing and mtDNA results, which might take weeks, even months.
- Getting the crime lab to extract DNA samples out of sheets, towels, and carpet pieces; results from swab samples from the bathroom sink, countertop, and the single bedside table taken from the by-the-hour hotel room where Trina had possibly been killed.
- Expecting the South Korean American Embassy to locate Mr. Soon-Lee—not top priority for them.

CHAPTER FIFTY-ONE

Outskirts of Marietta, Oklahoma

"Is this how you run this cheap-ass cemetery? You pile up corpses on each other because you don't have enough land? " Idabel Stout ground out between clenched teeth.

"Mrs. Stout, we run an honorable business. We do not—I repeat, do *not*—bury bodies on top of each other." The elderly man wrung his hands, his wrinkled forehead bunched up as sweat beaded his balding head. How on earth could this have happened?

"Clyde's body needs to be moved without another body sitting on top of his casket. Do you hear me?" Her screeching voice pierced his eardrums, and his entire body tensed up, wanting to smack her into the netherworld.

"This is a matter for the police. Until then, there's nothing I can do."

"Clyde must be moved, do you hear me? He must be moved to our plot in New Jersey. Do you hear me!"

Well, no, duh. She was screaming like a banshee. Crud, even the dead could hear her.

"Yes, ma'am, I understand. I'll do my best to make it happen as soon as possible."

"I've got it arranged if it doesn't happen tomorrow, my attorney will be suing the pants off you and your cemetery!" Mrs. Idabel Stout turned and clomped off. The large woman got in her Lincoln. She peeled out spraying small white pebbles in the air onto the paved road.

Bernie Cooper watched the plume of dust following the Lincoln from the rear of his small family-owned mortuary/slash cemetery, Final Resting Gardens.

He hands shook as he punched in the number and waited.

"Marietta 9-1-1, what's your emergency?" the woman's voice sounded.

"I'd, uh, oh, my, I'd like to report a murder." He closed his eyes, his stomach churned, a new ulcer was forthcoming. He pictured the skeleton—bones of someone who'd not planned to be interred in his cemetery. And why did it have to be on top of Clyde Stout, of all people?

Police, CSU, the fire department, they were all there, including Bernie Copper's son, Ed.

"Interesting." Detective Jeff Larson looked at the skeletal remains of an unknown person with degraded clothing, on top of the burial vault of Clyde Stout.

He flipped his notebook open, glancing at the smaller headstone of Clyde Stout. "Either of you know who this might have been?"

Ed and Bernie glanced into the hole. "Not a clue. How about you, Pop?"

"No idea, "Bernie Cooper said with a quaver in his voice.

"Tell me why Clyde Stout is being disinterred." Larson put his pen to pad and waited.

With the handkerchief from his front jacket pocket, one he

reserved for the teary-eyed mourner, Bernie Cooper wiped his sweaty bald head. "The Stout family is well-known in New Jersey. They were in the process of getting land permits and building permits for a ten-acre family cemetery and large mausoleum back in '94. With all the legalities and paperwork, and sudden cash flow issues, construction, and plot planning was to begin sometime in 1999. Clyde's untimely death in 1994 buggered up their family burial plans."

The detective exhaled. "So, they buried the guy here and now they wanna move his body to New Jersey, what kinda deal is this?"

"Actually," Bernie said, "they simply leased the plot. Idabel Stout and I had a business arrangement once Clyde passed. When the family cemetery and mausoleum were ready, they'd transfer the body. It was unfortunate for the Stout family but there were a lot of other obstructions preventing the completion of the family cemetery. They had problems with building permits for the mausoleum, and Idabel had some serious health issues. All this combined with some cash flow concerns delayed moving Clyde's body for years."

"Uh-huh. Twenty-two years. Long lease for a temporary grave." The detective jotted.

"Detective Larson, Mrs. Stout and Final Resting Gardens have a legal contract, and have had it rewritten to accommodate the extra years."

"I'm not disputing you, Mr. Cooper. But this is big problem, and not just for Mrs. Stout either."

"Oh, dear, I can't tell you how unhappy this makes me. Believe me, I have no idea how this could have even happened."

Bernie Cooper's balding head bobbed. New sweat beads formed and his son patted him on the back. "Take it easy, Pop. We'll get this straightened out. Don't worry."

"When was the hole dug? You keep records?" Larson looked from father to son.

"Here," said Ed Cooper. "This is our log book. Hole was dug on the first date,"—he pointed—"that one in 2011, and the service was the second date. Last entry is the date we filled the hole."

The detective looked and his brows dipped. "So, you dug the hole, next day you had the service. Why'd it take two days to fill the hole?"

"See the notation underneath? Our backhoe wouldn't start. We left a cover on the open grave. Once the backhoe was up and running, he filled the grave. I mean, we can't fill a hole by hand. Shoot can't dig one by hand either." Ed's words were just matter of fact.

"Yeah, I get you. So, who's your backhoe operator? He here?" Larson glanced about looking at headstones, short, tall, wide, chipped, or leaning, one green lawn tent set up in the far backside, and saw the backhoe next to an open grave.

"He's in the maintenance shed," Ed replied.

Bernie Cooper was more than happy to let his son take the lead.

"What's his name? I need to talk to him."

"Larry Darrough, but he's only been with us for a year. He wasn't the operator back in 2011. Back then we had two guys."

Larson heaved a sigh. "Alright, who were your backhoe operators in 2011?"

Bernie Copper spoke up. "A guy named Garcia who went back to México in 2013. And Stan Wallen's gone."

"He skip town, too?" Larson was tiring of the games.

"Yeah," Ed answered. "He skipped the universe. The guy died, two years ago. If you wanna talk to him, he's over there." Ed thumbed back to the front of the graveyard. "They buried Stan beside his son, Dennis."

Detective Larson looked over his shoulder. "Well, shit."

"Sorry," a contrite Bernie Cooper said. "What else can we do to help?"

Larson tapped the tip of his pen against his notebook and said, "How about I get a record of all the holes Wallen dug and filled?"

"Gonna be quite a few holes. Wallen worked here from 1986 to

2012, be a lot of logs to sift through," Bernie Cooper said, still flustered.

"Uh, Pop, we can get the information the detective needs. I'll get it sorted out, don't worry." Ed gave Larson a look.

"How about you get the information together, then call me? Here's my card."

Ed nodded, then asked, "Can we get Mr. Stout's burial vault out so we can transport his body for reburial in New Jersey? It'd be nice to get Mrs. Stout off our backs about this ill-fated incident."

"When CSU's done. It'll be up to them to give you the go-ahead. Ask Harold Knox, but until then, stay outta the way."

"Of course, not a problem, right, Dad?"

Bernie Cooper nodded, his hands still shaking.

Somehow, in 1994, someone dumped a body on top of Clyde Stout's burial vault. Along comes Stan Wallen a few days later, never looking into the hole, and fills the grave. Or did he put the body in? Either way this wasn't good, not good at all.

Five hours later, bones, teeth, degraded clothing, wire metal possibly from a bra, old white tennis shoes, earrings, tarnished costume jewelry, a ring, and two bracelets were discovered, all pointing to a probable female skeleton. CSU sifted through the dirt until there was only dirt, getting samples to boot. Photographs in every angle inside the hole, outside the hole, ten feet from the hole, as well as the headstone and the top of Clyde Stout's burial vault.

"Mr. Cooper?"

Both Ed and Bernie turned and answered, "Yes?"

Harold Knox regarded them.

"I'm Ed, this is my dad, Bernie." He stuck his hand out and Harold took it.

"I'm Officer Harold Knox, lead CSU technician. We're done. Here's the form releasing the crime scene."

Ed took the paperwork. "Will there be anything else?"

"Don't think so. Sorry about your troubles. This'll be hitting the news. Be best if you spoke with your attorney on how to handle the situation. Good luck."

The Coopers watched them drive away, both father and son worried about how this was going to affect their flawless reputation in the community.

Detective Larson sat at his desk, his eyes glued to a light-gray screen. In the upper left-hand corner were the words, *Marietta Police,* with gold shield emblems next to them. In the center blinking box, he entered his password and pulled up reports, clicked on forms, and the drop-down menu populated the screen. Scrolling, he clicked "homicide" and hit "enter."

Name: J Doe. Sex: Undetermined. Age: Undetermined.

Undetermined—this was the dominant word for his case. All he had was a date the hole was dug and filled. Heck, the victim could've been dead for days, even weeks before being tossed into the open grave then buried a few days later, and no one the wiser. Larson's mouth twisted. Did these backhoe operators think to look into holes before they filled them? Or had Stan Wallen put the body in himself? The guy was dead. What was he gonna do, have a séance? Ask him, "*Hey, Mr. Wallen, who'd ya kill before you kicked the bucket?*"

Larson leaned back, closed his eyes, and with his thumb and middle finger he squeezed the bridge of his nose to ward off the headache he was looking forward to getting soon. This was news *The Marietta Mirror* would eat up, maybe spotlighting him as a fool. A few dickwads in town called him Barney Fife. He hated the stigma, because the towns he'd policed were small; hell, he had a bachelor's in criminal justice and was working toward his bachelor in cybersecurity. Piss on them.

Inhaling, his fingers poised over the keyboard, he typed and pulled up the National Missing Unidentified Persons System (NamUs) and waited. Once the program loaded, he input a date to research a few weeks before the hole was dug. He hit "enter" and again waited. Not like Marietta or the surrounding towns had a lot of missing people reported.

The list was longer than he'd figured, but still short. Larson scrolled, slowly looking at each missing person's case—the gender, age, when missing, current age, and name. One stood out immediately for no other reason than the name and the date last seen. Last seen, four days before the grave was dug for Clyde Stout; her name, Lydia Wallen.

Now he needed the full report. He clicked on cold cases, archives, Marietta, Oklahoma, the date, and the name, *Wallen, Lydia, D.* Reports stated she was never found and thought to have run off with her lover, a guy by the name of Stoltz, recently released from Huntsville State Penitentiary, five days before she went missing.

With his BOP number, Larson pulled up inmate *Stoltz, Jerry, R.* Under his breath he said, "Ah, what do we have here?" A new incarceration date, whatdaya know? Six months later, Stoltz committed his third felony. Strike three. This garnered him a ninety-nine-year sentence. What a loser. Larson scrolled to see the rest of Stoltz's stats. "Well, shit," Larson said under his breath. The words glared out at him. *Inmate Deceased; investigation closed.*

Jeff Larson was back at square one.

CHAPTER FIFTY-TWO

One Justice Way — Dallas, Texas

Kasper's hands came up and his fingers rubbed his eyes. Not enough sleep these past few days and weeks. He rubbed his jaw. He needed new razors and was almost out of shampoo. At least Harlowe was no longer bitching at him about zero food in his fridge and why he never slept. A few days ago she'd moved into an Extended Stay Inn close to the office. As luck would have it, it was close to Mick's hotel. He wondered but never said a word. It was her life, and she was an adult. In his head, though, Townsend and Bishop didn't seem like a possible coupling.

"Morning, Bergman, is there fresh coffee?"

"Yeah, just made a fresh pot." He pushed himself from his desk and got up. "Pour me a cup too, will ya, Frankie? Where's Lefty, didn't y'all ride together?"

Francine plopped her shoulder bag on her desk and went straight for the dark thick coffee. Columbian mud, she called it, Kasper's signature coffee. "He dropped me off and went to run clothes to the dry cleaners. Harlowe and Mick aren't here yet?"

"Nope. About her and Mick, really, you think?" Kasper took the cup from her and sipped.

Frankie did a closemouthed chuckle, then, "Strange bedfellows, but hey, opposites do attract. Mick seems one-hundred percent changed, different, and in a good way."

"Yeah, I was worried how this would play out, asking him to help. Sorta happy."

Frankie brows dipped. "Sorta happy? Why sorta?"

"Harlowe's a great gal, don't wanna see her hurt."

"Bishop's a big girl. She can handle herself."

"Mick, too, with a few Judo moves." A tired grin settled on his face.

Everyone dug in different areas, looking for Matt Wallen, and no one, not even the Oklahoma Police Force, had found a physical address. They'd put surveillance on the PO Box, got eyes on Wallen, taken a few photos, and passed them along.

"They spotted him at a small diner. He ate at the counter, went to the men's room, and must've left out the back because he never came out. Ardmore cops went in and Wallen all but vanished. He had to have left out a back door."

"Could be he's afraid Jason's looking for him," Harlowe stated matter-of-factly.

"Nah, I think the guy is just whacko. The cops say he might be homeless."

"Possibly, Lefty, but the guy has to sleep somewhere, under a bridge, in a tent in the homeless community, somewhere."

"Kasper's right," said Mick. "What if we get a private dick to follow him? Plainclothes, be less intimidating than uniforms, get me?"

"Yeah, I get what you're saying, Mick," Kasper answered, "but we're not about to hire a private dick, Lord, we're the effing FBI, man."

A soft ping alerted Frankie, and she focused on her computer screen.

"Uh, guys," she got their attention. "Someone just opened the missing person's file on Lydia Wallen."

"How do you know?" Harlowe asked.

"I put an alert on her file so if anyone opened it I'd know."

"You put a tracer on who accessed the file?" Kasper walked to her desk.

"Yep, sure did. Somebody opened this file at the Marietta Police Department, yesterday morning."

Kasper went back to his desk and retrieved his phone. "Let's make a call, shall we?"

Not over twenty minutes later he ended his call with Detective Jeff Larson of the Marietta PD, updated his team, and opened his email to find the information Larson sent.

The others stood behind his desk as he clicked open the file and they read the incident report from yesterday's ordeal at Final Resting Gardens Cemetery.

"Twenty-two years she been on top of this Clyde Stout and no one would have ever found the body if they hadn't wanted to move his body back to New Jersey. What are the damn odds?" Frankie said, astounded.

"If it really is Lydia Wallen, there's nothing to compare her bone DNA to?" Discouraged, Harlowe sulked.

"They might have to exhume another body, but they could match her DNA to Dennis Wallen," Lefty said.

"Yeah, that's gonna take too long, dontcha think?"

"Mick's right, we need another way to—"Kasper's cell phone chirped, and he saw it was Dr. Lam calling.

"Dr. Lam." He listened. His head nodded every so often and a smile crept on his face. "Thanks, Nikki, that's great, and yeah, dinner next week sounds good, see ya then." He hit "disconnect" and looked at his team.

"Dr. Lam's lab results came back on the semen found behind Nora Mendez-Finch's ear. Now all we need is a match."

"Fat chance that's gonna happen. You wanna call Greenberg and say, hey, dude, spit in a cup and mail it to me, would ya?" Lefty said, frustrated.

"I think we need to call him, bring him into the case."

"Are you crazy, Frankie, he'd catch on and then run."

"I agree with Mick," Kasper said. "We can't bring him in, too risky. Frankie, where's Greenberg working these days?"

In a short few seconds Frankie had his itinerary. "Currently the douche is in Lake Charles, Louisiana, FBI resident office. Looks like he's there twiddling his thumbs, he's not working a case."

"I am so sick of this spinning-the-wheels shit and not getting anywhere." A huff blew out of Harlowe's partially closed lips.

Kasper said, "Let's find another judge, tell 'em why we feel Matt Wallen is in danger."

"You think I haven't explained it to every judge I've contacted? We've exhausted our search capabilities. There's no sign of Matt Wallen. His DMV address got us zip, other than an out-and-out manhunt. Got any other ideas, Chief?" Frankie's concern for Matt was real.

"A phone call I can make, ask for a favor."

"Make the call, because if you don't I'll unofficially access the Social Security Administration's mainframe to get his whereabouts."

With a nod he pulled out his phone. His eyes scanned each face.

"Let me make this call in private." With that he walked out to the hallway, scrolled, then hit "call" hoping he was available to talk. He paced the length of the hall.

"West, Homicide."

"Hey it's Kasper, I need a favor—"

He relayed his case, cutting to the chase quickly, and Detective Jack West listened.

"Sounds like a humdinger of a case, Bergman. I can give Judge Carlson a call, kid. She's a well-liked judge in Houston and I'm sure she has friends everywhere."

Kid. Jack was still calling him *kid*, but it made him smile and homesick for Houston and the HPD.

"I appreciate it, Jack."

"You think this Matt Wallen is in danger?"

"Yeah, I do. I'm also 99.9 percent sure Greenberg is our guy. He's killed at least three other women, the transgender woman, and possibly his stepmother. I think he's also good for the missing Thackerville woman. The man is cleaning house, knocking off anyone who knows his past."

"What about this woman, Mera Soon-Lee?" Jack propped his booted feet up on the corner of his desk, his phone to his ear, his brows dipped wondering what Bergman had gotten himself into. Accusing a fellow agent was risky business. The kid had great gut instincts, though, and a good head on his shoulders.

Bergman breathed into the phone heavily. "I haven't mentioned it to the team yet, but somehow I think the brother, Dennis, was the perp for Mera Soon-Lee."

"Yeah, why's that?"

"Seems her disappearance and his suicide were awfully close to the same time; guilt, you think? Another reason I need to find Matthew Wallen, he might have insight."

"Alright, Bergman, let me get on the horn with Carlson, she always liked you, and I'll sweet-talk her, text you soon as I get her answer. What's your email, I'll see if she'll get who owes her a favor to email the warrant directly to you. Work for you?"

"Yeah, Jack, thanks, man. Next time I'm in town, I'll meet ya at Quins, buy ya a few boilermakers. You still drink those?"

"Damn straight I do, especially if you're buying! Later, kid."

The line went dead and Kasper smiled. He missed working with Jack West and the crew at HPD, but he loved his new job, too.

CHAPTER FIFTY-THREE

"Fingers crossed, team. Hope to get a warrant to request the Social Security Administration to give up Matt Wallen's physical address. Praying he has one that's legit. Just spoke with Jack, he's gonna see about asking a judge he knows to find a judge friend she has in Dallas who'll sign off on the warrant."

"Detective Jack West from Houston?"

"Only West I know, Lefty, so yeah, him."

"You discuss the case with him, get his thoughts?" Harlowe looked over the rim of her official FBI coffee mug.

"Robbs said keep our ducks in a row on this." He looked around. "Where's Mick?"

"Said he had a private call he needed to make," Frankie said as Mick came back in and took his seat.

"Everything good, Townsend?"

"Yeah, it's all good, just needed to call a friend." Mick sounded odd, but Kasper didn't press. He didn't want to not trust the guy, but hey, it was Townsend.

"So, Chief, what's next?" Lefty asked, his eyes on Mick, then back to Kasper.

"We need to find Matt Wallen, get his story, and pray our DNA results get here soon, and hope we hear from the American Consulate in Korea, all before we go after Jay Greenberg. I want an airtight case when we nail this friggin' bastard." Bergman gazed at each individual's face, landing on Bishop's, who was grinning ear to ear.

"Bishop? What's that smile for?"

"Well, Bergman, you know those photos of the twenty-two-year-old crime scene you got from Detective Larson?"

"Yeah, so?"

"I've been doing some digging." She took two photos to his desk and pointed. "See this?"

"Uh-huh, a bracelet. So?"

"Give her a minute," Lefty spouted.

Harlowe slid the other picture over. "See this?"

"Same bracelet, so?"

"No, they're different. Look closer. Use the magnifier."

His shrugged, took the magnifier, and examined them closely. They were both wide, with thin grooved lines and inlaid with what appeared to be diamonds and green stones, emeralds perhaps. The stones were dull, and the grooves filled with dirt, and the jewels had dirt caked under each set of prongs.

"Okay, so?"

"Look at the cleaned-up versions of these pictures." She handed him another photo.

"They look very nice, almost real."

Harlowe expelled a huff. "Kasper, you dope, they are."

"Fine, the dead person, woman I'm guessing, had some nice jewelry."

Lefty shook his head. "No, not if it was Lydia Wallen, because back then they didn't have piss to put in a piss pot. I checked the financials. "

"Okay, and?"

"Look." Harlowe handed him a photo of Annelle Mackey and

another of RJ Anderson, prior to him being called Rayna. "Use the magnifier again. Look at their wrists, closely."

Again his shoulders lift and he took the photos and magnifying glass and looked. He held one up to see better, raising the magnifier, and said, "I'll be damned."

"Yep, that's what I said when they showed me," Frankie agreed.

"Lemme see." Mick's outstretched hand took the photos and when he saw it, he whistled. "Well, motherfucker, where the hell did they get those bracelets if they were poor country kids?"

Harlowe jiggled the swear box under Mick's nose and he grumped at her. "Alright, alright, Miss Potty Mouth." He threw in the remaining change in his jacket pocket, all sixty-one cents. Then, "How much are these valued at?"

"The smaller one, five thousand for the jewels, a thousand for the gold content, the larger one, the diamonds alone equal a little over two carats, and the emeralds one and a half. The band is eighteen karats, valued at twenty grand, possibly a lot more."

"Whew." Kasper's brows wrinkled as he leaned back. "Any thefts in the area, anyone report jewelry being stolen back then?"

"Yeah, I thought about that, so I checked, and yep. Jewelry got stolen, alright."

"And?" He waved his hand. "It's like I'm pulling teeth, Bishop, spit it out."

"Stolen from Mabel Armstrong, a decedent buried at Final Resting Gardens. Mrs. Armstrong was wearing them at her service, but the jewelry wasn't supposed to be buried with her. She'd bequeathed this jewelry to her great-granddaughter but the family in their grief forgot about them until a few days later."

Kasper's eyes widened. "They exhumed her body to get her jewelry?"

"No, they didn't have to exhume her because the delivery for her burial vault got delayed, some glitch in ordering, so they stored her casket in the back of the mortuary for a few days—four to be exact. The great-granddaughter was filling out her college apps when she remembered those bracelets were her college tuition. Only when they go to unseal Grandma's casket, the bracelets aren't there. The family got their money because the old lady insured her jewelry. They investigated and everyone took a poly, everyone but the kids. Until today, it's been a mystery, one we just solved."

Kasper moved his eyes up to see her face. "You mean grave-robbing was going on, or should we call it casket-robbing, and Wallen was the perp?"

Her head bobbed. "Yeah, because his dad was the backhoe digger, and he had access, the sick bastard. Here's something. If Mackey and Anderson were wearing the bracelets, they were with him when this body got dumped, and by the size of the bones, I'm leaning toward this being Lydia Wallen, who was a large woman and missing around that same time."

A smile crept up his face. "Good work, Bishop, damn good job. The pieces are really falling together, dontcha think, team?"

Everyone agreed, but it wasn't over yet. They needed Greenberg in cuffs.

"Hey, Dennis Wallen's suicide, was there anything worth anything on the report?"

"Nah, it was a cut-and-dried case but his prints are on file, so is his DNA. Only thing about Greenberg/Wallen, he called it in because he witnessed the suicide."

"That's it?"

"Bishop, it's more than we had, and don't complain."

"Sure, just frustrated, Frankie, that's all."

Kasper's brain clicked on something, you could see it all over his face. Harlowe recognized that look.

"What, Bergman?"

Out of his seat, he went to the murder books and pulled out the third book on Soon-Lee. "Prints, that's what." Flipping through the book, he got to the page with prints.

"Whose prints are you looking for, the victims'?" Mick asked, looking over Bergman's shoulder.

"No, no, see..."—Bergman pointed to the page—"they pulled prints that didn't match hers off her purse, and we haven't matched them to anyone."

Frankie's eyes narrowed. "And whose prints do you want to match them to? Greenberg's prints are on file, same as ours, and they don't match. Plus, he had a solid alibi, so that's a bust."

"Did anyone think to check Dennis Wallen's alibi?"

Kasper went from face to face ending up on Harlowe's whose face crinkled in thought, and asked, "You think Dennis killed Mera? For what end?"

Kasper shrugged. "Don't know why. But she was in Oklahoma about a month before and he was at the cabin with Jason two weeks later."

Mick asked, "You're saying he felt guilty for killing Jason's girlfriend? So he ate his gun? "

"Dunno, but ain't gonna hurt to check it out," Kasper remarked. He took his seat, ready to call the print division, and his intercom buzzed and he snatched up the phone. "Yeah, Carol?"

"Agent Bergman, I have a man on line four who says he needs to speak with you."

"Do I know him?"

"You know a Chung Soon-Lee?"

"Carol, put him through forthwith."

"Yes, sir."

Kasper's heart picked up a notch.

"Mr. Soon-Lee, this is Agent Kasper Bergman."

The room was deathly silent, so silent that the sound of a pin dropping would've been like a grenade exploding, and no one seemed to breathe.

Harlowe reacted first, pointing at the phone, her ears, and mouthing the words, *put it on speaker*.

"Mr. Soon-Lee, fine, Chung, I've got my team here. May I put you on speaker? Good." Kasper hit "speaker."

"Team, this is Chung Soon-Lee. Chung, Agents Bishop, Ryder, Sebastian, and Townsend."

"Nice to meet you, but let me get to the point, since this an overseas call. I've recently gotten word you are looking into my daughter's murder, correct?"

"Yes, we are. Did the American Consulate finally reach out?"

"No, my ex-wife Gladys did. She told me a lady with the FBI came to see her. Agent Bishop, I believe it was you, and thank you, ma'am, for your kindness to my ex-wife. Since our daughter's death, Glad hasn't been well, never will be again, I am afraid, so tread lightly where she is concerned, please."

Kasper spoke, "We understand, and we are truly sorry for the loss you and she suffered. Did your wife call you about this, sir?"

"I was there about a month ago. She told me then."

"You didn't reach out, sir, why not?" Kasper was a bit put out.

"I wanted to. However, my business in the States kept me tied up. I was on a tight schedule and got back to Korea last week. Before you say anything, Agent Bergman, I may have something that could help you find my daughter's killer."

"We're listening."

Five sets of eyes glued to the speakerphone, holding their breaths.

"I recently had to clean out an old storage unit and found something of Mera's I'd forgotten about. My daughter mailed herself a package with two letters. In the first letter, she asked me to hide the box until she could retrieve it. Her second letter was a decoy for her mom. Gladys is a busybody. I never told her about the package, and apparently I hid it very well since I've just now found it or even remembered it. Look, before you reprimanded me, Agent Bergman, my daughter disappeared, and unless you have a child that goes missing, you can't understand where my head was. I couldn't think rationally. I'd hid the package, and you know, out of sight, out of mind. All I could think about was my only child was gone, and no one knew her whereabouts—not me, her mother, her close friends, coworkers, not even her boyfriend. That's a moot point now. Only by pure accident was Mera's body found and we finally got to bury her and let her rest in peace."

"Yes, sir, we'll never understand your pain, and again, we're sorry for your loss." Kasper's heartfelt sadness traveled through the airwaves eleven-thousand miles away, across the Pacific Ocean, to the ears of Mr. Chung Soon-Lee.

"Thank you, Agent Bergman. Now, about this box, I haven't opened it, don't have the heart to because I don't know what I'll find, but if it was important to Mera, then it was important. I'll FedEx it to you Priority Mail, and it should arrive one, maybe two business days. I ask one favor."

"That would be?"

"Find out who murdered my only child and bring him to justice, make him pay for what he took from us."

"Mr. Soon-Lee, we'll do our best, I can promise you. If need be, how can you be reached?"

CHAPTER FIFTY-FOUR

Two days later, the print division delivered results. They were able to match Dennis Wallen's prints to prints lifted from the inside of Mera's purse. The prints had not been in contact with the elements; they were damn lucky.

"Unbelievable what science can do these days, ain't it?"

Townsend was right, and FBI agents were thankful for modern science.

"Okay, so he kills her, but why?" This perplexed Harlowe.

"We may never know, unless maybe Greenberg knows and tells us."

"Yeah, but we got to catch him first, Frankie."

Kasper said, "Lefty's right, and we still have nothing to call Greenberg in on, yet." His eyes on the white whiteboard, he ran down what they had, as the others listened.

"Yep, we got a lot of circumstantial evidence, nothing concrete, except Dennis Wallen's prints, but no goddamned prints for anyone else at any scene and no fuck-all DNA or whatever. All we've got is a motherfucking theory."

"Harlowe," Mick said, "put a twenty in the swear box, you're behind and need to pay up."

A wry look crossed her face. With a forceful yank, she tugged open a drawer, pulled out her purse, dug out a twenty, and stuffed it into the box. "Fine, you *ass,* and I just paid for that." She stuck her tongue out and he bit back a laugh.

Frankie, her head into her computer, looked up. "Kasper, Jack came through, we've got the warrant. Now we can get into Wallen's Social Security info. I'll send it into the admin office, get clearance to pull his SSA records."

"How long will that take, Frankie?" Lefty leaned in to look at her computer screen.

"Not long. I just sent them a PDF of the warrant, noting *urgent.*"

"Call them, have an administrator handle this, get them moving," Kasper said, then to Harlowe and Townsend, "How about y'all make a trip to go pick Matthew Wallen up after we've got confirmation of his address? Call the Ardmore PD, have them sit on the guy until then, got it?"

"Got it. Come on, Bishop, let's go gas up the rental and get moving. Frankie, will you text us the address once you get it?"

Surprise on her face that Mick was taking charge, Frankie smiled. "Sure, Mick, will do."

"Come on, Harlowe, let's move. Traffic won't be as bad if we leave now."

Harlowe shrugged, grabbed her purse, then spied the swear box. Taking it, she handed it Kasper. "Guard this, it's a fund for after we've cleared this fucking case for a free night of drinking and cussing."

"What if that potty mouth of yours gets going while you're headed to Oklahoma?"

Mick grinned. "I've got it covered, Lefty. She can dump her swear money in the console."

Bishop huffed. "Great. Now, let's go, we've got an evil man to pick up. Oh, and if any new shit comes in, give us a fucking call." She reached inside her pants pocket, pulled out a dollar, and handed it to Kasper. Mick's laugh boomed as they walked out the door.

Thirty minutes later, Frankie had an address and called the Ardmore PD, telling them to pick him up if they found him and hold him for questioning. Then she texted Harlowe the plan and the address so if he wasn't home they could sit on his house.

Kasper drummed the top of his desk, then said, "Lefty, can you put a report together, like a diagram we'd do with a mob?"

"You mean put Greenberg at the top like the mob boss, and a diagram showing how each person's connected to him?"

"Exactly, and Frankie, pull all the pen pal letters plus the ones found with Soon-Lee, look at the dates, see when they were written and by whom. Find out if they're still in lockup or dead; if they're dead, find out when then died and how."

"Hey, Kasper."

"Yeah."

"You send Mick and Harlowe off together for any specific reason?"

"Yeah, Frankie, you just heard me. I want them to pick up Wallen."

"No, that's not what I meant."

Kasper's brows curved inward. He smiled. "Oh, I see what you're getting at. No, I didn't do it for that reason."

Francine Ryder grinned. "They make a cute couple, don't you think? Almost as cute as you and Dr. Lam."

Kasper blushed.

Lefty had entitled his diagram, "Jay Greenburg's Connection Org Chart." Greenburg was at the top, with each victim placed on the chart, in how they linked to his past. Next was a graph on where he was in each instance he allegedly murdered them. His father and brothers were on another section of chart, including his stepmother, Lydia, Sylvia Amos, and Gloria Manchester.

"So," Kasper said, eyeballing the chart. "We can link him to every victim, and with the exceptions of Soon-Lee, Amos, and Manchester, we can put him in the vicinity."

"Don't forget Lydia Wallen," Lefty pointed out.

"No, I'm looking at him for her murder, too. He had the means and the opportunity."

"Kasper, we saw the jewelry on Anderson and Mackey. We know they were there, maybe it was just them," Frankie was quick to state.

"Why, she wasn't their stepmother? Here's what I think. I think Greenberg had had enough, and she pushed him to the brink; he snapped. We know his father worked at the cemetery, be easy for him to dump her body, hell, maybe good ole dad was in on it and that's why he covered the grave without a thought."

Frankie nodded. "Huh, sounds pretty damned plausible, I gotta admit."

"Also, since they knew, maybe that's why he killed them...maybe they even helped him kill her."

"Okay, now I've got to ask—why did he wait so long to go after them? It makes little sense."

Kasper's mouth twisted up in thought, then his phone jangled and he picked up without responding to Lefty's question. "Hey, Carol, what's up? Be there in a jiff." Then, "FedEx delivered our overseas package."

The box gave off ominous vibes. Reaching inside his drawer, he pulled out latex gloves, snapping them on before slitting it open to find the original flat mailing box with Mera Soon-Lee's name and her parents' address. Kasper viewed the postmark on the box. "Look," he pointed out, "she mailed this from Ardmore, Oklahoma, nine days before she went missing. Frankie, look at the dates Greenburg was in Huntsville. How many days after she mailed this?"

She thumbed through a stack of papers. "Here, says he was there when she was in Ardmore. Was still there when she got back. Actually, he was there through the next week and she'd gone missing that same weekend by these dates."

"After her visit to Ardmore, she goes missing. I suspect what's in this box is the motive for her disappearance and murder."

With due diligence, they photographed the delivery box, then the parcel inside, getting great stills of the postmarks on both and the delivery origins.

A long steady sigh blew from Kasper's lips as he carefully cut open the flat mailing box to not damage the outside. It would have to be sent to the print lab, perhaps DNA, if possible. Bending the flaps back they looked inside. Different-colored spiral notebooks, old and worn, each dated in faded black Sharpie with a year—1988, 1994, 1996. Under the books were letters, some still sealed and marked, *Return to Sender*, others lay opened and flat. Kasper took them out one by one, reading each, then passed it to Frankie, who passed it to Lefty. Except for the sound of paper rustling, the room was eerily silent.

"Letters from cons, and letters written to cons." Frankie eyed the *Return to Sender* letters, with the Marietta address as the sender—Lydia Wallen.

"Guess now we know the origin of the letters found in Mera's purse. But how did she get this stuff?"

Kasper said, "I'd guess that Stan Wallen gave her these, didn't know what he had, or he'd have trashed this stuff. You know how it goes—you move out and leave all kinds of crap in your parents' attic."

No one spoke, thinking about this idea. It was a probable scenario.

"What, she pinches these letters and three composition books, which by the way I cannot wait to read. Afterward, she laminates a few and mails the rest to herself. Why?"

"Her objective in life was to be an investigative reporter. Maybe there was a story there, and she was gonna write it?" Kasper looked expectantly at them.

"Yeah, maybe use it as her reason to break up. But he was in Huntsville when she went missing. So?" Frankie reminded them.

Kasper said one word and only one. "Dennis."

"Yeah, "Frankie nodded and said, "She was there, got this crap, and maybe she confronts him about his older brother and what, Dennis goes into protective mode?"

"We've connected his prints to Mera's disappearance and murder."

"Yep, now we have a probable motive for his killing her, to keep the family secrets a secret. You think he told Jason, Jay, whatever, that he had to kill her and then felt guilty so he eats his gun?" Lefty went to the coffeepot, poured the dregs of the pot into a cup, and put on a fresh pot.

Frankie said, "It's the only plausible explanation and there's not a damn soul we can ask. She's dead, so is he."

Kasper reached into the box. "Here, Left, take '88, Frankie you take '96 and I'll dig into '94. He didn't know Mera yet, so probably nothing about her. He knew all the others, though, maybe he wrote about them. Let's read, because like I said we need to learn about Jason the boy, and now's our chance."

Each began, and as they read further into each year, they learned long ago a dormant evil lived inside a boy named Jason Wallen, who grew into a full-blown monster.

CHAPTER FIFTY-FIVE

Lefty sat his notebook down.

"You finished?" Francie asked, turning a page.

"Uh-huh. Get this, in '88, Jason was eleven and man, the kid had an enterprise going."

Kasper looked up from his read. "Like a business?"

Lefty's eyes pierced a hole in the top of his desk, his mouth set in a frown.

"What, mowing yards or what?" Kasper's curiosity piqued.

A deep-seated sigh fanned pages on Lefty's desk before he spoke. "Nope, it was grave-robbing."

Two heads, popped up, one belonging to Kasper, the other was Frankie; eyes wide with incredulous expressions, and Kasper said, "What the fuck?"

"Yeah, straight out of the caskets, sick kids." He went on, "They'd go to the funeral home with their dad the day of the viewings, feigning paying their respects. They'd dress in nicer clothes to make it look on the up-and-up. Smart bastards. They viewed the body looking for jewelry, trinkets, anything they thought might be of value. The night before the funeral they'd sneak in and remove items no one would be looking for. The day of the service, Jason writes families are clueless, because they're too sad and crying. If they got a chance before the casket was sealed, they'd look again, and then do things with the dead bodies. Him and the other boys performed sexual acts —he showed them how, told 'em it was okay because no one would ever see the body again."

"Now, that's just sick." Frankie's lips curled in disgust.

"Listen to this," Kasper read:

> *"Ray and Annie got scared, but I told 'em I'd make it worth their while if they helped me, so I gave them the bracelets cuz there was more where that came from. Idiots wore them around town, but no one noticed. Guess cuz we are all poor white trash."*

"Ah, so the bracelets found with the body, I see," Lefty stated.

Kasper nodded. "And there's more. This next entry is a month later. Jason wrote:

> *"Her eyes rolled up. The fat bitch was choking on her tongue; I laughed. It felt fucking great watching her lights go out, she would be nevermore, like that stupid Poe story about the fucking raven we had to read in school. RJ and Annie, those fuckers lost the damn bracelets when we dumped her fat ass in the hole and we had to get outta there fast. Besides, no one wanted to jump on her dead fat ass. 'Go to hell, bitch', I screamed at her dead fat ass in the hole."*

"Oh Lord, his stepmother was his first," Lefty said surprised.

"And," Frankie said, "Gloria was number two."

Kasper and Lefty looked at her, both slack-jawed.

"In '88, Jason mentions Gloria," Lefty said. "He calls her a good friend, a girl who's neat."

"His relationship with her changes in '94, because he says she's a fucking great lay and best girlfriend ever," Kasper disclosed.

Frankie went on, "In short, she was pregnant, not willing to abort.

They fought about it and two days later she was missing. Y'all wanna know who her BFF was back then? You guys ready? It was Sylvia Amos."

Kasper looked from one to the other. "The pieces are fitting together, team, all we need now is to verify this information and submit the evidence we have to the US Attorney."

"Uh, look, Kasper," Frankie jumped in, "these are the writings of a kid, not concrete proof, no DNA, no witnesses, because they're dead, and it's a 'he said, we think' sorta case. Unless he admits to this, we can't prove a damn thing."

"We need to talk to Matt Wallen. He's the last living person who knows anything about Jason Wallen. And we need to put the information together to close the case on Mera Soon-Lee Wallen, if for nothing else than the sake of her family."

"That, I know we can do; we've got prints and a timeline proving she was in Ardmore. How about to solidify the case we dig, locate any cell number Dennis Wallen had, trace his movements back then, and hers, see if they crossed paths? Not just where, but when. Wasn't her cell phone found with her body?"

"Yes, it was," Lefty said, then, "That's a great idea, Fran, and I can get Travis on that ASAP, he's a whiz."

Absently nodding Kasper looked up. "Do it. Soon we've got Wallen." His eyes steely, he said, "I want him here in this office and in an interrogation room. I want to catch this son of a bitch before he finishes cleaning house."

Ardmore, Oklahoma — Two and a Half Hours Later

Harlowe and Mick surveyed the rundown area, Culbertson Street. There were lots of older frame homes, older as in built when the earth's crust was forming. Harlowe spotted them right away in an unmarked car sitting on the opposite corner, two plainclothes cops watching the house. With an easy gait, she strolled to the driver's window which was already down.

"I'm Bishop, over there's my partner, Townsend." In her head the words *partner* and *Townsend* were never two words she would've associated with each other. She almost laughed aloud but kept it in check.

"I'm Harris, that's Carmichael,"—his chin jutted to the guy in the passenger seat."

"Which house?"

Carmichael thumbed to the house on the corner.

"That house, really? You sure it's not condemned?"

Little grass, mostly weedy overgrowth and dirt, windows boarded up, missing glass, and paint peeling off in front of their eyes. The wooden porch was dangerously concave and the front steps missing slats. The sidewalk cracked and chipped. Bushes resembling jungle covered the cyclone fence on one side, intertwined with trash. The gate was missing.

"It's the address your agent gave us. We asked a few neighbors, they said he comes and goes, stays away for days, very secretive."

"Hmm. Tell you what, say a 7-Eleven around the corner, we're gonna go get drinks and stakeout food, plus visit the facilities, then we'll relieve you."

"Sounds good. We've been here five hours and been a bit bored."

"If he shows, detain him until we get back. Oh, and that's the life of an FBI agent, most days."

"Ma'am?"

"Boring, most days our lives are boring."

Back in Dallas at One Justice Way

"Got something interesting here, guys," Frankie announced.

"More interesting than these horror stories in spirals?"

"Nah, Lefty, but damn near."

"Whatcha got?" Kasper asked, pouring a fresh cup of coffee.

"Every con is dead, and what's interesting is they all died while incarcerated."

"Death row, sickness, shanked, what?" Lefty leaned back, bouncing his chair.

"No executions. Most of the men on death row have been there twenty-plus years. Another prisoner killed most of the cons whose names are on these letters, and they've not solved the cases."

Kasper's eyes drew together. "Are you—we—saying this is not a coincidence?"

She shrugged. "Dunno. Let me see something, hold on." Frankie scanned a few pages and nodded. "Someone killed two inmates a week after Wallen was at Huntsville doing that clandestine shit, and no, I'm not putting money in the swear jar. One of these guys was writing from Hutchinson County, they found him in his cell, he hanged himself, but it was a suspicious hanging."

"They investigating it?" asked Lefty.

"Yeah, but the investigation is closed, no DNA, no prints, nada to go on, so they're calling it a suicide. Now, here's something else. Four of these guys writing to Lydia Wallen were murdered in custody."

"Where were they?" Kasper's interest was aroused.

"Two in the Oklahoma State Pen, one at FCI in Bastrop County, and another guy at Parchman Farm, Mississippi."

"Spread out, aren't they?"

"Uh-huh, but not the murders...they all happened on the same date."

Kasper and Lefty responded in unison, "What the hell?"

"These guys didn't know each other. Their only connection was being a pen pal to Lydia Wallen, Jason's stepmother," Frankie said.

Kasper's head moved side to side, as he said," He's cleaning house, isn't he?"

Lefty's eyes narrowed almost shutting. "You saying Greenberg called in hits on these men?"

"In my opinion, it's not too far-fetched. Frankie has the means, and he has reach."

"I dunno, Kasp, what would be the reason, what's a con gonna do to him?"

Kasper's face pulled in a shrug contemplating Wallen's thought process before he answered her. "If you were cleaning house, would you clean every corner, even if you couldn't see the cobwebs?"

Her shoulders hunched up. "I guess so."

"These men, the men his stepmother was writing to, you think they kept the letters she wrote?" He held up a hand. "Not a question for you to answer, I'm just saying, if they kept the letters and somewhere in these letters she mentions him and how she hates him, and how her boys are bound for jail, and what should she do..."

Her face registered what he said. "You mean they could've had letters incriminating him as a boy, back in the day. I see, but he was Jason Wallen then, not Jay Greenberg."

"Doesn't matter, because Jason Wallen is traceable to Jay Greenberg, and Greenberg to the FBI."

"Munn." It was all Frankie uttered.

"What?"

"I said Munn, what about him, you think?"

A look of uncertainty crossed Bergman's face. "Call Swisher, check on him; I could give a flea's ass about the guy, but even a dickhead like Preston Munn doesn't deserve to be murdered in cold blood."

Frankie dialed the prison and then waited.

"Warden Swisher, Agent Ryder. Yeah, I'm good, listen, is Munn still alive and kicking? Yeah, he is, good. Hold on a minute." She saw Kasper's hand reach out to take over the call.

"Warden, Bergman here. Listen, Munn's life could be in danger, we're not positive, just keep a closer eye out, will ya?"

"Will do. Besides, right now he's not being his usual nasty son of a bitch self."

"Oh," said Kasper, "something happen?"

"Guy got the hell beat outta him two days after you guys left, he's still in the infirmary."

"Too bad," Kasper remarked, but his words held no remorse.

"You don't sound too broke up over it, Bergman."

"Nah, Warden. The man's still alive and breathing, and can still do his time. That's what counts for me. Hey, keep me posted on his condition."

"Will do." The warden hung up first, then Kasper replayed the warden's side of the conversation.

"Too bad."

"What's too bad, Frankie?" Lefty asked.

"That Munn will live."

"You're becoming a real hard-ass, you know that, Ryder?"

"Yeah, so sue me or come give us a kiss instead."

"Bold, Frankie, very bold," Kasper snickered. But Lefty was a man of action; he got up, planted a big wet kiss on her, then went for coffee.

Ardmore, Oklahoma

Fifteen minutes later with two colas, two waters, a bag of chips, and two store-made yucky sandwiches to keep them sustained, Mick turned onto the street to find Officers Harris and Carmichael speaking to a thin, bedraggled man, and no one was fleeing.

"You think that's Wallen?" Mick asked, cutting the engine.

"I'm hoping, so maybe we can offer him the sandwiches. I wasn't looking forward to cardboard with a dot of chicken salad in the center." Harlowe opened the door, as did Mick. Over the top of the car he said, "I'm sorta scary looking. You talk to the guy, he looks like a puff of wind could blow him down the road for a mile. I don't wanna intimidate him."

Nodding, she walked up to the officers who stood on the curb with the thin, disheveled gentlemen.

"Ma'am, this is Matthew Wallen. Mr. Wallen, this is, uh..." He looked at her wondering if she wanted to be known as an FBI agent.

She stuck out her hand. "Mr. Wallen, I'm Harlowe Bishop. This is Mick Townsend, and we're with the FBI."

"I see." With a steady voice he asked, "Are you looking for me because of Jason?"

Harlowe and Mick exchanged a quick glance, and he said, "Yes, sir."

"I'd invite you in, but my place ain't too fitting for company. Anyway, I'd imagine you wanna talk to me downtown, right?"

"Mr. Wallen," Harlowe asked, "you up for a ride?"

"Where to?"

"Dallas."

The man pressed his lips together. Looking down, he nodded for a minute, then he looked up and said, "How many?"

With a narrowed look, it's Mick who asked, "People?"

"Yes." Wallen's eyes held deep sadness when he looked straight at Bishop and asked, "Trina?"

Bishop puts her hand on the man's arm. "Yes, sir, I'm so sorry."

Matthew Wallen buckled, collapsing to the curb.

After eating both sandwiches and gulping down the water, letting him process what little news they'd given him, Matthew Wallen fell asleep for the rest of the drive back to Dallas. Harlowe glanced back over her shoulder at him. He was a shattered young man who looked ten years older than his age, his face gaunt, dark rings under his eyes, bone thin. She felt a wave of sorrow pass though her.

After introductions and pouring young Wallen a hot cup of

coffee, he began. It was a horror story and several times he had to stop and compose himself. It was sorrow which turned to anger, to hate, and then back to sorrow. His emotions were all over the place, his frailty a constant concern for the agents. Kasper worried he'd have a stroke; Frankie worried he would succumb to his own mental health.

His story began with when they'd moved to Marietta and how Jason started cashing in on stolen goods from caskets and digging up bodies not encased in burial vaults.

"Jason was relentless. He found the graves of richer people. We'd dig them up after our dad taught us how to run the backhoe, and no, Dad wasn't in on it, and before you ask, we covered our digging by stealing grass from the grass farm on the other side of town. Late at night J would take Dad's truck, then me and Den would push the truck down the road before J would crank it up."

His story went on for hours: desecration of bodies, necrophilia, dehumanizing the dead.

"Ray, uh, we called him RJ. He vomited several times, but Jason said he had to cuz he got money and was in on the stealing so he had to take part in this, too. J didn't make me since Mom beat the hell out of me. He figured her beating me was my part, but I had to watch and that was more than enough for me."

"Matthew, the notebooks, this stuff really happened."

"I truly wish I could say he made it up, but it happened. Am I gonna go to jail, cuz I wouldn't last one second?"

"Matt," Frankie spoke, "You aren't who we want. We want the man responsible for the deaths of Lydia Wallen, Gloria Manchester, Rayna, uh, RJ Anderson, Annelle Mackey, and sadly for you, Trina Robinson. We'd also like to find the body of Sylvia Amos. Mera Soon-Lee, did you know her?"

A tear slipped, then another, and more followed as he nodded. "Yeah, and I really liked her too, but Dennis said she found those." He pointed to the notebooks in evidence bags. "He thought he'd gotten them all, and I told him she wouldn't say anything. She had nothing to show Jason to confront him but he said no, she had to go to protect our big brother. Den warned me to stay out of it or he would beat the holy shit out of me and tell Jason." Wallen cried into his hands. "Mera might be alive if I'd stopped him, only I was afraid of my brothers."

CHAPTER FIFTY-SIX

Wallen's tale continued.

"Dad wasn't around, he worked all the time. He had a part-time job since Mom never lifted a finger outside the house." Matt's chuckle was bitter. "Not inside the house, either. J, he wanted stuff, stuff we couldn't afford. That's why he started stealing from the dead people's caskets." Matthew had to stop a minute to collect himself, and Harlowe handed him napkins to wipe his face. "Thank you." He snuffed then blew his nose. "Hey, I'm not saying I approved of this, but heck, I was just a kid. Jason was boss. We did what he said all the time—all us kids, RJ, Annie, Gloria, even Nora when she came every summer to visit. J didn't boss Trina around, he wasn't mean to her either, because I asked him, for me, to be nice to her." Matt wailed, laying his head on the table, covering it with his arms.

Kasper uncapped a bottle of water and handed it to him once he'd stopped weeping. His eyes red, face blotchy, he gulped the water and exhaled. "Sorry, this is all fresh for me, it's like Trina just died. She was the one I loved, and you know how it was back then. I mean, she was black, and I'm white. I was also younger, but none of that mattered to us. But her father, no, his daughter couldn't love a white boy." Again, Matt cried into his hands.

"Matt," Kasper's voice was calm. "I need to ask you some questions about Jason's other girlfriend, Mera...Mera Soon-Lee. Did you meet her?"

"Yes, Dennis and I met her when she came to Ardmore. That was in 2011. Jason didn't know she'd come up, though, well, not until Dennis told him, and that was after she vanished."

"Do you know what happened?"

Nodding, his eyes welled up once more, and the tears quietly flowed.

"You up to talking about it?"

Matt wiped his eyes, this time with the sleeve of his shirt, and he snuffled up his tears. "Mera was beautiful. I was smitten because she reminded me a little of Trina—her skin coloring and her smile." Matt became wistful, stopping to exhale, letting his body relax into the chair, his eyes closed. "Dennis was terrified for Jason." He reopened his eyes. "After he shot himself, I badgered Jason to tell me what happened. I had to know." His face snarled, his hands balled into fists, and his tone changed. "My brother and Mera would be alive now if J had burned this crap." His eyes went to the notebooks, letters, and photos. "If Mera had never found them." He hung his head, closing his eyes again. "If," he said, "if," he repeated softly. "Agent Bergman, there are a lot of ifs in my life, and the biggest if is this. If our mother was a good person, Jason would've been a good man. I believe this with all my heart."

"Matt, when did you last talk to your brother?" Harlowe asked, curious about any contact they might've had.

"Once a month, he calls to check on me. The doctors diagnosed me years ago with PSTD, that's why I am on disability. I attribute it to the beatings my mom gave me."

His life with Jason was no picnic and his PSTD was inflamed by this as well. Matthew had his head buried in the sand if he didn't realize this. But why rub salt into this bony, weary man's wounds?

With a discernable headshake, he went on with his story. "I wrote Annie a letter to ask her if she'd heard from Sylvia, said I was worried after they reported her missing. I tried to reach RJ, but heard he'd skipped town with a new man in his life, and heck, I didn't even know he was trans. After that I tried to find Nora but didn't have her new last name. I didn't know where she was, and no one knew anything about Trina. No one kept up with each other. Believe me when I say I wasn't involved, I swear on a stack of Bibles I didn't want to believe Jason could be doing any of this...God, he's FBI. I thought, well, that he'd become a good man, finally..." He paused, then, "Guess I was wrong."

This was going to be tough. But Matthew Wallen deserved to know about Tobias Robinson, and him conceivably being his father.

"You said you didn't know why Trina's family moved?"

"They moved in a rush. She never wrote to me, which crushed me."

"Trina was pregnant."

Matt let Kasper's words sink in, opening his eyes wide, his words stumbled out. "Pregnant? Her and I, we, she had a baby?" Pain filled his eyes. "Did they make her...make her get rid of it?"

Kasper scooted his chair closer placing his hand on the man's arm. "No, she had the baby, a boy, and she raised him."

Stunned, Matthew sat, silently absorbing this news.

"Matt, you okay?" Kasper's eyes were full of concern.

"I'm, oh boy...I'm a dad, really? Where is he, what's his name, does he know? Can I, can I call him, see him?"

This news breathed life into a beaten man who now had something to live for.

"If the paternity test proves this, then yes, you're his dad. His name is Toby, and—"

"Toby?"

"Officially, it's Tobias, but he goes by Toby."

Matt's face broke into the biggest grin, and his eyes shone. "My middle name is Tobias—Matthew Tobias Wallen. Trina named him after me, God, how I loved her," he said, his eyes bright and his voice melancholy.

"She called you her soulmate, that's what Toby told me," Kasper said.

Another tear slipped from Wallen's red-rimmed eyes, a joyful tear this time. "Her soulmate...Lord, how I wished it had been different." He nervously looked up. "Does he? Would Toby want to meet me if the paternity tests prove I'm his father?" A worried tremor infiltrated his tone.

"He said he did."

A small grin flicked on his face, and then he looked at Kasper anxiously. "What do we do now, Agent Bergman?"

"I can bunk with him at the safe house," Lefty offered.

Then Kasper said, "Yeah, but our agents can access our safe house locations, and we can't take that chance."

Not involved in their conversation, Matt looked from Lefty back to Kasper. "You want me to go to a safe house? Why am I in danger? Is he, uh, is my son in danger too?"

"Not sure he knows about Toby, but you, yeah, maybe. From what you've told us, you're the last person alive who knows his past."

"Wait. You think he might come after me, to, uh, kill me?"

"It's exactly what I think, and we need to keep you safe. As far as Toby is concerned, we're going to keep him safe too, and away from Jason." Kasper called him Jason, not Jay, because Jay Greenberg was an FBI agent. Jason Wallen was a serial killer.

Lefty took Matthew's sizes and headed out to get him clean clothes and find a hotel they could stash him in. Frankie got food for everyone, and they waited on Lefty's return.

Matthew's hands shook as he ate breaking Harlowe's heart.

He asked if they had pictures of Toby, but sadly, no, they didn't.

When the paternity test results came in, they would let him know immediately. Kasper promised he would.

Frankie took a call and excused herself while the others ate, in a silence no one could describe.

"Matt," Kasper said between bites, "we'll need you to be a witness to make our case against Jason. You understand what I'm saying?"

Matt chewed, swallowed, and nodded. "I understand, and I'd like to make a request."

"Whatever you need and whatever is within our power," Kasper said.

"Witness protection? Is that possible?"

"Is there something you aren't telling us, Matt?" Real concern laced Agent Bergman's question.

"My brother knows people. I'm thinking not just law-abiding people either, know what I mean?"

It was a true enough statement. Kasper felt guilty he hadn't thought about this before asking him to be a State's witness.

"This is a possibility, Matt. If there is a need, then of course we can suggest WITSEC. And Toby, what about him in all this?"

Matt's head bobbed. "I find out he's my flesh and blood son, I won't lose him again, Agent Bergman. I can't."

The door reopened. Frankie stepped in, her face drawn and worried. Kasper spotted it quickly and stood. "Frankie, what? What's happened?"

"That was Warden Swisher. They pronounced Munn in the infirmary two hours ago."

"How?" Kasper cut his eyes from Frankie to Matt.

"Someone stuck a whittled-down toothbrush in his carotid, bled out in seconds."

"They know who?"

She nodded. "Yeah, an inmate they call Smitty."

"The same man who called me that night, you mean that guy?"

"Yeah, our supposedly mobbed-up prisoner, one who was helping write the letters for the faceless man."

Kasper looked from Frankie to Matt. "WITSEC is necessary, and Toby has no choice now. Jay Greenberg will have reach, he's made friends in dangerous places over the years with his many visits to multiple prisons. Toby's existence will come out during the trial, and to be honest, Trina may have told him about his nephew as a bargaining chip to save her life."

"And if he isn't my son?"

"It might not matter to Jason, he may still want his revenge."

"This dead man, who was he to Jason?" an emotionally drained Matthew Wallen asked.

Kasper began the long story.

It felt wrong going after one of their own, but Jay Greenberg had never been one of them. He began his life as Jason Wallen, a kid who'd lost a loving mother and gained an evil stepmother—his only excuse for why his life had spiraled downward. Impressionable and needing a hero, it was too bad he'd picked a scumbag like Preston Munn. He revered him because he didn't like whores who treated him bad, belittled him, hurt him, or laughed at him—all the things his stepmom did and more.

Lydia hurting her flesh-and-blood sons strengthened his hatred and his anger festered, as did his need to have what he wanted, get what he desired, and do it all his way. As the years moved forward, his demons took over.

An arrest warrant would need to be issued, then the team would head to the Lake Charles FBI office and take Jason Wallen AKA Jay Greenburg into custody, extraditing him to Texas to stand trial on charges of kidnapping and first-degree murder, beginning with the murder of Lydia Wallen.

CHAPTER FIFTY-SEVEN

Five FBI agents appeared at the doorstep of the Lake Charles, Louisiana, resident FBI office two days later. No one was aware of what was going to happen, least of all Greenberg, who stood when they walked through the door.

Leo Sutton, the lead agent, met them, heading straight for Mick Townsend.

"Mick, good to see you, and thank you for calling. It was quite unexpected."

The two shook hands.

His face devoid of any emotion, Kasper asked, "What's this about a call, Mick?" Inside his anger was rising, but he kept his tone in check.

"Since I knew we'd be visiting Leo's office, I wanted to make amends before we got here. I gave the guy hell at the Academy and didn't want any bad blood to come between me and him and the job. A visit from a classmate who was a dickhead. Well, I just wanted to clear the air."

Leo beamed. "Made me feel better, and I gotta say, Mick, was the nicest apology a man could get. Appreciate it. No one has ever done that, got bullied all my life, so thanks."

Harlowe, who stood beside Mick, looked up at his tall frame and she nodded her approval, a tiny light in her eyes, but stayed quiet.

Sutton introduced them to the other agents, Jerry Chavez, Fin Stevens, Nan Baxter, and Gus Nystrom. Each agent stepped forward offering their hand and a smile.

"And you guys already know Greenberg, over there in his own little world." No one missed the change of Leo's tone when the name Greenberg rolled off his tongue. His dislike apparent, Kasper figured Sutton would be overjoyed watching them escort Jay out in cuffs. It didn't bother him. Kasper felt Greenberg deserved a lot worse.

"Greenberg." Kasper nodded his acknowledgement, but the others said nothing. A mere look and nod was all they gave Jay; even Mick and Jay's face registered surprise.

"You guys look good, so how can we help you?" Leo looked from face to face, waiting for an explanation.

"Leo, you have an office we can speak in, in private?" Kasper kept his tone even.

"Sure, back here," he said and nodded pushing his glasses up off the end of his nose.

Kasper followed, after leaning in and telling Agent Sebastian something.

"Very good. We'll wait out here." With a no-nonsense manner, Lefty walked to the only door into the office and took a stance, Mick following his lead. The girls sat in guest chairs and no one spoke. Jerry Chavez, Fin Stevens, Nan Baxter, and Gus Nystrom went back to work. Greenberg's eyes darted from each agent's face who didn't give him the time of day, and he quietly exhaled, then went back to work. Evidently Leo was in trouble. He hated the four-eyed weasel and hoped he was out on his ass.

Less than twenty minutes passed and Leo escorted Bergman out of his small office and back to the main open area where agents sat in half-walled cubicles. Both men were somber and the atmosphere in the room changed drastically. Frankie and Harlowe stood, Corneal headed back to the area Greenberg sat, and Mick followed. Kasper stepped in front of them, pulled out an envelope, and Leo stood beside him.

"Agent Greenberg, I need you to relinquish your badge and gun," Bergman said, and Mick had his hand on his weapon.

A look of complete shock covered Jay's face. "What the hell is this, some kind of joke, Leo? Is this a prank?"

"Greenberg, do it." Leo paused a beat, his tone rougher, "Do it now!"

His hand came up to his suit coat, and Mick stepped in. "Two fingers, Jay. Be careful what you pull out of your inside pocket."

His hand slowly moved his jacket open to expose his empty holster, his eyes darted to the top drawer of his desk. Frankie took one step to lean in and open the top drawer and remove the 9mil Jay carried, as well as the badge lying next to it.

"Somebody gonna tell me what the fuck is going on?" His fist balled up, and he hit the top of the desk, the sound reverberated.

The envelope held aloft, Kasper said, "Jay Greenberg AKA Jason Wallen, you are under arrest for the murders of Lydia Wallen, Gloria Manchester, Annelle Mackey, Rayna Anderson, once known as RJ Anderson, and Trina Robinson."

"The fuck you say..." He backed up and into Mick, who grabbed an arm, wrenching it behind him, cuffing him.

Shock in the office was an understatement. How could an FBI agent, one they'd all worked with, broke bread with, drank beer with, be a serial killer? The details were not discussed, and they led him out, his cussing them the entire time, and calling out his revenge for arresting an innocent man, and how they couldn't prove a goddamned thing.

The news hit the Bureau in waves, and the media swarmed like buzzards.

Before any press release was made, Kasper called Chung Soon-Lee to inform him that the person responsible for his daughter's death had been Dennis Wallen, explaining it was all to protect his brother, Jason, and how he took his own life two weeks later. Mr. Soon-Lee, grateful for closure, wanted to tell his ex-wife, saying it would be better if Kasper gave her the news, and Kasper agreed.

Kasper and his team kept Matt Wallen hidden and out of the limelight as much as humanly possible, and the only thing that kept him going was the news that Tobias Theodore Robinson was his biological son. They had yet to meet face to face, but had spent hours talking on the phone, and Kasper saw the man blossom once more.

Jay Greenberg was stunned his brother would testify against him, speechless when they showed him the journals, letters, and the proof of the bracelets. The most damning evidence had been the DNA found by Medical Examiner Nikki Lam, which had been on Nora Finch, and matched Greenberg's DNA without a doubt.

Greenberg's fingerprints matched prints found in the hotel room where they found Trina Robinson's locket, by pure accident. Out of hundreds of prints taken in a room no one had cleaned in weeks, what were the odds they'd find one solid thumbprint on the underside of the freaking toilet seat? It matched Greenberg's.

The Attorney General and his adjutant sat across the table from Greenberg and his counsel. They squared off, eyeballing each other.

"This will go to trial and your client is going to face the death penalty. This is Texas, my friend." His adjutant smirked a little, his elbow propped on the corner of the table.

"We have a deal, and if you agree, my client, Mr. Greenberg, wants the death penalty off the table. He'll take life without parole."

The AG arched his brows, shaking his head. "What can your client give us that would make us take the death penalty off the table? He's a federal agent and will be the first to ever to be convicted as a serial killer."

"What if he gives you one more body, closes another murder case?"

"Oh, he wants to bring the body count up to seven, does he now?"

"We don't go to trial, save the taxpayers' money, you get your guy, and another family gets closure."

The AG leaned back watching a shackled Greenberg under hooded eyes, contemplating this offer. Death row was crammed full of men who'd been waiting, and putting another one on the list wasn't worth it.

"We get the information, if it all pans out, then okay, we got a deal, but if this is a crock of shit, well, your boy here fries with the other bastards on the row."

Talk about a full circle. Preston Munn gave up a body too, to get life, and he ended up dead by the very man who worshipped him as a fourteen-year-old boy. Greenberg called in his hit, had the man taken out to cover his own ass, nothing more; it was business only. A few months later, they dug up the remains of Sylvia Amos, right where Greenberg told them she'd be—in Ardmore, Oklahoma. Her bones were found buried on top of Old Man Jim Granby's casket in the cemetery, Final Resting Gardens. Bernie Cooper was ready to have a stroke and almost did. Winona Amos-Garza, the sister of Sylvia, cried, finally able to let her sister rest in peace.

What an odd turn of events. Munn gave them Corrine DeSoto to get life without parole; his prodigy, Jason Wallen AKA Jay Greenberg, gave them Sylvia Amos.

Officially, he was Jason Wallen again, and he'd spend the rest of his life in USP Beaumont, Texas, lucky for him, not in gen pop. Who knew if one day they'd figure out he was once a G-Man—a *good man* —who fell into the dark abyss.

CHAPTER FIFTY-EIGHT

5:00 am

In the main lobby of the Dallas FBI building, the five of them stood. Mick, Lefty, and Frankie were heading out to catch their flights home.

"You guys sure you don't want Harlowe and I to drive you to the airport?"

"Nah, and get stuck in the morning traffic on your way back? A cab is perfect." Frankie eyed the time. "Yellow Cab should be here in about five minutes."

"Well, it was fun while it lasted," Lefty said, shaking hands with Kasper and turning to Harlowe. "And you? Are you staying in Dallas much longer?"

"A few days, going to help Bergman here with the paperwork, then I head back to the glitz of Vegas."

Mick stepped up to Kasper, his hand out. "Bergman, it was great working with you."

"You too, Mick, and boy, I never thought I'd say that."

The five had a chuckle.

"Yeah, I can only handle so much fun, glad the roller coaster finally stopped, and there's our cab." Frankie hitched up her purse.

"Uh, Mick, a word?" Harlowe asked, motioning him away from the others.

"Sure," he replied, and followed.

While the two of them had their private conversation, the other three were placing bets on the possibility of Harlowe and Mick becoming an item, and how it would be her in Nevada, him in Kentucky—or would one put in for a transfer?

"I think they sorta make a cute couple," Frankie remarked.

Lefty snuffled and the air from his nose made a laughing sound. "And if she has to, Bishop can whoop his ass. Mick knows it too!"

"Yeah, she can." Kasper's eyes cut over at them, standing toe-to-toe, her neck angled up talking to him, his bent down listening, and it made him feel good. Bishop deserved a bit of happiness in her life with her recent circumstances.

The Yellow Cab honked.

"There's our ride. Hey, Mick," Frankie called out, "gotta go, wrap it up you two."

Lefty rolled his and Frankie's suitcases out, helping the driver load them into the trunk, and Frankie hugged Kasper. "Hope never to visit another prison again, Bergman, but it was definitely an experience."

"One day, Ryder, I'd like the chance to watch you in an interrogation room, cuz I got a feeling you could tear a guy a new one."

"Nah, I like the stuff, well, most of the time."

Both of then knew that what she'd found by digging into Greenberg's "special" files was not the sort of cyber she meant. The photos were disturbing and part of the reason they were able to convict him with seven counts of murder, which included kidnapping, rape, and necrophilia. All this, and the name that popped into Bergman's head had not been Preston Munn, it had been Bundy.

Goodbyes were said. Agents Sebastian, Ryder, and Townsend waved so long, and Kasper and Harlowe watched until the cab was out of sight.

"So."

"So what?" she asked

"You and Mick?"

"Dunno, but we're gonna keep in touch. I'm planning a trip to visit the lovely State of Kentucky."

Kasper didn't pry. If it worked out, he'd know, because they both felt like family. But, he saw a languid look in her eyes, her posture relaxed. She wasn't the same Harlowe he'd picked up at the airport less than fifteen days ago; she seemed happy.

Lefty and Frankie, Harlowe and maybe Mick, and how about him and Dr. Lam? He was eager to see how that would go as well.

DFW Airport — Two Days Later

"Thanks for putting up with me, for listening, for being a shoulder, and a good friend, Bergman." She crushed him with a bear hug.

"Hey, thanks for this case and a chance to lead a team. Learned some stuff about myself and my fellow Quantico classmates. Boy, also got the shock of a lifetime with Mick. Go figure."

"He's really a good guy. "

"I hope he doesn't disappoint you, Harri, or hurt you." His words were heartfelt.

"Shit, that motherfucker does, I'll put his fucking ass to the ground."

"Harlowe!"

Her laugh rang out, and she punched him in the arm. "Wanted you to know I 'm still me."

The announcement her flight was now boarding echoed in the air and her row number called.

"Hate being first on, means I'm last off, oh well. Keep in touch, Bergman, I'll do the same."

Kasper watched her vanish into the line of folks boarding, and he smiled, shoving his hand into his pockets. He turned to leave, headed back to One Justice Way and the chatter he'd missed for the past few days.

EPILOGUE

He stood back. Sunglasses perched on his nose, the bill of the hat shading his face, a satchel dangling from his arm, a *Dallas Morning News* folded in his hand. His shoes a little dusty, his trousers wrinkled, and the navy-blue jacket he wore zipped to his neck. He'd lost fifteen pounds, his hair was thinning, his face scruffy with growth he hoped would become a full beard. He hadn't tried to change his looks, yet he didn't look like himself, and hadn't for the past six years. Six years? Time had flown, and he'd been out of the country for most of those years with an occasional job here and there. Into the States and out as fast as he arrived.

This trip was different, though—personal. Oh, if they needed him they'd let him know. He'd be at their beck and call, which would never change. Only death would part him from this way of life.

Kasper Bergman was his thorn, and this sore spot festered into a disease, eating at him. With purpose, he put one foot in front of the other, keeping a suitable distance between him and his quarry.

His eyes on the target, his feet slow yet steady, he followed the young FBI agent out into the public space where people walked toward him, around him, and beside him, chatting, laughing noisily, and exiting the same door Bergman did.

When the automatic doors slid open, Kasper's gut seized once the air hit his face. A prickling sensation tickled the hairs on his neck, and he inhaled then exhaled. What the hell, he thought, was this after-case shock? The bad guy was in jail, his job was done, why was he jumpy?

The man in the heavy navy coat set his satchel down, taking a seat on a guest bench near the tram waiting area. He unfolded his paper and pretended to read, looking over the edge watching Bergman.

Kasper's dress shoes hit the street as he looked left then right and his eye caught the gentleman sitting on the bench reading the *Dallas Moring News*.

The man paid him no attention, turning the pages of the paper several times as if he were looking for the rest of the article he'd been reading.

Kasper stood still eyeing him for no real reason, then continued his walk crossing over and into parking garage, ready to get back to work. He would give Nikki Lam a call, ask her to dinner again, get to know her better, and maybe even give her a good-night kiss this time. He smiled.

The man on the bench smiled too, lowering the paper and slipping off his sunglasses for a moment. His face decorated every single post office wall, FBI wall, and every police station as well.

Theo Sykes hoped they'd at least used a flattering photo.

AUTHOR'S NOTE

Word-of-mouth is crucial for any author to succeed. If you enjoyed *When Good Men Fall*, please leave a review online—anywhere you are able. Even if it's just a sentence or two; it would make all the difference and would be very much appreciated.

Thanks,

Deanna

ACKNOWLEDGMENTS

My only research resources for this novel were found by typing and clicking, or perhaps by watching any show related to different branches of law enforcement.

I am extremely grateful and would like to take this opportunity to express my heartfelt appreciation to my beta readers, Sharon and Robert. Both of them have been an incredible support system, providing me with invaluable feedback and dedicating their precious time to read my work in its raw, unedited form.

I would like to express my gratitude to my editor, Lisa Petrocelli, who consistently provides me with invaluable guidance and support.

And to Chandra Fry's astounding diligence in crafting the covers for my books always leaving me amazed, and to Staci Olsen for her outstanding work in formatting to make sure that the printed version of the manuscript looks fantastic.

I want to express my deepest gratitude to my husband, Travis, for his unwavering support and willingness to spend hours listening to me read what I have written each day.

A special shout-out goes to my dear pups, Ruby Belle and Daisy May, who never fail to bring joy and laughter to my writing sessions. Thank you for the delightful distractions!

Maybe one day I will have a list of acknowledgments a mile long, but for now this is perfectly fine for me.

ABOUT THE AUTHOR

Deanna King is the author of *Twist of Fate*, *Lethal Liaisons*, *Vicious Vendetta*, and *Trust No One*, all part of her Jack West Series. Other genres she pens include one young adult fantasy, *Saving a Sioux Legacy: the Story of Blaze*, and *Gracie's Stories*, a children's book. *When Good Men Fall* is Deanna's first FBI Novel. Deanna lives in Texas with her husband, Travis, and one wild Yorkie named Ruby Belle and a very chill Toy Poodle named Daisy May.

Reach out to her any time @ deannakingwriting.com.

www.ingramcontent.com/pod-product-compliance
Lightning Source LLC
Chambersburg PA
CBHW011402010726
47495CB00009B/2735

* 9 7 9 8 9 8 5 6 9 8 2 5 1 *